Thundering Snow
Thundering Mountain Ranch
Book 5

Nicole Neiswanger

Calico
publications

Publisher: Calico Publications, LLC
Cover Design: Covers and Cupcakes, LLC
Editor: Telltail Editing
Digital ISBN: 978-1-960600-06-6
Print Edition ISBN: 978-1-960600-07-3
Large Print Edition ISBN: 978-1-960600-16-5

For my two handsome sons.

Chase your dreams
and
never let anything or anyone stop you
from achieving them.

Chapter 1

March 1, 1901

Stanley slammed his empty tankard of beer onto the scarred, sticky table and swiped the white foam from his upper lip. He waved and caught the attention of the bartender. He gestured for a new beer, and the man nodded. Within minutes, a full tankard was delivered.

He slouched low in the rickety wooden chair, his back against the saloon's rear wall near a large, black wood-burning stove. Although the heat from the packed bodies was enough to warm the skin on the coldest of nights, he still shivered. He'd lost count of the beers he'd had, but it didn't matter. Regardless of how much he drank, it couldn't erase what his former wife had done to him and his family.

A fight had broken out. Two men crashed into tables, glass mirrors, and even other men. They grappled with one another in an attempt to gain the upper hand. Beer splashed, food was flung, and tankards fell to the floor as the two men broke chairs, tables, and windows. Other men scattered, either trying to avoid the melee or having a reason to join. The bartender and a few burly men rushed to break up the fights, but it was clear those involved weren't to be stopped.

Brawls weren't unusual in the small railroad town of Pocatello, Idaho. It had been officially founded a mere seven years earlier and was bustling with activity from the railroad, establishing it as the Gateway to the Northwest. Stanley had been traveling for years, and it was the latest stop to hang his head, no better or worse than any other town he had visited in his pointless quest to find the woman who had ruined his life. Stanley should have been thrilled that Connie was truly gone, but he was still angry and even more so at his brother. It should have been Stanley who'd ended her, not Michael.

The fight continued to rage in front of Stanley, but it didn't stop him from imbibing his beer. He had no skin in the fight and was content to watch it play out. Entertainment in town was limited to the women in the saloons, gambling in the game halls, or attending church services on Sundays. Not that attending church was entertainment, but one couldn't be too choosy.

Suddenly, a soft body encased in light pink silk crashed into his table and then tumbled into his lap. A full, curvy warm one who smelled like his ma's rose-scented perfume. She had a head full of light brownish hair streaked with yellow that reminded him of the stalks of wheat after a fruitful harvest.

Startled, he dropped his tankard, spilling what was left onto him, the woman in his arms, and the floor. She screeched with outrage. He didn't know why, but considering he hadn't held a woman in his arms in quite some time, he wasn't inclined to let go.

Her frilly dress seemed out of place for a saloon, but who was he to judge the women who worked in them? As he took a good look at her, however, he questioned his initial perception. Her hair was piled high on her head in an elaborate arrangement of curls covered in an expensive hat, and her dress was made of the finest quality of silk.

It was something he hadn't seen since the woman who wasn't really his wife, had worn while he lived and worked on what he thought was his inheritance until he learned she had forged his pa's will, killed his pa with the help of a ranch hand, and cheated on him with the same ranch hand. All of this to take what his ma and pa had labored and built.

The woman's gown, having been pulled down slightly in the melee, barely contained her. He got quite a pleasant eyeful and would've continued to enjoy it until she slammed her sharp elbow into his gut. He grunted and released her. She scrambled from his lap and backed against the wall. She held her parasol in front of him as if she were wielding a sword she'd use to slice a man in half.

He chuckled before jumping out of his chair to get out of the way of the pointy end of her makeshift weapon. Although it would likely do little damage, he wasn't inclined to see what she could do with it.

"Don't touch me, you… you… ingrate," she screeched. The concoction of bows and ribbons that adorned the side of her head fell forward, covering the left side of her face before she shoved it up and out of the way. Her gaze never left his, as though he was the one who had pushed her into his lap.

Two men collided into the table next to them, the fight around them worsening by the second.

"Ma'am," he said, shimmying out of the way. "I certainly don't know what happened, but I can safely say I'm not about to lay a hand on you." He held up his hands to show he posed no threat.

"But you… you…"

Stopping her before she could say more, he said, "I caught you when you fell into *my* lap while I was enjoying *my* beer." He waved to the spilled tankard that rested on its side. "I didn't force you there, nor did I do anything inappropriate for a lady such as yourself." That might have been a slight stretch, as he couldn't have helped but get a handful of her when she landed in his lap. If he had known she was a lady, he wouldn't have taken such liberties.

Her cheeks flared bright red with embarrassment. She continued to hold the parasol in front of her as though that could stop him or any other man from taking what most women offered willingly in a saloon. He was a gentleman, or at least he had been before his life unraveled years before. He'd never take advantage of a woman, but he did see the need to get a lady out of such a place.

"May I be of some service?" He jumped out of the way of another man flying through the air.

"As you can see, things are getting a bit out of hand."

She narrowed her eyes and tilted her head as if contemplating his measure. "I… Just keep back."

"I won't hurt you." He looked down and brushed at the liquid dripping from his trousers and got a whiff of his stench. He hadn't had a bath in days and likely presented as a swine of the worst order. He might be drunk and stinky, but he still remembered the manners his ma had pressed into him when he was but a young lad. "I apologize for my lack of cleanliness and rank odor, but I'd never touch a woman, especially one who wasn't encouraging my advances."

She started to lower her parasol when another body struck him, that time from behind and not of the delightful kind. He stumbled forward and into her bountiful bosom. She dropped her parasol in surprise as he once again got a handful of her soft curves beneath the pink silk. His face was smashed into her chest, and he couldn't help but enjoy the feel and the view. Before he could fully appreciate the woman, she pushed him back, stomped on his foot, and kneed him in the face when he bent forward. He fell back on his hindquarters in stunned and painful amusement.

"My dear, are you all right? Did this swine harm you?" The high-pitched voice then proceeded to smack him over the head with a wooden cane.

He grimaced at the jolt across his head and tried to protect himself, but she didn't stop. His hands smarted from the whip of the cane. Thank goodness she had a horrible aim. If she'd gotten a good whack, he might've been knocked unconscious.

She abruptly stopped and went to stand near the girl's side, clucking like a mother hen. "Why did you come in here, Charlotte?"

He grinned. Charlotte was the name of the woman in pink. He rubbed at the top of his head, searching for any bumps and luckily didn't find much, but his favorite black hat had fallen in the scuffle. It was likely lost in the frenzy occurring all around them. He raised his head and pulled his knees to his chest. He was enjoying the show, albeit at his expense.

Charlotte smiled at the older lady and patted her on the arm. "No one hurt me, Aunt Martha." She jumped as a glass shattered against the wall next to her. "Although I certainly don't look like it, now do I? I got caught in the scuffle looking for Father and fell into this poor gentleman's lap." She didn't seem to be bothered by the fracas blooming at an alarming rate around them.

He shook his head as he was the *poor gentleman* now, and tried to contain the chuckles that threatened to erupt. If he hadn't been there to witness it, he would've thought he was watching a play on the stage of the local theater in Helena. Everything that had happened in the past few minutes had been just as ridiculous as the melodramas put on by the local theater troupe his ma and pa had taken him and his older brother to when they were young. He remembered watching in wide-eyed wonder as the actors exaggerated their movements and their speech to raise laughter from the crowd.

"Where is your father?" Martha asked. "Did you really see him?"

Another plate skittered next to him with what looked like a perfectly good steak and potatoes. His mouth watered. He was downright hungry all of a sudden. He'd have to get a bite to eat at the hotel if he got out of the saloon in one piece.

"I don't know. Maybe." Charlotte tilted her head, a quizzical expression on her lovely face. "I thought I saw him, but I might've been wrong." She pushed at her fallen hat, but it toppled once again. She quirked her lips in irritation.

A chair slammed into the wall behind Stanley, and he jolted from the impact.

"Oh my, poor dear. You keep looking for Marcus, and he doesn't want to be found."

"I know, but I can't help it. I want... No, I need to find him."

He wondered who Marcus was, but before he could ask, a man flew into another table next to them and grunted from the impact. It was time to go. Stanley jumped to his feet. Enough of his woolgathering. He had to get these women to safety—if they let him.

He glanced at the floor and saw his hat under the crumbled remains of the table. He bent, swiped it up, and slapped it on his head. Didn't want to lose that. Grabbing each woman by their elbow, he said, "As much as I'd like to continue to watch you two engage in this tete-a-tete, I think we should leave."

"Unhand me, you—" Martha pulled at his grip, but he didn't let go.

"Yes, I know. I'm an ingrate, swine, wretch, blah, blah, blah."

Martha looked at him in shock, opening and closing her mouth like a baby bird waiting for its mother to bring it a worm to eat.

"You can berate me later, after we get you to safety." He pulled them toward a door next to the bar. The saloon had erupted into a full-fledged bar fight with bodies and furniture flying every which way. It was a wonder they didn't get hurt.

"My parasol," Charlotte muttered, trying to pull away, but he held fast.

"Sorry, ma'am, but I think your parasol needs to be left behind. Unless, of course, you want to ask the men lying on top of it to gather it for you?" She swung her chest across his arm to look behind them, irritation on her face. "I'm sure they'd be happy to help a nice young lady like yourself."

Charlotte gasped but stopped fighting him. She let him lead her out the door and into the back room of the saloon. He practically threw the two women inside before he slammed the door shut behind them. He grabbed the nearest chair and positioned it under the door handle to keep men from coming after them. It wouldn't hold for long but would perhaps give them enough time to find a way out in one piece.

The door jostled as someone tried to get in, but the lock and chair held for the moment.

Fluttering her hand in front of her, Martha took great breaths, her rapid breathing causing her chest to rise and fall from exertion. She struggled to gain her composure and plopped heavily in a chair next to a worn, wooden table that held empty bottles of liquor. "Young man, I don't know who you think you are, but—"

"Shh, Aunty Martha. He saved us from that disaster out there." Charlotte waved her arm toward the door and what lay beyond.

Martha pointed her cane at her niece. "We would've never been in here if you hadn't once again chased after a man who looked—"

"Enough." Anger flashed in Charlotte's eyes. "We don't need to air our dirty laundry in front of Mr…?" She stared at Stanley with questions in her eyes.

"Seymour," he said, bowing his head. "Stanley Seymour's the name."

"Mr. Seymour," Charlotte said. "Thank you for saving us, although you certainly didn't act the gentleman when we first met."

He laughed, as her words were in direct contrast to what had happened just moments before.

"I don't understand what is so funny, Mr.

Seymour," Charlotte said, affronted by his laughter. She rested her hands on her hips.

Tears leaked from the corner of his eyes with the force of hilarity that suddenly overtook him. Bracing his hands against his knees, he took a couple of deep breaths to calm the chuckles racking his frame. She didn't think he was funny, but he sure did. "I didn't act the gentleman."

"No, you certainly did not. Why you… you had your hands all over…" Her cheeks were bright red. She was quite adorable with that blush, not to mention her plump red lips just begged for a man's thorough attention.

"I caught you when you fell into my lap, and then I was pushed into your…" He waved toward her bosom.

"Oh, you're insufferable," Charlotte muttered. "Maybe you aren't a gentleman if you have to mention—"

"I never claimed I was a gentleman." A wide grin lifted his cheeks. A grin he hadn't had in quite some time. That woman was the first to make him smile, and he would enjoy it no matter how long it lasted.

Chapter 2

March 1, 1901

Charlotte scowled at the man in front of her. "You might not have claimed to be a gentleman, but your clothing, your demeanor, and your speech patterns suggest otherwise." Oh my, she sounded like a stuck-up prig, but that was the only way she could preserve what was left of her honor in the ridiculous situation.

His smile diminished.

"Not to mention the fact that, if you had been anything but a gentleman, you would've left us to fend for ourselves out there." Charlotte took a deep breath to calm her rapidly beating heart, but with just one look, he practically made her swoon in her impractical silk slippers.

She hadn't intended to get caught in the brawl, but when the man who looked just like her father headed inside the saloon, she had forgotten where she was and had run after him. It had been reckless, but after looking for her father for over a year, she wasn't surprised she lacked caution. Lead after lead had amounted to nothing.

Nine months ago, the private detective she'd hired sent word that her father had been seen at various locations along the route to Pocatello. She had traveled hundreds of miles from her hometown of St. Louis to the wild, western part of the country with the hopes that, for once, the information would be correct.

Stanley's grin returned, reminding her that she and her aunt were in a precarious position. While he didn't seem the type to take advantage, Charlotte could never be too sure. When she fell into his lap, her skin had burned, especially when he'd skimmed his large hands across her. She wouldn't admit it, nor would she agree that maybe, just maybe, the situation she'd found herself in was partly her fault. Instead, she'd straightened her shoulders and glared at him.

He stunk to high heaven, but my, oh my, he was a strikingly handsome man. Broad shoulders, dark blonde hair that curled around the nape of his neck, and a scruffy beard all worked to enhance his rugged appearance. He stared at her with golden brown eyes as though he was truly seeing her for who she was. His clothing was cut from the finest cloth, although it was clear he hadn't seen a laundress in some time, but there was no hiding he came from wealth.

The door rattled once again with force. Stanley quickly scooted around them and opened another door on the far side of the room. It opened to a dimly lit hallway. He grabbed a lantern from the shelf. "Follow me, ladies. We can continue this conversation later when we aren't likely to get tackled by the drunk men out there."

"Aren't you drunk?" Charlotte muttered as she helped her aunt from the chair.

"Well, I was, but I'm afraid that's no longer the case." He smirked. "Take hold of my arm, ma'am."

He grinned at her aunt with a smile that could charm a snake into submission. Her aunt blushed and took his arm like a queen holding on to her king. He quickly and efficiently led them down the hall and to relative safety. Once they were outside and far from the saloon and imminent danger, he asked where they were staying.

She opened her mouth to tell him it was none of his business and that they could make their way on their own, but her aunt beat her to the answer. "The Pacific Hotel."

"Right this way, ladies," Stanley said with a wide grin. "I'm staying there myself."

How fortuitous indeed that they were all staying at the same hotel. He'd get a chance to see Charlotte again if he played his cards right.

Charlotte stumbled, and he grasped her elbow to steady her, grazing his fingers against her soft skin.

"Thank you," she mumbled, avoiding his gaze. She bent her head, allowing him to glimpse her long neck where wisps of her cornsilk hair dangled teasingly across it. He wondered what she would do if he were to place a gentle kiss behind her ear.

Stanley didn't know where those images were coming from. He hadn't had thoughts of any woman since before he'd met the evil Connie. Considering the fallout from that miserable mistake, he hadn't desired any woman in years. He couldn't afford to make the same error twice, so it'd be best to keep his distance.

Charlotte stopped, carefully removed her elbow from his grip, and stared him straight in the eye. "I haven't seen you in the hotel. How do we know you're telling us the truth?"

"Miss"—he pushed the brim of his hat up his forehead—"I was raised to tell the truth, and my ma would've been appalled if I did otherwise. I arrived four days past, checked in, and have been frequenting the establishment we just left. I assure you I'm not lying. The clerk at the front desk will verify my story."

Charlotte reached for her aunt's arm and practically dragged her down the dirt road, leaving him standing behind them. Shaking his head in laughter, he followed. Charlotte might not want him near them, but he was a gentleman, albeit a filthy one. He would hate for them to be accosted while walking along the dimly lit road to the hotel, and he'd make sure they returned safely whether or not Charlotte wanted him to.

Stanley also couldn't help but want to understand why they had entered a saloon. It'd give him something else to think about other than his own pathetic existence.

The sun had fallen. The days were short, but

they'd grow longer soon. Spring would be a welcome change from the dark and dreary nights of winter, although winter surely fit his melancholy moods.

When they reached the doors to the hotel, he pulled them open before Charlotte could argue. "After you." He winked at her aunt.

Martha blushed and swatted his arm before sweeping past him and inside, her cane banging against the wooden floors. When they arrived at the front desk, Charlotte asked the clerk for their key before turning to him. Good manners dictated she stop and thank him, although it was clear she'd rather do anything but.

"Thank you for escorting us back to the hotel, Mr. Seymour."

Her impertinent tone made him want to laugh, but he contained the chuckles.

Stanley removed his hat and bowed a bit formally, even if he did look a fright and could use a bath.

She shook her head and tried to contain a

smile, but it was of no use. He saw it and couldn't help but be encouraged by it.

"It was certainly my pleasure, Miss Charlotte. May I escort you and your aunt to dinner tomorrow night? I promise I'll take a bath and won't be quite as... Well, I'll be much nicer to your olfactory senses tomorrow."

She brought her hand to her mouth and covered her lips. "As kind as your offer is, Mr. Seymour, I think we'll have to say no."

"Now, now, Charlotte," Martha said. "There's no reason to turn down his kind offer. We'll likely be here for quite some time. We can certainly have a nice evening with a gentleman." She patted Charlotte's arm. "We'll be happy to join you, Mr. Seymour. We'll meet you in the hotel dining room around six tomorrow evening."

He nodded. "That would be lovely, Mrs....?"

"Martha." She pinched his cheek. "We'll see you tomorrow. Have a nice evening."

With that, Martha turned and let Charlotte guide her to the grand staircase and up to their rooms.

"Mr. Seymour," the clerk said, "your key." He wrinkled his nose as he got a whiff of Stanley and tried without success to smile through it.

Stanley palmed the key between his grubby fingers, the dirt beneath his fingernails a stark reminder of his stench. "Thank you. Can you have a tub and warm water sent to my room? I reckon I'll need to wash if I'm going to enjoy their company tomorrow evening." He lifted an eyebrow.

"Yes, sir," the clerk said, brightening significantly. "It'll be sent up momentarily. Anything else we can help you with?"

Stanley also ordered a hot meal. That steak and potatoes from the saloon had looked mighty inviting. He hadn't had a decent one in weeks, as his appetite had been mostly nonexistent. It was time to fix that, as he suddenly had a ravenous appetite.

The sudden change in his well-being had nothing to do with the sweet and charming Charlotte. Nothing at all.

* * *

"Why did you agree to have dinner with him?" Charlotte asked once she closed the door to their hotel room. She ripped off her ruined hat and threw it on the table next to the fireplace. Then she pulled off her soiled gloves, rubbing at the stained leather. "We don't know him, and he was in that saloon."

Charlotte would have to inquire if the hotel had a laundress in the morning. She worried the stains on her gloves and dress would set if she didn't get them cleaned soon. Who knew what had been on the wall and floor in that horrendous place?

"The same saloon you ran into without any thought to your reputation or to what you might find?" Aunt Martha ignored the furious look on Charlotte's face, shuffled to the armchair, and carefully sank into it. "I think you have no cause to judge the man. He certainly didn't have to rescue us." She kicked off her kid boots and reached to massage a stockinged foot between her fingers.

"I really need to learn to wear something just a bit more comfortable when I'm out with you. My feet are not thanking me right now."

"He didn't rescue us," Charlotte said as she pulled out hairpins. She scratched at her scalp and groaned as the heavy weight fell to her shoulders. "I could've gotten myself out of there just fine. I was just caught unaware when that fight started between those men."

"Humph," muttered her aunt. She wiggled her toes, lifting her feet from the floor, and stretched her arms above her head. "I'm famished. I'll ring down to the desk and get something sent up." She pushed to stand and shuffled across the floor to the new contraption they called the candlestick phone.

The Pacific Hotel was surprisingly modern and had a switchboard. You could pick up the handle of the phone and it would ring to the main floor. All kinds of new inventions had been developed over the past few years. It was an exciting time in their new modern world. Who knew what else the turn of the century would bring for them all?

Ignoring her, Charlotte sat, carefully removed her slippers, and extended her legs, stretching her feet before dropping them to the floor. The slippers were not meant for the harsh terrain they found themselves in and were likely ruined as well. She would have to stop at the mercantile and see if she couldn't purchase a sturdy pair of boots. She might also have to look into a more serviceable skirt and blouse for the weather and conditions of Pocatello. The railroad town was far from the high society of St. Louis. Her gowns made her stand out in a crowd like a beacon of flashy sophistication.

Charlotte stood and curled her toes into the plush rug before walking to the window, listening to her aunt as she barked into the phone. Her brisk and efficient tone brokered no argument from the one on the other end.

"Yes, brown gravy and green beans would be perfect. Hot rolls and plenty of warm butter. Oh, and two slices of chocolate cake." Martha ended the call a moment later.

Charlotte gazed into the night sky when a poke on her backside made her yelp and swing around. She rubbed at the spot. "Aunty, why did you do that?"

Not looking a bit contrite, Aunt Martha said, "Young lady, if you hadn't gone into that... that din of inequity, I wouldn't have had to follow you. Do you realize how close you came to damaging your reputation? Thank heavens that handsome Mr. Seymour was there to escort us out. If he hadn't been willing to help, I shudder to think what would've happened to you."

"Nothing happened to me. I'm perfectly capable of defending myself."

"Are you? I saw that man grab hold of you before he was pushed from behind. He had every intention of having his way with you, and I'm positive you wouldn't have enjoyed it." She tapped her cane on the ground and frowned.

Charlotte bowed her head. Her aunt was right, although she'd never admit it. Charlotte was going too far in her quest to find her father, but he was all she had left. She had to know why he'd left St. Louis from his own lips, not from what her grandfather always told her.

"That may be the case, but if I—"

"Stop it, young lady. You know you shouldn't have gone in there. If you'd seen your father, we could have asked for help, but instead, you rushed inside without thinking. It could've cost you your life, not to mention your virtue."

"Aunty—"

"Don't aunty me." Her aunt's glare made Charlotte cringe with shame. "Your mother would be appalled if she saw what you were up to, not to mention what your grandfather would think."

Charlotte's grandfather was determined to see her married off to a man of his choosing unless she could convince her father to return home and stop him. She could ignore her grandfather's wishes, but he threatened to withhold her inheritance if she did. She could live without all of the frivolities she'd had since she had moved in with him, but she needed the money if she were to open the children's home. So many children were without loving parents. She wanted to do something positive with her life other than be a mother and a wife.

Charlotte took the cane from her aunt's fingertips and put it aside. She took Martha's hands in hers. "I'm sorry. I didn't mean to frighten you. I shouldn't have gone inside the saloon." She gently squeezed her aunt's hands. "I just saw my father, and I couldn't take the chance he'd disappear again."

Her aunt pulled away and placed her soft palm on Charlotte's cheek. "I know you want to believe it was your father, but we've been chasing him across the country for months with plenty of sightings that have amounted to nothing. You need to be careful."

"I will. I won't do it again."

Her aunt shook her head, a slight smile on her face. "I highly doubt that, but I know you will try. For me, I hope?"

"Yes, yes. Of course I will."

Appearing appeased, she patted Charlotte's

arm. "I'm going to rest for a few minutes. Please, let me know when the food arrives." She grabbed her cane and hobbled to the other end of the suite to the room she would call home for the next few days or as long as it took for Charlotte to determine if her father had been in Pocatello, if he was still there, or if he had left town.

One way or another, she was going to find him.

Chapter 3

March 2, 1901

Stanley glanced in the mirror of his hotel room, smoothed down the edges of his navy suit jacket, and flicked at a piece of white lint on his chest. He cleaned up nicely once he took the time to do so.

He questioned his motives for taking Charlotte and her aunt to dinner. Stanley couldn't pursue her. He had nothing to offer, but he had committed to taking them to dinner. He wouldn't go back on his word, even if he thought he wanted to.

Earlier that morning, he had rifled through his belongings and realized he had nothing appropriate to wear. He'd rushed to the first floor and asked the desk clerk if any men's clothing stores were nearby. Lucky for him, one had just opened across the railroad tracks and provided ready-made suits. He was able to procure one for a tidy sum, the store clerk grinning widely at the giant sale he had made when Stanley needed to be outfitted from head to toe. For some reason, he was compelled to make a good impression, even though there could be nothing between them. There couldn't be. He was only in Pocatello for a few more days before he'd leave once again for parts unknown. He never stayed anywhere for long and hadn't for years.

He grabbed a clean white handkerchief, folded it into a square, and placed it into his suit pocket. He glanced at the clock. It was time to leave. If he wasn't careful, he would be late, and he didn't want to make a bad impression.

When he reached the dining room, he found the maître d' and requested a table near the windows. The sun was slowly moving behind the mountains and would set soon. Candles flickered on each of the white tablecloths, and gaslights hung on the dark brown walls. There was a dim hum of voices and utensils clinking. Stanley thanked the maître d', sat in the chair facing the door, and asked for a whiskey. He needed liquid courage. If the women arrived, he'd have that going for him, and if they didn't, it would numb the pain that never went away, no matter how hard he tried.

A few minutes later, the whiskey arrived. As he lifted the drink to his lips, he saw a vision in gold. Her thick hair hung down her back, held away from her face with gold clips that matched the vibrancy of her gown. He wasn't the only one who had noticed. Men across the rooms stopped what they were doing and were awestruck by her beauty. She stopped at the entrance, spoke to the maître d', and then scanned the room until she met his gaze.

A crackle of chemistry flared between them, and he felt the jolt all the way to his toes. He shifted in his seat to eliminate the feelings of unrest springing up inside him. Who was this woman, and why was she having such an impact on him? Before he could even dissect the thoughts roaring through his mind, Charlotte and her aunt were led to his table.

He shoved his seat back and fumbled a bit before standing. The cloth napkin he'd placed on his lap fell to the ground. He bent, snatched it from the floor, and slapped it none too gently onto the table. His nerves were getting the best of him. In the past, he wouldn't have been so clumsy, but his confidence was shaken.

Charlotte bent her head, covering her mouth with her white-gloved hand as she once again tried to contain her laughter at his embarrassment and clumsiness. She had every reason to laugh. He wasn't acting as a grown man should. Instead, he was acting like an overeager young man who'd never been around a proper young lady. If he wasn't careful, he might stumble and fall at her feet, fawning over her like a moon-sick calf.

He took a visible deep breath. "Welcome, ladies. I'm so glad you could join me tonight."

Martha smiled and reached for her chair.

"Oh, please let me," he said and walked to Martha's side. He pulled it out and waited for her to sit before gently pushing it forward. He reached for Charlotte's chair to do the same. Charlotte opened her mouth to likely give him a scathing rebuke, but she shared a glance with her aunt and snapped it shut, stopping whatever thought had crossed her mind.

Charlotte placed her reticule on the table before smoothing her gold skirt and settling into the plushness of the armchair. He nudged it forward. Her long hair was draped across her shoulders. He raised his hand ever so slightly to touch it but caught himself from pushing his hands into the thick strands.

He'd almost made a monumental mistake. You didn't touch a lady without her permission, especially one you didn't know. He stepped away and ran his sweaty palms along his suit jacket before he returned to his seat, praying his composure was in place before he faced them.

"Would you both care for a drink?" he asked, picking up his napkin.

"I certainly would, young man." Martha waved to the nearest waiter and ordered glasses of red wine for her and her niece. She also asked for a bread basket. "I'm famished. I need a bite to eat before we order or I'll fairly faint. And that wouldn't do if I want to keep my niece here properly chaperoned." She picked up a napkin, shook it, and placed it in her lap. "And if I did faint right here, you"—she wiggled her eyebrows—"might even try to steal a kiss."

"Aunt Martha," Charlotte said, bright red streaks blooming across her cheeks within seconds of her aunt's words.

He laughed but then swallowed the guffaws when Charlotte's gaze swung to him. "We certainly don't want to see you faint with hunger." He then asked the waiter for a few other tasty tidbits while they perused the menu.

The waiter returned a few minutes later with

an overflowing bread basket, a warm crock of butter, jams and honey, and their drinks. Martha dug in while he glanced over the top of his menu and gazed at Charlotte. He tried to appear nonchalant but feared she'd notice that he was looking at her with lust-filled eyes.

The waiter took their orders and quietly slipped away. Then silence reigned. Stanley's mouth went dry, and he lost whatever small talk manners he used to own. He hadn't sat with a proper young lady in years and hadn't had a meal with anyone other than miners, cowboys, and criminals, so he was unsure what to say.

Martha glanced between the two of them and sighed. "Tell me, Mr. Seymour, what brings you to this small railroad town?"

He didn't want to talk about his past and didn't know what to do with himself since his former wife was gone. Talking about the mess of his life wasn't normal dinner conversation, and he didn't want to be the cause of a somber mood.

Martha looked at him quizzically. "Did I ask a complicated question?"

"No, no," he said. "It's not that... It's just not something I like to discuss."

"Aren't a lot of things?" Martha ripped off a piece of bread and slathered it with a thick layer of creamy yellow butter before she popped it into her mouth. She raised an eyebrow, waiting for him to continue.

He took a sip of his whiskey to give him a moment to gain his composure. "I guess you could say I've been on a mission, and I've stopped here to take a rest."

"What kind of mission?" she asked, her gaze probing.

He squirmed under her scrutiny.

"Aunt Martha, don't you believe that's invading his privacy? He said it wasn't something he likes to discuss," Charlotte said.

"Nonsense, I'm just making small talk. Asking why someone is in a small town in Idaho is a reasonable question."

"It may be reasonable, but pushing him to

further explain when he's already given an answer is pushy," Charlotte said.

"Phssh, I'm an old woman. I'm entitled to a few eccentricities." She took a sip.

Charlotte shook her head but smiled. The love the two women had for one another was obvious, even to the common onlooker.

"Now, what was I saying?" She raised a finger to the corner of her lips. "Oh yes, what is your mission, Mr. Seymour?"

The waiter returned with a platter of cut meats and cheeses and warm savory tarts, allowing him a moment to consider his response. A few minutes later, Martha waved for him to continue. It appeared she wouldn't let him get away from answering her questions, but he didn't want to face his past and his inability to save his pa.

When he couldn't take the silence, he said, "I'd been looking for the woman who had a hand in my pa's murder, and I'm deciding my next path now that she's dead."

"My, oh my. I'm sure there's a story behind

that, and dare I say, a difficult one at that. I won't presume to ask what happened… Unless, of course, you wish to share." There was a glint in Martha's eyes that spoke of her curiosity to know more.

"Aunt Martha, we cannot presume to ask Mr. Seymour what happened to his father. It was rude of you to press. This has to be a very painful topic for him. He certainly doesn't need to explain." Charlotte was clearly trying to get her aunt to stop her inquisitive questions.

Martha glared at her niece but nodded. "I apologize, Mr. Seymour. I certainly don't want to bring up painful memories for you."

He smiled to ease the tension. "It's perfectly all right. You couldn't have known. It was an innocent enough question, one perfect strangers might ask when meeting one another for the first time." He sighed. "In full openness, my former wife, Connie, murdered my pa. She hid her intentions and deceived all of us. When we discovered what she had been up to, it was too late."

"Has she been found?" Martha asked.

"Yes," he said. "In November, she finally paid for what she did to my family."

"My, that sounds ominous," Martha drawled.

Stanley tried to smile but failed. He was tired and couldn't find the energy to return home. Instead, he wandered aimlessly from town to town, having no idea what to do next but unable to face the censure in his brother's eyes. He didn't feel right living at his family's ranch or anywhere near his brothers. Connie had callously weaved a scheme that hurt his family to its core. "She'd been running for years but returned last year to Helena, where my brothers caught wind of her presence. She had resources, friends, and a means that far surpassed anything we ever expected. What she told me about her past was far from the truth, but we'll never know the fullness of what she had been up to."

"That's quite the tale, Mr. Seymour," Martha said.

"It is, isn't it?" He lifted his lips into a painful

smile. Her questions had dredged up memories he tried to forget but likely never would.

* * *

Charlotte squirmed when Mr. Seymour explained why he was in Pocatello. She loved her aunty dearly, but sometimes she pressed too far and didn't know when to stop. Thankfully, their food arrived and gave her aunt something to concentrate on other than Mr. Seymour and his tragic past. She could tell with one glance, however, that Mr. Seymour was not eating. If he'd been hungry, it was no longer the case. He pushed the food around his plate, and the occasional bite was met with a grimace.

When they arrived, she'd been excited to see him, although she would've never admitted that to her aunt. Her Aunt Martha was on the prowl for a husband for Charlotte. She had already expressed her lack of desire to marry to both her grandfather and her aunt, but neither listened. The difference being her aunt wanted Charlotte to marry for love, while her grandfather had picked a man who worked for him. Different motives, but ultimately the same price.

When her gaze met Stanley's across the full dining room, the air had stilled and then tightened as though an invisible tether pulled her to his side with one slight movement. Other sounds had disappeared. Tingles had run across her skin, and blood had rushed to her cheeks. It was a wonder she hadn't broken out into an unladylike sweat.

She'd wanted to impress him, and that scared her. She'd almost told her aunt she had a headache, but when she saw him, she hadn't been able to stop herself from gliding toward him. His eyes were dark magnets that drew her in like butterflies on a warm spring day. He was the first man to have ever caught her attention and hold it.

But then her aunt had probed into his private life. When he admitted his pa had been murdered, her heart had broken for him. She too had lost her mother although she'd been able to say her goodbyes. From Stanley's tone, he'd not been granted the same opportunity.

As they finished their meal, Charlotte tried to salvage what remained of their disastrous conversation. "I want to apologize for my aunt, Mr. Seymour."

"You don't need to apologize for me, young lady," her aunt hissed. The glare Aunt Martha gave her indicated she'd get a talking-to when they were alone in their rooms.

"Oh, I do, Aunty." Turning back to Mr. Seymour, she said, "Please accept our condolences on your loss. I, too, lost my mother, although not in the same manner."

"I'm sorry to hear that, Miss Charlotte. May I call you Charlotte? I don't think you ever told me your surname."

"I didn't, did I?" she said, and frankly, she wasn't about to. Not until she knew more about the man. "Charlotte will do."

He nodded but smiled at her obvious attempt to ignore his not-so-subtle question. "Before we continue, I insist you call me Stanley. Calling me

Mr. Seymour makes me think you're talking to my pa or my older brother." His eyes twinkled, and the grin on his lips caused heat to flare across her cheeks.

"I don't know, Mr.—"

"Stanley," he said firmly.

"Oh, all right, Stanley. If you insist."

He nodded. "May I ask why you two are visiting this fine territory?"

Turnabout was fair play. Her Aunt Martha had asked the same question, and it would be rude of her to ignore him. "We're looking for my father."

"Oh, is he lost?"

His humor fell flat, but she couldn't find fault in him trying to make light of the situation.

"Yes, you could say that he is." Lost or not wanting to be found. It could go either way.

Seeming to realize his misstep, he frowned. "Is there anything I can do to help?"

"No..." She paused. "Unless you can track down a man who doesn't want to be found."

"Oh, I might have my ways. Why don't you

tell me what you know?" Stanley settled more comfortably in his chair, a glass of whiskey between his fingers as though he had all the time in the world. Somehow, that irritated her and caused the fine bristles at the back of her neck to stand straight up. It was as though he was making fun of her attempts at finding her father.

"Now, why would I trust you... A stranger? Someone I don't know."

He bent his arm, crinkling the fine fabric of his suit. The white cuff of his shirt poked through the coat sleeve, and a gold cufflink sparkled in the candlelight. He fingered his mustache as though contemplating a very serious question. "Maybe because a stranger would have a different take. Might see something you've missed." She opened her mouth to respond, but he spoke first. "Not that I think you've missed a thing, but because he's your father, you might not see things as clearly."

Stanley had poked through her insecurities. She'd been wondering the same thing just that morning, and now he bared them on the table for her to examine.

When she stayed silent, he continued. "I'm someone with no stake, who has, dare I say, some experience in looking for someone who doesn't want to be found. Not that I'm saying he doesn't want to be found, but I'd be happy to lend my services. If you're interested, that is?"

"I don't know," she said, while a part of her screamed yes.

"I think we should hear him out, my dear," Aunt Martha said. "He's offering to help, and don't you forget, he helped us just last night."

Charlotte could strangle her aunt. She was trying to push Charlotte into Stanley's arms and wasn't subtle about it. Her aunt had lost her beau at a young age and had never married, which gave her an insatiable desire to make sure Charlotte wouldn't be left alone, no matter how she had to go about it.

Chapter 4

March 18, 1901

Charlotte wondered why in heaven's name she had agreed to Aunt Martha's latest crazy scheme. Having Stanley's help in looking for her father over the past two weeks was sending her emotions on a wild ride, and she found herself waiting for a glimpse of him every day she didn't see him. She didn't want to be attracted to the man, but her aunt conveniently disappeared when Stanley was around, especially if propriety allowed for it. Charlotte almost felt like a young girl with her first schoolyard crush.

Stanley had interviewed several men, both in her presence and out of it. The two of them had followed countless leads that led to nowhere. It had been quite exhilarating at times to observe Stanley's dogged determination to track down every person who might have seen her father. While she was flattered he seemed willing to help, irritation prickled her skin because she couldn't do it on her own. She had started on this journey wanting to find her father but found herself needing Stanley's help to continue.

Being in Stanley's company made it difficult to resist him, although it was completely one-sided. She was sure he didn't regard her as anything more than a way to distract himself from the weight he carried. He certainly didn't look at her like a lovesick calf, the way she found herself looking at him when he wasn't paying attention.

"Charlotte, you're keeping Stanley waiting," Aunt Charlotte yelled from the front room of their suite, thumping her cane on the hard wooden floors not covered in rugs.

Charlotte had just donned her woolen bonnet, grabbed her fur-lined mittens, and smiled to herself. She didn't have a moment's peace when her aunt was on a mission. Stanley was waiting for her at her aunt's insistence, she was sure.

She swallowed the thick pile of saliva that had pooled in her mouth. Stanley stood next to a window, and the light shined on him like he was a Greek god. All magnificent, proud, and delicious. He had to know what he did to women. She had to shake herself free from the unwanted thoughts. Their relationship was a business one, nothing more.

At first, Charlotte hadn't believed he'd take her aunt up on her request to help them locate her father. Why would a perfect stranger want to help them? But when her aunt mentioned the amount, Stanley's mouth had fallen open, and it was a wonder he hadn't caught flies with it. He couldn't say yes fast enough, although Charlotte wasn't altogether sure it was strictly the money that intrigued him. There appeared to be another ulterior motive for his willingness to help, but she couldn't pinpoint what it was.

She forced her gaze away from Stanley and instead looked out the windows, trying to distract herself with the thick snowflakes falling from the dark sky. She didn't know what was wrong with her. No man had ever made her feel this way, and she wasn't sure she liked it. It was distracting her from why she was in Idaho.

"What are the plans for today?" Charlotte asked once she tamped down her beating heart. Her path was straightforward. She couldn't let a handsome man derail her.

"I heard talk of a man fitting your father's description in a saloon on the east side of town. I thought I'd question the man who saw him while you and your aunt—"

"I'll go with you," Charlotte interrupted.

"I don't think that's a wise idea. It isn't safe for a young lady like yourself."

"I don't think I need you to tell me what's safe." She raised an eyebrow, just begging him to argue with her.

"I wasn't hired to guard you." Anger flashed in his eyes along with a hint of impatience.

"I don't expect you to, Stanley. But I hired you—"

"No, your aunt hired me." He shifted and opened his coat to reveal a pair of silver-handled six-shooters sitting on his hip.

If Stanley thought showing his gun belt would scare her, he was surely mistaken. Plenty of men wore them strapped to their sides. While things had become civilized, one still had to be mindful. Stanley seemed more sophisticated than a common gunslinger, but now that she knew he was comfortable wearing them, he'd be useful to her, especially on that side of the railroad tracks.

"I won't argue with you. We don't have time for this. I'm going with you." She slapped the mittens against her hip.

"No, you're not," he said. "I can't search for him as well as make sure no harm comes to you."

"We've been looking for two weeks, and this

is the first time you've been concerned. Has something changed?"

He shifted and avoided looking her in the eyes. "No, not exactly."

"Then there is no reason to dawdle. Besides, I have this." She reached into a hidden pocket on the inside lining of her coat and pulled out a small derringer. It wasn't the most powerful of weapons, but it fit nicely inside and would work in a pinch. She also had a knife stashed in her boot and one in the boning of her corset. "I'm not some powerless woman who can't protect herself."

A devilish smile reached far across his cheeks that he unsuccessfully tried to hide by shaking his head, but it was too late. She had seen it and won the argument.

"Now"—she put the gun back into her pocket—"are you ready to leave?"

He picked up his black hat, gave her aunt a quick kiss on the cheek, and opened the door. "After you, my lady."

Sarcasm laced his words, but she wasn't about to let it bother her. She had gotten her way, and she'd expected nothing less. He might think he was all-powerful, but she had a few weapons at her disposal as well.

Chapter 5

March 18, 1901

Stanley watched Charlotte flounce out of the hotel room and down the hall. At least she hadn't worn a fluffy, shimmery dress that spoke of impracticality. Instead, she had donned a serviceable skirt, blouse, and thick coat to protect her from the cold. There was an air about her that spoke of class and wealth, and it wasn't something she could hide, no matter how hard she tried. All eyes were drawn to her the moment she walked into any room.

He followed her down the stairs and out the

front doors, where they had to maneuver across the railroad tracks, being careful of any advancing trains. The Union Pacific Railroad had built the hotel right against the tracks, making it convenient for guests and workers alike. It could be downright dangerous crossing the multiple tracks, but it was easy enough as long as you watched your step. The saloons, brothels, jailhouse, general store, livery, and churches sat on the other side of the rail lines.

Once across the wooden rails, they dodged stray dogs, freight wagons being dragged behind mules and oxen, and men on horseback before reaching a rough, wooden walkway. It was survival of the fittest on the other side of the tracks. Stanley prayed he hadn't made a mistake in agreeing to let her come with him, even though he was quite sure he couldn't have stopped her.

Suddenly, a large black dog barked furiously from down the road, bared his teeth, and ran straight toward them. Charlotte yelped and practically climbed onto his side as if he were the nearest tree trunk. Trying not to laugh as her screeches of outrage pierced his eardrum, he couldn't help but place his arms around her slim waist. When a squirrel or bird caught his attention, the dog abruptly stopped and ran the other direction, leaving them unscathed.

"It's all right, Charlotte."

She dropped her arms from around his neck, her face bright red and her breath heavy from fear. "I'm so sorry. I don't know what came over me."

He chuckled. "No reason to apologize. I wasn't sure what that dog was going to do. If you hadn't climbed onto my waist, I might've done the same to you."

She brushed at her skirts, her hands shaking.

Realizing he might've embarrassed her, he changed the subject. "Let's continue on shall we?"

Stanley held out his arm. She avoided his gaze and placed her hand on his.

A few men had stopped to watch their antics. With any luck, they wouldn't be accosted, for he wasn't in the mood to find himself in jail for shooting any man making advances on the charming young woman next to him.

Though he'd argued with her earlier and told Charlotte she shouldn't go with him, he'd known she wouldn't sit waiting like an obedient housewife. She'd insisted on accompanying him on most of their jaunts in his effort to find her father. He'd put up a slight fight, less Martha think he had ill intentions, but he was intrigued by Charlotte. Wanting to see how far she'd go in her quest to find her father, he would do what he could to stay in her presence even though it wasn't the best idea he'd ever had.

He'd been shocked when Charlotte pulled the small black, one-bullet derringer from her coat pocket, but he shouldn't have been. While she dressed and acted as a proper society lady, there was a toughness to her. He wouldn't be surprised if she had a knife or two stashed on her as well.

Snow had fallen the night before and covered everything with a sheen of blinding white crystals, but it had grown dark brown and gray from the horses, cattle, and foot traffic that never ended. They would be much more comfortable in front of a roaring fire instead of outside in the elements, but they had a mission.

Brisk wind swirled around them. Stanley pulled up the collar of his thick, fur-lined coat and tightened the scarf around his neck. Growing up in Montana, he'd learned that being unprepared in wintery conditions could lead to frostbite or even death. He glanced at Charlotte and wondered if she was reconsidering her desire to be out in the frigid gales ripping around them. From the firm set of her shoulders, he figured she'd never admit it, especially if she had a stake in the outcome.

"It's mighty cold out here, Charlotte. Are you positive you want to come with me? I'm happy to question the man and return with the details." He took her elbow to help her over a particularly large snow drift. Her boots sank into the dirty snow, but she seemed unaware that the hem of her skirt would be wet and filthy by the time they returned to the hotel.

"I'm perfectly content to continue." She pulled from his grasp and turned to look around them. "Which way are we to go?"

He wondered at her stubbornness and had tried to be a gentleman by suggesting she return to the hotel. Later, when she complained about her frozen nose and toes, she couldn't say he hadn't asked.

A few minutes later, they arrived at the Elk Horn Saloon. He had visited it the night before, which was how he'd learned about the man they were looking for. The saloon had a honky-tonk girlie show and the finest selections of beer, although he wasn't sure what Charlotte would think of the place. A din of inequity wasn't the type of place he'd normally take a proper lady. His pa would've been horrified that he'd taken her to a place like that. He had taught him better, but Stanley was learning he couldn't tell Charlotte what to do or how to do it. She had a mind of her own, and who was he to dictate a word to her? He wasn't her pa, brother, or even her husband. He was just the lucky sap who'd agreed to her aunt's request.

Looking at the two-story saloon and brothel, she let go of his arm, grasped the railing of the porch, and stomped her feet to remove the snow. She looked over her shoulder and cocked an eyebrow at him as if to ask what was taking him so long. She was feisty and would make some man very happy one day.

He moved his coat to display his sidearms. He wouldn't enter a saloon with a lady by his side without letting the men know he wasn't afraid to fight and defend her honor.

Pushing open the swinging doors, he ushered her inside. It took a moment for his eyes to adjust. Little light pierced the grimy windows. With it being the middle of the day, there was no need to turn on the gas lamps or light lanterns until the place filled for the evening show. Only hard-core drunks who imbibed from sunup to sundown with bleak gazes, worn bodies, and solemn moods were the only ones who frequented the place during the day. It'd become livelier in the evening when the ladies entertained, but just then, no music played from the scratched and worn upright brown piano. A few rough-looking whores lined the edge of the bar, looking for someone willing to take them up on what they offered.

One whore ambled to their side. She raked her bloodshot eyes across his frame, her gaze appreciative. She tried a come-hither smile but failed with her missing teeth and a body that had seen better days. He wasn't interested and shook his head. She dropped her smile and swung around in disgust as though he weren't worth the trouble, that he was the one missing out on a good time.

Ignoring her, Stanley scanned the room and saw the man he'd been looking for. Placing his hand against the small of her back, he led Charlotte through the tables and around those whose attentions were solely on the drinks in front of them. A few lifted their heads as they passed but looked at his sidearms and fierce expression and ignored them. They didn't appear inclined to get into an altercation with him any more than he did with them.

When they reached the rear of the saloon, the man they were searching for took one look at Charlotte and stumbled to his feet. He awkwardly removed his hat, trying to push back the stringy strands of gray hair that remained. He was an older man with a rounded back and a scruffy gray beard across his gaunt cheeks. His clothes were threadbare but clean. He might not be a man of means, but he had a keen gaze, even with the unexpected lady in front of him.

"Ah, I... Um, I wasn't expecting to see you with someone, Seymour."

"My apologies, Billy. May I introduce my companion, Miss Charlotte? Charlotte, this here is Billy. He might have valuable information on your father."

"Her father," Billy said. Bulging eyes stared at them like a pair of ripe red apples. "I... Um, not really sure I can help." He slapped his hat back on his head and lurched around the chairs and table.

Stanley stopped his departure and glared at him. If he had to restrain Billy, he wouldn't have a problem doing so. While Billy was a good man, he'd been dealt a rotten hand and was skittish at the best of times.

Billy raised his head, looked at Stanley, and then plopped back into his chair. "Maybe I can after all."

Stanley pulled out a chair for Charlotte, and she gracefully sank into it. She removed her mittens, dropped them onto the table, and then rested her hands on her lap. He followed suit, except he took a chair against the wall. It was never wise to have his back to the room, especially in a saloon. He needed to see everything that was going on so he could stop an attack before it arose.

"Mr. Billy," Charlotte said, nodding to the man.

"Oh, no mister, pretty lady. Just Billy. I don't cotton to no highfalutin words. I'm a simple man from a simple place." He slapped his chest. "No meaning any disrespect and all."

"None taken, Mr.… I mean, Billy." Charlotte smiled to cover her blunder. "Can you—"

She stopped when Stanley put a hand on her knee and squeezed in a too-familiar gesture, but he needed her to be quiet. Billy was skittish enough as it was. He didn't need Charlotte discomfiting him and then Billy disappearing before they could ask him questions.

Her eyes flashing in warning, she quieted after appearing to recognize his nonverbal cues. This was his world, not hers, and she'd do well to remember that.

"Billy," Stanley said, his voice stern, quiet, but clearly authoritative. "Last time we spoke, you told me you might've seen who we're looking for."

"Well, as I told you the last time, I'm making no guarantees." He fiddled with the strap of his brown suspenders.

"I don't expect guarantees, but we'd appreciate it if you'd tell us what you know."

Stanley reached into his front pocket and pulled out the coins he'd set aside for the man. That would help speed up the information gathering. He dropped a few on the table but kept them just out of reach of Billy, giving him the enticement without giving him the benefits.

"I'm a bit thirsty," Billy said, settling farther into his chair and crossing his arms.

Stanley waved to the barkeep, who sent a barmaid over to them. "Charlotte, would you care for something to drink? Coffee, perhaps?"

She shook her head. Stanley ordered two beers—one for Billy and one for himself. Sometimes you had to loosen a tongue to get a satisfactory answer.

A moment later, the barmaid placed two giant tankards in front of them. Billy took a lusty drink before wiping his mouth with the back of his hand and grinning a toothy smile. "Now, don't that hit the spot?"

Stanley took a much smaller sip of his beer. He was smart enough to know he had to keep his wits about him with Charlotte sitting by his side. Although it was quiet in the saloon at the moment, that could change within the blink of an eye.

"So the man I saw, he fits the description—"

"Yes," Stanley said. "What can you tell me about him?"

"He came into town a month ago and has been skulking around the rail depot. Don't knows as though he's working there or not, but I've seen him a time or six."

Stanley rubbed his chin. "What makes you think he's who I'm looking for?"

"He's out of place. His hands aren't rough, his boots are new, and he's never done a solid day's work in his life." Billy took another gulp of his beer. At the rate he was going, Billy would finish the thing in two more gulps.

"There are plenty of men like that around here." Stanley wouldn't assume that was Charlotte's father and just take Billy's word.

"Maybe, but they don't be hanging out at the depot lookin' like they're up to no good."

Stanley nodded. That made sense, but he

needed more. "Charlotte, did your father work for the railroad?" He didn't want to reveal where Charlotte was from. Nefarious people could take that information and pretend to know her father to extort money. As it was, the money Charlotte had paid to find information was staggering. Stanley was glad he wasn't funding that adventure of hers.

"No," she murmured.

"What else, Billy?" Stanley asked.

Billy scratched at his scalp. "I heard he hailed from Missouri."

Charlotte straightened in her chair.

Stanley caught her eye and gave her a slight shake of his head. With any luck, she'd understand that it'd be best to let him do all the talking. "Did you ever speak with him?"

"No, but I heard somethin' else that was purely interestin'."

"And what was that?" Stanley asked. The man being from Missouri could be a coincidence. The conversation was likely another dead end. They'd had their fair share of them the past few days. People claimed to have seen her father when none of them had any helpful details.

"I heard he was looking for lost gold."

Stanley stiffened and looked at Charlotte. She appeared as shocked as he.

"What do you mean, lost gold?" Stanley asked.

Billy grinned, lifting his cheeks enthusiastically. He was pleased to have given them information they hadn't expected, although Stanley wasn't sure if it would help find Charlotte's father.

"You know, my memory is a bit sketchy these days. It might take some time to remember everything." Billy looked pointedly at the money Stanley held under his fingertips.

The information was going to cost him. Stanley reached into his pocket and pulled out a few more coins, placing the bigger denomination on top of the others.

Billy's eyes twinkled. "Yes." He tapped his fingers on the wooden tabletop. "It appears things are coming back to me but are still right there on the edge. I just can't seem to recall it."

Stanley pulled a bill from his pocket and slapped it on the table. It was an outrageous sum, more than the man deserved, but if it gave them what they needed, well, then Charlotte could afford it, as it was her money. He slid the money across the table but kept his fingers on it. If the information wasn't worth every penny, he wouldn't have any problems removing it from Billy's grasp. "Has your memory returned, Billy?"

"Well, miracles amaze me. Yes, siree, it certainly has"—he pointed—"just now, as a matter of fact. Must be divine intervention."

"What can you tell me... Umph." He grimaced as Charlotte poked him in his side. "I mean us." He rubbed his ribs where she'd dug her finger into his flesh. "About this lost gold?"

"It's quite a story." Billy relaxed farther into his chair, picked up his tankard of beer, took one look inside, and dropped it on the table. "Looky there, my beer has disappeared. I might need another for this long tale."

Stanley smothered a groan and waved for the barmaid to bring him another. If he wasn't careful, Billy was going to be drunker than a skunk before he could tell them everything.

Once Billy had another full tankard of beer in front of him, he took a giant swallow. "Have you heard the tale of the blood-soaked treasure?"

Stanley shook his head.

"In 1865, the Overland Stage Line sent a treasure of gold from Virginia City in the Montana territory just after the War Between the States. Four men held up the stagecoach, one of which was a crooked sheriff from Boise. Imagine one of those." He laughed and then emitted an enormous belch. "The story goes one man rode the stagecoach as a passenger, and the other three waited in the Portneuf Canyon. A shoot-out occurred, left a bunch of dead passengers, and the outlaws got away with two strongboxes of gold worth roughly eighty thousand dollars."

Stanley whistled. "That's quite a lot of money. How true is this?"

"Oh, it's true, all right. It's quite the legend."

Billy bounced enthusiastically in his seat now that he had their undivided attention. He was a storyteller and enjoyed regaling those who'd listened with whatever yarn he could spin. "Anyways, the survivors made their way to Miller Ranch Station, where they identified the men who robbed the stagecoach. The insurance company even put up a ten-thousand-dollar reward for the return of the gold. Eventually, the outlaws, including the sheriff, were killed, but they never found the gold. It's believed to be buried somewhere in the canyon."

Intrigued, Stanley said, "What does this have to do with the man I'm searching for?"

"I'm getting to that. Hold your horses." Billy took another drink of his beer, his arm shaking. "He's been asking lots of questions about the robbery and the men involved. I overheard him saying he knew a relative of one of 'em."

"I wonder why he'd be looking for gold. Does he need the money?" Stanley asked, more to himself than anyone else.

Charlotte stiffened next to him. He looked at

her, but before she said a word, Billy spoke up again. "I was told he was looking for the hidden gold so he could prove to his daughter's grandpappy that he was worthy."

"Worthy of what?" Stanley asked.

"Don't rightly know. He's just saying the grandpappy is controllin' and ran him off. Grandpappy thought he married his daughter for his money, but he wouldn't give him nothing 'til he proved himself. Then grandpappy took his granddaughter away and told him to disappear."

"That's right interesting," Stanley said. He'd gotten little information from Charlotte and her aunt about the disappearance of Charlotte's father. If this was her father, then Stanley was even more curious as to what had happened in St. Louis. "Anything else I should know?"

"Nots really."

"Are you sure?" Stanley pressed.

"Wells, he seemed..." Billy took another drink of his beer, the liquor running down his chin where he missed his mouth. Clearly, the two beers Stanley had provided him were not the only ones he'd had that day.

"He seemed?" Stanley prodded.

Billy's eyelids drooped, and he bobbed his head.

"Billy? Billy?" When he didn't move, Stanley reached over and pushed at his shoulder.

"What? What was that?" Billy pushed at the table and sat up, looking around them, confused for a moment. Seeming to recognize Stanley, he said, "Whats did I miss?"

"Nothin' much," Stanley said. "Can you tell us more?"

"Like what?" Billy said.

"Do you know where he's staying?" Stanley asked.

"Who?" He tilted his head and wiped at his greasy hair.

Stanley shook his head in frustration. "The man looking for the gold, the one you saw at the depot."

"Oh him. No, no. I don't know where he's

staying, but there ain't that many places to sleep here in Poky."

Stanley had heard the town referred to as Poky by the locals and thought it had a nice ring to it. "Do you know if he's still in the area?"

"No."

"Do you want to share anything else?"

"No." And with those last words, Billy promptly fell asleep.

Stanley sighed. He wouldn't get any more information out of the man, considering his snores would wake the dead. Stanley started to stand, but Charlotte stopped him.

"We can't leave. Wake him," she demanded. "He might know more about my father."

"We don't know for sure the man he was talking about was your father."

"Yes, we do. That was my grandfather he mentioned. I know he ran my father off, but I didn't know why—until tonight."

"That doesn't prove it was your father. It could be any man trying to prove himself to his daughter's grandfather."

"No, it *was* my father. He's here." She slammed her fist on the table, and the rickety wood shook near their feet. "I saw him the night I met you. Aunt Martha didn't want to believe it was him, but I know it was. This proves it."

"I think you're hopeful, and perhaps it was him, but we won't know for sure until or *if* we find him."

"Then wake Billy so we can question him more." Her voice had grown shrill and was attracting attention.

It was getting late, and what light came from the sun had diminished. More men had come inside the saloon, and many of them were not drunk. Stanley had noticed a few rough and rangy ones staring at Charlotte with lust and smacking their lips. He should've ended the conversation with Billy long before then, but he had gotten caught up in the interesting tale. It was the best lead they'd gotten all week.

"Charlotte," Stanley said, whispering in her ear, "if we don't leave now, we're going to have some big ole problems. If you haven't noticed, there are men in here who aren't likely to let a pretty young lady like yourself leave without…" He let the sentence hang, as he didn't need to explain what they were up against. He prayed she wasn't as innocent as she looked. He straightened and held out his hand.

She looked over her shoulder and shuddered. She grabbed his hand, squeezed it tightly, and let him tug her close.

"Stay near me," he said, "no matter what."

Chapter 6

March 18, 1901

Charlotte gripped Stanley's hand as if it were her lifeline. She hadn't been paying close enough attention to how many men had stepped inside the saloon during Billy's story. The men were eyeing her like she was a juicy steak or a sweet cake they wanted to devour. She reached her free hand into her coat pocket and fingered her derringer. She was confident she could get a shot off if needed, but the men in the saloon far outnumbered them. Plenty of drunks rambled by, and the number of calico queens had increased too.

She was sure Stanley could fight some of them, but not all of them. She had been impulsive in insisting she go with him. Her independent streak was something she should learn to keep in check, but she had to know what had happened to her father. It was imperative that she find him and soon. Time was running out.

They maneuvered through the growing crowd. Charlotte tried to stay as close to Stanley as she could without jumping into his arms. The slaps and pinches on her rear, as well as the brushes against her arms and chest, made it clear that if they didn't remove themselves from the saloon soon, there would be a fight. She wouldn't let any man take advantage, although she wasn't sure she'd be able to fend them off, but she'd give it all she had.

Just as the door to the outside was a few steps away, a burly man stepped in front of them. Stanley was a tall man, but the man put

Stanley to shame. She swallowed back a lump of fear as the man widened his feet and folded his arms across his chest. A beaver hat covered his head and ears, and a brownish-black, rangy bear coat rested across his vast shoulders and hung to his knees. A thick, black beard covered his chin and cheeks, and a horrendous smell wafted off him. It was a stench unlike anything she had ever experienced. A mix of skunk, dried blood, horse manure, rank onions, and heaven knew what else that she couldn't quite identify. She coughed, the scent seeming to wrap around her slight frame and choking her. Releasing the derringer in her pocket, she covered her nose with her hand. Maybe that was rude, but she couldn't help it. The smell was appalling.

Stanley stopped and pushed her behind him, but she didn't need protection. She raised her gaze to the man and changed her mind. She gripped the back of Stanley's coat and prayed he wouldn't kill them. When no sounds of pounding flesh hit her ears, she leaned to the side to get a look at what the man wanted, but her attention was soon diverted to the sounds behind her. She swiveled her head and gasped. A pack of dirty, drunken men was closing in on them. Clubs and knives were held in their hands. Their eyes were anything but kind, and they licked their lips in anticipation. They weren't worried about Stanley.

They were coming after her, and nothing was going to stop them.

She patted Stanley's shoulder, but he didn't budge. She nudged him again, but he still didn't move. Stubborn man. She reached for her derringer, flipped around with her back to Stanley's, and held it out in front of her. The men just laughed and surged forward. She screamed as she got off one shot that flew above their heads and burst through the wooden railing on the second floor.

They guffawed, hit one another's shoulders, and continued toward them. They weren't scared of her and her small derringer. Stanley whirled around and shoved her out of the way. The burly man who had stopped them from leaving the saloon roared past them, holding his arms wide, a large club held in one hand.

All havoc broke loose.

* * *

When Charlotte screamed, Stanley's blood had run cold. By keeping her behind him, he thought she'd be safe, but he'd underestimated those left in the saloon. He hadn't made an error like that in some time. Coincidentally, the last time had been with his friend and mentor, Jacob.

Stanley hadn't seen Jacob in years, not since he tried to prove to his pa that he was capable of taking over the family ranch. In one of his rebellious stages, before Stanley married Connie, he'd gotten angry with his pa one night and had left the ranch determined to make his pa eat his words. He'd been nigh on about eighteen, thinking he could show his pa and his brother Ben that he was more than they believed. Of course, they'd been right, but he'd learned a valuable lesson.

Jacob had saved him more times than he could remember, and tonight would again be one of those times.

Stanley hadn't recognized him at first. It had been many years since he had last seen him, but when Stanley pushed Charlotte behind him, the man had smiled, and the face he remembered had morphed into the older man standing in front of him. Before Stanley could welcome his friend back into his life, Charlotte had screamed. Jacob then ran into the melee defending them both without question. He didn't even ask who Charlotte was.

Jacob brandished his club and knocked out two men before they even saw him coming. Stanley pushed Charlotte out of the way and reached for the special club he had made for himself years before that he had shoved into his boot. He had modeled it after the one Jacob had. Small and compact, it was heavy and surprised even the most seasoned fighters. Stanley swung it and took out two more, but others kept on coming. When a fist hit his belly, Stanley grunted, but he fended off the attack.

Before long, flying bodies landed on tables, and chairs were smashed. He and Jacob had moved to fight with their backs to each other. The drunken men soon retreated once they realized the two of them were a force to be reckoned with.

When he could take a breath, Stanley eyed the room. Charlotte was pinned against the wall. A man kept her contained with his hand on her cheek and his lower body pushed into hers.

With a primal roar that sounded unlike anything he had ever uttered, Stanley rushed toward them and whipped him around, jamming his tight knuckles into the man's face with one solid punch. The man dropped like a bag of bricks. Stanley grabbed Charlotte around the waist and backed out of the saloon, with Jacob finishing off the last of the men.

They ran along the snow-packed road and turned down an alley, with Jacob following close behind. Slowing when it appeared no one was following, they came to a stop against an old wooden doorway.

"Haven't had that much fun in ages, little buck," Jacob said, wiping blood from his cheek.

Stanley chuckled. The fact that Jacob found that skirmish a fun time was reminiscent of plenty of tussles the two of them had gotten into when he was younger.

"It's been quite some time. Never expected to see you out here," Stanley said.

"I'd have to say the same. You're far from home." Jacob lifted an eyebrow.

Stanley rubbed the back of his neck. He didn't know if Jacob had heard about his pa, but then wasn't the time to explain the whole sordid mess. "Seems we both are."

They reached a set of horses and mules tethered along a hitching post. "Where you staying?" Jacob pulled a sugar cube out of his pocket and let the horse nibble it from his hand.

"At the Pacific Hotel next to the depot," Stanley said. "Meet me in the dining room just before sunrise tomorrow. I'll buy you a meal. My treat."

"I don't need no charity," Jacob said, rubbing his horse's muzzle as it pushed his head into Jacob's coat, looking for more.

"Didn't say it was charity. Got a job for you. If you're interested." Stanley recognized Jacob's pride and wouldn't do anything to question it.

"I'd like that." Jacob mounted his horse. A pack mule loaded with supplies was tied to the horn of his saddle. "I'll see you tomorrow then. Evenin', ma'am." He doffed his hat. Within seconds, Jacob had all but disappeared in the swirling snow that had arrived while they'd been inside the saloon.

Stanley took Charlotte's hand and escorted her back to the hotel. It wouldn't take long for those in the saloon to come outside and find them if they were angry enough. He wanted to be far away when they did.

* * *

Charlotte held Stanley's arm as he pulled her through the rapidly dropping snow. They struggled through the snowbanks, but Stanley was relentless. He didn't let her lag behind, lifting her when she got stuck and keeping her from slipping on any hidden ice. Before long, they reached the front of the Pacific Hotel.

He urged her up the steps of the three-story hotel. The wooden canopy prevented the snow from dropping onto their shoulders and gave them a chance to take a breath. Stanley brushed his hands against her shoulders, removing the snow, and then lingered far closer than appropriate, but she didn't mind. With her on a single step above him, they could see eye to eye.

He pushed a fallen strand of hair behind her ear, resting his fingers against her neck before falling away. Tingles zipped through her, and she wished he'd kept his fingers near.

It had been an eventful afternoon of discovering crucial information about her father. When the fight broke out in the saloon, she'd had a moment of panic, but Stanley had kept her safe from harm—both he and that strange man he called Jacob. There was a history there. She had so many things she wanted to ask Stanley, but it wasn't her place to question him. They weren't friends. They were just... She didn't know what they were, but she couldn't ask such personal questions.

He had been hired to do a job and was trying his best to fulfill that promise to her aunt. Charlotte thought that was all she had wanted, but something had shifted. The air had changed between them. She wanted something more from him, but she wasn't sure what that was.

"You best go on inside now, Miss Charlotte," Stanley whispered. His voice was a caress against her ears, as if a butterfly had softly flapped its wings before drifting away. "The snow's getting worse, and you'll catch your death of cold."

"I'm not cold," she said and then promptly shivered as an icy breeze blew between them, lifting her skirt and the ends of her scarf. She giggled at the contradiction to her words.

He smiled, his brown eyes soulful. "Maybe not, but it won't be long before you freeze." He clasped his hat on his head to keep it from flying away. "I'm sorry about tonight. I should've done a better job of keeping you from those rough men."

She reached for his free hand and held it between her thick mittens, slowly rubbing up and down his bare palm. He had left his gloves in the saloon, and his fingers were bound to be icy. She lifted them to her lips and blew. He shivered and tried to pull them away, but she held tight and blew once more before letting go.

She pulled off a mitten and touched his cheek. "You protected me like a true gentleman. I'll see you in the morning." She leaned forward and brushed her lips against his whiskered cheek. "Good night, Stanley."

Before he could see the blush blooming on her cheeks, she turned and went inside the hotel. A blast of warm air welcomed her inside as she left him standing alone in the snow.

Chapter 7

March 19, 1901

Early the next morning, Stanley found Jacob sitting with his back against the far wall of the hotel's dining room. The maître d' appeared affronted that the man sat inside the pristine room. Knowing Jacob, he probably still smelled as if he'd rolled in a pile of buffalo dung.

It had been some time since they had seen one another, and much had happened in those intervening years. Things that couldn't be changed or removed from their shared history. Jacob might've been a friend and a surrogate father, but Stanley didn't know if he'd still be willing to help him considering what had happened the last time they'd been together.

Jacob also didn't know about Stanley's biggest mistake, and once he discovered that, he'd likely leave Stanley to his own devices. Jacob didn't tolerate stupidity, and Stanley had that in spades both then and now. How many chances would Jacob give him once he learned Stanley was the reason Stanley's pa, Cole, had died? Jacob had been a part of Stanley's life since he was a young child and was bound to be disappointed in him.

Jacob stood when Stanley reached his table. He had a wide grin and pulled Stanley into a warm bear hug, his furs enveloping him like a dusty cave. Stanley's nose itched, and he had to pull away to sneeze, not once but twice. The thick furs draped across Jacob's shoulders needed a laundress and a good smacking with a dust broom. It hadn't seen a lick of soap in months, if not years, as evidenced by the smells and dirt floating off it.

"Little buck, how ya doin'?" Jacob said, gripping his shoulders once Stanley finished sneezing.

Jacob was scruffy, and Stanley could barely tell it was the man he used to know. His rough voice and big smile were what Stanley remembered, and it brought him a measure of comfort he didn't know he needed.

"I'm still waking up and taking a breath every morning," Stanley said, which was a far cry from the truth, but he wasn't going to lay his troubles at Jacob's feet. He would likely tell him to buck up. Jacob didn't cotton to laziness or excuses and believed you were the owner of your circumstances.

Slapping Stanley once more on the back, Jacob sat, and a cloud of dust floated around him.

"It's been years, Jacob. Whatcha you doin' here? The last time I saw you, you were hunting outside of Trapper Peak."

"That was some good hunting in those days." Jacob relaxed in his chair, finished the last drop of his coffee. He dropped the cup and waved for another. A few minutes later, two hot mugs of coffee and a bread basket were deposited on the table. Not wasting any time, they both ordered eggs, steak, and warm potatoes but waited to discuss the real business until after the waiter disappeared.

"Why aren't you at your pa's ranch?" Jacob asked, skipping right past the normal pleasantries. He was nothing if not direct. "I heard you inherited it and then subsequently lost it." He lifted an eyebrow.

Stanley squirmed under the scrutiny. He wouldn't have expected Jacob to have known, but Montana was a relatively small community, and it took little for information to pass from one mouth to the next. "It's a long story."

Jacob scratched at his bear. "Not as though I've got anywhere to go."

Stanley shook his head and picked up his mug of coffee. He'd been drowning his sorrows in plenty of liquor as of late, using it to mask the pain, but it was a bit too early to imbibe. Seeing

Jacob the night before had made him realize he had to stop. His family had been through enough in the past year, and helping Charlotte gave him a purpose outside of his mindless pursuit of his former wife. It wouldn't be easy, as he craved the liquor on many nights, but he'd at least try.

He wasn't looking forward to telling Jacob everything that had happened over the years. He wanted fortification for that conversation, but he'd live without it. If he couldn't find the strength to talk to the one man who meant the most to him outside of his deceased pa, he'd never be able to fully help Charlotte or himself.

Over the next hour, Stanley told Jacob the unvarnished truth about what had happened eight years prior. How he had married a beautiful, yet unbelievably conniving woman. How she had convinced a ranch hand to kill his pa. How she'd had an affair with the same man and then tried to have Stanley killed. Everything had been a giant scheme to gain control of the family ranch his ma and pa had worked so hard to build. Connie hadn't loved him. She had only loved the money, land, and what it could have given her.

When Stanley finished, he leaned forward, clenching the sides of his coffee mug in a pathetic attempt to avoid looking at Jacob. He was ashamed of his behavior. That was why he had left the ranch. Ben had wanted him to stay once the truth had been revealed, but his guilt over his part in bringing that woman into the family had eaten him alive. He'd believed their pa had left him the ranch when, in truth, it had belonged to Ben all along. His father had left each of his children parcels of land, but the main part of the ranch belonged to his oldest son.

Stanley hadn't questioned the forged will like he should have. Instead, he had gone along with it at Connie's insistence, and not wanting to upset his *wife,* he'd kicked his brothers off the ranch and almost sent his sisters to boarding school, all for the love of a woman who had never loved him to begin with.

"Seems you created yourself quite a pickle,"

Jacob said after a long moment of silence. He circled the top of his coffee mug with his fingers.

Stanley nodded just as the waiter delivered their food. The piping hot steaks and fluffy eggs should have made his belly growl with anticipation. Instead, it revolted now that he'd spoken the truth of his actions.

Once the waiter disappeared, Jacob took a large bite of the eggs. He swallowed and said, "But your family forgave you and wanted you to stay. Why you running?"

"I'm not run—"

"Don't lie to me." He pointed his fork at Stanley. "You're running, and until you face that... you'll never find the peace you're lookin' for."

"What makes you think I'm lookin' for peace?" Stanley muttered.

"I know you, probably more than you know yourself." Jacob cut his steak and took a bite of the meat, chewing thoughtfully for a moment. "So, who's the little lady you had with you last night? She don't seem the type you'd take to a saloon. Thought your pa taught you better than that."

The piece of bread Stanley stuffed in his mouth stuck in his throat, but he forced it down. Pangs pierced his chest with what his pa would have thought if he'd been there. "He did, and normally I wouldn't have, but she insisted—"

"Insisted? Didn't realize you let a woman lead you along by her apron strings."

Stanley's face burned with embarrassment. Jacob made it sound as though he let Charlotte dictate his actions. "I'm not her husband, brother, or father, so I don't have any right to tell her what to do."

"Maybe not, but ya shouldn't have taken a lady in there unless... she ain't a lady." Jacob's eyebrows lifted suggestively.

Stanley glared at Jacob. "She *is* a lady, and don't you say nothing more about her."

Jacob grinned. "I thought so. Don't get your hackles up. I just wanted to see what you'd say. The gal is important to you, then?"

"What? Oh, no, nothing like that." Stanley's

collar tightened around his neck, and he scowled.

"You protest much?" Jacob chuckled.

"Her aunt hired me to help find her father."

"All righty then," Jacob said. "And you took her to the Elk Horn Saloon because…?"

"I hadn't planned on it. In fact, I didn't want to, but she felt she needed to go and—"

"And you let her decide that going to a saloon was in her best interests. A place that's not safe for any woman, especially a lady, and considering what happened, she could've been killed. Not that I don't trust your ability to hold your own in a fight, but if I hadn't shown up, what would've happened?"

Stanley bowed his head in shame. "I shouldn't have let Charlotte sway me into taking her. I'm ashamed I did, but I'm glad you showed up 'cause I don't think I could've taken them all on my own."

Jacob reached over and slapped him on the shoulder. "Then I'm glad I did."

"How'd you find me?" Stanley asked.

"I wasn't looking for you. I was hunting for someplace warm and a bite to eat. When I pushed open the doors, I saw you trying to escape a growing crowd behind you. Kind of surprised you'd find yourself in a situation getting so out of control." The twinkle in Jacob's eyes disappeared.

Stanley shook his head at what he had been unprepared for. "I got distracted and wasn't paying attention to how many men had arrived. Not one of my smartest decisions, that's for sure."

"I hope not," Jacob said. "What were you doing in that saloon, anyway? I wouldn't have expected to find you in a place like that."

"You'd be surprised where you'd find me these days."

Jacob frowned, and Stanley's embarrassment grew.

"I had a lead on Charlotte's father, and the man who had that information wanted to meet me there. He was supposed to be reliable, and I believed it was better to meet where he was most comfortable. I'm glad you showed up when you did, however, 'cause you saved my bacon."

Jacob nodded. "Just like old times." He lifted his coffee in salute before downing the rest in one big gulp.

* * *

Charlotte stood at the edge of the dining room and watched Stanley with the man who'd helped them escape the saloon the night before. She didn't know what their relationship was, but it was clear they recognized one another.

The man had given her quite the fright, but she was grateful he'd arrived when he did. She would need to thank him, but in that quiet moment, she could observe Stanley once again without him being aware of her perusal. She caught herself watching him when he wasn't aware, admiring his tall frame and the easygoing smile he had when he thought he was alone. She needed a few moments to collect her thoughts before she approached, as she was playing a dangerous game and wasn't sure how it was going to end. She had a mission, and it didn't include finding a husband.

When Stanley questioned Billy at the saloon, her impression of Stanley had skyrocketed with his composure and his ability to extract information. She still couldn't believe what Billy had told them. Her father trying to find lost gold seemed strange, but for years, he had tried to prove himself worthy to her grandfather and had failed. She wasn't sure finding lost gold stolen from a stagecoach over forty years ago was the best way to change her grandfather's mind.

As much as she loved her father, there were things about him her grandfather had every right to be disappointed in. He hadn't taken care of her mother like he'd promised. After her mother's death, he'd gambled away what had been left of her mother's dowry, and his debts had climbed to a staggering level. If her grandfather hadn't stepped in, he would've been strung up by furious debtors and left Charlotte with little to no food to eat.

"Excuse me, miss. Can I help you?"

She jumped at the question and found the maître d' standing behind her. The man was in a crisp black suit, his hair slicked back. He narrowed his eyes at her clandestine behavior. She blushed. He had found her hiding behind a column, gazing at a man. She may be in an uncivilized part of the country, but that didn't mean she shouldn't act like a lady.

"Oh, yes, yes." She raised a hand to her forehead to push back a strand of hair. "I'm supposed to be meeting Mr. Seymour. Have you seen him this morning?"

The maître d' looked at her strangely. She had to hold back the embarrassed chuckle that was rising in her chest. The maître d' had seen her staring at Stanley, and she likely looked like a fool. The dining room was empty save for Stanley and his friend, but she had to at least give off the pretense that she wasn't acting like a wanton woman and instead was the respectable woman her mother had raised.

The man held back a grin. "Yes, miss. If you'll

follow me, please." He then led her through the tables to the one she had been staring at just moments before.

As soon as Stanley saw her, he scooted back his chair and stood. "Miss Charlotte, I wasn't expecting to see you this morning."

The maître d' lifted an eyebrow. Stanley's statement was in direct contrast to what she had just told the man when he found her hiding behind the column.

Trying to cover her blunder, she said, "I'm sorry. I thought we'd agreed to meet this morning." Knowing full well they hadn't. "I thought we could discuss the information we received from Billy last evening."

"Would you care to do it later? I wouldn't want to discuss your family business in front of Jacob without your permission."

"If Jacob... May I call you Jacob?" She looked at the man, lifting her lips into an engaging smile.

Jacob's gaze was strong and unwavering. He nodded. "Of course, little lady."

She turned her gaze back to Stanley. "If Jacob is a friend of yours, then I trust him if you do." She nodded to Jacob sitting across from them. He looked just as scary as he had the night before, his horrendous smell still as strong. She resisted the urge to hold her handkerchief to her nose. She didn't want to appear rude, but heavens, it was a pungent smell. With any luck, she'd get used to it, but she wouldn't hold her breath. Although that might be the thing to do to keep the smells at bay.

The maître d' held out her chair, and she sat gracefully into it. "Thank you."

"Miss Charlotte, it certainly is a pleasure," Jacob said, a grin creasing his beard-covered cheeks. She relaxed. He might've smelled something fierce, but his smile put her at ease. "I was just asking little buck here why he took a lady such as yourself to a rowdy saloon."

"Little buck?" She tilted her head and looked at Stanley. "Does he mean you?"

Stanley's neck turned red at her question, but

she didn't have to hear him say the answer to know it was true.

"Yes," he said. "I've known Jacob here since before I could walk. Ain't that right?"

"That sounds about right," Jacob said. "I remember this one time. He was just a boy trying to be a man when I caught him trying to kill a buffalo, and he didn't know what he was doing. The buffalo near gored him to death, but I yanked him out of the way in the nick of time. Good thing too 'cause I ain't too sure I'd had so much entertainment if he'd been gored to death. He kept me laughin' for a few years 'til he got his feet under him."

"Oh, I'd love to hear stories about my new friend here," she said with a wide grin.

"Nothing interesting there, I'm sure," Stanley muttered.

Jacob chuckled, the laugh coming from deep in his gut and enveloping everyone in its mirth. "I could tell you some stories, miss."

"I'd love—"

"Maybe another time, Jacob," Stanley said, interrupting her.

She hid a smile behind her white cloth napkin. Stanley clearly didn't want Jacob to tell her any other humiliating stories.

Not wanting to further embarrass him, she changed the subject. "What did you think of Billy's tale? Do you believe he saw my father and that he's the man looking for the lost gold?"

"Lost gold," Jacob said. "What's this all about?"

After getting Charlotte's permission to continue, Stanley recounted what Billy had told them. After hearing the information a second time, she was even more convinced it was her father looking for the gold. The description and his reasons for finding the gold fit. It had to be him. Combine that with the fact that she had seen her father in the saloon the night she met Stanley, that was all the proof she needed.

"I'm not convinced he's Charlotte's father, but it's a compelling lead," Stanley said.

"Do you believe he might stay at a nearby hotel?" Charlotte asked.

"If he's low on funds, I wouldn't count on it." Stanley took a sip of his coffee. "I'd likely look at the rooms rented by a saloon or perhaps a boarding house. Those might be more affordable for a man down on his luck."

Charlotte nodded. According to her grandfather, he didn't have much, and whatever her grandfather had given him had likely been gambled away. The fact he'd made it that far suggested he was finding the cheapest place he could lay his head.

"What do you know about your father's day-to-day activities?" Stanley asked.

"Not much, I'm afraid," she said. "He left St. Louis when I was fifteen. He sent a few letters over the next couple of years, but they were very few and far between. Then nothing over the last three years. No letters, no telegrams, nothing."

"What made you decide to look for your pa after so long?" Jacob asked.

She wasn't willing to share all the details, but

she could at least share a modicum of the truth. "I've wanted to look for him, but my grandfather wouldn't hear of it. I asked Aunt Martha to speak with him. She convinced him to give me a year to find him and resolve whatever I needed to with him—his words, not mine." When she and her aunt first met Stanley, she hadn't wanted him involved. After two weeks of being in his presence, she couldn't imagine her quest without him.

"What do you plan on doing once you've found him?" Stanley asked.

She hesitated. That was the one question she asked herself every day. While she needed his help in convincing her grandfather that marrying was a bad idea, it was more than that. "I'm not really sure, but I would like to convince him to come home with me to St. Louis. My grandfather is getting up in years, and I want to have my father in my life. My grandfather filled his shoes in all the ways he could, but I miss him something fierce."

Chapter 8

March 27, 1901

Stanley slammed the tankard of beer down with such force, the liquid sloshed over the rim and sprayed the bar top. The man behind the counter at the Royal Exchange Saloon glared at him but wiped away the beer with his wet rag. Stanley didn't care. It had been a week of useless information, and the rotten day he'd had was the cherry on top. He was near to bursting with frustration. When he saw that woman who had looked just like Connie, for a moment, he had been struck senseless. Then she had turned, and he'd realized it wasn't her, but in that moment, his fury had boiled over. He knew she was gone but there were times when he'd see someone who reminded him of her and it brought forth pain he'd like to forget.

Stanley had found men who swore they'd seen Charlotte's father, but none could say where he was holed up or what he was doing. The only thing they had were rumors about a man looking for the lost gold. He would come into different saloons, have a beer, and then disappear again. He was slippery as an eel in an ocean, or at least how Stanley'd imagine one.

Stanley eyed the bartender. "I've been told he's been here a number of times, and you can't tell me for sure that you've seen him!"

Normally, he controlled his temper, but his nerves were frayed. It was freezing outside, the snow was thick on the ground, and Charlotte was on his mind every single waking moment and his non-waking moments, for that matter.

He was overrun with thoughts of her, and having her by his side was driving him near to insanity. He thought he could control his urges, but in moments of insanity, he wanted to pull her into his arms and kiss the sweet daylights out of her. But he had to remember it wasn't appropriate. While she had kissed his cheek the other evening, he had no doubt it'd been driven by impulsivity and nothing more. She was only in his life because she needed help in finding her father.

The bartender slapped his rag on the counter, braced his hands against it, and stood nose to nose with Stanley. "Do you know how many men come in here daily? How am I supposed to remember one cowpoke gold dreamer for another?"

Stanley huffed, picked up his tankard, and settled into a chair at the rear of the saloon. There was no point in continuing to harass the bartender. Stanley had tried giving him money, but the man had laughed. He'd told Stanley he didn't need it and to keep it. Others might have taken the money and told him whatever he wanted to hear, but the bartender had a semblance of integrity and refused it.

An hour later, Stanley was good and drunk. He'd told himself he would limit his drinking, but he was tired, frustrated, and randy as a cowpoke after a long cattle drive. Before long, he'd had too many drinks to count. Earlier, he'd left Charlotte at the hotel so he could investigate the latest lead at that blasted saloon, and like all the others, the lead had gone nowhere. Every situation that week had instead resulted in uncomfortable altercations. He was nursing a black eye, sore ribs, and more bruises on his arms and chest than he'd had when he'd gotten into fights with his brothers back home in Montana.

It would be wise to return to his family's ranch, but instead, he was in Idaho helping a woman who not only drove him to distraction with her demands but also with her sweet charm. He told himself over and over again that he couldn't get involved with another woman until he resolved his anger toward his dead ex-wife, but instead, he drowned his sorrows even though it fixed nothing. Stanley had brought that vile woman into his family. If he'd never married her, his pa would still be alive, and the nightmare would've never started.

A burst of female laughter and loud music knocked him from his painful memories. He looked at his tankard. It was empty. Raising his arm to wave for another, he slowly dropped it when he saw Jacob push through the swinging doors. Stanley considered slinking down in his chair, but then he'd be a coward. He didn't need any more guilt over his actions, even if the censure he'd receive was well-deserved.

Skirting the tables, Jacob walked toward him. He only had to look at a man to make him scurry out of his way. He was larger than a bear and stronger than an ox.

"Wallowing again?" Jacob asked, grasping the chair in front of him.

"Didn't ask for your opinion," Stanley muttered. Jacob's question raised his hackles.

"Wasn't giving it." Jacob yanked the chair,

flipped it around, straddled it, and rested his forearms on the back. "Trying to avoid me tonight, I gather?" After he waved for his own tankard, the barmaid scurried over to them with a beer and set it in front of Jacob. "Thank you kindly, miss."

The young barmaid blushed and stuttered a response before walking away. When Jacob smiled, women swooned at his feet.

"Ignoring my questions?" Jacob lifted the beer to his lips and settled more comfortably into the chair.

"Nothing important to answer," Stanley slurred.

"You trying to get yourself killed?" Jacob raised his thumb and forefinger to his ear and pulled on it.

"Nope, just trying to get a moment's peace. Enjoy my drink, that's all." Stanley ran his fingers across the top of the wooden table. Sticky residue was every few inches.

"Don't ya mean drinks?" Jacob lifted an eyebrow.

"Does it matter?" Stanley said, casting his gaze downward. "I don't appreciate the interrogation."

"Just having a conversation, little buck." Jacob's voice was low.

"I ain't a little buck anymore," he slung back.

"Couldn't tell from the way you're behaving."

Stanley caught the humor laced with worry in Jacob's eyes. "Humph." Stanley took another long drink, the beer dribbling down his chin and onto his chest. "Why don't ya go on back to the hotel and leave me be?"

"I would, but since you couldn't fight yourself out of a bullpen with an angry steer, you ain't gonna be able to defend yourself against anyone, especially if someone picks a fight with you."

"No one's gonna mess with me," Stanley said, raising his tankard in salute while Jacob expanded in front of him. "Did you grow a friend?" He chuckled at his own joke.

"Not sure I follow you," Jacob said. His face

grew large, shrinking and then expanding once again into three hazy bodies.

Stanley swayed in his seat. He closed his eyes tightly, trying to shake himself out of his stupor, but it was too late. The alcohol had done its job. He relaxed in his chair, sliding forward until no more thoughts entered, and all was quiet within.

* * *

Pacing back and forth in her hotel room, Charlotte muttered obscenities under her breath. Her aunt would be appalled if she heard the words Charlotte really wanted to shout. When they returned to the hotel earlier that afternoon, Stanley had promptly disappeared. She couldn't decide if it was what had happened while they were out or the innocent kiss she'd placed on his cheek the week before. He had been standoffish and unlike himself ever since.

Sometimes, as he gazed at her with fondness, his smile sent a zing straight to her toes. Other times, she'd find him looking into the distance, sadness oozing off him. She'd wanted to smooth out the wrinkles on his face, run her fingers against his whiskers, and feel his warm breath on her skin.

Improper thoughts ran through her mind, but she couldn't help herself. He was breaking apart her defenses, one day at a time. A part of her almost didn't want to find her father for fear that, once they did, Stanley would disappear from her life. She was falling for him and falling fast.

She hadn't given him a reason to stay, and she wasn't sure she could. Whatever was eating at Stanley was far more complicated than she could ever solve. It had something to do with his former wife, and there was nothing she could do to ease that pain.

"Would you quit your pacing, young lady?" Aunt Martha said from her chair in front of the roaring fire. The room was chilly, but the flames helped to cut the cold. Her aunt was reading one of her novels and had been buried in it when Charlotte returned to their room.

"Sorry, Aunty. Are you famished? I could call the front desk and have them send up a meal?" She picked up a glove she had dropped and placed it back on the table next to the door.

"No, my dear, but you order something. You haven't eaten since this morning." Her aunt turned her nose back to her book and pulled the thick woolen throw more securely around her waist. Her aunt loved her books and insisted on bringing a trunk full of them on their trip. The porters at each of the railroad stops always grunted with effort every time they had to move the trunk on and off the train, the weight almost breaking their backs.

Charlotte's stomach rumbled. She was hungry, but she'd rather know what Stanley was up to. He had been spitting mad when they returned but had controlled his temper in her presence. However, as quickly as he had deposited her at the hotel, she knew he was plenty angry. Just because he had fallen into a pile of horse manure while chasing a man down the street wasn't her fault. Neither was the fact that once he caught the man, the man had up and punched Stanley in the eye. If Stanley had talked to the man like a gentleman instead of insulting him, he might not have hit Stanley. Not that Stanley would've believed that. By that time, Stanley had been furious. His horse had thrown him right before they rode into town after he'd been stung by not one but two bees.

It had been a series of unfortunate events, most of which he couldn't control. Well, outside of insulting the man he'd been chasing. She couldn't blame the man after Stanley had called him a low-down rotten swindler, and then, frustrated, Stanley had thrown the horse manure he'd just stepped into at the poor man's face. If Stanley had done that to her, she would have hit Stanley herself.

She wasn't sure what had come over Stanley in that moment, but she was sure it had nothing to do with looking for her pa. He had stopped, looked into the distance, and seen something that had seemed to freeze him before he hurled insults. If things hadn't been so serious, it would've been like a schoolyard tussle fighting over a game of marbles gone wrong.

She reached for the candlestick phone and ordered warm food and wine. She couldn't let Stanley's actions ruin what was left of her evening. When done speaking with the front desk, she pushed the thick drapes away from the tall windows and looked out at the snowy night. It had snowed every single day since they'd arrived. Lots of white, fluffy snow as far as she could see. They would get snow in St. Louis, but not like that and not with such strength and power. Even the mountains were covered in it. Only the tips of the tall pine trees could be seen.

The snow drifts were high and thick every morning. Horses and people struggled to get through, but perseverance always won. Those living there didn't let a bit of snow stop them. Men were covered in thick furs and tall leather boots. Women were wrapped in woolen skirts and fur-lined coats, their summer bonnets replaced with thick stocking caps. People dressed for warmth, not for fashion. It was a world full of survivors, and only those with a force of will and strength lived and survived there.

As she watched the never-ending sight of activity below, she wondered at how vast the area was. A man could hide for months, and no one would be the wiser. She didn't know if she would ever find her father. He was proving impossible to find, and their search was becoming an insurmountable task.

A knock on the door startled her. Their food had likely arrived. The hotel clerk pushed a fully laden cart into the room. He lifted steaming plates and bottles of red wine and placed them on the dining table. The wine was a fruity blend that she had tried a few nights before and would pair well with the food. She might have ordered too much, but everything sounded delicious, and she hadn't been able to decide. Charlotte handed the man a few coins. He shoved them into his vest pocket and left. She closed the door behind him, leaned against it, and sighed. Anticipation filled her belly. Roasted chicken, hot rolls, and candied carrots were among a few of the items waiting for her.

After dinner, Charlotte grabbed her thick woolen shawl, left her aunt, who had fallen asleep in her chair, and walked to the lobby. She couldn't sit still in her room and wanted to see if she could find Stanley. She had to make sure he had recovered from his mishaps, and if she were truly honest with herself, she wanted to catch another glimpse of him before he left her life for good.

It was late, but too many unanswered questions peppered her mind. Her father had to be in town somewhere. Pocatello was small compared to St. Louis. There were only so many places he could hide. They had been from one end of town to the other, but they were always a step behind him. It was as though her father knew they were after him and was determined to keep them at arm's length.

The lanterns and gaslights flickered as the wide front doors of the hotel were opened, and an icy breeze blew in. When she reached the bottom of the stairs, she scanned the wide lobby but didn't see any sign of Stanley. She was on a fool's errand, but it didn't stop her from turning her gaze toward the dining room and wondering if he was inside, although she'd more likely find him in the bar with a decanter of whiskey in his hands. Stanley drank quite a bit. She wondered if he liked it as much as he seemed or if he was using it to forget his tumultuous past.

Not finding him in the quiet dining room, she went back across the lobby to the bar. It was on the other side of the hotel, far from the stairs that led to the rooms above them. It was nowhere near as lively as the ones across the railroad tracks, and for that, she was thankful. Otherwise, the noise might have kept her up at night.

Once again, the front doors opened. The breeze prickled her skin. A large man stumbled in with another slung across his back. It was Jacob. He swung around to close the door, and she gasped. Stanley was hanging from his shoulder. No movement came from his lanky form.

She raised her fist to her mouth, but Jacob's

casual nonchalance with having Stanley across his shoulder eased her concerns a bit.

Jacob raised his head, and recognition lit his eyes. A smile lifted his round, whisker-covered cheeks. "Well, hello there, little lady. Whatcha doing down here? It's late, and you should be up in your room behind a toasty fire." He shook his head. "It's bitter out there. Looks like you're shivering."

She looked at her arms and the goose bumps that pricked her skin. "Don't mind me. What happened to Stanley? Is he hurt?"

"Nah," he said, shifting the weight across his shoulders as though Stanley's long and brawny form weighed nothing more than a rabbit pelt or two. "Just a bit of overindulgence tonight, that's all."

"Overindulgence?" She tilted her head.

"Yep, he had a tad too much to drink."

She furrowed her eyebrows. "Oh." Her concerns about Stanley were valid. He had clearly tried to forget about the rough day he'd had.

"He doesn't know when to stop." Jacob widened his stance.

"He was pretty angry when he left me this afternoon."

"Oh, did something happen?" Jacob asked.

"Just a few mishaps. Nothing to be concerned about, but I fear that Stanley was none too happy when he returned me to the hotel this afternoon."

"That might explain why he was a bit deep in his cups when I found him."

Charlotte grimaced. "I should have stopped him from leaving me here."

"Little lady, you wouldn't have been able to stop him. He's got some mighty big demons he's got to work through."

Stanley groaned but didn't stir. Jacob looked over his shoulder at Stanley's slack form.

She sighed. Even though Jacob didn't appear to be straining under his weight, it wasn't fair to keep him from leaving. "Well, I guess I should let you… get him to his room."

"Thank you kindly." He doffed his hat toward

her like a true gentleman. Covered in his thick furs, he looked further from any gentleman she had ever known.

As Jacob carried Stanley up the stairs, she stood alone in the lobby and wondered why she was determined to follow a man who imbibed himself into oblivion. Stanley had an addiction that could be dangerous if left unchecked and reminded her too much of her father's addiction. Her father had gambled everything her mother had and left her destitute. Would Stanley do the same but with liquor?

Chapter 9

March 28, 1901

Stanley rolled over and groaned. He ached from the beating he'd taken yesterday from the man on the streets, the bee in the meadow, and the countless beers he'd downed. The pounding inside his head was fierce, and he barely contained the nausea rolling through his belly.

He pushed off the bed and stumbled to the water closet, where he promptly lost what he'd drunk the night before. After heaving everything that remained, his belly settled, at least for the moment. He sat back on the cold floor, sweat lining his forehead, and swiped at his mouth. He grimaced at the smells coming from him and the privy. The hotel had some of the latest gadgets, and he was very grateful for them at that very moment. He reached for the pull handle and listened as it swished the contents away. If only it could wash away his raging headache just as quickly.

After a few long moments, he stood and threw water on his face, shivering at how frigid it was. It wouldn't wash away the grime and sweat, so he'd need to call the hotel clerk for warm water if he wanted to have any semblance of cleanliness. While the hotel had some of the latest modern conveniences, only cold water poured from the pump.

He couldn't remember exactly what he had done after he'd returned Charlotte to the hotel and headed to the Royal Exchange Saloon. After the debacle in the street with the horse manure and his ill-begotten fight with a man who had been unlucky enough to be near him, he'd thought downing multiple tankards would ease his aches and pains, but like always, it never did.

He should return home to Montana, but rather, he'd found himself embroiled in another emotional ride, one he didn't want or need. But he'd been unable to walk away from Charlotte. He was going down a dangerous path, but he couldn't seem to help himself and only wanted to spend more time in her presence.

A loud knocking on his hotel room door made the incessant pounding in his head far worse. He groaned and prayed it wasn't Charlotte. He looked a fright and smelled something awful.

"I'm coming," he yelled and grimaced at the sound of his voice.

The person behind the door only pounded harder.

"Hold your horses," he croaked as the pain intensified. It was too early in the morning.

Growling, he ripped the door open, practically pulling it from the hinges. He opened his mouth to issue a scathing rebuke but instead was stunned silent. He swallowed painfully.

It was his youngest brother, Michael. Stanley hadn't expected him to show up unannounced, and he wasn't pleased he had.

"Can I come in?" Michael asked when Stanley didn't wave him inside.

"Why are you here?" he growled.

Michael removed his hat, ran a hand through his dark brown hair, and sighed. "Are we going to do this in the hallway?"

Grunting, Stanley backed out of the way to let his brother inside. The two of them had had words when Stanley was at the ranch in December, and things hadn't ended well. Michael was the peacekeeper in the family, always happy and jovial. But when Michael tried to smooth things over with him, Stanley had said things he shouldn't have. Michael had meant well, but it didn't mean Stanley was ready to have it out with him again, especially then and there.

Michael sauntered into the room and whistled under his breath. "Nice room you've got here, big brother."

The pleasant tone of Michael's voice grated

on Stanley's nerves. He closed the door and leaned against it, crossing his arms across his chest. If he kept his fists closed, he might stop himself from beating his brother into a bloody pulp. The feelings of unrest and rage he had toward Michael were unfair, but they were there, nonetheless.

"So glad to see you, too," Michael said when Stanley kept quiet.

Stanley ignored Michael's attempt at levity. "You're the last person I expected to see this morning."

Michael frowned. "I know you're still mad at me."

"I'm not mad," he muttered.

"Lying to me won't solve the problem." Michael moved across the room, likely knowing if he came within arm's reach of Stanley, he'd pay for it.

"I'm not lying."

Michael sighed and flopped into an armchair in front of the fireplace. "Sit down," he said, pointing to the other chair. "This is gonna take time to resolve."

"I'm fine," Stanley said. "And there's nothing to resolve." He was being stubborn and uncooperative.

"Have you always been this pigheaded and I failed to see it?" Michael slouched low in his seat and ran his fingers across his thighs in a nervous twitch.

Stanley shook his head. He stalked to the liquor cabinet and pulled out a bottle of whiskey. "Care for a drink?" he said, lifting the bottle up for Michael to see.

Michael shook his head. "Isn't it a bit early for a drink?"

Stanley stopped and glared at his brother. Michael returned the glare, his typical merry twinkle having long disappeared. Instead, it was filled with severe disappointment and disgust at what Stanley had become.

Stanley slowly dropped the bottle back onto the table without pouring a drink. It *was* too early, but he needed one to get through the upcoming conversation, and that was a problem. But he wouldn't give Michael the satisfaction of knowing he might be right.

He stalked to the chair and sat, trying to keep his head from bobbing too much. The throbbing behind his eyes was growing at an alarming rate. "Why are you here?"

"Plenty of reasons," Michael said, finally answering the question that Stanley had asked when he first opened the door. "The biggest of which is fixing what's gone wrong between us."

"There's nothing wrong." The lie slipped past his lips. Was that what had become of him? Lying to his brothers, avoiding them at all costs, hoping he could somehow make up for what he had done.

Michael pushed forward in his chair and braced his hands against his knees. "There's plenty wrong. It started years ago when you married that woman, brought her into our home, and then kicked us all off the ranch."

Stanley felt as though he had just been gut-punched. It was difficult to hear the truth from the one brother who forgave everyone before they had a chance to say *I'm sorry*.

"I'm…" The words trailed away. He couldn't respond.

Sorrow filled Michael's eyes. "I'm not here to berate you, Stanley, but I am here because you can't let it go. None of us are holding a grudge, and we don't blame you. You had no idea what she was up to. None of us did, and you couldn't have stopped it. But the fact that you're still avoiding the family and drinking"—he waved to the bottle Stanley had just dropped—"yourself into oblivion isn't doing anyone any favors."

"I'm not drink—"

"Don't lie to me. You were falling down drunk at Luke's wedding, and it clearly hasn't stopped. Drowning your sorrows in liquor isn't gonna bring back Pa and won't heal that hole in your soul."

"You don't know what you're talking about. I don't need this from you, of all people."

Michael gripped his knees, the nervous twitch replaced with anger. "Don't you mean the person who killed Connie and ended her reign of terror on our family?"

"Dammit. I don't want to do this now." He was going to say something he'd regret if Michael continued to push him.

"If not now, then when?"

Stanley slammed his fist onto the edge of his armchair. "You had no right."

"I had no right," Michael muttered, shaking his head. "Then I guess I should've just let her kill Luke so you could get your revenge. That would make you feel better? To lose another member of our family?"

Stanley's heart seized with pain. "That isn't fair, and you know it."

"Life isn't fair, big brother, and it's time you realize it."

Stanley's anger had built to a fever pitch. "I'm well aware life isn't fair."

"Then why are you still blaming yourself for what happened?" Michael's mouth was set in a grim line, a look Stanley was unfamiliar with.

Michael never got angry or upset, but the situation had been a long time coming.

"Because I'm responsible!" Stanley yelled. His chest heaved with frustration, anger, and sorrow.

Michael stood and paced back and forth in front of him, not speaking for a long moment. "You're not responsible for what that woman did."

"I married her."

Michael stopped abruptly. "She trapped you."

Stanley shook his head. Michael didn't understand and never would.

"Listen to me," Michael said, his voice low. "She sought you out. She had a plan all along."

"I know that. She wanted the ranch." Stanley's voice broke.

"It's more than that. We tried to tell you when you came home, but you refused to listen."

"I didn't—"

"Stop." Michael slapped the top of the sofa. "You didn't listen. You refused to sit down with Ben, Luke, or me to hear what we'd discovered about her plans and how she came into our lives."

"She married me. That's how she did it." He didn't understand what the point was. He didn't need his brother telling him what Connie had done or how she'd done it.

"You were a means to an end for her. She was angry with Pa, and it had nothing to do with you."

"It had everything to do with me," Stanley said. Why couldn't everyone understand that he was the only person responsible? "I married her."

Michael ran his hands through his hair and braced his fingers against the back of his neck. "Yes, you married her, but she always planned on killing Pa. She's Uncle Howard's daughter, Stanley."

"What?" Stanley gagged. "I married my cousin?" His stomach rolled with revulsion. He'd slept with his uncle's daughter. It was worse than he could have ever imagined. "I'm going to be sick."

"You didn't know," Michael said. "None of us

did, but don't forget Uncle Howard wasn't Pa's brother in the true sense of the word. His ma had him by her first husband. If that eases your mind a bit, Connie wasn't blood."

Stanley had to take a few deep breaths, trying to swallow back the acid in his throat. His heart raced faster than a galloping horse. Their Grandpa Harvey had married Howard's ma when his pa was just a few years old. Their grandpa had given Howard his name. "Not sure that helps. If you wanted to make me feel worse than I already do, then you've succeeded."

"That wasn't my intention." Michael braced his hands against the sofa, bending his back and lowering his head.

"Then why?"

Michael slowly lifted his head and stared hard at Stanley. "Are you ready to listen?"

Stanley sank back against his chair and waited. If Michael had come that far to talk to him, he'd do well to listen. It was the least he could do, even though he'd rather be doing anything else.

Michael paced once again, clearly agitated until he took a deep breath. "From what we've been able to gather, Uncle Howard visited a brothel that Connie's ma worked in. He must've gotten her pregnant during one of his visits, but we don't think he knew he had a daughter." He stopped in front of the fireplace and rested his thumbs in the edges of his brown suspenders under his coat. "A few years later, Uncle Howard came to visit Ma and Pa. Pa introduced Howard to a local neighbor and his daughter, Beth Ann. Howard married Beth Ann and took her back to Texas, not knowing Connie's ma had given birth. At some point, Connie's ma approached Howard, but he denied the child was his and refused to offer support. Connie's ma became desperate and hounded Howard for years, but he never believed Connie was his."

"Maybe she wasn't," Stanley said. "Uncle Howard wouldn't have denied the child if'n it was his."

"Maybe, maybe not. We'll never know for sure."

The hard edge to Michael's voice was difficult to hear. Stanley was the cause of it, no matter Michael's protestations.

"Uncle Howard should be able to tell us, especially if he was aware that Connie's mother claimed she was his."

"Well, that's the thing. He passed away a few years ago."

Stanley tilted his head. "That makes no sense. We would've heard. Someone would've let Ben know."

"But they didn't. We don't know if anyone tried or not, but word never reached us," Michael said, moving to the window and leaning against it.

"What about Beth Ann?" Stanley's chest hurt from what that might mean.

"Turns out, she died in 1892, about the time Connie showed up in your life."

"Are you saying she had something to do with Beth Ann's death?" He swallowed back the idea of what Connie might've done to Beth Ann.

"No idea, but nothing is surprising anymore," Michael said.

"What a mess," Stanley muttered. "Still doesn't explain why Connie was after Pa."

"She blamed Pa for Howard not taking care of her. She told Luke that if Pa would've never introduced Beth Ann to Howard, he would've married her ma and she would've had a better life. Connie thought everything should've belonged to her and had been planning on eliminating all of us. She almost killed Luke. He came so close to dying, Stanley." He paused, resting his hands on his hips, and glared at Stanley. "I had no choice but to take her out, and I'm not sorry I did."

Chapter 10

March 31, 1901

Charlotte hadn't seen Stanley in days, not since Jacob had returned him drunk and unconscious. She'd sat in her hotel room, growing impatient, twiddling her thumbs, and wondering what Stanley would do next. She'd tried writing a letter to her grandfather to inform him of their progress, but instead, she crumpled every single piece of paper after a few lines. Nothing she wrote sounded promising. Finally, she gave up and stared out the window while all manner of thoughts ran through her mind.

Aunt Martha had been feeling under the weather and had fallen asleep, leaving Charlotte to her own devices. Not wanting to disturb her, Charlotte grabbed her wrap and left for the dining room. She was restless and while she didn't enjoy eating alone in a public dining room, if the maître d' would seat her at a secluded table, it might help calm her thoughts.

Within minutes, she was settled into a small alcove next to the roaring fire, away from most of the hustle and bustle of the other dining room patrons. She ordered a glass of red wine and asked for the chef's special. She pulled a small journal and stubby pencil out of her pocket and settled into her chair, the flames next to her keeping her nice and warm while she put her thoughts about the past few weeks to paper. While she couldn't find the words to write a letter to her grandfather, she had no problem writing about her adventures.

Fully engrossed in her writing, she barely acknowledged the waiter when her food arrived. As she picked at the butter and garlic potatoes, roast beef, and bacon green beans, her attention was focused on her memories. She would have continued to be oblivious if shouting and the clatter of dishes against the wooden floors hadn't pulled her from the pages.

Another fight had broken out between two men. It seemed she had seen an endless array of brawls, skirmishes, and vicious fights over the past month and wondered if that was all men did in that western town. It constantly amazed her how the men found nothing wrong with expressing their frustrations with their fists.

She was far enough away from the melee that she didn't need to move, but she could no longer concentrate. Placing her journal into her skirt pocket, she picked up her glass of wine when one of the men involved spun around. His gaze met hers and widened in shock.

It was her father.

Before she could say a word, he fell forward onto a table, not ten feet from her. She jumped to her feet, and the edge of the table hit her hip, but the pain shooting down her leg paled in comparison to the pain in her heart.

Horrified, she watched the table crash under her father's weight. Food and dishes flew through the air. Women screamed, men jumped out of the way, and waiters rushed to help those hurt in the fracas. Chaos reigned.

The two men continued to grapple viciously. The man fighting with her father got the upper hand, yanked him up, and slammed a fist into his face. Charlotte cried out. She wanted to help and stop the fighting, but she would only be in the way.

Her father struggled to stand. Once he got to his feet, he swung a wooden table let at his adversary's head. Blood splattered like raindrops across the room and the men standing nearby. The man's head swiveled with such force it was a wonder it stayed attached before he crumbled to the ground in a heap. Her father dropped the leg and braced his hands on his knees, his chest heaving with exertion. Two hotel clerks grabbed her father's arms and pulled him away. He stumbled back from the force of their grip.

She scurried around the table to get to him, but the crowd had grown in size. She pushed her way through the mass of people, not apologizing for her rudeness. Stepping on toes, she elbowed men and women alike as she moved to get to her father. By the time she made it through the crowd, her father was gone.

Looking around in disbelief, she grabbed the first person near her. "Where did he go?"

The man glared at her in disgust, his handlebar mustache seeming to mock her, and pulled from her desperate grasp. His arm slipped from her fingers, and he stomped away.

Seeing a hotel clerk, she ran to his side. "Where did they take him?"

The hotel clerk pulled on his vest, scrunching his eyebrows. "Take who?"

"The man who was in the fight." Her voice was shrill to her ears, but the fear of losing him again and making sure he hadn't been harmed overrode any good sense she might've had left.

"They took him to the doc," he said.

"No, no, not that one. The one who hit him."

The hotel clerk's lip curled in disgust. "The no-account? Why would you want to know about him?"

"Please, can you just tell me where he went?" She sounded hysterical.

He straightened his black string tie. "Why, they took him to jail, where he belongs and where he'll likely rot to death. We don't appreciate men fighting like animals in our fine establishment."

The hotel clerk turned to another guest who was begging for his attention, leaving her standing in dumb disbelief. She had finally found her father, and instead of the happy reunion she had envisioned, he'd found himself in jail, and there was no telling when she'd get to speak to him.

✳ ✳ ✳

An hour later, Charlotte left the jailhouse and wiped the wetness from her cheeks. The sheriff had refused to let her see her father until the following morning. He had no sympathy for her. The sheriff said she'd have to wait, just like everyone else, except she wasn't like everyone else. Women didn't just barge into jailhouses demanding to see a man who had almost beaten another man to death. The sheriff had been stringent in his stance on following the rules and didn't care for her tears or pleading cries.

She tugged her woolen wrap tightly against her slight frame. She should have dressed warmer, but she hadn't expected to leave the hotel and find the jailhouse when she'd gone to the dining room that afternoon.

She stumbled forward. The man who shoved her continued past, muttering obscenities under his breath, unsteady on his feet with a glass bottle held in one hand and his other extended to push all out of his way as he moved to his destination. The man was drunk and was going to remove her out of his way without a care for her well-being.

She moved out of the path and leaned against the nearest building. Her heart was heavy, and her body was chilled both from the cold and the dread that her quest to find her father would end without the resolution she'd been looking for. She should return to the hotel, but she was restless and didn't want to explain to her aunt what had happened. Charlotte wanted to go somewhere where she could forget the pain of forever being disappointed by him.

Not knowing the real reason for his disappearance ate at her morning, noon, and night. She needed to know if she was the cause of him leaving, but she wasn't sure she'd ever get the answers she sought. However, she wouldn't get her answers standing outside on a cold March evening.

Loud laughter and music blared from the left, but quiet spoke to her from the right. She stomped her way down the snow-covered road. She meandered along, kicking the snow and watching it fall back to the ground, almost as though she were walking in a winter wonderland. It wasn't though, and if she didn't find shelter soon, she might find herself frozen to death. Her teeth chattering, she tightened her grip on her wrap. While it kept her warm in a chilly room, it did nothing for the cold weather outside.

A dim light beckoned. It wasn't bright, but it cast enough of a glow for her to follow. Squinting and stomping through the mounds of snow that had accumulated in the hours since she had left the hotel, she reached the light and pulled on the door to the white clapboard church. Soothing, cheerful music and gentle voices filled the space.

She shuffled to the stove on her left, letting it warm her frozen limbs. A mixture of young and old men and women congregated at the front of the chapel, standing in rows while a thin, spindly man in a black shirt and trousers, likely the pastor, led them in song. Their sweet voices lifted her spirits and made her feel at home. She hadn't been to a church service in months and hadn't realized how much she missed it. She wasn't overly religious, but she enjoyed the friendships she'd made over the years attending in St. Louis.

Once her limbs stopped tingling, she quietly walked to a worn wooden pew and slid into the seat so she could listen. The choir sang song after song, some happy, some soulful, but all uplifting her spirits. As her fingers and toes warmed, so did her heart. She'd been far angrier with her father than she wanted to admit. Now that she had found him, she could finally let him know how she felt. Let him know how much he had hurt her when he disappeared and left her without a mother or a father.

"May I sit?" a voice asked.

Charlotte jumped. A tall young woman stood in the aisle to her right.

"I'm sorry. I didn't mean to startle you," the woman said.

"No, no, please don't apologize." Charlotte smiled. "I was lost in thought. Please sit. I could use the company."

The woman had kind brown eyes and a bright

smile. She wore a nicely cut, thick coat, dressed more appropriately than Charlotte for the weather outside.

"Thank you." The woman sat next to her, removed her brown woolen gloves, placed them on the wooden pew, and untangled the scarf around her neck. "You must be freezing with just that thin wrap as protection. Do you need help?"

Charlotte smiled. "No, I just made the mistake of leaving the hotel without a proper coat."

"Oh." She wrinkled her nose. "Which hotel are you staying at?"

"The Pacific Hotel."

"The Pacific? Why, that is over a mile from here. There's no way you can return with just that as protection. Would you allow me and my driver to take you back?"

"Oh, I couldn't do that," Charlotte said. What a kind soul she had found while trying to temper her anger and soothe her soul. It'd been serendipity to step inside the church tonight. "It was my mistake. I made it here, so I'm sure I can get back to the hotel without incident."

The young woman raised an eyebrow. "How long has it been since you've been outside?"

Charlotte looked at the windows and grimaced. "I… I'm not sure, to be honest. I think I've lost track of time."

"It's grown dark outside, and the snow has been coming down in sheets for the last hour."

Charlotte then noticed the woman's shoulders and skirt had remnants of snow. An icy breeze ripped through the sanctuary as the double doors at the rear opened.

Charlotte shivered. "I can't believe how late it is. I've been so enthralled with the music and my thoughts, I wasn't taking care. I'll just—"

The woman shook her head. "Nonsense. My driver will take you back. I insist." She patted Charlotte's knee. "Where are my manners? Here I am insistent that my driver take you back to your hotel, and I haven't even introduced myself. I'm Bertha Fairbanks." Bertha had turned slightly and gazed at Charlotte, her smile kind and generous.

Charlotte realized her pride had to be shelved. If she wanted to live for tomorrow, she had to take the kindness offered. She held out her hand. "Charlotte McVicker. It's a pleasure. Considering I've been an imbecile for wandering so far from the hotel and in the midst of a winter snowstorm, I would be most grateful for your assistance in returning to my hotel."

"Good," Bertha said. "Now that we have that settled, what in heaven's name were you doing outside without a proper coat?"

"I… It's a long story."

"Oh, listen to me." Bertha's grin was infectious. "I'm impertinent. My mother tells me I just don't know when to stop with my questions. I'm inquisitive by nature and am intrigued about why people come to our tiny railroad town. Honestly," she said, barely taking a breath, "I'm quite bored and never have an opportunity to mingle with proper ladies. I can tell by the cut of your dress that you're a lady of the finest quality." Bertha flicked a droplet of melted snow from her coat pocket. "Where are you from, Charlotte?"

Charlotte grinned, her mind trying to keep up with Bertha. "St. Louis."

"Oh, how exciting." She pulled on a brown curl, twirling it around her finger. "I've always wanted to travel but have never been given the opportunity. Maybe one day, but first, I'd have to find someone suitable enough to marry. Someone who has the funds to take me across the country." Bertha undid the top buttons of her overcoat. "My, it's getting a touch warm in here, don't you think?"

Charlotte hardly thought so. While it wasn't frigid inside the sanctuary, they were sitting in the back near the doors that opened and closed frequently. Before she could say a word, Bertha continued with her monologue, barely giving Charlotte time to answer her questions. It was easier to nod and smile encouragingly, letting Bertha hold the conversation on her own. The young lady was engaging, although quite the chatterbox, but she did help Charlotte forget about her troubles.

"May I ask why you are visiting Pocatello?" Bertha asked. "And does your family know you're out here?"

Charlotte was startled by the question. She wasn't sure how to answer that. She didn't want to divulge that she was looking for her wastrel of a father who was behind bars, but she didn't want to lie, especially to someone she'd just met.

"Oh, I'm so sorry. That's none of my business." The excitement dimmed in Bertha's eyes. "I'm asking you so many questions and have hardly given you a chance to speak. I have a tendency to talk quite a bit, especially when I'm nervous." She tittered and wilted with that pronouncement.

Not wanting to give the poor girl a reason to frown, Charlotte reached for her hand and squeezed. "No, you're fine. It's a perfectly reasonable question to ask. It's just not an exciting story and is... Well, it's not something I'm proud of."

"You certainly don't have to share if you'd prefer not to." Although, Bertha fairly frothed at the mouth. It was clear the girl didn't get out much if she was that interested in someone she had just met.

"It's not that I have anything to hide." Charlotte sighed. There was no reason to be ashamed of why she was in Pocatello. "I came here to find my father."

"Oh, is he lost?" Bertha tilted her head to the side.

Charlotte laughed, though it wasn't a happy laugh. "No, he's not. In fact, I found him tonight."

Bertha's hands raised to her mouth. "Oh, my heavens. That's wonderful news. I hope all is well."

"I wish it was." Charlotte frowned.

"I'm not sure I understand."

"My father is, well, he isn't…" She didn't want to go into too many details. "I haven't seen him in years. He left me in the care of my grandfather when my mother passed away."

"Oh, I'm so sorry, Charlotte. Losing your

mother must've been so difficult." She reached for Charlotte's hand and squeezed it. "My mother drives me batty on the best of days, but I can't imagine not being able to see her and confide in her when I need it most." Her chest rose as she took a deep breath. "Why, just the other day, I had this encounter with a man who asked my pa if he could court me, but the man was not someone I would ever notice." Bertha squinted, and a scowl grew on her lips. "He's older than dirt, and he's as round as a grizzly bear with matted hair that has mold growing in it. Not to mention he smells like old, dirty socks. I told my ma that I may be desperate to find a husband but not desperate to marry one older than my pa and moldier than month's old bread."

Charlotte grinned at that pronouncement and had to hide the bubble of laughter in her throat.

"But listen to me, once again, I just go on and on without giving you a chance to respond." Bertha let out a sigh, the brown curl next to her cheek fluttering from the force of her breath.

"My ma passed a few years ago, so I've

come to terms with it, but thank you for being so kind." Charlotte scratched behind her ear. "It's been years since I've seen my father, and my grandfather would like me to marry. He's even picked out the gentleman he believes is the one for me."

"Oh, how exciting. The men around here are purely boring and interested only in the railroad or their ranches. I want someone who is sophisticated, debonair, and who'd sweep me off my feet." She sighed dramatically.

Charlotte raised an eyebrow.

Bertha blushed and waved her hand. "Oh, no, I'm sorry. I don't mean it's exciting that you haven't seen your father in years but that your grandfather wants you to marry."

Charlotte laughed. "I wish I was excited, but I'm not. The man works for my grandfather, but he only wants to marry me so he can inherit my grandfather's money."

"Is he at least handsome?" Curiosity filled Bertha's eyes.

"Yes, he is. Too handsome, if you ask me.

Smooth, sophisticated, and an absolutely dreadful bore. I can't imagine spending the rest of my life doing as he bids. He's an old-fashioned fuddy-duddy, and he'd marry my grandfather if it got him what he wanted."

Bertha's smile faded with Charlotte's blunt words. "My, that is—"

"Blunt, yes, I know. The man is the worst." Charlotte shuddered at the thought of Colin touching her. Leaving St. Louis and him had been a blessing in more ways than she could count. Unfortunately, if she didn't find her father, she'd soon have to return. She might be forced to marry the man, and that was something she couldn't let happen.

Bertha raised an eyebrow. "Are you going to marry him?"

"Not if I can help it." There was no way she was going to become a broodmare for that overbearing, overconfident pain in her behind.

Chapter 11

April 13, 1901

Charlotte opened the door of her hotel room and found a clerk waiting for her. His shiny face was filled with enthusiasm and youthful exuberance.

"Ma'am, I have a message for you." He handed her a folded piece of paper, bowed his head slightly, and then scurried down the hall before she could find her reticule and give him a coin. She was surprised he didn't leave scorch marks on the rugs with how fast his feet moved.

It had been a long two weeks as she tried to wait patiently for information about her father.

When she returned with Stanley to the jailhouse the morning after he was arrested, her father had already been released. They'd tried to question the sheriff, but he'd said it wasn't any of their business, and if they didn't want to find themselves locked up, they'd leave his jailhouse. He'd said he was plenty busy and had enough to do with the criminals he had resting in the cells than to answer their annoying questions about a man who'd already been released.

The sheriff's smug smile had been infuriating, but there'd been nothing they could do. He'd dismissed them without a second glance, calling her an impertinent young lady. That had been after she'd told the sheriff he was a stain on society. The sheriff hadn't taken well to her insult, and Stanley had had to drag her out of the jailhouse before they found themselves behind bars.

Frustrated, Stanley had enlisted Jacob and his brother Michael to help, and the three of them had practically disappeared over the past two weeks. Occasionally, she would get a note from Stanley letting her know they were still looking, but he gave her no other information on the whereabouts of her father or if they were any closer to finding him. It was driving her near to distraction not to know anything. Stanley refused to take her with him after the altercation in the saloon, claiming it wasn't safe for a lady such as herself. Unfortunately, her aunt agreed with him and insisted Charlotte was to stay behind.

The only thing that kept her from pulling her hair out with frustration was her new friend, Bertha. Charlotte enjoyed her company, as she was a vivacious young lady, but her enthusiasm was at times too much. Bertha wanted to know all about St. Louis—the musicals, the balls, and the theater. Bertha was determined to leave Pocatello and was going to find the man to take her.

It seemed such a lifetime ago to remember the frivolous activities Charlotte had participated in before she and Aunt Martha left St. Louis. As they traveled from place to place, she'd matured and was looking for something more fulfilling.

She couldn't imagine going back to endless balls and senseless activities that had nothing more to them than nonsensical gossip. Charlotte wanted to do something meaningful, and she relished the idea of opening a home for young children who were without any loving parents. Charlotte wanted to follow in her aunt's footsteps, doing something more with her life than being a dutiful wife.

One thing was for certain—she'd never marry the man her grandfather had picked. Colin Steed was not the man for her and never would be. She didn't know who she wanted to spend the rest of her life with, but she wouldn't marry just because her grandfather believed she should.

"Charlotte, close that door. There's no telling who could be out there. It's dangerous."

Charlotte had been standing at the door far longer than she should have. She bowed her head to hide her smile but did as her aunt bid.

"Who was that, my dear?"

"It was a hotel clerk with a message, Aunty."

Charlotte opened the folded piece of paper and quickly read it.

"And what does that message say?"

Charlotte looked at her aunt nestled on the sofa, a blue afghan in her lap and a ball of spun wool and knitting needles in her hands. She was comfortable whittling away the morning. Between her books and her knitting, the woman never let her hands sit idle. If they had been in St. Louis, her aunt would've been involved in one of her many charities. The woman was a ball full of fire, always on the go, always taking part in worthy causes, and when not doing that, reading her precious books or knitting blankets and caps for the children in the orphanages that were full to the brim of little ones who needed love and care.

Charlotte sometimes wondered if her aunt would bring children home if she thought she could get away with it. She had always wanted children, but she had given up on love and had never had any of her own.

Her aunt was the most compassionate and

hardworking woman in Charlotte's life. Her aunt never sought the accolades, but the inheritance her mother had left her gave her the ability to give generously to her causes. Those worthy charities benefited both from her pocketbook and the time she offered. Charlotte's grandfather had no knowledge of the impact his sister had on the St. Louis community and likely never would.

The only reason Charlotte knew as much as she did about her aunt's good works was because one day, she'd run into one of Martha's closest friends who extolled her virtues. She'd been happy to tell Charlotte about how wonderful and generous her Aunt Martha was. With some digging, Charlotte had discovered numerous people who had nothing but wonderful things to say about her aunt.

Charlotte had to wonder if her trek to find her father wouldn't harm her aunt and the causes she loved. Her aunt loved Charlotte like her own and would do anything for her, hence why she'd been one hundred percent behind Charlotte's quest. In fact, her Aunt Martha had been the one to convince her grandfather to give her the year to find him.

"Charlotte, Charlotte." Aunt Martha's high voice pierced through her complicated thoughts.

"Yes, Aunty?" She raised her head to look at her aunt.

"Are you listening to me?" Her aunt's smile was mischievous. "I think your mind has wandered. Does the note contain good news?"

"Yes, Aunty. It's from Stan..." She blushed. She shouldn't be referring to Stanley by his given name. They were business associates, or that was what she tried to convince herself every time she was in his presence. He had demons in his past that left no room for a romantic relationship with anyone, at least not then. "I mean Mr. Seymour."

"And what does Mr. Seymour have to say?" Her aunt pushed her spectacles up her nose.

"They might've discovered where my father went when he was released from jail."

"That is good news, my dear."

Charlotte wondered if her aunt meant it. The

look Martha gave her wasn't of joy but of caution, but Charlotte wouldn't let it stop her. Her aunt wasn't a fan of her father, Marcus, but she was aware of how important this was. While she might have reservations, she respected Charlotte enough to let her see it through to the end.

"Yes, it is." Charlotte held the paper to her chest. "He wants to meet us for dinner tonight."

"Hmm. I think I'll let you go in my stead. Please give him my regards, but I'll take my dinner up here." Her aunt picked up the knitting she had dropped, the click-clack of the needles filling the silence.

"Is everything all right, Aunty?"

"Of course, my dear. I do have a slight headache, so it'll be best if I stay here." She kept her gaze on her hands and didn't spare Charlotte a glance.

"Do I need to call for the doctor?"

"No, no." She released the knitting with her one hand and waved the question away. "It's just a slight headache that a little peace and quiet will fix. You go to dinner with Mr. Seymour and see what he has to say. You can fill me in when you return."

* * *

Stanley and Jacob sat at a table next to the enormous fireplace a few minutes before six that evening. Michael had decided to take his dinner in his room. He had gotten a touch of the flu and didn't want anyone to get sick on account of him.

Stanley had arrived early to make sure they had a warm place so Charlotte wouldn't be uncomfortable. While the days were growing warmer, the nights were still chilly. You never knew what to expect in the Rocky Mountains.

He'd been shocked when Jacob had stepped into the dining room. He'd taken a bath, shaved his beard, and donned a suit that fit him like a glove. He seemed a different man and reminded Stanley too much of his pa. While the men were different in appearance, Jacob's personality was achingly familiar, and it brought back memories that were both comforting and painful.

The waiter brought them glasses of whiskey, and they clinked glasses before taking a sip. It was an expensive brand that went down smooth as silk, and Stanley finished it in a few quick gulps.

"Do you really believe Charlotte's father headed out of town?" Stanley looked around for the waiter to ask for another whiskey. When he caught his eye, he pointed to his glass.

"It appears he did." Jacob's expression was pensive. "As best as I can reckon from that man I ran into late last night, it was to a place the locals call Robbers Roost."

"That's quite the name," Stanley said. The waiter brought him a second drink.

"You gonna limit your whiskey tonight?" Jacob asked.

Stanley hesitated and slowly dropped the glass on the table. "You trying to tell me something?"

"Don't need to tell you something if you

already know the problem. Seems to me you're smart enough to realize if there is one and smart enough to do something about it."

Shame filled Stanley. He had been drinking too much, but he'd been using it to forget where he had gone wrong in his life. He had thought he would slow down, but the stress of not finding Charlotte's father was catching up to him.

Stanley averted his gaze and swallowed the thick lump that had grown in his throat. The fact that Jacob had noticed he was drinking too much was humiliating.

"All the gold hunters look there, as that was where the stagecoach robbery occurred," Jacob said. "Not that anyone's found it, or at least that's what the rumor is. Every few years, a new set of gold hunters arrives desperate to find it."

"With any luck, we can find him there." Stanley moved the whiskey out of the way.

Charlotte appeared off to his right. She was the picture of perfection, dressed in a blue and white gown that hugged her slim waist and flared to the floor, and every man in the room stopped what they were doing to look at the mesmerizing vision. He couldn't take his eyes off her.

His inappropriate thoughts had to stop. He was being paid to do a job, not to ogle the woman. Until he got a handle on his mess of a life, he had to keep her at arm's length. It wouldn't do her or him any good to drag her into the problems he had created for himself, especially since he wouldn't be a complete man until he came to terms with what had happened eight years before and the one he had created when he ruined his relationship with Jacob.

She smiled as she caught his eye. She raised a hand to her head and smoothed back flyaways as though she too were nervous to be in his presence. He had to be reading too much into her innocent movements, and instead, he needed to concentrate on what he was there for.

"She's here, Jacob," he said, although from the smirk on Jacob's face, it was clear he had already figured that out. Jacob lifted his glass in salute and then took a drink, the motion similar to a father telling his son *go get 'em*.

Stanley stood, reached for Charlotte's hand, and led her to the empty chair. Once she sat, he pushed it forward and had a hard time stepping away. He wanted to touch her shoulder, to brush the hair away from her neck, to run butterfly kisses against the creamy skin.

Slightly shaking his head, he backed away. He had caused enough trouble by losing his mind over one woman. He couldn't let another one do the same. Charlotte was as far from Connie as possible, but he was still the same man, wasn't he?

Stanley's wobbly legs barely held him upright as he walked to his chair and clumsily collapsed onto it. He glanced at Charlotte to see if she had noticed, but she was busy fiddling with the napkin in her lap. This woman was causing emotions he hadn't ever expected to feel again, and he didn't know what to do with them.

"Howdy, little lady," Jacob said. "How you doin' this fine evening?"

"I'm well, thank you. You look different." She slapped a hand over her mouth, her cheeks bright red with embarrassment. "I'm sorry. That was awfully rude of me."

Jacob laughed, emphasizing the creases near his eyes. He pulled on the lapels of his suit jacket. "That's the nicest thing anyone has ever said to me." He had a wide smile. "I thought it was time for me to clean it up a bit. When my stench makes my nose twitch, it's time to do something about it."

She giggled. "You didn't—"

"Oh yes, I did. But enough about how handsome I am." He smoothed back his hair. "How about we get something to eat and then get down to brass knuckles about what I learned last night?"

Charlotte nodded enthusiastically. Jacob raised a finger, and a waiter materialized within seconds at their table.

"I'd like your finest wine," Jacob said. "And how about a tray of cheese, fruit, and cut meats before we decide on our main meals?"

The waiter nodded and scurried away. Minutes later, he returned with the wine and took the rest of their food order. Jacob's sophistication surprised Stanley. Who was this man that he'd always known as a fur trapper and hunter? Jacob didn't appear to be anything of that sort, at least not anymore. A lot had changed since Stanley had seen or heard from him, and perhaps there was more to the man than he'd realized.

They exchanged small talk until their meal arrived. Before long, they happily relaxed in their chairs, stuffed to the brim. While they had business to discuss, it'd been nice to forget about the things on his mind, and he surmised both Charlotte and Jacob had similar thoughts.

While he had a glimpse of the weight Charlotte was carrying, he had no idea of the pressures Jacob may be under. Stanley had been so self-centered all those years ago and had never been concerned if those around him had their own problems. If he were perfectly honest with himself, he'd never thought to ask either. These were the many reasons he refused to go back home, even though his family begged him to return. Having Michael in town was unsettling. Stanley was discouraged and dismayed that it had come to that. His brother had to hunt him down and beg him to return to the ranch, but he couldn't—not yet.

Jacob shifted in his chair, and his expression changed from jovial to serious. He leaned forward, placed his elbows on the white tablecloth, and rested his fingers around the sides of his glass.

Stanley followed suit. It wasn't a conversation he'd imagine they wanted any of their neighbors to hear. Stanley leaned forward. "What can you tell me… us about Charlotte's father?"

Chapter 12

April 13, 1901

Charlotte was wary of the information Jacob was about to tell them. She didn't know if she could take any more bad news. Jacob's somber expression told her it likely wasn't good. At that point, though, any information was welcome regardless of the pain she might experience.

Charlotte dropped her napkin onto the linen-covered table, placed her shaking hands in her lap to hide them from the men's scrutiny, and focused her attention on Jacob. She braced herself.

Jacob scanned the room before he settled his gaze back on them. One hand stroked his chin while the other tapped the white linen-covered tabletop. With the storm blowing outside, very few occupied the surrounding seats. Only one family of four remained, and they were on the far side of the room. The two little boys were quite precocious, and their merry laughter made her smile.

"I found the man who paid the fine to get your pa out of jail, but," Jacob said, holding out a hand, "he wasn't willing to give me much information. He's sporting quite the black eye and broken ribs but insists it was a misunderstanding. I asked him why he was willing to help the man who'd beaten him."

She wondered the same thing. It was strange and raised a multitude of questions.

Jacob shifted in his seat, straightening one leg, and winced as though something pained him. "He says he thand your pa were discussing a business proposition when another man stormed into the hotel lobby and demanded Marcus pay up, that he was a pathetic..." Jacob paused when he saw the stricken look on Charlotte's face. "He claims Marcus didn't realize who he'd been hitting, but I don't believe him. The man was lying."

"Why did you think that?" Charlotte said.

Jacob lifted his drink and took a sip. "He wouldn't look me in the eye and kept on insisting that if we saw your pa, we needed to detain him so they could continue with their business. He asked me what I knew about your pa, what he was up to, where we had seen him, and such."

She frowned. It sounded ominous.

When Jacob hesitated, she said, "Please don't stop on my account. I'm not naïve. I know he's made mistakes. He left me when my mother passed away, for heaven's sake, and when he saw me both in the saloon and the hotel dining room, he didn't even acknowledge me." She resented what her father was doing, but it didn't stop her from wanting to find him. "Instead, he's hiding from me, determined to stay away. If I were smart, I'd head back to St. Louis and forget about him, but I can't." Her voice broke. She blinked back the tears that threatened to fall. She'd hold them until she was alone and no one could see or hear her.

Jacob nodded. "He said he bailed your pa out of jail because of their misunderstanding." Jacob's voice grew gruff. "He's determined to hold your pa to his end of the bargain."

"What bargain?"

Jacob flicked a crumb off the table. "Ain't that the question. I think the man knew, but he wasn't willing to tell me, or at least not yet. He hinted that the information came at a price." He took another drink and swiped at his upper lip. "While I don't have a problem paying for information, I don't have what he's looking for, and I'm not sure we should pay the man."

"I have money and will pay for it," Charlotte said. "I don't want that to stop us from getting the information we need."

"That's the thing, little lady. I'm not thinking you're gonna wanna do that. The man knows you're here, knows who your grandpappy is, and I'm afraid he'd try and milk you for all it's worth."

Charlotte's spine straightened with resolve. No one was going to scare her away from her mission. "If he can tell me where my father—"

"At what price, though? Good people don't extort pretty young things like yourself," Jacob said.

"I don't know—"

Stanley rested his hand on hers. "Let's think about this for a minute, Charlotte. We know your father is looking for the gold. And he got into a vicious fight where he repeatedly struck back, and it landed him in jail."

She yanked her hand from under his. "I don't understand your point, Stanley." Irritation pierced the back of her neck.

"Sounds to me as though both men are likely after the gold and are not working well together. I wouldn't be surprised if they're trying to outmaneuver one another."

"My father is not..." She rubbed her forehead. A sharp ache was working its way across it. It was a lot of information to absorb. She'd been worried for months, and to be this close to finally finding him made it difficult to see reason. She took a deep breath. "If we don't pay this man for information, then how are we going to find my father?"

"Well, it seems to me if your pa is looking for the gold, then he's likely headed to where the gold was last seen."

"Where the stagecoach robbery happened?" Charlotte asked. Her excitement grew at the thought that perhaps they could finally pinpoint his location, and she'd be able to talk with him for the first time in years.

"Yep, that's what I'm thinking," Jacob said, looking at her as though she were smarter than the average bear.

"I wonder where that is?" Stanley asked. "Wait. Is that the Robbers Roost you were telling me about before Charlotte arrived?"

"Robbers Roost? That's an interesting name for the place," Charlotte said.

"It is, isn't it?" Jacob said. "Kind of a fittin'

name, if you ask me." He chuckled and pulled out a piece of paper from inside his suit coat. "I did some more digging and found a few reliable gents who gave me a map to where we should start looking." He laid it out on the table, the paper crinkling with the motion.

The waiter walked up to their table. He held a bottle of wine in his hands, with a white towel wrapped around the base.

Jacob flipped the paper over to hide the information from the waiter.

"Excuse me for interrupting," the waiter said, his voice high and nasal. "This wine here is compliments of Mr. Edward Smith."

Charlotte wondered who that was and looked at Jacob and Stanley quizzically. Both of their expressions were unreadable.

"Are you sure you have the right table?" Stanley asked. "I'm not sure we know who that is."

Jacob lifted his fingers. "Oh, we do. You can leave that right here." He pointed to the table.

The waiter popped the cork, placed it in the wine bucket, and quietly slipped away.

Once the waiter was gone, Stanley asked, "We do?"

"You don't, but I do. He must think that by bribing us, we'll help him find Charlotte's father." Jacob grinned and poured himself a generous glass of wine. "While I don't cotton to bribery, I ain't about to let this fine wine go to waste. Anyone else care for a sip?" He held the wine bottle and looked at the label. "Wowzah, this sure is a nice bottle. It's worth more than my last decent haul of furs."

"You haven't fur trapped in years," Stanley said, laughing.

"I know," Jacob said, a wide and mischievous grin on his lips.

Charlotte wasn't about to miss a good wine even if it did come from a nefarious source, so she held up her glass and let Jacob pour some of the dark red wine into her wineglass. She swirled it, took a sniff, and smiled appreciatively. Jacob was right. It was a very expensive bottle.

"Well, don't keep us in suspense. Who is Edward Smith?" Stanley asked.

Jacob took a gulp and smacked his lips. "That is pure deliciousness right here."

"Jacob?" Stanley prodded, crinkling his eyebrows.

"What? Oh, yep, sorry." Jacob leaned forward, placed the glass down, and rested his elbows on the table, his navy suit in sharp contrast to the white tablecloth. "Mr. Smith is the man who was fighting with your pa and who paid the fine to get him"—he pointed over Charlotte's shoulder—"out of jail."

"What? He's here?" Charlotte turned to see who might be watching them, but no one had entered. Only the family of four remained.

"No. I don't see 'em, but I ain't going to let this wine go to waste. I'm sure going to enjoy it." Jacob took another long drink.

Charlotte shook her head. Wine was meant to be sipped, savored, but he was drinking it as if it was water for a hot, thirsty body.

"Why would he send us a bottle of wine, I wonder?" Stanley said.

"Probably to let us know he's watching us, I gather." Jacob flipped over the piece of paper he had removed from his pocket before the waiter interrupted them. "He wants that cache of gold just as much as our little lady's pa does. I'd be willing to bet he's going to use whatever resources he has to find it, including watching our Charlotte here like a hawk."

Charlotte's spine tightened, and unease trickled through her. Her quest for her father had taken a turn she hadn't expected.

"You believe Charlotte is in danger, don't you?" Stanley asked.

"I do," Jacob said. "From what I've been able to gather, numerous stagecoaches have been robbed there over the years. As you already know"—he shared a glance with Stanley—"the four involved in the robbery hid the gold within ten miles of the place. They wouldn't have been able to make it far with just their horses. Considering that the four accused were caught, killed, and hanged within a year of it, and the gold was never recovered, it stands to reason it should be hidden somewhere in that canyon."

"They could've hid the gold anywhere. It could take forever to find it," Stanley said, tapping his finger on the table. "If someone hasn't found it already. Seems a foolhardy mission after all these years."

Jacob nodded. "You would suppose so, but apparently, one of 'em left a map with a loved one about where it was hidden. Somehow your pa got ahold of that information." He picked up the piece of paper and handed it to Stanley.

"What's this?" Stanley asked.

"That there is a map to show us where Robbers Roost is. That way we don't get lost ourselves." Jacob leaned back in his chair and folded his arms across his chest.

"The fact that someone has a map to where the actual gold is hidden sounds too good to be true." Stanley examined the piece of paper in front of him for a minute before sharing another glance with Jacob. "If a family member had that kind of information, why would they not tell anyone about it for over forty years?"

"Good question. I haven't the faintest clue," Jacob said. "But one thing's for certain. If we don't go looking, we won't know the answer either."

* * *

Stanley met Jacob in the lobby after escorting Charlotte back to her room. The two of them were headed to a nearby saloon where Stanley could question Jacob further. Jacob seemed elusive, and Stanley wondered if he was holding something back that he didn't want Charlotte to hear.

Thirty minutes later, they arrived at a nearby saloon and honky-tonk. The place was near full, but Jacob slipped the bartender a few coins, and they landed a table near the front to enjoy the show. Stanley wasn't particularly interested, but Jacob was plumb tickled about seeing it.

They settled into their chairs with tall

tankards of frothy beer. The roar of the crowd was loud and made it difficult to hear one another without yelling.

An older man with a bright blue vest and shiny, black boots jumped onto the stage. Black whiskers lined his ruddy cheeks, but he grinned from ear to ear and waved to the crowd. Whistles could be heard as men urged others to quiet. Soon, the crowd's enthusiasm subsided, and the cacophony of noises dimmed. All that was heard was an occasional boot hitting the ground or a glass being dropped heavily onto a table. The men were anxious to see the women, but the show wouldn't start until the old man was ready.

"Gents, welcome to the best honky-tonk in town. Have we got a show for you tonight."

Raucous catcalls bounced off the walls, and the man grinned enthusiastically. "Firstly, we have Miss Lilabeth to delight you, followed by the engaging trio of Fanny, Penny, and Milly, who will certainly captivate and entertain you."

The room erupted into a blast of clapping, stomping, and loud cheering. The sounds bounced against the walls, causing empty glasses to dance across wooden tables.

The old man waved his hands to quiet the room. "Now, without further ado, I give you Miss Lilabeth."

He jumped off the stage. The fiddler and the piano man struck the first strains of an upbeat and cheerful song, and a dark-haired beauty pranced onto the stage, her clothing leaving nothing to the imagination, but her sweet voice was music to the ears. She captured the attention of every man in the room. While she was scantily clothed, there was an ethereal radiance to her that begged men to watch her but also kept them at a distance.

Miss Lilabeth sang a few songs before the musicians took a ten-minute intermission. Jacob jumped up and sauntered to the bar to get them fresh drinks. A few minutes later, he returned.

"You gonna tell me what you kept to yourself at dinner tonight?" Stanley asked with the momentary pause in the loud music and cheering. The men inside the saloon had been temporarily appeased with the entertainment from Miss Lilabeth and were likely waiting in high anticipation for the next act to start in a few minutes.

Jacob had been mid-lift with his drink. He paused, a strange expression on his face before he continued to take a sip. When done, he wiped the beer foam from his upper lip. "I wasn't sure you'd caught that."

Stanley shook his head. "Yeah, I did, but I figured you didn't want Charlotte to hear so I didn't press you."

Jacob nodded. "About that. Smith acted as though he was fairly friendly with Marcus, but something didn't ring true for me on that." He drummed his fingers on the wooden tabletop. "If they were friends, they wouldn't be getting into a fight so bloody that Marcus almost killed the man. There has to be some serious anger for someone to lose control like that."

"Perhaps Marcus is volatile and has a vicious temper." Stanley didn't believe that of Charlotte's father, but what other explanation could there be?

"That is something to consider. Has Charlotte ever said anything like that about her pa?" Jacob looked around the room, his gaze never stopping as he likely considered each person he saw and whether or not they were a threat.

"No. She told me that while he'd had a gambling problem, he didn't drink and never raised his voice in anger to either her or her mother, but she also hasn't seen him in over ten years. Who knows what she saw or didn't see as a child?" Stanley should have likely questioned Charlotte more about her relationship with her father, but he hadn't wanted to upset her unnecessarily, as it was clear she was sensitive about him.

Jacob pulled at his collar. "So why would Marcus lose control like that?" He held up his hand. "I don't expect you to know the answer to that. It just seems odd and out of place with what Smith claimed when I questioned him. Besides that particular observation making the hairs on the back of my neck stand on end, I asked around, and a few fellers told me that Marcus has racked up some gambling debts and actually owes Smith a tidy sum of money."

"Is Marcus really looking for gold that doesn't exist?"

"I wonder. The fact that no one has supposedly found the money in over forty years doesn't make much sense. Either it was hidden so well that no one will ever find it or someone found it and kept quiet about it. Either way, I don't think Marcus is going to find it no matter how hard he searches."

"So why is he avoiding Charlotte and continuing to look for it?"

Jacob shrugged. "Maybe he's trying to bide time, perhaps trying to keep Charlotte safe. Or Smith threatened Charlotte and Marcus is trying to protect her. I suppose it could be that he really doesn't care about his daughter and wants to find the gold before Smith does."

"I hope that isn't the case." Stanley would hate for Charlotte to realize that her father was only after the money. "With any luck, we're wrong, and he's really trying to protect Charlotte."

"Regardless of Marcus's intent, I have no doubt Smith is lying about his relationship with him, and Charlotte is going to pay the price someway."

"I sure hope not," Stanley said. "I can empathize with her. My supposed beloved wife did something worse. She murdered my pa."

Jacob frowned. "You really haven't told me much of what happened with your wife."

Stanley needed a stiffer drink than the beer sitting in front of him before he told that story, but that wasn't going to happen. He took a long pull of his beer and dropped it on the table. "It's not a happy-go-lucky story, Jacob. Not something I'm proud of." He lowered his eyes. "I let a pretty face sway me into marriage and into sending my brothers away after we lost both Ma and Pa. Then I come to find out she'd been cheating on me the whole time with a ranch hand before she attempted to have him kill me."

"I'm sure your pa—"

"My pa would've been horrified to know I let a woman do everything *she* did. He raised me better than that. He taught me to be mindful and—"

"And your pa would've been sorry to discover what she'd done. He wouldn't blame you." Jacob placed his hand on Stanley's arm, but he pulled away.

Jacob was wrong. His pa had been appalled when he arrived at the Thundering Mountain Ranch with Connie by his side. She'd been everything his pa despised. His disappointment was something Stanley would never forget. While his pa had welcomed Connie, his pa's actual feelings had emerged for a split second. Not only had Stanley brought home a wife unsuited to the harsh realities of ranch life, but he had brought one home who was nothing like his pa would've ever imagined him marrying.

Stanley had even distressed his ma. She'd always dreamed of her children marrying on the ranch. He'd taken that from her by marrying Connie with no one's knowledge.

What had transpired after that had been eighteen months of pain for everyone. His parents had tried to welcome Connie, but she'd been unhappy. She'd gone to Helena every chance she got and spent money faster than he could earn it. She'd run through what Stanley had saved for years within the blink of an eye. When he told her she had to stop, she had thrown such a tantrum it was like looking at a five-year-old child pitching a fit because a toy had been taken away.

Connie had been furious that he hadn't built her a home and instead made her live with his ma. He'd really believed she wouldn't mind. He'd planned on asking his pa if they could live in the original homestead, but once Connie saw it, she'd refused to move there. She'd said she would've rather lived with his ma than live in that hovel.

The cabin wasn't large, but it would've been enough for a new couple. Unfortunately, he hadn't understood, or he'd ignored the warning signs. Money was her motivator, and when that ran out, she'd gotten even nastier. He'd just been stupid enough to ignore it. He was still unclear as to when she'd forged his pa's will, making him the sole heir and then having her lover, the ranch hand, smother his pa to death.

Realizing he had disappeared into his thoughts, Stanley shook his head. "The past is hard to remember. I can never ask for his forgiveness. I tried for years to find her and bring her to justice, but she was slippery. I had no luck in finding her until she popped back up in Helena last year."

"Sorry to hear that." Jacob's gaze was probing.

"Don't be. She's in hell, where she belongs."

"That's good news, isn't it?"

"I guess," Stanley muttered.

"I don't understand."

"Dammit, Jacob." He slammed his fist onto the table. "I was the one who brought her into the family. It should've been me who took her down, but I failed. Michael had to kill her when she tried to kill Luke."

Just then, the curtains on the stage opened wide, the piano man pounded out the strains of a new song, and three girls with long legs, frilly multicolored skirts, and petticoats graced the stage, swinging their skirts and kicking their legs to the delight of the men.

The noise from the music and the hollering and whooping drowned out any remaining conversation. It was good timing, as Stanley was done reminiscing about the mess he'd made of his life. Jacob might've had good intentions, but nothing could change the fact that he was the one who had brought Connie into their lives and ruined what was left of his family.

Chapter 13

April 21, 1901

A week later, Charlotte left her aunt sleeping peacefully to meet Stanley outside the general store. After a few days of dodging Charlotte's questions, her aunt had admitted that she'd run into Stanley. He had concerns about Charlotte's father, and when he told her he was uneasy about her father's involvement with questionable men, her aunt had become unsettled. She wanted Stanley to ensure Charlotte's safety, and while he had tried to assuage her aunt's fears, she wasn't sure her aunt felt any better. Thinking it over and not wanting her aunt to fret, Charlotte had considered giving up her quest. She didn't want to put her aunt through any more unnecessary pain, but she couldn't seem to let go of the need to understand why her father had left her.

Charlotte had been unable to talk with Stanley, as the three men had disappeared for a few days. They'd finally returned the night before and there had been some unmistakable tension between the two brothers. Not wanting to pry, she hadn't asked any questions, but she certainly wondered about it.

Stanley had asked her to meet him that morning. He told her to wear a warm riding skirt, a thick coat, and a pair of sturdy boots. They were taking her to an abandoned stagecoach station, and while spring had arrived, there was still snow on the ground.

"Ready?" Stanley said, approaching her from behind.

She almost jumped out of her boots. Raising

her hand to her chest to calm her rapidly beating heart, she nodded.

"Shall we?" Stanley said, holding out his arm.

"Yes," she said and wrapped hers around his. "Where's Michael and Jacob?"

"They're meeting us at the livery."

The sun wasn't high in the sky, but it was bright blue with a few puffy white clouds scattered in the distance. It hadn't snowed in a few days, and the temperature was actually pretty pleasant. With any luck, the weather would hold, and it'd stay pleasant for their trip.

"How far away is this stagecoach station?"

"Not far." He patted her hand. "It'll take us about an hour to get there."

He halted and looked across the rail tracks to make sure no trains were coming and then helped her across the uneven and, at times, dangerous wooden lines. Depending on the time of day, it could be quite busy, but three trains had just rumbled along the tracks and away from the station. No others could be seen so it was safe to cross.

A few minutes later, they reached the livery. Jacob stood waiting for them. His beaming smile was a welcome sight, and he opened his arms in welcome. Unable to resist, she let go of Stanley's arm and bounded across the dirt road. If she'd been lucky enough to have an older brother, she would've wanted him to be like Jacob. Warm, welcoming, and loving, Jacob was a happy and jovial man who loved life and those around him.

Jacob pulled her into his arms and enveloped her in a warm hug. It was as though a furry cuddly bear had wrapped himself around her— giving her comfort and love when she needed it most. She hadn't realized how much she needed that until that very moment.

A few seconds later, he released her but held her upper arms, looking into her upturned face. "You're a pretty sight for these ugly ole eyes of mine," he said, a mischievous grin on his lips. "If'n you ever decide Stanley ain't the man for you, you can come callin' to me. I'd be happy to make you my wife."

Shocked, she dropped open her mouth.

"Stanley isn't... I mean, we aren't..." She gulped. Her face was likely as red as a ripe tomato.

He chuckled heartily, leaned down, and whispered in her ear, "You might not be now, young lady, but this heart of mine is never wrong. You're meant for one another. Just give him a chance. He's had a bad run, but he's a good man."

"But—"

Jacob placed a finger across her lips, silencing her. "Don't say nothing. Just know if you ever need me, I'm here to help, but he'd protect you with everything he had." Before she could respond, he stepped away and dropped his hands.

Charlotte stumbled back, flabbergasted by Jacob's words. If she looked at Stanley, she might blush unbecomingly and make a fool of herself.

Stanley's brother stepped out of the barn, leading four horses. She walked up to them, taking a few breaths to slow her pounding heart.

Jacob had put into words the things she had been thinking but was too shy to admit.

She brushed her hand against the muzzle of the smallest horse. It snorted and pushed against her. She giggled and whispered in its ear. She didn't get to ride as often as she'd like, and it was a joy when she could. Her grandfather had a few horses that he stabled on a property outside of St. Louis, and they would go there during the heat of the summer. When she was younger, she would ride for hours.

The more she was around Stanley, the more she wondered if Jacob was right, but she didn't know if Stanley was someone she should pursue. It might lead to heartache. He drank far too much, was furious with his ex-wife, and looked at her with heavy-hooded eyes that sent waves of awareness from the base of her neck all the way to her toes. He made her want to swoon whenever he smiled at her.

She was in serious trouble.

* * *

Stanley scowled watching Jacob envelop Charlotte in a warm hug. He was as old as his pa and treated all women with care, but a surge of jealousy roared through Stanley like the freight trains that had just left the station. He didn't want any man touching her, including the man who meant the world to him and would never cause him intentional harm.

When Jacob released her, he whispered something in her ear, and she blushed something fierce. Shaking his head, Stanley walked to the horses Michael held. He had to get his jealousy under control. It was misplaced, but he was curious about what Jacob had said to her to make her cheeks turn a becoming bright pink.

"Ready to go, little buck?" Jacob placed his large hand on Stanley's shoulder and squeezed affectionately.

Stanley couldn't be mad at him. He was like that with everyone and would protect Charlotte like a daughter. "Yes, let's ride." Stanley took the reins of a black stallion and checked the straps.

"Do you need help, Charlotte?" He nodded toward the saddle.

Grinning, she grabbed the pommel with one hand and her skirts in the other and lifted herself up into the saddle. Her skirts bunched around her knee, revealing her small foot and shapely calf. He shouldn't have looked, but he couldn't resist. Licking his dry lips, he had to tamp down the ardor springing up inside of him.

"Whatcha waiting for? Let's go," she said, gazing at him beguilingly.

Jacob mounted his horse and leaned against the saddle's pommel, trying to contain his laughter. He had caught what Stanley had been gazing at and likely knew the thoughts that were running rampant through his mind. Stanley had never been able to hide anything from him.

"Everything all right, big brother?" Michael asked, a wide grin on his face. "Need some help?" Michael too had likely seen what Stanley had been looking at and would give him a hard time for it if given half a chance.

Stanley glared at Michael, mounted, and

pulled the reins of the horse to the south. He didn't wait for them to follow. If he continued to stare at Charlotte like a lovesick calf, who knew what other boyish actions he might take.

Having Michael in town was grating on his nerves. Michael insisted he wasn't leaving until they talked, but Stanley refused to speak to him about what had happened last year. Stanley was being stubborn and unfair, but his anger was overriding his good sense.

An hour later, Stanley pulled his horse to a stop, the reins held loosely in his hand. He lifted the brim of his hat and stared at the abandoned stagecoach station. It must've been a bustling place in its prime but had fallen into disrepair over the years.

An old barn with a gaping hole in the roof sat to the left. Corrals with missing and broken rails sat to the right, and the old outpost buildings had seen better days. Some were still standing while others were barely hanging on to the supports that had held them strong once upon a time. The only thing that remained of the main house was a large stone fireplace. It'd likely been where the stationmaster and any passengers had rested for the night.

Charlotte led her horse next to him and wiped at her forehead with a pale pink handkerchief. "Why are we here, Stanley?" Those were the first words she'd uttered since they left Pocatello.

"This is one of the stations we believe your father thought the gold was buried, or at least ways that's been what we've been able to ferret out."

She sat straight in her saddle and looked around as though her father might pop up and say *I'm here*, but no one stood and announced themselves. The four of them were the only ones for miles around. They had seen no one on their trip, which was surprising because forty-five years ago it had been a hotbed of travelers before the railroad built its tracks and changed transportation forever.

Stagecoaches still existed, but many of the stations had closed with the decrease in business. They were living in a new world, and searching for lost gold was a memory best left in the past. Until Charlotte had answers, though, he'd be there to help her through it.

"We're alone, Charlotte," Stanley said.

She turned in her saddle and glared at him. "I can see that, so please tell me why we're here." Her tone was curt. He didn't know what had changed her attitude, but he wouldn't let it get to him.

Dismounting, Stanley tied his horse to a hitching post. Jacob and Michael followed but kept their distance from him and Charlotte. They likely saw a storm brewing and didn't want to be around when it erupted. A moment later, Charlotte heaved a loud, exasperated sigh, swung her leg over the pommel, and slid down the side of her horse.

Stanley had to hide a grin. She was plumb irritated with him, and he'd never admit it to anyone other than himself, but he kind of enjoyed it. Seeing her riled up caused her cheeks to glow and put a sparkle in her eyes, although she likely wouldn't agree with him because they sent daggers to him at the same time.

She wandered away and walked slowly to what remained of the stagecoach station, stepping cautiously across fallen lumber, rocks, and dull red bricks. She had no fear, and while she had nothing to be afraid of, he was glad she was mindful and didn't rush headlong into the unknown.

Not wanting her to walk into danger, he called out to stop her. "As far as we can tell, your father was out here about ten days ago."

"How do you know that?" Her back was to him as she glanced around the valley.

"We tracked his horse to this location."

She whipped around, a few strands of her blonde hair flying in the wind. "You did?"

He leaned his foot against a broken fence post and braced his hand against his knee. "Yes, ma'am, we certainly did."

She stiffened. "Why didn't you mention that before?"

"You didn't ask." He was being an arse, but he couldn't help himself.

Her hands were fisted at her hips, but she relaxed them when she caught his glance and muttered something under her breath that he couldn't hear.

"Did you say something?" he asked, even though he was certain she wouldn't tell him what she had said, as it was likely a curse of some sort directed at him.

"What did my father do while he was here?" She moved closer to him.

Stanley had no simple answer for Charlotte, but he could show her what they had found. He pushed away from the fence post and waved for her to follow. He led her behind the crumbling barn and pointed to a path created by many more before them. The snow had melted, and only trampled dry weeds remained. The area was remote and hadn't been disturbed in some time with the exception of the path they were on. It had struck him as odd when they'd been there before, but it hadn't taken long for them to discover why the path was still there after years of neglect on the station.

Jacob appeared behind them and placed his hand on Charlotte's shoulder. "We followed the path for some time."

"And what did you find?" she asked, turning her head, hope in her wet eyes.

"I'll show you." Stanley reached for her hand. He was mildly surprised she didn't pull away and smiled to himself when she held on tight. Her small hand fit perfectly within his palm. Contentment rolled through him like fluffy clouds on a warm spring day. Knowing she trusted him enough to place her faith in him made his chest puff out with pride. Unfortunately, he was about to squash that contentment.

Leaving Jacob, they walked through the brush and followed the path before he stopped. She gasped, pulling her hand away when she saw what was before them. He couldn't blame her. He, Michael, and Jacob had been surprised as well.

Chapter 14

April 21, 1901

When Stanley touched her hand, Charlotte briefly thought she should pull away, but as his warm hand tugged her along, she couldn't let go. It felt right somehow, but she had to remember they didn't have a future together, no matter how much these small moments made her hope for something precious between them that could, with time and attention, blossom into something more substantial.

Hundreds of holes littered the valley. Some were freshly dug, and others had tall, dry stalks growing out of them, showing they'd been dug sometime before. Her father wasn't the first and likely wouldn't be the last to search for the gold that might be hidden behind the barn at the abandoned stagecoach station. The place had been ravaged by greedy men all determined to find that elusive gold. There was no telling who might have found it or if it was still buried deep beneath the rocky landscape.

They certainly didn't want to be walking or riding their horses there after dark. A horse could stumble and break a leg, and it could be days, if not weeks, before anyone found them, with no guarantee that anyone would.

"Do you think he found anything?" Charlotte asked, running her hand against the back of her sweaty neck. The hot sun was high in the sky, and while still cool, it could bake her exposed skin. She'd likely get freckles if she stayed out there too long.

"Who? Your father?" Stanley had a stick in his hand and was poking random holes with it. She wasn't sure what he was doing, but it made her want to laugh. He looked a bit ridiculous.

"Yes." She coughed to hide her giggles. He didn't notice and continued to wander. She couldn't take it any longer. "What are you doing?"

"Me?" He stopped and paused to look at the stick in his hands. Stanley chuckled. "Looking like a fool, I'm thinking."

She shook her head. "You aren't a fool, but it's definitely been interesting watching you. You'd think you were throwing a line and trying to catch a fish with the way you were pushing that stick into the ground."

He shook his head. "I'll admit that poking holes wasn't my finest moment."

"Maybe not, but it gave me a giggle or two."

He dropped the stick alongside a dead tree and rested a foot on the rotting wood. His expression was pensive. "We think he must've come here and dug a few of these holes. Either that or he took a gander and thought if there had been anything here, it'd been taken long before now."

"But where would he have gone from here?"

He raised the brim of his hat, letting her see the brown of his eyes. They were dark and serious, the light-heartedness of the past few minutes gone. "I really don't know, Charlotte."

"Why did you bring me here, then?" She rested her hands on her hips, not understanding what the point of the trip had been.

He stared at her for a long moment and then pushed away from the log. "Because I wanted you to see that finding him won't be as easy as you might think."

"I never thought it was going to be easy, Stanley, but I know he's here. I saw him with my own two eyes. If he's determined to find this gold, then he's got to be near. We just have to be patient. We will find him. I know it in my heart." She pounded her fist against her chest.

He sighed, a frown on his lips. "I'm not trying to hurt your feelings or give you no reason to hope, but—"

"No. You can stop right there. I'm this"—she held up her thumb and forefinger, holding them barely apart—"close to finding him. I'm not giving up now."

"I'm not asking you to give up, but you need to be realistic." He had softened his tone, but it only infuriated her more.

"Realistic." She stomped her foot on the hard ground, and while the movement had a certain dramatic flair to it, it didn't produce the sound she wanted it to have. "I've been looking for him for months. I'm not giving up now."

"Charlotte—"

"Don't you dare Charlotte me," she roared. "If you don't want to help me any longer, then just tell me."

"I didn't say that." He held up his hands as though he was going to ward off her anger.

"You didn't have to say it," she cried. Her shallow breath likely caused her face to redden. "I know you have your own problems. You only agreed to help me because my aunt cornered you and made you feel guilty."

"That's not what—"

"Why don't we just end this? You can go on your merry way, and I—" Her words caught in her throat when he abruptly yanked her into his arms and kissed her silent. She swallowed her protestations as her eyes closed and fireworks exploded in her mind in a cascade of bright reds, blues, and greens. She couldn't think, couldn't breathe, couldn't do anything except enjoy the taste of his mouth against hers.

He suddenly pulled away, a smirk on his lips. "Are you always this stubborn?"

She stumbled back and raised her fingers to her mouth. Her thoughts were scattered, but she was aware enough to take issue with his question. She glared at him. "I'm not stubborn."

He shook his head, shrugged, and walked around some larger holes and back toward the trail they had come from. It was as though the kiss hadn't affected him at all.

"Where are you going?" *Don't leave me after that delicious kiss.*

"Back to the horses," he called over his

shoulder, his back straight, his focus forward and away from her.

Her gaze roamed over his backside, heat blooming inside of her. She was glad he didn't look her way, for she'd likely burst into flames if he did. However, in that very moment, she didn't think that would have been a problem. She would've likely let him do anything he wanted if it meant he would give her the love she craved but hadn't realized she wanted from him.

"Are you coming?" he called, his voice fading as he proceeded farther away.

"I'm not done looking." She sounded like a petulant child, but she didn't like that he had kissed her and then said nothing about why he'd done it. Instead, he was leaving her to fend on her own. The man was infuriating, maddening, but oh so delicious she could swoon in his arms if he gave her half a chance.

"When you're done, come find me," he said. Before she could stop him, he disappeared from view.

He was as irritating as a wasp circling her

head, but heavens, could he kiss. A radiant smile crossed her face as she walked back and forth, being careful to watch her step. While her heart still pounded from the touch of his lips against hers, she couldn't forget why she was there. She'd consider the ramifications of his kiss when she was alone and could ponder what it meant and how it had made her feel.

She had gone on a fool's mission in trying to find her father. Seeing him in the brothel and the hotel lobby had been an answer to her prayers. The problem was, he was like a mouse, always finding a hidey-hole to disappear into and doing his utmost to keep away from her.

Charlotte groaned. She looked to the trail where Stanley, Michael, and Jacob were waiting at the end. She didn't want to admit defeat, but maybe she'd have to, after all. She couldn't continue to chase after a man who was not willing to be found.

What would it take before she finally admitted defeat?

* * *

Stanley left Charlotte, his feet faster moving than a hare being chased by a fox. He couldn't believe he had kissed her. Her face had been red with irritation, and when he couldn't get a word in, he'd acted without thinking. While he should be ashamed of himself, he wasn't. He had enjoyed that kiss far more than he cared to admit. It'd be hard not to do it again, not when she looked at him as if he hung the moon.

He strode to the front of the dilapidated barn and searched the open field for Jacob and Michael. He didn't think they would've returned to town without them, but he could never be too sure what Jacob might do. He did what he wanted and when he wanted it, and Michael was never predictable. While Michael was still congenial, he had changed over the years, and Stanley didn't know him like he'd thought. He would've never expected Michael to be the one to pull the trigger to end Connie's life.

Unfortunately, seeing Michael brought back

feelings he didn't want to face. He wasn't in love with Connie, but he was outraged and even more so now knowing she might've been related to him. The whole thing just didn't make sense. His Uncle Howard had been a good man and wouldn't have harmed someone on purpose. There had to be more to the story, but Connie was gone, and there was no way to get the truth from her.

A hand gripped his shoulder and squeezed. He yanked out his revolver and flipped around, shoving it into the man's side.

"Now hold on, little buck. Didn't mean to startle you," Jacob said, holding his hands in front of him and backing away.

Stanley released the hammer, shoved the revolver into his gun belt, and wiped his forehead of nervous sweat. "I'm as anxious as a newborn kitten out here. I didn't realize it was you."

"I would've thought you could've heard me clomping through the brush," Jacob said, a grin lifting his red cheeks.

"I was in my own mind, I guess. Thinking about things." Things he'd rather forget.

Jacob reached into his shirt pocket and pulled out a piece of jerky. He offered it to Stanley, but he waved it away. Jacob shrugged and then took a bite, chewed, and swallowed. "Mind me asking what those things are?"

Stanley trusted Jacob, but he wasn't sure he wanted to answer his question. Jacob's gaze was piercing, thoughtful. He always had an uncanny knack for seeing what Stanley wanted to hide. He usually just let the silence drag on long enough that Stanley would tell him all the details. It was a particularly unique tactic, and while Stanley had figured out his method years ago, it still didn't stop him from spilling his dirt.

"Just ruminating on information I learned about my pa from Michael."

"Oh." Jacob lifted an eyebrow. "And what information is that?"

"Where's Michael?" Stanley said, ignoring the question.

"Around here somewhere, I suppose. He'll be

back soon, I'm sure." Jacob kicked at a clump of dirt and lifted the piece of jerky to take a bite, then hesitated. "What did you learn about your pa?"

"Nothing really important but interesting, nonetheless."

Jacob waited. He was like a dog after a bone, not letting go even when Stanley tried to change the subject. Before Stanley realized he'd fallen for his tactics once again, he explained what Michael had told him about Connie's claims and that his Uncle Howard had passed away.

When he finished, Jacob grimaced. "I don't remember your pa ever saying anything untoward about Howard's marriage to Beth Ann."

"You knew Howard and Beth Ann?" Stanley scrunched his forehead.

"Of course I did." He smiled. "I met your pa long before you were born and his brother too."

"I didn't know that."

"I've known you since you were a tyke, little buck. Didn't you realize I knew your pa's family too?"

Stanley ran his fingers through his hair. "I guess I never thought much about it."

"Remember when you ran off that summer?"

"How could I forget?" That summer had been a hard one between him and his pa. He had been headstrong and stubborn, thinking he knew better, and had run off half-cocked determined to prove to his pa that he could be on his own.

"That was actually the last time I saw your uncle. I was visiting him and Beth Ann when your pa sent word asking if I could find you, and lucky for you, I did. If I hadn't caught up with you when I did, we'd be having a mighty different conversation right now."

Stanley had gotten himself mixed up with a pack of dangerous men who'd been hell-bent on destruction. Jacob had plucked him out of the mess before he could get himself more caught up in the havoc they'd been causing and had set him on the straight and narrow.

"You helped me when I needed it the most. I'm most appreciative."

Jacob chuckled with mirth. "You say that

now, but when I grabbed you by the scruff of your neck and stopped you from going with those men to rob that there bank, you weren't thrilled. In fact, I remember you being quite belligerent and petulant, trying to be a grown man when you barely filled out those boots you'd been wearing."

"I certainly wasn't, was I?" He was exasperated by his immaturity at the time. "I'm surprised you kept me in check, to be honest, but considering every one of those men died during that robbery, as well as those two bank tellers, I'd be in a mess of hurt if you hadn't interfered."

Jacob's jovial expression dimmed. The memory of that time was difficult, but yet Jacob had intervened at just the right moment and had saved him from a death sentence or a life in prison. Both of which would have ruined his life forever.

"Anyhow," Jacob said. "Right after your ma and pa bought the ranch, Howard came to visit. They were living in that small cabin that I believe your brother-in-law and wife are living in right now."

"Ma and Pa loved that homestead," Stanley said. "They always said that if they hadn't kept on having us, they would've likely stayed there for life. Ma said it was a reminder to them of what they stood to lose if they didn't keep their family close. I never really understood what that meant, but after they built the other main house, the two of them would sneak off for a night or two alone to get away from us, especially once Katie was born. With six of us running around, we were quite the handful."

"Yes, you were, but they loved all of you fiercely." Jacob cast his gaze over the remains of the homestead, his face pensive. "Howard met Beth Ann at a barn raising that first summer and fell head over heels for her. He couldn't marry her fast enough, and he took her back to his Texas ranch soon after."

"I didn't realize you knew so much."

"There are plenty of things you don't know about me," Jacob said, slapping Stanley on the back. "Where's the little miss?" He looked over Stanley's shoulder.

"She's back behind the barn." Stanley pointed to where he had left Charlotte.

"You left her there?"

"Yeah, we had a minor tiff. She ain't too happy with me right now."

"And why's that?" Jacob said, a twinkle in his eye. "Did you finally kiss her silly like you've been wanting to from the day you met her?"

Chapter 15

May 15, 1901

It'd been three weeks of endless searching and they were in no better shape than they'd been when Stanley started the endeavor. He said good night to Jacob and Charlotte and then walked to the hotel's front desk. He should've told Charlotte they were done after they'd left the first stagecoach station, but he hadn't had the heart to disappoint her.

They'd then visited numerous other abandoned stagecoach stations, chased men who claimed to know nothing, or found ones whose eagerness to help was just a way to take as much money from Charlotte as they could without sharing any valuable information. In the months since he'd met her, they were no closer to finding her father than when they started.

Michael had returned to Helena after they visited the first stagecoach station near Robbers Roost. That had been their best lead, even though it had resulted in nothing worthwhile other than the opposite of what he thought it would have done. Instead, it further emboldened Charlotte to continue looking for her father. After that trip, he'd thought for sure that she would've called it quits but she hadn't.

It had also been the last time he'd let himself be alone with her for fear he would kiss her again or perhaps do something more. He couldn't stop thinking of her and how she'd felt in his arms. His control was slipping, and he either needed to give up and tell her she needed to head home to St. Louis or do something about the fire raging inside of him. Though a visit with a whore might solve the physical problem, he was afraid nothing would satisfy what he really wanted, and that was her.

When they returned to the hotel that afternoon after another fruitless search, Charlotte had murmured her thanks. Her spirits had clearly been down, and she'd trudged up the stairs to her room, hanging her head in defeat. Jacob had also said his goodbyes and left for the boarding house where he'd rented a room. The hotel wasn't for him, he'd said, laughing when Stanley had offered to secure one for him weeks before. He kept offering, but Jacob was insistent he didn't need the upgraded room.

"I don't need these fancy digs. Mrs. Little's boarding house works just fine for me. A soft bed, fresh water, and a hot meal every night. Not to mention a bit of lovin' when she's in the mood." Jacob laughed heartily. He always had a love for women and they flocked to him as though he were a colorful peacock, his bright blue and green feathers always open and welcoming them, but never favoring one over another.

As Stanley waited in line at the front desk, a man stood in front of him complaining about the size of his bed. Stanley had to contain his laughter at the spectacle the man was making of himself. The clerk expressed his apologies for the man's inconvenience and offered him another room. The man, unhappy with that, muttered something under his breath and then stomped away. The clerk waved Stanley forward, his expression apologetic.

Stanley leaned against the desk and took a piece of paper and a pencil stub to send a telegram to his brother Ben. He hadn't heard if Michael had returned home safely and felt it only right he at least reach out and inquire.

"Oh, Mr. Seymour." The clerk smiled. "I'm so glad you stopped by. We received an urgent telegram for you." He turned and looked at the numbered key rack where they stored the messages and keys. Reaching for the one in slot twenty-nine, the hotel clerk pulled out a folded message and handed it to Stanley.

Stanley dropped the pencil and furrowed his brow. He hadn't been expecting anything but flipped it open.

STANLEY SEYMOUR, PACIFIC HOTEL,
POCATELLO, ID
ANNE AND CHILDREN HOME SAFE STOP
COME HOME IMMEDIATELY STOP
BEN

His heart stopped for just a moment but then he sighed with relief. His sister Anne and his brother-in-law, James's children had been missing for months. Stanley hadn't known what had transpired until he returned home for Christmas. During Michael's visit, Michael had told him that their brother-in-law, James, was in Idaho somewhere looking for them, but they hadn't been sure where. Anne and the children's return was good news for everyone. Ben had been worried sick for months, but the responsibilities of the ranch and his own family had kept him from helping with the search.

Stanley scratched out the message he'd been planning to send and instead wrote a new one.

BEN SEYMOUR, THUNDERING MOUNTAIN
RANCH, HELENA, MT
MESSAGE RECEIVED STOP
WILL SEND WORD WHEN ON MY WAY STOP
STANLEY

After handing the message to the hotel clerk, he pulled out coins to pay for the service.

"I'll get this to the telegraph office right away, Mr. Seymour." The hotel clerk placed the coins in a lockbox. "Is there anything else I can do for you?"

Stanley shook his head but then realized he did have an additional request. He scratched out another two notes, one for Jacob and one for Charlotte. "Could you have this one delivered to Ms. Charlotte McVicker in room twenty and this one to Jacob Jones at the Blooming Flowers Boarding House?" He pulled additional coins from his pocket and handed them to the clerk. "For your help."

The clerk smiled, especially once he noted the number of coins. "Right away, sir." He snapped his fingers for a bellboy. Handing both of the notes to him, he gave the boy quick instructions.

"Thank you." Stanley pushed away from the desk when he realized he hadn't asked one important question. "One more thing. Do you have the train schedule for next week?"

The hotel clerk frowned and scratched his chin. "No, it hasn't been delivered yet. I can send word to you when it arrives, or you can go to the ticket office in the next building over and they'll have that information readily available."

Stanley nodded. While he had promised Charlotte he'd help her, his family had to come first. If Ben was demanding his return, he couldn't ignore it. He'd have to return to Thundering Mountain Ranch for a few days, and if all was well, he'd return to Pocatello to pick up where he had left off. The search for Charlotte's father would have to wait.

*** * ***

Charlotte stared in dismay at the message that had just been delivered. Stanley was leaving to head home to his family's ranch. He said he'd let her know his departure date as soon as he purchased a train ticket and would return in a few weeks once all was well back home.

She crumpled the paper between her fingers. While she understood his family's needs came first, it didn't lessen the pain of knowing she was once again on her own. They'd grown close, and yet there was still a chasm between them. She didn't expect him to return, and he had no reason to, even though he had promised her aunt he would help them. Charlotte couldn't ask him to come back and had to release him from his promise. It was the right thing to do, although it pained her to know she would never see him again.

The past few weeks had revealed nothing. Her father could have discovered the gold, but the more likely situation was that he was searching for a treasure that was long gone and had been since it had first been taken over forty-five years ago.

She did not want to return to St. Louis with her tail between her legs, but it was time to face reality. She could ask Jacob to continue in Stanley's stead, but he had only helped because he was Stanley's friend. For all she knew, Jacob was returning to Helena with Stanley.

"What's wrong, my dear?" Aunt Martha called from the sofa where she sat knitting.

Her stomach rolled at the knowledge that, once again, her plans were thwarted. Not sure how to respond to her aunt's questions, she handed her the wrinkled note.

Aunt Martha placed her knitting to the side, reached for the spectacles perched on her head, and squinted to read the note under the gas lamp.

Not wanting her aunt to see the devastation that was likely written all over her face, Charlotte walked toward the fireplace and stared into the flames, trying hard to contain her composure. She wasn't a crier by nature, but she wanted to act like a two-year-old and throw a wild tantrum over the things that continued to get in her way.

"Well, my dear," Aunt Martha said. "This is certainly unexpected, but you can't blame the man for needing to return to his family."

"No, I don't blame him. I'm just..." Charlotte swallowed, emotion growing thick in her throat. "I just hoped we would've found my father by now. I should just admit defeat and go back to St. Louis." She whirled to face her aunt. "I don't want to go home, Aunty." She clenched her fists, her posture stiff and unyielding.

Her aunt placed the note on the table, grabbed her cane, and struggled to stand. Charlotte should help, but her aunt would only protest.

Aunt Martha shuffled to her niece's side and took her hand in hers. Her small hand was firm and sure, even with the wrinkles and age spots that lined the top of it. That hand had seen a lot in life, both good and bad. "I didn't realize you were that set against going home."

Charlotte tried to pull away, but her aunt held firm.

"I don't want to marry Colin." Tension crackled in her voice.

"You don't have to, young lady. We aren't living in the dark ages anymore." She tried to lighten the mood, but Charlotte was too despondent to smile.

"I do, unless I can find my father."

"What has made you believe your father has any say in the matter? Do you really think my brother is going to listen to him?" Her aunt's voice had softened.

"But that's why we came."

"No, that's why you came, Charlotte."

Charlotte pulled away from her aunt, and that

time Aunt Martha let her go. "I don't understand."

"You do, young lady. There's no point in denying it. I've been going along with this search of yours, and it's high time we discussed it."

"There's nothing to discuss, and you're wrong." Charlotte turned to walk away.

"No, I'm not." Aunt Martha hit her cane on the wooden floor, abruptly stopping Charlotte. "Don't you turn your back on me. I was planning on doing this eventually, but Mr. Seymour's leaving has just made me do it sooner."

Slowly, Charlotte turned around. Her aunt's expression was one she had never seen before, and Charlotte didn't know what to think. Anger, frustration, and sadness were rolled into one hard look. Her aunt had always been on her side, always encouraging and loving, but in that moment, she was anything but.

"Sit, Charlotte." Aunt Martha's arm extended stiffly against her cane.

When Charlotte opened her mouth to argue, Aunt Martha hit her cane again on the floor and pointed to the sofa. Snapping her mouth shut, Charlotte obeyed.

Aunt Martha groaned as she dropped slowly into the chair. Charlotte cringed with shame. Her pain was due to Charlotte dragging her across the country. Aunt Martha had agreed to come along because she hadn't wanted her niece to be alone, or at least that was what Charlotte had believed. She wondered if there was something else to her aunt's willingness to accompany her.

Her aunt rested her cane against the arm of the chair, folded her hands in her lap, and stared hard at Charlotte. She squirmed under the glare, but she wasn't sure what to say to the woman who meant the world to her.

"Now, this has to stop. I went along with this harebrained idea of yours because I wanted you to be safe. Your grandfather would not go along with it unless I accompanied you."

"But—"

"No. You are going to let me have my say."

Charlotte nodded. She respected her aunt

and would grant her the courtesy she was asking for.

"Now." Aunt Martha pushed at a strand of her hair that had come loose from her coiffure. "When you asked me to come with you, I was happy to do so. Living in St. Louis has been hard on you since your mother died. I thought an adventure might be good for you." She sighed and shifted in her chair. "But I also thought you'd learn that your happiness would come from within and not from your father."

She held out a hand to stop Charlotte from once again opening her mouth. Aunt Martha had an uncanny ability to know what Charlotte might do before she even did it.

"I have no doubt you saw him here, but Marcus doesn't want you to find him. He won't stop my brother from trying to marry you off to Colin. I know you don't want to marry him, and I understand why. He's just a mini version of my brother, and that's not a good thing." Aunt Martha reached for her mug of coffee and realized it was empty.

Charlotte jumped to her feet. "Let me get a fresh cup for you, Aunty."

She held the mug for Charlotte. Charlotte carefully touched the sides of the coffee pot on the dining room table to see if it was still warm and poured a full cup. "Cream or sugar?"

"No, my dear." Aunt Martha reached for the mug with two hands and took a whiff of the powerful brew. "Mmm, that smells delicious. Thank you."

Charlotte murmured, "You're welcome." She sat, wishing she had poured herself a cup, but it'd have to wait until her aunt had her say.

"Now, where was I?" Aunt Martha said after she took a sip. "Oh yes, my brother, your grandfather." She tapped the side of her lip with her forefinger. "He has good intentions, always has, but he's determined to have things his way. His interference caused problems with your mother and father."

"I always thought that was the case but didn't want to assume without talking to Father," Charlotte said.

"It was between adults and not fit for a young girl's ears. We did try to keep the harsh things from you."

"I haven't been a child for years, so why didn't you tell me when we left on this trip?" She wrinkled her nose, a sneeze blooming, but she held it at bay.

"And what would I say? That your father was as worthless as your grandfather believed or that your mother was aware? Because your grandfather was stubborn and muleheaded, she stayed with your father just to spite him, especially after you were born and her life became more difficult." The words rushed out of Aunt Martha's mouth so quickly, Charlotte's head spun at the implications.

"I…" That was unexpected. Her grandfather hadn't thought highly of her father, but she hadn't expected Aunt Martha to feel the same. "I didn't realize you don't like my father."

"I never said I don't like your father," Aunt Martha said. "He didn't have the strength to fight your grandfather on what he thought your mother deserved, just as he won't be able to fight your grandfather on what he thinks you deserve."

"I'm trying to understand, but I'm not sure I do."

"Charlotte, your father won't have any influence on your grandfather's desire for you to marry Colin. The only person who will help you… is you."

"But—"

"But nothing, young lady. You've used the excuse of finding your father instead of facing your grandfather. Even if you find him, he won't help. He's too scared, too broken to do anything. Marcus could have stood up to your grandfather years ago. He didn't have the strength and, let's be honest, the will to do so. He was only after his next payday, his next gambling adventure." She took another sip of her coffee, her gaze hard as she stared at her niece over the cup's brim.

Charlotte grew uncomfortable with every word her aunt uttered. She wanted to get up and leave, but it would be rude to do so. Instead, she sat patiently just as she had been taught.

"If he's here and looking for gold, then it's the same thing, just in a different place. Marcus doesn't want to work. I'm a bit surprised he spent the time digging for that gold, but he'll never find it. It's been forty-five years, and no one has found it, or if they have, it's long spent by now. He's chasing a dream and isn't inclined to help you. If you found him and could talk to him, what makes you think he's going to return with you to St. Louis?"

"To help me," Charlotte cried, knowing in her heart that everything her aunt was saying was correct. Ultimately, she'd have to face her grandfather, but she wasn't sure she had the strength to do that.

"He won't help you, and it's time you face it. You do have the fortitude to fight your grandfather. You just have to find it." She pointed at Charlotte. "He loves you, and I believe if you stand firm, he'll acquiesce and still give you your trust fund. Honestly, if you end up marrying someone respectable, he'll agree regardless. If he doesn't, then you'll be under your husband's care and—"

"What if I don't want to marry?"

"We both know that isn't true." She smiled to soften the harshness of her words. "You've always wanted to marry, likely for the wrong reasons, but you still want someone strong and compassionate in your life. Perhaps someone like Mr. Seymour." Her aunt's eyes gleamed at the not-so-subtle hint she had just dropped in Charlotte's lap.

Chapter 16

May 16, 1901

Charlotte left the small café on the other side of the railroad tracks. She'd spent the morning wandering aimlessly through the various stores along the primary thoroughfare, her arms full of packages as she tried to take her mind off Stanley's imminent departure.

She'd ventured into a dressmaker's shop earlier and had been speaking with the owner when her stomach growled loudly, startling both of them. They'd been admiring a new shipment of fabric that had arrived just that morning. The dressmaker had smiled and suggested the new café when Charlotte laughed to hide her embarrassment.

She had taken a seat near the window and had been surprised by her appetite. Once the tasty treats were in front of her, she hadn't resisted. Restless that morning, she hadn't eaten ahead of leaving the hotel, but the tidbits the café owners presented her were worth it, and her belly appreciated both the sweet and savory tarts the owners had suggested.

She and her aunt had talked long into the night, and while Charlotte wanted to disagree, deep in her heart, she knew her aunt was right. Her father wouldn't help her. Instead of being the woman her grandfather had raised, she'd been running scared. Charlotte's grandfather loved her, but he had a fierce temper and always got his way. If she defied him, she took the chance it could change her future forever, but perhaps it was time for her to take that chance.

Stopping at the edge of the railroad tracks, she saw Stanley. She waited for him, although he appeared distracted and out of sorts. He didn't catch her eye and passed her by without saying a word. His indifference and lack of recognition sent a painful tug to her heart. She meant nothing to him.

"Stanley." He kept on walking and didn't appear to hear her. "Stanley," she said, that time a little louder.

He turned as he searched the pathway in front of him before he stopped his gaze on her. "Charlotte, I didn't see you there."

She tried to smile, but she was sure it was a frown. The fact that he hadn't seen her and admitted it was even worse to her battered heart.

"I received your note last night," she said. There was no point in pretending she wasn't upset. She might as well get it out in the open and confront it before she lost her chance to be near him one last time.

He removed his hat and slapped it against his leg, looking sheepish for sending her a note instead of telling her himself that he was leaving Pocatello. "Good, I'm glad you got it. I'll be back in a few weeks, and we can continue—"

"No, it's over," she snapped, her tone harsher than even she expected. "I'm going home to St. Louis. This has been a fool's mission. I'm sorry I dragged you into it."

He swallowed hard a few times, his Adam's apple bobbing with each one. After a long moment, he said, "I didn't mean for things to happen this way, but my family—"

She shook her head. "No. You don't have to explain yourself. You have your family to think of, and I need to return to St. Louis. My grandfather expects me to marry—"

"What? You're going back to St. Louis to get married?" He looked like she had just thrown a punch into his gut. Was he jealous?

"Yes. I mean, no—"

His brows snapped together, wrinkles lining his forehead. "I don't understand. You never said anything about getting married."

She stared at him, searching his eyes. Her grandfather wanting her to get married wasn't something Stanley should be concerned with. She had never mentioned it because she wouldn't marry the man, no matter her grandfather's intentions.

"It wasn't any of your business." Her hands struggled to hold all of her packages and maintain her composure.

"I can't believe—"

"You can't believe what?" She waited as she tried to discover why he was so concerned.

He sighed. "I just assumed you'd be waiting when I returned."

She shook her head. "I've been praying for a reunion with my father that was both unrealistic and a schoolgirl's foolish dream. I should've realized sooner that this was a useless mission. Every single abandoned stagecoach station we visited just cemented the fact that my father is only concerned with finding the gold. He has no interest in being in my life. It's time for me to return home and forget about a man who doesn't want to be my father. I've been stupid and reckless."

"You haven't been stupid or reckless," he said, showing a hurt she hadn't intended to inflict.

Regardless of what Stanley said, she'd been stupid, thinking only of herself. Dragging her aunt across the country, all so she could have someone else stand up to her grandfather. Her father couldn't stop his plans. It would be up to her. Her conversation with her aunt had shown her that the only way forward was to be honest with her grandfather. She wouldn't marry Colin. She was going to do something worthwhile, and she just had to express herself to him and live with the consequences.

"I won't belabor the point," she said, straightening her back with resolve. "I won't be here when you return... If you return."

* * *

After he bid Charlotte goodbye, Stanley left the train depot with a ticket in hand. He should've offered to help her with her packages, but she hadn't given him a chance to say anything before she disappeared into the growing crowd of people on the warm spring day. He was afraid he had hurt her feelings, but he hadn't addressed it when he had the chance and was afraid he wouldn't have time now to mend the sudden rift.

He'd leave for Montana in a few days, giving him just enough time to see if he could try one more time to find Charlotte's father. She said she was done, but as adamant as she'd been in trying to find him, Stanley didn't believe she truly wanted to be done. She had determination in spades, so he couldn't understand what had changed. It couldn't be because he was leaving, especially since he said he was going to return. It had to be something else.

Ben's telegram was clear. Stanley needed to go. He had been distant and unreliable for years. His time with Charlotte had shown him that his aimless wandering needed to stop. He had been drinking too much and had too much anger and resentment toward his brothers and those who loved him. It wasn't fair to continue to be a drain on the family's resources, nor was he being fair to himself. Connie was gone, and he had to come to terms with it.

He just prayed that Ben would forgive him for being absent for so many years. Michael arriving in Pocatello had been a swift kick to his pants. His brothers no longer held grudges for his part in bringing Connie into their family, but it still gave him pause to know that if it hadn't been for him, his pa would still be alive today. After Michael left, his guilt had intensified. He hadn't trusted his brother and had made it difficult for Michael to make amends. He was ashamed of himself and had to fix what had broken between them, as well as everyone else in his family.

He placed his train ticket into his billfold as he walked inside the hotel's lobby and glanced at the large clock that rested against the far wall. The day had gotten away from him. He hadn't eaten and was right hungry, but he didn't want to eat alone. Stanley had grown to enjoy the meals he shared with Charlotte and Martha and would miss them.

He glanced into the dining room and scanned the occupants, when he saw Charlotte's aunt. She appeared to be alone. He hesitated, not wanting to intrude, but at the same time, it would be the perfect opportunity to speak to her alone and return the money she had given him to find Charlotte's father. Stanley hadn't found Marcus and didn't feel right about keeping it when he hadn't delivered.

Removing his hat, he smoothed down his hair and straightened his vest. He spoke to the maître d' before he skirted around the tables and patrons. He reached Martha's table and stopped in front of it. She was mid-bite and hesitated. After a moment, she placed her fork back on her plate, picked up a white cloth napkin, and dotted it across her lips before smiling.

Stanley hadn't been sure of her reception considering the note he'd sent to her niece the night before, but her grin made him think perhaps he hadn't ruined things with Martha as much as he had with Charlotte.

"Mr. Seymour," she said. "What do I owe for the pleasure of your company?"

"Martha, I was hoping I'd run into you."

She raised an eyebrow as though to tell him she didn't believe him, but she went along with his ruse. "Would you care to join me?" She waved a hand at the empty chairs in front of her.

"I'd enjoy that very much." He sank into one across from her.

She gestured to a waiter, and he scurried to their side most efficiently. "Please bring Mr. Seymour..." She paused and looked at him. "May I?"

He nodded. It was usually the man who ordered for the woman, but it appeared Martha had different ideas.

"Please bring him the special of roast beef, mashed potatoes, brown gravy, two—no three rolls, and some green beans." She looked at him to make sure he agreed, and he gave a slight nod. "He'll also have your best whiskey."

The waiter scribbled on his white pad of paper and disappeared. A few moments later, he returned with a large basket of rolls and a glass of whiskey. Stanley should have refused the whiskey, but he didn't want to be rude. He'd only take a sip and drink the glass of water instead. He thanked the waiter and licked his lips. The fresh smell of bread caused his stomach to rumble.

Martha lifted her glass to her lips and took a quick sip. "You better eat one of those rolls before you starve to death."

Stanley laughed and didn't hesitate to reach for the warm bread. He smeared on a thick slab of the softened butter and took a large bite, trying not to moan at how grand it tasted.

He lifted his head and caught Martha staring at him. He grinned sheepishly. "I apologize, ma'am. I haven't eaten today, and I guess I was right hungry."

"Don't apologize to me. I appreciate a healthy appetite." She cut her roast beef and took a bite.

"I'm glad I ran into you," he said after he had finished one roll and was busy slathering butter on the second.

"Oh, really? And why is that?" She quirked an eyebrow.

"I… Well…" He was at a loss for words and didn't know how to broach the subject.

"Yes. Spit it out. I don't have all day. I'm not getting any younger." She softened the harsh words with a smile.

He took a deep breath. "I hate that I'm leaving you and Charlotte before finding Marcus. I know how much it meant to you both—"

She held up her hand. "Let me stop you right there, Mr. Seymour. You aren't leaving us in the lurch, as you might believe. Charlotte was on a goose chase, and it was good she finally realized it." She picked up her fork and pushed the food across her plate. "I do hate that our association is ending so soon, but your family needs you. You've been right gentlemanly in trying to help. I'm grateful. However, I'm not upset that we aren't looking for that wastrel of a man any longer."

"You're not?" Stanley was surprised.

"No, I'm not." She placed her fork on her

plate and took a sip of her lemonade. "I love my niece dearly, but she was misguided. He never tried to be a good father when he was in her life and definitely wouldn't be now if she had found him."

"That seems harsh." He'd thought Martha was just as determined to find Marcus as Charlotte was.

"It isn't harsh. It's the truth." She slapped the table as if to prove her point.

He picked up the glass of water the waiter had placed next to his whiskey. "It's fortunate that she has your support then. It's hard for me to imagine not having a pa who cares."

The twinkle dimmed in Martha's eyes. "I feel the same way. My father was nothing like Charlotte's. I wish she could've had someone as caring and loving as he was."

"What was your pa like?" Stanley asked.

The beaming smile on Martha's face told him everything. She clearly had favorite memories, and sometimes people needed to share them. "Ah, no. You don't want to hear an old woman go on and on about things from the past."

He reached across the table and took her withered hand in his. It was small, and he imagined at one time it had been smooth as silk. She was ever the lady. "Yes, I do. Tell me about him."

She covered his hand with her other one, patting it for a moment before he pulled away. "Why don't you tell me about your pa first, Mr. Seymour? Then maybe I'll tell you a thing or two."

He considered what she said for a long moment and then nodded. She was certainly inquisitive. "My pa was a fine man."

"I'm sure he was if he produced a son as strong and trustworthy as you," Martha said.

He frowned. "I'm not sure I was the vision Pa had for an obedient son."

"Now, I can't believe that." She shook a finger at him. "Look at what you've done to help my Charlotte."

His neck burned as heat bloomed up his

chest. He wasn't sure Martha would think so highly of him if she was aware that he'd kissed her niece or that he'd had too many lustful thoughts concerning her. "I haven't done more than anyone else would've done." He'd probably done more than he should have, but he'd keep that to himself.

"Oh, phishaw. We both know that ain't true, but that's neither here nor there. Now tell me about your mother and father."

He bent his neck to hide his smile. "Where should I start?"

"The beginning is always a good place." She picked up a roll and tore off a piece, smearing blackberry jelly on it before popping it into her mouth.

He shook with laughter. "My pa, he was a force to be reckoned with, but he loved us. He spent plenty of time with each one of us— teaching, guiding, but he wouldn't take no flak from us either."

"He sounds like a good father."

"He was." Stanley smiled at the memories. "I

remember this one time, I was nigh on ten years old. We had lived at the ranch for a few years at that point. Ma wanted to name it Thundering Mountain on account of a ferocious thunder and lightning storm the night we arrived at the ranch. She said it was appropriate due to the thunder that crashed and shook the earth." He fiddled with the collar of his shirt, his mind in the past. "He had me and my older brother, Ben, help him cut down tall pine trees to create the archway to the ranch. He'd showed us how to strip the branches off, cut them to the right size, and then we nailed 'em together before we lifted them into place." He took a bite of the creamy mashed potatoes. "When we were done, he stood between us, put his arms around our shoulders, and called us men that day." He chuckled. "We were far from men, but he said we had done the work of a man and that he was proud of us. Ma then came down the long drive carrying my youngest sister, Katie. The look on her face was one I'll never forget."

"And what was that?" Martha asked.

"It was one full of love for my pa and for us, of course, but I'll never forget the look that passed between them. I can't describe it, but I knew right then and there that I wanted what they had. Years later, I thought I had…" He shook his head, emotions tightening his throat. He should have worked through these feelings by then. "Well, it doesn't matter what I thought."

"You've been hurt far more than you show, haven't you?"

He raised his head, and her compassionate gaze was almost his undoing.

"I don't mean to be nosy, but I know a bit about the hurt someone can do to you, especially if you think they are the one for you." Tears filled her eyes. She raised her fingers and quickly wiped them gone.

He wouldn't ask her, but the empathy in her eyes told him she did. He nodded and downed his water in one gulp. He wanted the whiskey, but drinking to dull the pain was no longer an option, not if he wanted to start to make amends.

"I certainly didn't mean to make things uncomfortable," Stanley said.

"Oh, you haven't. I was the one asking the questions. I apologize if I made you think of things best left in the past." She cut her roast beef but didn't take a bite. Instead, she picked up her napkin and wiped at unseen crumbs on her fingers. "But I do want to say one thing."

"Yes," he said. She was a sweet old woman who had good intentions, so he'd be happy to listen to her.

"Don't let one woman…" She held up a finger to stop him from disagreeing.

He snapped his mouth shut.

"Don't let one woman ruin your future. Grieve for what might have been and remember the happy memories. File the painful ones in the past and look forward to the future." She took a deep breath. "Don't close yourself off. Otherwise, you might become an old, bitter woman who could've had more but let anger ruin her for everyone else." Martha's eyes shined with unshed tears, but they were still bright as she stared at Stanley. It was as though she was trying to convey something more than just her words.

He reached across the table and took her hand in his, squeezing for a moment before letting go. "I'll remember that."

* * *

"Aunty," Charlotte exclaimed when her aunt walked through the door of their hotel room. "Where have you been? I expected you hours ago."

"Now, Charlotte," Aunt Martha said, shuffling across the floor. "I was enjoying a delicious meal with your Stanley."

Heat rushed to Charlotte's cheeks. "He isn't *my Stanley*."

"Tsk, tsk. Whatever you say." She sat on the sofa across from Charlotte, kicked off her shoes, and rubbed one foot. "These shoes, while delightful to look at, are not kind to my feet."

"Do you want me to ring the front desk to ask

if they can send up Epsom salts and a small tub?"

"Oh, would you, my dear? That would be splendid and most welcome."

Charlotte nodded and did as she bid. After speaking to the front desk, she said, "It'll be brought up momentarily."

"Thank you. I don't know what I would do without you."

"Would you like a cup of tea?" Charlotte reached for the pot of hot water that had been delivered right before her aunt had arrived.

"No, I had plenty to drink while I was talking with Stanley." She winked at Charlotte.

Charlotte groaned. Her aunt was forever playing matchmaker. "Now, Aunty, enough about that. Mr. Seymour is leaving—"

"He may leave, but he doesn't have to disappear from our lives. If you know what I mean." She tittered with glee.

Charlotte was not amused. "No, I do not. He's heading north to Helena, and we are heading south to St. Louis."

"We don't have to go south. We can go north."

Charlotte paused, holding the warm teapot with both hands. "Now, why would we go north when we need to go south?"

"We haven't seen that part of the country. Perhaps your father is headed that way."

Charlotte stared in dismay at her aunt's wild idea. "There's no sign that my father went north. If anything, he's still here trying to find that elusive gold." She placed the teapot back on the table, rattling her cup and saucer. "I'm sorry. I don't mean to be rude."

"You aren't being rude, my dear. You're only speaking the truth."

Charlotte picked up her cup and saucer and sat across from her aunt. "And the truth is, we need to head home, not north."

"I don't know. I've always wanted to see Montana."

Charlotte had just taken a sip of her tea and almost spat it out with the ridiculous statement her aunt had just uttered. Placing the teacup down before she spilled it all over her lap, she lifted her feet and rested them next to her on the sofa. "You've never mentioned wanting to see Montana."

"Of course I have." Aunt Martha couldn't hide her grin. She was still up to her matchmaking ways.

"What are you up to?" Charlotte asked, squinting at her aunt.

A knock sounded at the door, stopping her aunt from replying.

Charlotte stood but pointed at her. "We aren't done discussing this."

"Now, now. Don't keep the hotel clerk waiting. Besides, my feet are begging for those salts." She rubbed her foot to prove her point.

Tightening the sash of her wrapper and holding the top closed at her neck, she opened the door.

The hotel clerk pushed a small cart with a bag of salts and a small tub of warm water inside. "Where would you like me to put this, ma'am?"

"Right here would be just fine," Aunt Martha said, pointing to the floor.

The clerk did as her aunt said. Charlotte gave the clerk a few coins and thanked him as he left.

Picking up the bag of salts, Charlotte poured the crystals into the warm water, stirred it with her hand for a few seconds, and then stood. "Let me grab you dry towels for when you're done."

Her aunt had removed her stockings and moved her skirt and petticoats to her knees. Sticking first one foot and then the other into the warm water, she muttered something unintelligible, leaned back, and closed her eyes. "Thank you. That feels heavenly."

"You're welcome." Charlotte took a deep breath. "Now, do you want to—"

Her aunt raised her hand and flicked her fingers. "No, I do not want to discuss why I've always loved the thought of going to Montana, but I already purchased two tickets. We leave on the Tuesday train."

Chapter 17

May 17, 1901

The next morning, Charlotte tried reasoning with her aunt, but Martha was adamant they were going to Helena. Her aunt was plotting to put them on the same train as Stanley with the hope that something would develop between them. It was a ridiculous notion. While he might have kissed her, Stanley didn't see her as anything more than an acquaintance or perhaps a friend. She wouldn't embarrass him by asking or approaching the subject. It was best to leave it in the past.

Charlotte told her they should return to St. Louis, that they had been gone for far too long, but her aunt argued she'd traveled across the country with no complaints and had been nothing but supportive. She insisted Charlotte could give her one fun trip before she went to her maker.

Charlotte had said no more. She *had* dragged her aunt hundreds of miles on a trip that had ended in a small Idaho town with absolutely nothing to show for it, so she couldn't argue with her aunt's outrageous request.

Leaving her aunt in the hotel room, Charlotte headed to the dry goods store to pick up some nonperishable food items for their trip. She didn't know how edible the train food would be, but her aunt was particular. Charlotte wanted to make it as nice as possible for her.

She also needed to send a telegram to her grandfather to let him know they were leaving for Helena. She didn't think her grandfather would be thrilled about the extra stop, but with any luck, he'd be appeased with that knowledge that they would return to St. Louis soon after.

After looking both ways before crossing the railroad tracks, she hurried to the dry goods store. It was a gorgeous May morning. The sun was bright, and it wouldn't be long before she could replace her thin coat with cotton blouses and lighter petticoats. She could even start wearing cotton skirts as opposed to the thick wool ones.

The dry goods store was not far, and it was nice to get outside, even if it was for a short walk. Before long, she reached the stairs leading up to the wide doors that were propped open with barrels of nails and tobacco. Large, brown burlap bags of flour and sugar rested next to the barrels, with baskets of carrots, onions, and red apples catching her eye. She stepped inside and was surprised by how cheery the store was, considering it was packed wall to wall with anything and everything imaginable. Bearing in mind how far west they were, the store was surprisingly well-stocked. A few ready-made skirts and blouses along with heavy bolts of fabric in a variety of colors were also available.

After giving the storekeeper a list of supplies, she browsed aimlessly while he gathered the items she had requested. He'd been enthusiastic, especially after he saw what was on the list. The storekeeper was likely adding up the money she would pay, especially when she said it would be in cash.

She eventually reached the ready-made clothing. She didn't need anything new, but she couldn't help herself. A pink blouse with delicate lace beckoned her. She held it against her chest and looked down, admiring the cut and feel of the fabric. She found a mirror off to the side and smiled. The color was nice and would be a treat.

"That is quite the becoming blouse."

Charlotte jumped and whipped around. Jacob stood to the side. He had crossed his arms against his chest and wore a cheeky grin. She raised a hand and rested it against her beating heart. "Jacob, you startled me."

His beaver cap dangled from his fingers.

"Sorry about that, young lady. I certainly didn't mean to. Didn't think anyone would miss my big ole clomping footsteps."

She grinned and grazed her fingers against his arm. "I was so enamored with this blouse, I didn't hear a thing." She glanced at the lovely fabric, sighed, and went to return it.

Jacob stopped her. "Now, why would you want to put that back? Looks like it belongs on you."

She stroked her fingers against the soft fabric. "It really is pretty, isn't it?"

"It sure is. I'd be willing to wager that it'd look mighty fine on you as well."

She blushed. "Oh, you are too kind, Jacob."

"Nope, not kind. Just stating facts."

Peering at it once again, she decided to be impulsive. "Why not? I haven't purchased anything new in some time. I think I just might buy myself something for the next leg of our trip."

He tilted his head and lifted a bushy eyebrow. "Oh, you planning on leaving Poky?"

Folding the blouse, she placed it in her basket. "Yes, my aunt has a hankering to see Helena."

He smirked and waggled his eyebrows.

Before he could say a word, she said, "No, no. It isn't what you're thinking."

"And what am I thinking, little lady?" He clearly wanted to chuckle but hid it under that mischievous smile.

"That—" What could she say without confirming what he was obviously thinking—that they were following Stanley? "Please, forget I said a word."

She scooted around the table full of folded shirts and skirts and marched over to another one that had cotton stockings. She grabbed two pairs and placed them in her basket next to the blouse.

Jacob cleared his throat, his eyes sad. "I didn't mean to make you uncomfortable."

"No, I'm sorry." She placed her hand on his arm and squeezed affectionately. "You meant nothing by that." She sighed. "It does appear we're following Stanley. I haven't told him, and with any luck, we'll be on a different one so he doesn't get the wrong impression."

"What about your pa?" he asked. "Do you think he went to Helena?"

"No. I'm sure he's still here, searching for that elusive gold. He has to know I'm looking for him, but he doesn't want to be found." A sharp pang pierced her heart. Knowing how much her father didn't want to see her hurt more than anything else could. "After Stanley let us know he was returning home, I decided my search was over and that I needed to return to St. Louis where I'll…" She didn't want to tell Jacob that she had to confront her grandfather. It wasn't important. "I'll find something worthwhile to do."

"Why are you headed to Helena, then? 'Cause I hate to tell you, that's not exactly in the right direction."

She chuckled. "Yes, I'm aware. Aunt Martha insists that she's always wanted to see Montana. Between you and me, she wants to see me and Stanley in a relationship, which will not happen.

He has zero interest in me that way but has been very generous in helping look for my father."

"Are you sure about that?" Jacob shifted and leaned against the nearest wall, his shoulders so wide it was a wonder they didn't knock off the items on the shelves behind him.

She lifted an eyebrow. "Of course I am. Stanley had no intention of staying here until my aunt strong-armed him."

His large hand touched her elbow. "Stanley doesn't let anyone make him do a thing. He wanted to help and was happy to do so."

Jacob clearly thought there was more there than there truly was, but she wouldn't belabor the point. "Regardless, there's nothing between us. He's returning to Helena for his family, and I'm headed there to appease my aunt. The likelihood of us running into one another would be rare, especially since we'll stay at a Helena hotel. If I understand it correctly, his family's ranch is outside of Helena."

"Yes, Thundering Mountain is an hour east of Helena."

"What an interesting name. Have you been there?" she asked, drifting forward.

Jacob pushed away from the wall and ambled next to her side as she walked the aisles full of goods. "I have. It's been over ten years, back when their pa was still alive. Probably the last time I saw Stanley, truth be told. It was before he married that woman."

"Oh," she said. "The one that killed his pa."

Jacob nodded. "She was a conniving woman who was after the ranch, but Stanley foiled her plans, although she'd done enough damage after having killed Cole." There was a tremor in Jacob's voice, and she hated that she might've been the cause of it.

"I'm sorry for your loss. I didn't mean to bring up something painful."

"You didn't, little lady. Cole was a good friend of mine, and while we didn't see each other often, he meant the world to me. I enjoy remembering the good times. I can't bring him back, but I can recall the memories that warm my heart."

She halted, her heart breaking at what they'd all gone through. She squeezed his hand. "Thank you for sharing that with me. I think I can understand the haunted look in Stanley's eyes now. What a horrible thing to have endured."

"A few months back, his brother Luke almost died in a gunfight with her and her goons. If not for Michael, Luke might not be here with us today." Jacob paused. "I shouldn't be telling you this, but it might help you understand him better."

She pinched the skin between her brows to stop the headache that had just developed. "I feel awful for not understanding the depth of his pain. He shouldn't have had to be dragged into my problems in trying to find my father."

"No, no. I don't want ya feeling bad. You didn't do nothin' wrong." He fiddled with a button on his shirt. "He wanted to help you and was happy to do so. I imagine he feels lousy about not finding your pappy before he got the telegram asking him to come home. I'm sure he'd return to Poky and continue to look for him in a few weeks."

"Yes, he mentioned that." It was time to let her father go. "I have no doubt he'd keep his promise, but I have to face the fact that my father doesn't want me to find him. As much as it pains me, it's time to move on."

* * *

An hour later, Charlotte waved goodbye to Jacob, her basket full. She worried Stanley's way of coping with the tragedy would harm him in the long run, if it hadn't already. He had so much to give someone, but he was still stuck in the past. Until he forgave himself, he wouldn't be able to move forward.

As she weaved through the clogged streets, it seemed everyone was enjoying the pleasant afternoon. Wagons and carriages clambered down the dirt roads, horses neighed, and wheels turned. A dog scampered across the dirt with a bone dangling from his jowls. A butcher chased him, a cleaver in his hands, hollering something unintelligible. She had to hide a chuckle at the display the two of them made.

Children laughed and played at a small park behind a nearby church. Their screams of joy and giggles warmed her heart. She turned in the direction of the park and sat on a small bench under a large tree to watch them. Women strolled through the cobbled and dirt paths, pushing carriages, grasping toddler's hands as they tried to walk, and holding babies in their arms. Loving couples had their arms wrapped around waists, and even one hid behind a tree, eager to find a moment alone. Families picnicked on the grass field, enjoying cold meats, lemonade, and one another.

A tall, lanky gentleman with a tall top hat stopped and sat next to her. He reminded her of some of the dapper men in St. Louis who wore the finest cut of cloth but had nothing between their ears except hot air. He seemed a bit out of place in the small railroad town, but who was she to judge?

The man tugged at his waistcoat and then straightened his hat. Charlotte wasn't trying to be nosy, but she couldn't help but notice him. He had red hair, a handlebar mustache, and thin lips.

Realizing she'd been staring, Charlotte averted her gaze back to the children playing around them.

"It is a grand day, isn't it?"

Charlotte startled at the man's question. "Yes, it certainly is."

"Are you from here?" His voice was nasal.

Tingles of discomfort crept up Charlotte's spine. She didn't know the man but had been raised to be polite. "No. I've been visiting."

"And where do you hail from, if I might ask?"

Charlotte turned to face him. "St. Louis."

"My, oh my. You are far from home." He stroked one edge of his mustache. "Why would you ever come to this frontier town?"

"I've been trying to find my father," she said, the words slipping past her lips before she could stop them. She didn't know why she had just told a perfect stranger her personal information.

He had no need to know and meant nothing to her.

"Oh, and have you had any luck?" The man stared straight ahead, seeming not particularly interested in Charlotte's response.

"Unfortunately, no."

"So a wasted trip, then." His voice was condescending, with a hint of malice in his tone.

Charlotte swallowed back her ire. She didn't know the man and had no quarrel with him. Holding back her desire to say something rude, Charlotte wondered if perhaps the man's sophistication was a mask for a tough life. She wouldn't judge, although she'd likely be better served to say her goodbyes and leave the man to his business.

"I wouldn't say it was wasted, per se," Charlotte said.

The man nodded but didn't respond. Instead, he focused his attention on the children playing in front of them. "Such messy creatures, aren't they?"

"The children?"

"Yes," he drawled. "Screaming with high-pitched voices, always playing in the dirt, dragging their filthy hands and faces onto every surface, not to mention how sticky they are." He curled his lips into a sneer.

"They are quite a bit of work, but they do bring joy." Charlotte disagreed with the man wholeheartedly. The more he spoke, the more Charlotte wished she hadn't taken the time to sit on the bench.

"Do they?" he said, arching a brow.

Charlotte didn't think the man deserved an answer. The two of them clearly had different ideas regarding children.

"Charlotte, if I may call you Charlotte?"

Startled, she glanced at him, immediately wishing she hadn't. "How do you know my name?"

"You should be careful of the company you keep." He circled the ivory cap of his cane with his fingers.

"Excuse me?" Charlotte bristled with irritation. "Who are you?"

"That matters little," he said. "But I'd suggest that if you aren't careful, you could get yourself into a mess of trouble."

"You don't know me, so what gives you the right to say that to me?"

He chuckled, but it was filled with malevolence. His gaze was focused on the children playing, and he didn't look at her or move.

She didn't want to be near him any longer. The hairs on the back of her neck stood on end. She needed to get away from him. Charlotte stood and picked up her basket.

The man turned and smiled, but there was a malicious evil to his gaze. "So quick to leave, just when we were getting to know one another."

"I don't want to get to know you. I need to return to my aunt."

He stood, tall, overbearing, making her want to cower in fear, but she wouldn't give him the satisfaction. "Ah, your Aunt Martha, I believe."

Charlotte jerked her head sharply. "How do you know my aunt?"

"I know plenty about you—your eccentric aunt who is right now resting at the Pacific Hotel, how you have been cavorting with two men, and…" He paused dramatically as though he were dragging out the crescendo to a song. "Your wastrel of a father that you've been unsuccessfully trying to find. If you do find the man, you might want to warn him that if he double-crosses me one more time, he'll wish he never met me."

Charlotte's heart raced. "My father isn't what you say." There might be some truth to the man's words, but she wasn't about to admit it.

He glared at Charlotte, sending an unnerving and sinister chill up her spine. "Oh, he is and always has been." He lifted the brim of his top hat. "It seems you might not know him as well as you might think. It could be in everyone's best interest if you were to leave Pocatello on the next train. Otherwise, you might get caught in the crosshairs of something you'd regret."

Charlotte straightened her back, tightening her fingers on the arm of her basket. Was this the man who had been working with her father? "Are you Mr. Smith?"

His lips pursed. "It matters little as to who I am. Just heed my words."

"Charlotte?"

She turned and trembled with relief. Jacob and Stanley were in the distance. While she didn't think the stranger would harm her in public, there was no doubt he was dangerous. She could feel it.

Charlotte waved to Stanley and Jacob and then turned to tell the man to leave her alone, but he was gone. She scanned the park and didn't see hide nor hair of the man. He had vanished into thin air.

Chapter 18

May 17, 1901

Running into Charlotte in the park had been both sweet and painful, but Stanley was glad he had. The last time they had seen one another had been uncomfortable. He hadn't known what to say and had been shocked when she told him her grandfather wanted her to marry another man.

That morning, Stanley had attended to a few errands, and on his way back to the hotel, he'd run into Jacob, who'd been happy to tell Stanley about his conversation with Charlotte. Stanley had had to fight back a surge of jealousy knowing that Jacob had spoken to her. Jacob had then convinced Stanley to come with him to find her, and they'd soon spotted her in a nearby park. Seeing her sitting on the bench had sent a tug of longing so hard through Stanley's gut, he'd had to breathe slowly until the feelings eased.

She had been talking to a man whose top hat had obscured his face, but it was of no mind to him. Many people walked in the park. Stanley only had eyes for Charlotte, and that was concerning, especially since they would part in just a few days. He'd been trying to tamp down his desire for her, but it wasn't working.

Stanley had hoped to find another clue about her father, but nothing had developed. He should leave well enough alone, but he still wanted to make sure she hankered no ill will toward him.

He called out to Charlotte. She turned, a radiant smile lifting her pink cheeks. Charlotte glanced behind her before walking toward them, her gait hurried as though something had been chasing her.

"Stanley, I didn't expect to see you this afternoon." She glanced at Jacob and grazed her fingers against her lips. "Jacob, if I didn't know any better, I'd think you were following me." She giggled, softening her words.

"Why, little lady, I just can't help but be in your presence. It just warms my heart." He slapped his chest.

She blushed, and with the hand not holding her basket, she patted Jacob's arm. His cheeks reddened. Stanley watched in awe as Charlotte turned Jacob into a lovesick calf. He couldn't blame the man. Charlotte was a delightful young woman, and when she looked at you, it was right special.

"I'm going to miss you, Jacob. You always make me smile." Charlotte beamed with amusement.

Stanley hated that he'd never see her again. *Why didn't she talk to me that way?*

"Pocatello ain't gonna be the same without you. If you ever come back, be sure to look me up," Jacob said.

"Are you planning on settling here, Jacob?" Stanley asked. Jacob had always been a wanderer, so to think he might settle was unexpected.

Jacob shrugged. "Don't know if it'll be here or somewhere's close by, but I'm getting up in age. My bones could use a good rest."

Stanley placed his hand on Jacob's shoulder and squeezed with affection. "Well, don't forget you're always welcome near us. There's plenty of open land in Montana."

Jacob grinned. "I might just have to consider that. Although, the weather there can get mighty brisk, and that wind"—he shivered—"whips through you, chilling even the most padded places."

"It's not much better here, either," Stanley said. "But you're right. The open spaces near us do cause strong winds that'll near split you in half if you ain't prepared for it."

"Ain't that the honest truth," Jacob said, laughing. "Your pa always tried to convince me to come up there. I remember one February when I'd taken him up on his offer. Your family had just moved to the ranch the summer before and were living in that small cabin before he built the main house."

Stanley remembered all of them crammed into that cabin. It'd had two bedrooms and a loft. With six children and their ma and pa, they'd been living on top of one another like barrels of salted beef. The boys had the loft, and his sisters were in the room next to their ma and pa. While tight and, at times, loud and uncomfortable, there'd been a lot of love in that tiny house. His ma and pa couldn't keep their hands off one another, and the love between them had been nothing short of amazing. They'd get into some serious rows, but they'd always resolved it before they went to bed.

He remembered plenty of nights looking over the side of the loft. He'd see his pa holding his ma from behind, swaying in front of the fire, murmuring in her ear. He never could hear what his pa said, but the smile on his ma's face had told him plenty.

Realizing he'd missed what Jacob had said, he murmured an apology. "I appear to be woolgathering. I couldn't help but remember how we lived in that cabin, all on top of one another but with lots of love."

"Yes, that's about right. Your pa loved your ma something fierce. It's a shame they were taken from us far too soon."

Stanley's heart hurt knowing it was his fault his pa was gone. He might not have been able to stop his ma's demise, as she had died from that awful sickness, but knowing he had brought Connie into their life and—

"You can stop right there. I can see where your mind is a-goin'. You had nothing to do with your pa's death." Jacob's voice was harsh, father-like, and it stopped Stanley from uttering a nasty rebuke, especially since they were in the company of a lady.

"We shouldn't be arguing in front of

Charlotte," Stanley said, "but we'll both have to agree to disagree. We know my involvement. He'd still be alive if I hadn't married her."

"Maybe, maybe not, but doesn't matter no more. Your pa wouldn't want you carrying this burden. He'd want you to get on with your life, find a pretty lady..." He looked at Charlotte. "Like this lady here, wooing her and making her your own."

Charlotte's face turned bright red. She brought her hand to her mouth to likely cover her disgust. There was no way she'd be interested in a man who'd caused his pa's death. Besides, his own face was likely as red as a hot poker from a smithy's fire.

"Ah, I didn't mean to make everyone uncomfortable," Jacob said, although Stanley knew without a doubt that Jacob didn't feel a bit remorseful. He'd been trying to push Stanley toward Charlotte since the moment he met her. While Stanley could appreciate how charming she was, she had her own demons. There'd be no future between them. Too many obstacles stood in their way.

"It's all right, Jacob," Stanley said. "I know you have good intentions. Let's just not make Charlotte uncomfortable."

"Oh, no," she said, "I'm not. Please don't think that. I can see that you care for Stanley very much, Jacob."

"He's like a son to me," Jacob said. The conversation had turned serious. They had a close relationship, but Stanley hadn't realized the depth of Jacob's feelings.

"Jacob, I don't know what to say—"

"There's nothing to say. Now that we've gotten serious and maudlin, we should let Charlotte get on with her day."

Stanley nodded. "I'm sorry if we've kept you from—"

"Oh, no." She touched his arm, sending a surge through her fingers straight to his gut. He could see why Jacob had blushed like a schoolboy. She had touched him before, but in that moment, with her eyes appearing wet, something more snapped between them. "It's nice to see you both. I'll miss you, but I understand why you're heading back to Helena."

"What about your father?"

She avoided his gaze and instead stared off into the distance as though looking at him might be too painful. "I'm done." She took a breath before continuing. "As I told you yesterday, I've spent far too long trying to find him without success. He has to know I'm here. I know he saw me when that fight broke out in the hotel. The fact that he continues to avoid my inquiries tells me he doesn't want to see me. I just had to come to the realization that I can't force what doesn't want to be found. I can go home now with a clear conscience and the knowledge that I tried my best. He's the one who's losing out on knowing his daughter."

"I'm truly sorry we weren't able to find him for you, though," Stanley said.

"You have nothing to be sorry for. I appreciate everything you and Jacob have done for me. I do fear my aunt derailed you from finding what you were here to find."

Stanley shrugged. He had been on a path of destruction, and she had likely saved him from falling into further despair. "Don't feel that way. If I hadn't wanted to help, I wouldn't have. Besides, it gave me the honor of getting to know you both."

"Oh, yes. Aunt Martha does think highly of you. Perhaps if you have a free night before you leave, you'll grace us with one more dinner."

"I'd like that very much, Charlotte."

Her blonde hair shimmered in the glaring sunlight. "Good. Send a note when you're free." She turned and looked at Jacob. "Please join us as well, Jacob. Aunt Martha would hate to leave without saying her goodbyes."

"Awe, shucks, little lady. I'd be honored."

She pushed back a lock of hair. "Gentleman, I must be going. I've been gone far longer than I expected. I'm sure my aunt is fretting."

"We don't want that," Stanley said. "Until later?"

"Yes," she said, waving as she left the two of them. Just as she was about to go out of sight, she turned, and their gazes locked.

He was going to miss Charlotte something fierce.

Chapter 19

May 17, 1901

Charlotte berated herself for keeping quiet about her travel intentions while she had talked with Stanley and Jacob. Plenty of opportunities had presented themselves, but she hadn't said a word. Jacob had looked at her a few times, raising his eyebrow as if asking if she was going to tell Stanley that she and her aunt were headed to Helena, but she never did.

It was embarrassing to know her aunt was trying so hard to push the two of them together that she struggled with how to tell him. It'd be far easier to keep the information to herself and pray they'd never run into one another. Stanley had too much on his mind and didn't need to know her aunt was playing matchmaker.

Charlotte's mind was elsewhere as she walked back to the hotel, but as she got closer to the railroad tracks, she raised her head and stopped in shock. It was as though a herd of buffalo had just been spooked on the wide-open plains and rushed past her, nearly ending her life. Her father stood mere feet away with his wide-brimmed hat in his hands, looking the same as she remembered outside of the gray streaks in his hair. He didn't run and appeared contrite. She wasn't sure what to think. She could be dreaming, but he was too real.

He shuffled his feet and ran a shaky hand through his hair before resting it behind his neck. He said something, but she couldn't hear it due to the loud clanging in her ears.

He moved toward her until he was standing within a hairbreadth of her.

"Father?" While she knew in her heart it was him, she needed confirmation.

He nodded, sadness filling his eyes.

She was unable to speak and didn't know what to ask him. She'd been looking for so long, and for him to suddenly appear made her uncomfortable and unsure of herself.

"Charlotte, I have much to explain. Could you… Would you consider talking with me?"

Joy should have filled her heart, but instead, trepidation filled her soul. He'd avoided her for so long she feared the conversation would be unpleasant. She didn't want it to be, but considering how evasive he'd been and the earlier threat from the man in the park made her hesitate. Whatever her father was involved in was far more sinister than she realized. It had to be more than just finding the missing gold treasure.

When she didn't turn and leave, he led her to a quaint bakery shop with small café tables nestled in front of the large squeaky clean windows. Guiding her toward the far end, he held out a chair for her to sit. He acted as a gentleman should, but she was wary of his intentions.

"Would you care for something to drink? Coffee, lemonade?" He twisted the brim of his hat, the only sign of his trepidation of their impending conversation.

"Lem…" She swallowed and tried again. "Lemonade, thank you."

He scooted around the tables and went inside the bakery, the door closing softly behind him. Would he return, or was it just a way to get her hopes up before he disappeared again? She placed her basket on the ground and then scooted her chair closer to the table, trying to get under the bakery's awning and the shade it provided. It was warm, and there was no wind to help cool the hot sweat that was building behind her ears and down her back.

Ten minutes later, just when she thought her father had disappeared once again, he walked out of the bakery holding a tray. It held two glasses of lemonade and bite-sized cakes and pastries that, on a different day, would've caused her mouth to water with anticipation. Now, they just made her belly churn in disgust.

He looked at her closely before setting the tray on the table. "I wasn't sure if you were hungry, but I asked for a selection of pastries if you'd care for a bite to eat."

Instead of responding, she reached for the glass of lemonade to wet her lips and soothe her dry throat. Her belly clenched with unease as she swallowed the overtly sweet liquid.

After the silence stretched between them for a long moment, her father coughed. "I suppose you're wondering why I finally appeared."

"Yes, I am. I've..." She swallowed, trying to gain her composure. "I've been looking for you for months."

"I know, and I'm sorry for that."

Fury ripped through her, and the words fell out of her mouth like a gushing waterfall after a long drought. "Are you sorry? You've been gone for over ten years. You had to have known I was here looking for you. I saw you in the saloon, and I know you saw me in the hotel dining room. Why have you been avoiding me?"

He grabbed a pastry and ripped it in half, placing one piece in his mouth and chewing it slowly. It appeared he was trying to come up with an answer that she would believe. She narrowed her eyes. Was he trying to hide something from her?

When he finally swallowed, he said, "I haven't been avoiding you on purpose, but I didn't want you to get caught up in my latest mess."

"And what mess was that?" She knew the answer but wanted to hear him say it.

"That doesn't matter."

"Of course it matters. Is it the gold?"

He dropped the other half of the pastry onto the table. "How do you know about the gold?"

"You couldn't believe I wouldn't find out? I'm not that young girl you left behind." She slammed her fist onto the small table, and the plates clattered against the wooden surface before slowly settling back into place.

He looked ashamed at her words, and he well should be.

His voice was low. "I know you aren't, although in my heart, you always will be. I just wanted what was best for you."

"I was heartbroken when Mother died and then"—she pointed at him—"instead of being a father, you left me with my grandfather." She stared at the man she'd been desperate to find, but she wondered if the ache in her heart was worth it.

"I didn't leave you with your grandfather," he snapped, pounding his fist on the table and startling the other guests. Realizing he had spoken too loudly, he shuddered and leaned forward. "He took you from me and threatened to throw me in jail. He said if I came near you again, he'd make sure I rotted in there."

"That is preposterous. Grandfather would never do that."

"Wouldn't he?" He shook his head. "I'm sorry. I don't want to argue about him. We will never agree about him. I can't change the past, but I'd like to explain if you're willing."

She wondered if there was a measure of truth in his words. Her grandfather had no love for her father and had done everything he could to convince her not to go on this trip. He hadn't wanted her to have anything to do with her father and had done everything in his power to keep it that way.

"Why would Grandfather not want me to find you?"

"I don't know," he said, anger simmering just below the surface. "That's not true. I do know. He never wanted me to marry your mother."

"That isn't anything I didn't already know. When I told him I wanted to find you, he was none too pleased. He said that the two of you eloped and took the choice out of his hands."

He gripped his cup of coffee and looked down, avoiding her gaze. "I suppose we did, but I loved your mother and would have done anything for her. But he was furious when I married her and even more so when she passed."

"That doesn't sound like Grandfather." Although, she wasn't being completely fair. Her grandfather was stubborn and willful. She'd seen it firsthand with his determination to see her married to the man of his choosing.

"It is like him. You were a child when all of this happened. I was heartbroken when she passed, not in my right mind. He had money, power, and I had nothing but a broken heart and a little girl who needed me. Your grandfather saw a way to ruin me even further and took you away. There was nothing I could do."

"You could have fought for me, stayed and—"

"And done what? I had no money, nothing. He blamed me for her illness and said that if I didn't leave you behind, he'd call in my debts and have me thrown into jail."

"But—"

"But nothing, Charlotte," he muttered. "I

know you don't understand and likely never will. I realize I could have tried to fight him, but I had just lost the one person who thought I could do anything. She was gone, just like that." He snapped his fingers. Shuddering, he took a small sip of his coffee before resting it back on the table. He ran his thumb over the edge and then finally raised his eyes to look at her. "I'm sorry, more than you'll ever know."

Charlotte trembled. What her father described didn't sound like the man who had raised her after her father and mother were both gone, but at the same time, she also understood how powerful her grandfather was. If she were perfectly honest with herself, she'd admit that it was within her grandfather's power to do exactly as her father said.

Her father smiled, his softening gaze focused on something over her shoulder as though he were remembering a beautiful memory from the past.

When he was quiet for a few moments, she wondered if she had upset him. "Father?"

"What? Oh, sorry." He rubbed a hand across his brow and dropped his shoulders. "I was remembering your mother." The smile on his face was reminiscent of memories that were once sweet and precious. "She was something special. I'm sorry you didn't get more time with her."

Tears filled her eyes, but she blinked them away. "I wish, well, I wish things had turned out differently."

"I do, too, Charlotte. I truly do."

"Why are you here now?"

He leaned back in his chair and pulled the brim of his hat down over his forehead. He flitted his eyes back and forth. It was as though he feared for his life, and considering the man who had stopped her just that morning, there was likely a threat of epic proportions.

"I didn't want you to be involved with... with what I've been searching for."

"The gold?" She tilted her head, hoping he would be honest with her.

He shook his head. "No—"

"Don't, Father. I know all about it. How the stagecoach was robbed in 1865. How the authorities believed a passenger was involved. How the gold disappeared. How the authorities found and killed the perpetrators, but the gold had disappeared. I've even been to the stagecoach station where you were digging for it."

He appeared surprised, as though he hadn't believed she'd truly learned of his schemes while in Pocatello.

"Tell me," she said. "Have you found the gold?"

His sad eyes settled on her as unspoken words hung between them. All their pain couldn't be settled in one conversation, but she hoped it was the beginning of something. They may never be the father and daughter they should have been, but perhaps they could at least start anew.

"No," he said. "I've been on a useless chase for something that was never there."

"What makes you think that?"

"It doesn't matter now. Just know that I'm

done looking, although my former partner believes otherwise." He avoided looking at her, instead focusing on the table.

"You mean Mr. Smith?" He had to have been the man who had threatened her earlier that day. It all made much more sense. The pieces clicked into place.

"You know of him?" His shaky voice made it clear he hadn't expected her to know even that much.

"He sent over a bottle of wine one night while I was dining with Stanley Seymour and Jacob Jones." She hesitated to tell him of the man's threat just that morning. Something had obviously changed between the two of them if she were visited by each one in the space of a few hours.

He picked up another pastry and popped it into his mouth, chewing slowly for a long minute. "The two men you employed to help find me?"

"You know about them?"

"Yes," he said.

Her father had been keeping an eye on her

even if he hadn't wanted to be found. "Jacob spoke with Mr. Smith, who told him the two of you were working to find it and that he was the one who bailed you out of jail. Somehow Jacob discovered you were going to be looking near Robbers Roost and that you had gotten a hold of a map that told the location of the stolen gold."

Her father sighed. "Well, you know much more than I expected, but not all of it's correct."

She took a sip of her lemonade, the heat outside growing. "What part is inaccurate?"

"It doesn't matter, not anymore. There's no gold, and I'm leaving Pocatello tomorrow." He tugged on his suspenders.

"No! You can't leave me again. Not after everything I've been through to find you," she cried. She hated that she sounded like a child. She'd put everything on the line to find him. Now that he was right there in front of her, she didn't want to lose him again.

He removed his hat and wiped away the sweat that had gathered on his forehead before slapping it back on and making sure it rode low on his forehead. He clearly didn't want anyone to recognize him.

A nervous chill tingled the back of her neck. "Are you hiding from someone?" Was he hiding from Mr. Smith?

"Why would you think that?" He avoided her gaze.

She scoffed. "Why wouldn't I think that? You've been hiding from me for weeks, and now you're leaving tomorrow. What I can't understand is why you finally showed yourself to me?"

"I needed to tell you to be aware, to stay away from Mr. Smith. He's not a good man. I worry he'll come after you."

"Why would he come after me? I have nothing to do with this. He has to know we haven't seen one another in years."

"Yes, he knows that, but he also knows..." Her father reached into his jacket pocket and pulled out a picture, his eyes softening at the image before he handed it to her. "He knows how much you mean to me. He threatened to hurt you if I didn't find the gold."

Dread slithered around her like a venomous snake preparing to strike its prey. The man who had stopped her in the park had to be Mr. Smith. He had told her to leave Pocatello, but did he know her father was leaving as well? So many unanswered questions, but she didn't believe her father would be honest with her if she asked.

The picture was one she had never seen before. She must've been about five when it was taken. She was sitting on the floor, the ruffles on the coverlet of the bed being replaced when she was older, but she remembered many days lying in that bed thinking she was a princess. Charlotte handed it back to him. He stroked the front of it, tears filling his eyes before he blinked and returned the photo to his pocket.

"He saw me with the photo one night when I... Well, when I was too drunk to know what I was saying, and I..." He shifted in his seat while playing with a pastry, tearing it to pieces but not putting anything in his mouth. "I told him how much you mean to me. How I regret not defying your grandfather and taking you with me when I left St. Louis." The words tumbled out of him in a rush.

She hadn't expected him to say that, and her heart broke. It was so different from what her grandfather had told her, what she had always believed. While she was desperate to believe him, there had to be more to it, but she didn't think she'd ever be told the truth. Neither her father nor her grandfather was being completely honest with her, and she had to accept that.

"So why are you leaving Pocatello if you haven't found the gold yet?"

"I told ya. There is no gold. It's been a waste of time."

She tilted her head, trying to understand. "Then why would Mr. Smith be after me?"

He sighed. "He doesn't believe me. He thinks I'm hiding the gold and keeping it from him. That's why I'm leaving tomorrow. If I leave, he'll follow me and leave you alone."

"Where are you going?"

"That's not important. I just want you to be

careful. Please know I did everythin' out of love for you."

Why had things gone so wrong between them? "I want to believe you, I really do, but—"

"I understand. I don't expect you to forgive me, but I want you to know that I love you." He raised his hand and reached toward her but then yanked it away. "I always have. Your mother was my world. While I made tons of mistakes, of which I'm sure your grandfather"—his voice turned to one filled with disgust—"had no trouble telling you."

"He—"

"It's all right, Charlotte. I know you love him, and he's always treated you well. He took care of you when I couldn't. I know he lavished you with gifts and everything you could've ever wanted."

"How would you know that? You left me over ten years ago."

"I…" He looked away from her.

"Yes?"

"A maid in your grandfather's house took pity

on me. She sent me letters with updates on how you were doing over the years."

"I didn't know that." Her anger was receding. Perhaps he had cared.

"We agreed you'd never know. She didn't want to lose her position, and I wanted to know you were being taken care of. It was easier that way."

"Easier for who?" She was so frustrated. Too much wasted time.

"Easier for you. You were devastated the morning I left, and I—"

"Yes, I was." She gripped the edge of the table. "I had just lost my mother. You told me you were leaving and that I'd never see you again. I was only fourteen years old. I didn't want to lose my father, too."

"I had no choice." He held up a hand to stop her protests. "While I know you don't believe that, that is what I felt. Did I regret my choice? I absolutely do, but I can't change it."

"Then why can't you tell me where you're

going? I can follow, and we can get to know one another again."

"Charlotte." He reached across the table and took her hand in his. She tried to pull away, but he didn't let go. "I'm not good for you. I wasn't then, and I won't be now. You're much better without me."

She wrenched her hand away. "You don't know what's good for me."

"In this, I do." He slid his chair back and stood. "I'm sorrier than you'll ever know. Perhaps coming to you was a mistake, but I had to warn you. Please be mindful of your surroundings. If Mr. Smith approaches you, be wary and be on guard. He's after me. I don't want him to hurt you."

She shoved her chair from the table and picked up her basket, her movements stilted and abrupt. "I'll be mindful."

"Thank you," he said. "I've got to go now. Take care of yourself, my darling girl."

She nodded, tears filling her eyes at everything that hadn't been said. "I... I appreciate you warning me. Can you send word when you're safe?"

He stared at her hard, as though memorizing her features, then reluctantly nodded.

Before she could stop him, he walked briskly away and disappeared. If she hadn't just sat there with the man she'd been desperate to find for months, she might've thought she had dreamed the whole encounter.

Chapter 20

May 19, 1901

Charlotte woke from another sleepless night. They were supposed to leave for Helena in two days, and she was dreading the trip. Her aunt was excited and brimming with joy over the next adventure. It likely had more to do with the possibility that they would run into Stanley and had nothing to do with seeing the wide-open spaces of Montana like she claimed.

Charlotte told her aunt about finding her father. While her aunt was satisfied that Charlotte had talked with him, she was displeased that he'd left his daughter again. Charlotte did have to accept that her grandfather wouldn't want Marcus to return to St. Louis, and it didn't sound as though Marcus was too keen to see her grandfather.

There was one bright spot in all the turmoil. Her father had agreed to send word when he was safe. That was probably the best she could hope for.

She forced herself out of bed. Lying around all day wouldn't finish the packing or fix the problems with her grandfather. Stanley and Jacob were meeting them for an early dinner, so she had to get moving.

Hours later, Charlotte sat on the sofa, exhausted. Her aunt had left to do some shopping, leaving Charlotte to finish the packing. It made things easier if Charlotte did it without her aunt's input. She tended to complain if Charlotte didn't put things in the exact place she thought they needed to be. She would hover, tapping her cane, pointing her finger, and muttering under her breath with every wrong move Charlotte made.

As Charlotte rested, she scanned the numerous trunks and satchels scattered in front of her. She was amazed at how much they had purchased over their trip. They would need another trunk, and Charlotte would have to check with the dry goods store to see if they had one in stock. There was no way her aunt was going to leave any of her new purchases behind. Charlotte had to find a solution.

She poured herself a cup of coffee and then immediately spat it out. It was cold and unpalatable, tasting like sludge. She rubbed her temples to ease the ache brewing between her eyebrows, but it didn't help.

She was tired and irritated with her aunt for forcing the trip to Helena. While she wasn't looking forward to discussing her future with her grandfather, it would be nice to be home. There was nothing for her in Montana, no matter how much she wished Stanley would look at her differently.

Charlotte loved her grandfather and missed him, even if he was high-handed in his opinions concerning her future. It had been a long few months, and while she'd seen beautiful parts of the country and experienced things she never would've without the trip, it was time to end her quest, especially after she talked with her father. It was clear he would never come home. She'd been a fool to think otherwise.

Her only regret was that she hadn't told Stanley how much she enjoyed being in his company. Tonight was the last time she would see him. He made her laugh and dream of things she never thought possible. She still didn't know what she wanted to do with her life, but she wouldn't discover what that was by continuing to avoid her grandfather.

She had more important things to do than daydream about something that wasn't in the cards for her or for Stanley. Slipping off her soiled blouse and skirt, she quickly washed. She picked up her reticule and room key and walked down to the lobby.

When she reached the front desk, the hotel clerk smiled. "Good afternoon, Miss McVicker. What can I do for you today?"

Handing him the key, she said, "Would you make sure my aunt gets this if she returns before I do?"

He whisked it away. "Absolutely. It'll be my pleasure. Is there anything else I can help you with?"

"Yes." She pressed the side of her eye, her headache not easing. "We're leaving on the Tuesday train for Helena, Montana, and will need our trunks picked up and delivered."

"Yes, miss. I have a note from your aunt to pick them up first thing Tuesday morning. We'll ensure they're safely on the train and deliver your claim tickets an hour before the train is scheduled to leave."

"Thank you."

"You're certainly welcome. Have a wonderful afternoon."

Waving goodbye, she walked out the open doors. A sizable crowd waited for several trains to rumble down the tracks. The crowd grew with each passing second. She received an occasional elbow or two in her side, but apologies were murmured, and no harm was done. To prevent a smashed foot or a black eye, she moved to the far end of the tracks to wait.

Ominous rain clouds had rolled in and blocked the sun causing dark shadows to form. A chilly breeze whipped through the buildings. Her skirt rippled in the wind, and she tugged her shawl around her shoulders. She sensed movement behind her and turned to look when a burly arm wrapped around her waist and yanked her close.

A hand slapped over her mouth, and the man whispered menacingly in her ear. "If you scream, your aunt will die. Cooperate and she'll live to see another day." He dug his fingers into the soft skin around her mouth. She tried to get away, but it was of no use. "If you don't stop now, I'll send my friend to the hotel, lure your Aunt Martha somewhere, and kill her. Do you want that?" he hissed.

Chills ran along her spine. This wasn't a random event. She had no choice but to cooperate.

"I'm going to remove my hand now. We're going to walk calmly across the tracks. You do what you're told, and she'll live. Understand me?" He paused. "Nod your head if you do."

She didn't move, and he tightened his hand across her lips, his intentions quite clear. Reluctantly, she nodded, and he eased his rough hand from her lips. It was as though he anticipated her to scream. When she didn't, he relaxed his hold and then nudged her forward once the last train rumbled past. The man held her close, digging his fingers into her belly and holding her arm with his other hand. His grip was solid and sure. He wasn't about to let her escape.

She tried to catch someone's eye, but no one paid them any mind. People had places to go, minding their own business and not worrying about a random woman being led through the streets by a man. They likely appeared to be a couple who'd had a spat and were headed home to air their grievances in private.

The man muttered obscenities under his breath when she stumbled, but he never once loosened his grip. Instead, he held her tighter. "Keep walking. I ain't got much time."

"Where are you taking me?"

"Don't you worry about that none. You listen, do as you're told, and things won't go so bad for you. If you don't, well, your aunt will find an evil end, and you'll wish you'd listened to me to begin with." His voice was filled with hostility. He was not to be trifled with.

Things wouldn't end well, no matter how much she cooperated, but if she did as he said, hopefully, the man would keep his word. She could never live with herself if harm were to come to the most precious person in her life.

Twenty minutes later, the man pushed her into an old dilapidated house on the far end of town. The place looked as though the former occupants had left in a hurry. A thick layer of dirt and dust coated every surface. Tables, chairs, and an old blue velvet sofa with a worn afghan across the back were all that remained. Dirty metal dishes lined the kitchen counter, raggedy drapes dangled limply across the windows, and a kerosene lantern hung on a hook on the wall. The lantern provided the only light in the room, and dark shadows were present.

He pushed her toward a second room, but before she could get a good look at him or utter more than a yelp of pain after he pinched her arm, he pulled a black hood from his pocket and yanked it over her head. He then pushed her forward. Her feet tripped over a broken floorboard, but he pulled on her arm to keep her from falling, cursing at her clumsiness. He then shoved her into a chair, keeping his hand on her shoulder to hold her in place. The fear of what might happen next overrode her good sense, and she screamed.

The man squeezed her shoulder. "I told you if you scream or don't do as you're told, I'll kill your aunt. Don't make me do it now when you did so well on the way here." His words penetrated

Charlotte's distress and her need to escape. She quieted, gulping hard.

He pulled her arms behind her back and tied each one to the spindles near her armpits, then he secured her legs. She was confined to a wooden chair with no way to break free.

"Now don't you be going anywhere," he hissed. A moment later, the door slammed shut, and she was left alone, tied to a chair with a black hood over her head.

She tried to sit quietly, but the black hood was tight and suffocating. She pulled at the ropes, the chair rocking against the floor. The door slammed open. The man grabbed the back of Charlotte's head and yanked. He whispered harshly in her ear, "I thought I made myself clear. Right now, I won't touch you or take your innocence, but if you continue to make noise, I won't stop myself from taking what every woman wants to protect, *if* you know what I mean." He ran his finger along the exposed skin above the neckline of Charlotte's blouse and flicked open the top few buttons.

"Please stop," Charlotte cried. "I'll cooperate, I promise." Tears soaked the hood, making it even more difficult for her to breathe, but the alternative was far worse.

"Now, now. That wasn't so hard, was it?" The man released his hold on her. "Enough of you fighting the ropes. Sit there quietly, and nothing more'll happen. Your friend here learned real quick to do as she was told. I suggest you follow her example."

"Friend?" Charlotte asked. Who else had he taken?

"Yes, your dear, dear friend Bertha. The two of you will do just nicely for what we've got planned."

"I don't understand," Charlotte said, shaking her head and pulling once again at the ropes binding her to the chair.

"You will soon enough, don't you worry. Now, stop trying to get away or what happens next will be far worse than you could've ever imagined. Trust me, when I say you're gonna want to get in my good graces. Otherwise, I'll throw you to the wolves."

* * *

Stanley walked through the lobby of the hotel, eagerly anticipating the early dinner with Martha and Charlotte. Martha had sent him a note asking him to meet them at four, and it was nearly that. It would be the last time he'd be able to spend any real time with them. His train was leaving the day after tomorrow. If he were honest with himself, he'd acknowledge he was going to miss Charlotte, but he wasn't ready to do that, and it was likely too late to do so. Perhaps after he resolved his situation at home, he'd make a trip to St. Louis.

He chastised himself. That was a ridiculous notion. St. Louis was hundreds of miles from Helena, and he'd have no reason to go there. He'd avoided his responsibilities for far too long, and Ben had been more than patient. Staying away from family hadn't served him well. He hadn't contributed to the family's coffers, and while he had taken little, he had been living without the weight of responsibility.

He had wanted his pa's ranch and had loved owning it for a brief time, but once he lost it and realized what his wife had done, his self-worth had been decimated. Turning to the bottle, drowning his sorrows, and claiming he'd been searching for her had just been an excuse. An excuse that no longer held. It was time to face his family and the pain he'd caused them.

Stanley wished things could have been different with the woman who had quite literally fallen into his lap. He'd acted like he had been doing them a favor to search for Charlotte's father, but in reality, Charlotte and Martha had done him a favor. They had given him a purpose, a reason to do something more than ruminate on what had gone wrong in his life.

He considered the past few months and hadn't realized how much Charlotte had crept ever so slowly into his heart. While their conversations had been engaging and fun, there shouldn't have been enough there to develop into a serious relationship, so why was he sad they would have to part?

"Mr. Seymour. Mr. Seymour," a quivering voice called from across the lobby. Martha was shuffling toward him. Her hair was in disarray, and her lips were pursed into a frown. She appeared upset.

He hastened to her side. "Martha, what's wrong?"

She shook her head, her breath heavy.

He took her arm and led her to a plush sofa in the lobby. "Are you all right? Shall I send for a glass of water?"

"No, water. I'm fine."

"Where's Charlotte?" he asked once she was settled and had a moment to catch her breath.

She dropped her cane and took his hands, gripping them tightly with her gnarled fingers. "I don't know. I returned from my brunch expecting to see her, but she wasn't there. I thought perhaps she had gone to procure another trunk, as she'd been packing. But it's been hours, and there's been no sign of her."

Her anxiety-laden voice gave him cause for concern. He tried to smile reassuringly, but his neck tingled with foreboding. Charlotte wouldn't leave her aunt with no idea of where she'd gone. Something was wrong. He just didn't know why or what it could be.

"I called down to the front desk. The nice man told me she'd left hours ago, but he hadn't seen her return. Where is she, Mr. Seymour? This is not like her. Something must've happened."

"I'm sure she's fine," he said.

"Mr. Seymour," she said, anger in her voice. "Don't placate me. I'm not a doddering old fool, although I may walk like one. I still have all my faculties and can remember every detail of my life." She pulled her hand away and poked a finger into his chest. "Something *is* wrong. She wouldn't have left without leaving word. She was so looking forward to having dinner with you tonight, and she's not here."

"Yes, ma'am. I understand, and I know you're

not a doddering old fool." He smiled to soften his words.

She relaxed, her shoulders dropping since she had his attention and he was taking her words to heart. "You've got to find her. She means everything to me."

"I understand, Martha, but first things first. Charlotte would want me to make sure you were all right."

She raised a hand to her forehead, brushing back wisps of gray hair that had fallen from her messy coiffure. "I'm fine," she said, but her hand shook. She noticed and immediately dropped it to her lap, trying to hide it from him, but he was too observant.

"Perhaps, but have you had anything to drink or eat?" He didn't need her fainting. The last thing Charlotte would want was for her aunt to suffer.

"I had brunch, but I'll admit, I've had nothing since."

"Let's get you up to your room, where you'll be safe. I'll order food for you." He reached for her hands, but she pushed him away.

"No," she cried. "You need to find Charlotte. I'll be fine."

"I know you will." He patted her knee, trying to comfort her. "But I won't be able to search for Charlotte unless I know you're all right as well."

She shivered. "If you insist."

"I do." He picked up her fallen cane and took her hand, helping her to her feet.

Once in her room, he picked up the candlestick phone and called down to the front desk to order some food and a large pot of coffee. They were going to need it.

He knew deep inside his soul that Charlotte hadn't just forgotten the time. She'd either been hurt, someone had delayed her, or something worse. He just didn't know where the threat was coming from, but either way, he would find her.

Chapter 21

May 19, 1901

Charlotte had no idea what the man had planned, but after his threats, time was not on her side, and she had to find a way to escape.

She sat still in the chair, the hard wooden spokes digging into her back. The dark hood was still over her head, but at least the man had let her be. After what seemed like hours but was nowhere near as long, she strained to hear if her captor was still nearby. She couldn't hear him and hadn't for quite some time.

Deciding to take a chance, she bent her head

and upper chest and tried to shake off the hood. After a few minutes and with luck on her side, it fell and dropped into her lap. Her eyes smarted with the light coming in through cracks in the walls, but they adjusted after blinking a few times. Raising her head, she saw what appeared to be her friend Bertha, tied up on the other side of the room with a black hood over her head, just like Charlotte.

"Bertha," she whispered.

Bertha didn't stir.

Charlotte said her name again, that time a tad louder.

Bertha pulled at the ropes, grunted, and then tilted her head. "Charlotte, are we alone?"

"Yes. Are you all right?"

"I'm spitting mad," Bertha snapped.

Charlotte couldn't contain the grin. While it wasn't a laughing matter, it was good to see and hear that Bertha hadn't been hurt. "Can you shake off the hood covering your head?"

"I don't rightly know."

"Bend forward, hang your head, and try shaking it off. That's what I did."

Bertha groaned but did as Charlotte suggested. A few moments later, the hood fell into her lap and showed the pure rage on her face.

"I'm so sorry," Charlotte whispered. Bertha likely hated her, for Charlotte had to be the reason why Bertha was tied to the chair.

"Don't apologize," Bertha hissed. "This isn't your fault. That man lied and told me you needed my help. I mistakenly followed him to this place. I know better."

"Do you know who he is?"

"No." Bertha cocked her head. "I thought you knew."

"I don't. A man grabbed me and put the hood over my face. I never saw him."

"Then what's going on?" Twisting to look behind her, Bertha moved this way and that as she fought the ropes holding her in place.

"I wish I knew," Charlotte said.

"Do you have any enemies?" Bertha asked,

grunting as she pulled at her bindings. Her movements caused the chair to rock back and forth.

"I don't know anyone in Pocatello other than you, Stanley, and his friend Jacob." Although, it could be related to her father, but she didn't want to believe he was involved. It was likely Mr. Smith, but that also seemed unreasonable since he had just told her to leave Pocatello, and she had been planning on doing so. Besides, it hadn't sounded like him, so it had to be something else.

Bertha stopped fighting the ropes around her and regarded Charlotte thoughtfully. "Well, you must know someone who's out to sell us to the highest bidder."

"I don't know anyone like that." She was lying to her new friend, and it made her skin crawl.

Bertha shook her head. "I overheard two men talking before you got here. One of them said they have men willing to pay top dollar for innocent girls."

Charlotte's belly pitched and rolled with revulsion. "You don't mean—"

"Yes." She scowled. "We've got to get out of here."

"He said if we tried to escape, he would kill my aunt."

"I don't mean to be insensitive to you or your aunt, Charlotte, but I'm not going to sit and wait. I stayed quiet while they were here, as they threatened my own family, but it doesn't sound like they are here now. My pa always told me if someone were to take me—"

"Take you? Your pa thought there would be a chance you'd ever be taken?"

"Well, yes." Bertha grunted as she continued to pull at the bindings around her arms. "My pa's rich. I don't mention it very often because people want a lot from me knowing how much he has."

"I'm sorry, I just assumed…" From her first encounter with Bertha, she had just assumed she was a farmer's daughter. She hadn't acted like the rich society ladies Charlotte was used to dealing with back in St. Louis.

"No need to apologize. It's not as if I go around telling people that my pa's richer than dirt. He certainly doesn't act like it and tells me I better never act that way either. He says money can go just as easy as it can come and to never take it for granted. Besides, he'd never let me." Bertha giggled.

"He sounds like a very loving father." A father Charlotte wished she had, but instead, she'd been stuck with a gambler who had left her when she needed him the most.

"He is." Bertha tried lifting her foot, but it was tied firmly to the chair. "Blast it! Pa always said if I was ever taken, I was to do as they said to keep myself as safe and as unharmed as possible. Then they'd likely get complacent, overconfident, and then that would be my chance. *This* is our only chance." Bertha paused and scrunched her forehead as though trying to decide what to do next. "If they want to hurt your aunt, they'll do it regardless if we cooperate or not... *unless* we get to her first. My gut says they're just saying whatever will work to get you to do as they say."

"I can't take that chance."

"Charlotte, do you want to become a whore?" Bertha's voice was hard, her glare even more so. "'Cause I certainly don't."

"What?" Charlotte stuttered.

"A whore, woman of the night, harlot, calico queen? Because that's exactly what's going to happen to us if we don't get out of here. They won't let us go. It's up to us to figure out how to escape. If we do that, then we can get to your aunt and the authorities to protect us all."

Bertha's words finally pushed through the fear pulsating through Charlotte. Bertha was right. Charlotte's aunt wouldn't want her to give in or capitulate. If she did, her life would have horrors she hadn't even begun to imagine.

She took a deep breath. It was time to fight back. "You're right. They have plans we don't want to be a part of. Are your bounds tight?"

"Yes. That stupid man made sure there was no give. What about you?"

"The ropes are getting tighter with each move I make."

Bertha muttered under her breath. "There's got to be something we can do." She looked to the right and the left. "This chair is old and rickety. What's the condition of yours?"

Charlotte wondered at the odd question but rocked back and forth. "It's old, too. Why?"

"I'm wondering if I rock my chair and fall to the floor, then maybe the impact will cause one or two of the joints to loosen or break."

"You could get hurt, Bertha." She didn't want her friend to take any unnecessary chances. Whatever was going on had to be Charlotte's fault. Her friendship with the strong, fiercely stubborn woman had pulled Bertha into this fiasco.

"I could, but I'd rather have a few cuts and bruises than experience whatever those two men are planning." With that, she started rocking back and forth, the chair groaning and creaking under the movement.

Charlotte shrugged. If Bertha was going to go for it, then she would too. "I guess we have nothing to lose."

Bertha grinned and then emitted a small shriek when the chair rocketed to one side and crashed to the ground. "Humph." She didn't move for a few seconds.

"Are you all right?" Charlotte asked, trying to keep her voice low and praying that if the men were still in the house, they hadn't heard them. Luckily, no one came running.

"Yes," Bertha said, lifting one arm free from the chair. A wooden spoke dangled from the rope around her wrist. She twisted around on the floor until she freed her other hand and then undid the ropes around her ankles.

Groaning, Bertha pushed to stand, but she didn't let whatever damage she'd done to herself stop her. Amazed at the strong woman, Charlotte didn't know if she could have done the same thing without Bertha's nudging.

Bertha ran to Charlotte's side and untied the ropes around her wrists, allowing her to bend forward and pull the ropes off her ankles. Bertha moved to stand next to the wooden door. She pulled it open a crack and peered through the opening. They had to be alone. No one had come running with all the commotion they'd been making. Their captors were secure enough in the belief the two young women wouldn't be able to free themselves.

Charlotte said a quick prayer of thanks. Without Bertha, Charlotte would still be trussed up like a calf off to auction. She shivered at what that could have meant, and while they had broken loose from their bindings, they still weren't free.

Until they were out of that house and back in a safer part of town, they were still in danger.

Chapter 22

May 19, 1901

After they had eaten, Stanley tucked a warm blanket around Martha's legs. She had fallen asleep on the sofa, exhausted with fear over Charlotte's whereabouts. He had wanted to look for Charlotte almost immediately but hadn't been comfortable leaving Martha alone until she had calmed her nerves. She'd been distraught, and he feared her heart would give out. He believed Charlotte would prefer he care for her aunt first before he started looking for her. Martha's soft snores let him know she was truly and completely asleep.

Leaving her on the sofa, he made a few phone calls, being careful to keep his voice low. The front desk patched him through to Jacob's boarding house. He quickly told Jacob what was going on, and they agreed to meet in the hotel lobby in twenty minutes.

As he ended the call, a knock sounded at the door. He hesitated and wondered who it could be. It wasn't Jacob, and Charlotte would have gotten a key from the hotel clerk. It was either someone from the hotel or something far more worrisome.

Wishing he had thought to grab his revolvers when he'd left his hotel room earlier, he slowly walked to the door, being as quiet as possible. He picked up a heavy silver candlestick and held it behind him. If it was a threat, he didn't want to be empty-handed. It might not be much of a weapon, but it could stun an assailant for a brief moment.

He cracked open the door and braced his

foot against the wood. One of the hotel clerks stood outside in a crisp white shirt and a black shoestring tie around his neck, a wide smile on his lips, and a folded piece of paper in his hands.

"Message for Miss Martha Evans."

Placing the candlestick on the table and opening the door wide, Stanley took the paper and handed the young man a coin. "Thank you. I'll make sure she gets it."

The man hurried to the stairwell, unconcerned with anything more than doing his job. Stanley closed the door and locked it securely behind him. He turned and found Martha staring at him. She had woken from her nap.

"Who was that?" she asked. "Is it news on Charlotte?"

"I don't know," he said, handing her the note. "Someone sent this. It's for you."

She took it from him snd, with trembling fingers, opened it. A moment later, she cried in anguish.

"What's wrong?" Stanley asked, although he already surmised that it wasn't anything good.

Shaking, she handed the note to him, tears filling her eyes. He took the note and scanned the contents. Whoever had taken Charlotte was demanding a significant sum of money. It had to be related to her father and the missing gold. They were obviously done waiting for Marcus to find the treasure and instead thought Charlotte's aunt would give them what they were asking.

"They want so much money," Martha said.

"I'll get it." He would have no issues with acquiring the funds they wanted. He had more than enough in his bank account in Helena. The problem would be in getting it fast enough. They wanted the money to be delivered first thing tomorrow morning, before the sun rose and the bank opened.

"No, I can't ask you for the funds," she said. "I can get it. I just have to go to the bank in the morning."

"They want the money before the banks open," he said, immediately wishing he hadn't told her. She hadn't read the details closely enough. Otherwise, she would've known that wouldn't have helped.

"I don't have that much cash on me." She clutched her throat. "What are we going to do?"

"You let me worry about that, Martha. I'll get the funds, and I'll bring Charlotte home to you, mark my words."

***

Charlotte and Bertha crept down the short hallway, each footstep more careful than the last. Charlotte tried to be silent, but it was difficult with how rundown the place was. Every few steps, one of them would step on a creaking, crackling, or snapping board. Charlotte jumped at every single sound, but they eventually reached the main part of the house. Her heart racing uncontrollably in her chest.

Peering through a grimy window, Charlotte didn't see anyone standing outside. She wasn't sure how they'd gotten so fortunate, but she wasn't going to stick around to find out why the men had left the two of them alone in the house. It was their opportunity to escape, and they were going to take it.

Out the door, Charlotte and Bertha ran down the steps and toward an alleyway running alongside the house. Being mindful that they weren't free yet, the two of them stayed close together. Charlotte gripped Bertha's hand as they looked around corners, taking precautions to avoid the men who'd taken them. Charlotte didn't know what the man who had grabbed her looked like, but Bertha had seen at least one of them and she was keeping her gaze sharp. Hopefully, they'd be able to avoid them until they were far from danger.

Panting, Charlotte rushed up to another building and abruptly stopped when she heard voices. Bertha yanked Charlotte back up against the building and placed her finger to her lips.

Charlotte nodded, her breath caught in her throat and pushed back her tangled hair. She was a frightful mess. They both were. It was minor and nothing to be concerned about, but if she didn't put her attention on something inconsequential, she'd melt into a puddle of nerves.

Bertha took a deep breath, braced her fingers against the building, peered around the corner, and then visibly sighed with relief. "It isn't them."

They weren't safe yet, but Charlotte smiled grimly. "Let's keep going. Until we reach the sheriff or someplace safe, I'm still worried they'll find us."

Bertha grabbed Charlotte's hand, and the two of them ran past the two men who'd been ribbing one another. The men stared in shock at the two women hurtling down the road.

They turned another corner and ran into a bustling crowd of women, children, and men who were tending to their afternoon activities without a care in the world. Not wanting to appear any more crazed than they already were, the two of them slowed to a walk and tried to blend in with the crowd.

Charlotte's heart was beating rather fast, and

she struggled to keep up with Bertha, who was resilient and determined to get away from the place they'd been held captive. Charlotte wasn't sure what she would've done if she'd been alone. Bertha was a blessing in so many ways.

Bertha jerked to a stop, her hand halting Charlotte.

"What is it?" Charlotte asked, scanning those around them, but she didn't see what or who had caused Bertha to stop their movements.

"It's one of them," she hissed. Bertha yanked Charlotte close to her side and pointed across the crowd at a man standing in a grove of thick trees. The man was of average stature with dark blonde hair. He was facing away from Charlotte, and she couldn't see his face. The man who had taken her had felt much taller.

"That isn't who took me," Charlotte said, but then the man turned and Charlotte uttered a cry of dismay. "That's my father."

Bertha stumbled back a step. "What? He's the one who convinced me to come to the house."

"I… I don't understand." Why was her father involved with the man who'd taken her? "This doesn't make sense."

"You're right, it doesn't," Bertha muttered, "but we don't have time to discuss this. We have to get out of here, find the sheriff, and find help. I'm not willing to let them come after us again."

Charlotte's gaze shot to the people standing around her father and zeroed in on the man her father was standing with. It appeared they were arguing, but he was the man who had sought her out in the park, warning her of Stanley. "I know that man. The tall one with the red hair."

"You do?"

"Well, not personally, but he sat next to me in the park the other day. He told me to leave Pocatello."

"But why would he be with your father?"

"I have no idea, Bertha, but they're arguing. Maybe all isn't as it seems."

Bertha glanced at her, her eyes bugging out of her head. The words sounded false even to Charlotte's own ears.

"He wasn't the one who had taken me, though. I would have recognized his voice. There's got to be at least three of them," Charlotte said.

Her father shook his clenched fist, and the other man smiled, a look of pure evil on his face. Her father's ominous words were coming back to her. He had told her he was leaving town to keep her safe but his plans to leave must have failed. But why he had lured Bertha to the house was something she didn't understand. That was not the man she had thought was her father.

"We have to find help before they see us," Charlotte said. It broke her heart to know her father was involved in Bertha's abduction, but she didn't have time to consider why. Her friend had suffered at the hands of her father. Charlotte's personal feelings had to be shut down, and help needed to be found.

Chapter 23

May 19, 1901

An hour later, Stanley stood on the rickety old porch as the horses galloped away. He held his revolver in one hand and a knife in the other, but it was too late. Charlotte and Bertha's captors had escaped.

Bertha had given them quite detailed directions to the old house the two of them had been stashed in before they escaped. It helped that Bertha had lived in Pocatello her whole life and knew the place like the back of her hand.

Charlotte had gotten lucky in befriending the engaging young lady.

Bertha had been spitting mad when they'd burst through the open doors of the hotel and found him and Jacob. They hadn't been able to find the sheriff, and Charlotte had convinced Bertha that finding Stanley was the next best thing. Stanley wasn't sure he was, considering he just let their captors disappear, but he was honored Charlotte had that much faith in him.

He couldn't just stand there and watch the horses disappear. If Charlotte thought he could catch them, then he had to try. He shoved the gun into the back of his pants and the knife back into his boot and ran down the steps and around the corner to where his horse was waiting. Jacob was nowhere to be found. Maybe he'd seen them leave and had gone a different direction to head them off, but Stanley couldn't wait to figure that out. Time was of the essence.

Stanley grabbed the pommel and mounted. The horse shifted uneasily beneath him, sensing

Stanley's urgency and agitation, but raced down the street when Stanley urged him forward.

Wagons, cattle, stray dogs, and people clogged the streets. Stanley drew back on the reins, slowing his horse. He was further delayed by a particularly large herd of cattle that lumbered along. The cowhands kept them from stampeding, but they were meandering as though they had no cares in the world.

Stanley cursed under his breath. The riders had disappeared. After an agonizing few minutes of maneuvering through the herd of cattle, he peered down streets and alleyways, swiveling his head before looking at the front of the herd. He was at a loss as to which way to go. For Charlotte's sake, he really hoped it wasn't Marcus who had lured Bertha to the same house Charlotte had been taken to.

Frustrated, he hit the pommel of his horse and startled the poor gelding, who pranced with agitation, unsure of Stanley's intentions. Sighing, he pushed up the brim of his hat and adjusted on the saddle, the leather creaking under his skin.

The morning had grown warm, and his collar stuck to his neck. He reached a finger between his skin and the fabric, pulling it away.

Suddenly, a galloping horse blew through what remained of the cattle herd. The rider yanked on the reins, and the horse and rider abruptly stopped. Dust billowed around them like a mini tornado.

Stanley waved a hand in front of him, trying not to inhale the dirt, but it was useless, and he coughed in earnest. He yanked a handkerchief from his shirt pocket and wiped at his watery eyes and the dust that had settled on his face and neck.

Once he could see again, he lifted his head and sighed with relief. "Jacob, where have you been? I was worried you'd gotten hurt or worse."

Jacob grinned and lifted the cap off his head. "Don't need to worry about me none. You should know better than that. I always get myself out of any scrapes. And speaking of scrapes, you need to come with me right now."

"What? Why? I need to find them."

"Little buck, we don't have time. Let's go." A tight-lipped frown lined his mouth.

Jacob guided his horse to turn and urged him into a gallop.

* * *

Charlotte paced back and forth in the hotel's lobby while Bertha sat in an armchair in front of the roaring fireplace. Stanley and Jacob had run out of the hotel the moment she and Bertha arrived, leaving them in the safekeeping of the hotel clerk. Although, Charlotte wasn't sure the young man behind the desk could fend off any attack, even if he had good intentions. He was inexperienced but had put on a good front, removing a revolver from behind the desk and placing it on the counter. She'd had to hide a grin when he'd thrown back his shoulders and told Stanley quite proudly that he would defend the two women against any and all attacks.

"Are you going to wear a hole in that floor, Charlotte?" Bertha asked.

Charlotte stopped and rested her hands against her hips. "Perhaps, but I can't sit still."

"I'm well aware of that. You haven't stopped moving in over an hour."

"What if they get hurt?"

"It's a little too late to wonder about that now." Bertha leaned back in her chair, resting her forearms on the arms. She wasn't concerned in the least.

"Are you not worried about them?"

Bertha grimaced and pushed to stand. "Yes, but I can't do anything about it right now. You told me to trust Stanley, so that's what I'm doing. If you want me to get irrational, weepy, or angry, I can do any of those, but I'd rather not, as it won't solve the problem we have now."

Bertha's straightforward and matter-of-fact attitude pulled Charlotte from her worry. She was right. There was no point in expressing emotions she didn't have to, at least not until they knew more.

The hotel doors banged open, and an older man with peppered gray-black hair and a woman with dark blonde hair rushed into the hotel. They looked harried and troubled. The man pulled the woman with him and rushed to the desk, not paying any mind to the two women.

The woman said, "My daughter, where is she?"

Bertha jumped from her seat. "Momma."

The woman whipped around and gasped. She ran toward Bertha, and Bertha met her halfway. Her mother enveloped her in a tight embrace. The man followed and soon had both women in his arms. Tears flowed, but generous smiles graced their lips. Charlotte averted her gaze so she didn't intrude on what was a poignant private family moment.

Whispered words of comfort and love were expressed between Bertha and her parents, and it made Charlotte's heart tug at all she had lost with her parents. Her mother had loved her, but she had been taken from Charlotte far too soon. Once she was gone, Charlotte had subsequently lost her father, and now, when she thought she had finally found him, it turned out that he was involved in taking both Charlotte and Bertha for money. For that blasted gold. That was all her father thought about. He had sacrificed her safety and the safety of her new friend, all so he could be rich. He had never loved her. If he had, he would've never been involved.

"Charlotte?"

She raised her head. Bertha's eyes were filled with a compassion Charlotte didn't deserve. Bertha stood between her parents. Her father's arm was around her shoulders, holding her close. Their love was clear and unwavering. Jealous for something she could never have again made Charlotte want to wallow in misery, but she wouldn't. Bertha had come to her rescue and had become a dear friend. She shouldn't have been dragged into the mess of Charlotte's life.

"I'd like you to meet my ma and pa."

Charlotte straightened her wrinkled blouse and smoothed back wayward strands of hair from around her face, trying to move it back as best she could. She looked a fright, but she tried to quell her nervousness at meeting the two most important people in Bertha's life.

"Mr. and Mrs. Fairbanks, it's a pleasure. I'm so sorry—"

"No apologies are needed, young lady," Mr. Fairbanks said. "Our Bertha here told us what happened."

"Then she told you it was my father—"

"You are not responsible for the actions of your father," he said. "And while I don't condone what he did, and I fully expect him to pay for his actions, sometimes we don't know why someone does something in a moment of weakness or desperation."

Charlotte swallowed back a lump in her throat. She hadn't expected his compassion. She'd expected him to blame her and be furious that she had brought harm to his daughter. She blinked furiously to hold back her tears and swallowed the thick lump in her throat.

Bertha stepped forward and pulled Charlotte into her arms, giving her the comfort Charlotte hadn't realized she needed.

After a long moment, Charlotte pulled away and wiped the wetness from her cheeks. "Thank you for being so kind to me after everything that has happened. Without Bertha, I don't think I would have made it out of there alive. You taught your daughter well. She was brave, determined, and found a way for us to escape. You should be very proud."

Mr. Fairbanks smirked, a twinkle in his eyes. "I guess she must've listened to what I had to tell her for once. She's a handful but has always known her mind, so I'm glad a few of my words penetrated that thick skull of hers."

Bertha giggled. "Oh, Pa. You know I always listened to what you've had to say. I just don't always agree with it."

He snorted. "Ain't that the truth?" Then his eyes grew solemn. "I'm so glad the two of you made it out of there alive. When I got that note with their demands, my heart near stopped." He brushed a curl from Bertha's cheek, his touch tender. "Your mother and I would've paid any amount to get you back."

He reached for his wife's hand and pulled her close. "Have you spoken with the sheriff yet?"

"No. He wasn't at the jail, so we came here. Charlotte's been working with Mr. Seymour and Mr. Jones. They were in the lobby getting ready to search for us when we burst inside. Charlotte's aunt received a similar note."

"Oh, no," Charlotte said. She had been foolhardy and selfish.

"What?" Bertha said. "What's wrong?"

"My aunt. Stanley said she was worried, but I was so distracted I forgot to send word to let her know I was all right. She's probably worried sick."

"Go," Bertha said. "Go let her know you're all right. I'm famished, and Pa says we can get a bite to eat. Once you've checked on her, you're both welcome to join us."

Charlotte told them she would be back once she saw to her aunt. If there was any reason why she couldn't come back downstairs, she would call the front desk and have them notify Bertha and her parents. Bertha shooed her away, and Charlotte ran up the stairs.

She was a horrible niece. She had known her aunt was worried, but she had been so distracted with her worry over Stanley and Jacob that she had plumb forgotten to let her aunt know she had returned safely to the hotel.

Chapter 24

May 19, 1901

Charlotte stuck the key in the lock, pushed open the door to her hotel room, and rushed inside.

"Aunty Martha, I'm so sorry I worried you." Charlotte dropped to the floor in front of her, grabbing her hands. They were cold to the touch. "Aunty, what's wrong? Why aren't you saying anything? Do I need to call for the doctor? I'm so sorry I didn't get up here as soon as I got free, but there's so much to tell you—"

Aunt Martha shook her head, placed a finger over Charlotte's lips, and effectively silenced her. Then she pointed. In her haste, Charlotte hadn't seen the man sitting across from her aunt, a revolver held in his hands, until it was too late.

Charlotte swallowed a gasp when she saw the tall, red-haired man from the park. "What... what are you doing here?"

The man chuckled, although the laugh was far from merry. "Oh, that'll be a surprise for you, one that you won't enjoy. You should have listened and done as you were told. Now, you and your aunt will suffer."

"Why are you doing this?" Cold chills ran up the back of her neck.

"I told you before that you should've never come here looking for your father. That was your first mistake."

"Why would looking for my father matter to you?" Her voice trembled. She didn't want to show fear but it was hard to hide.

"Because he became distracted," he snapped.

"I don't... I don't understand." Sweat

gathered at the back of her neck and trickled down her back.

"It doesn't matter now. You defied me, caused me to lose a sizable sum of money, and frankly, I just don't like you." His sneer grew with each word he spoke.

Unease crept up her spine. "My grandfather will give you what you want. I just need to send him a telegram. Give me a couple of days, and you—"

He slammed his cane on the ground. "Oh, shut up, you sniveling girl. I don't have time to wait for your grandfather to wire me funds. That'll take too long. But don't worry, you'll pay."

"Pay how?" Charlotte said. She couldn't let him hurt her aunt. "If it's what I believe, then I won't do it. You can't make me."

He cackled. "Oh, quit your blathering. I don't have time for this. You'll do exactly as you're told. Get up! Both of you." He waved the gun, making his point clear that she shouldn't argue.

"Go where?" Charlotte asked as she stood, helping her aunt to her feet. It wasn't the time to fight back, not with the chance that something could happen to her beloved aunt, but if she found a moment to get her aunt to safety, she was going to take it.

"To your new home, of course." An evil smile lined his thin lips.

"My home is in St. Louis." Charlotte held her aunt's arm.

"Not anymore, it's not." His steady arm pointed the revolver at them. "Go out the door and to the back staircase. You'll do as I say. I'm not afraid to use this."

"I'll need my cane," Aunt Martha said.

"I don't think so," he snapped. "You can use that as a weapon. I'm not someone to trifle with."

"If you don't want me to fall down or keep you from getting wherever we're going, you'll let me use it. I don't walk well without it," Aunt Martha said.

He muttered an obscenity under his breath. "Grab the cane, but don't even consider doing something stupid with it. I'm not afraid to shoot either of you."

Aunt Martha grunted but nodded. "Charlotte, my dear, it's behind the chair over there." She pointed to the armchair on the other side of the room.

Charlotte squeezed her hand before grabbing the cane.

"Enough with the delays. Go toward the door. Don't make any sudden moves."

Charlotte held her aunt's elbow as they walked down the back stairs and out the side door of the hotel. It was dark outside, daylight having long disappeared. The only lights came from the buildings across the railroad tracks and what shined through the hotel windows. The man forced them across the tracks, and her aunt struggled to keep up. Charlotte was worried she would fall and hurt herself, although what the man planned was likely going to be worse than falling and skinning their knees.

Charlotte had hoped they would see someone who could help, but it was as though everyone had gone inside and hidden from the dark shadows that sprang up once the sun dropped behind the mountains. The man kept a close eye on them, walking next to Charlotte's aunt, the revolver pressed in her aunt's back to remind the two of them that if they made the wrong move or the wrong step, he wouldn't hesitate to shoot Aunt Martha.

Bertha had shown her she could fight and escape, but that time was different. Charlotte couldn't sacrifice her aunt's safety. If she found a moment where her aunt would be far from danger, then she would fight the man. She wasn't going to go willingly if the opportunity presented itself.

"How much longer?" Charlotte asked after her aunt stumbled once again. Her aunt dug her fingers into Charlotte's arm, piercing the skin. Her fear was almost as great as Charlotte's, but Charlotte had to be strong. She should have gone to her aunt as soon as she'd returned to the hotel. This was all her fault. She had mistakenly worried about Stanley's safety instead of her aunt. He could take care of himself while her aunt could not.

"Don't you worry your pretty little head," the man sneered. "We'll be there soon enough."

He led them through the dark streets, his confidence in walking through the black night unwavering. He wasn't afraid, but then he had a revolver in his hands while Charlotte and her aunt had nothing more than a wooden cane.

A few minutes later, he stopped them in front of a rowdy saloon. Music from a piano and a fiddler mingled with raucous laughter, screams of glee, and moans from customers inside. Charlotte shuddered in revulsion. It was not one of the nicer saloons, not that any saloon was nice, but some were worse than others, and that one was in the horrendous category. The smells emanating from inside made Charlotte wish she had a handkerchief to cover her nose, but she was out of luck.

"Why are we here?" Charlotte asked.

He laughed. "Why, it's your new home, Charlotte."

"No," Aunt Martha said. "Over my dead body."

"That can certainly be arranged, dear darling Martha. You can either wish your dear niece good luck and good wishes or find yourself in an early grave." The man stopped and stepped just to the front of them, greed and revulsion in his eyes. "Your grave will come sooner than planned."

Charlotte had mistakenly believed if she cooperated with the man, her aunt would be safe. From the sound of it, she had cooperated for nothing. "No. You can't hurt my aunt. I've done what you asked. She is no threat to you. I'll go inside and do as you ask. No fight, no argument. Just please let her go."

"You gave up that right to ask for anything when you and Bertha fled earlier. If you'd stayed like the good girl your aunt thinks you are, she wouldn't be facing the end of her life. You can blame yourself, Charlotte. This is all your doing."

Charlotte's throat closed. She had underestimated him and what he would do. She should have fought the man before they left the hotel. Now, they were standing in front of a saloon with drunk men who would have no interest in helping them.

"Say your goodbyes to your aunt. This has gone on long enough."

"No," Charlotte said, jutting her jaw forward. "I won't be going inside there. You can't do this. I won't become a whore. If you're going to kill her, you can kill me, too."

"You don't have a choice. If you push me, I'll make your aunt suffer. A bullet in the leg, perhaps one in the hip. I'll let her bleed out slowly and make her watch you lose your innocence." He held the gun against her aunt's chest.

Charlotte looked around in vain. There was nowhere to go, nowhere to hide, and no one who would save them. She stood frozen. She couldn't go inside that saloon. Whatever awaited her had to be worse than anything she could ever imagine.

The man muttered under his breath before swinging the gun and slamming it against her aunt's head. Aunt Martha didn't see it coming and fell to the ground.

"No!" Charlotte reached for her aunt, but before she could prevent her aunt from getting hurt, the man grabbed her by the arm and yanked her away. Her aunt smacked her head against the dirt road, her limp body unmoving as blood trickled from behind her ear.

"You hurt her," Charlotte yelled, trying to pull free. Her worst nightmare was coming true.

"You gave me no choice." He tightened his grip on Charlotte's arm and shoved the barrel of the gun into her belly. "I have no patience for insolent brats who don't listen. While I need the money you're going to bring, don't think if you push me too far I won't hesitate to pull the trigger and blow a hole in your side so wide that you'll die bleeding out here on the street, all alone and in certain agony." His words sent an ominous chill through her. "Now, get moving and walk toward that saloon before I decide you aren't worth the effort and kill you anyway."

* * *

Stanley followed Jacob as they wound through the maze of streets. Dim light from lanterns cast shadows on the nearly empty thoroughfares. Families had returned to their homes, and miners, cowboys, and gamblers could be found inside the numerous saloons and brothels.

Jacob held a finger to his lips. Stanley nodded, and they both dismounted, taking care not to make a sound. They tethered their horses to a hitching post.

Stanley stood next to one of the seedier saloons and whorehouses across the tracks and a fair distance from the hotel. The saloon had seen better days, but the place was loud and booming with activity. There was no shortage of men and women inside enjoying a good ole time. He didn't know why Jacob had brought him here, but he was sure Jacob wouldn't lead him astray.

He followed Jacob as they crept along the west side to the rear and went inside through the back door. The hallway was dark, and sounds were muted, although an occasional burst of laughter or a particularly hard press of the piano keys would echo in their ears.

They'd snuck into an empty stockroom full of liquor barrels and shelves containing filthy spittoons, broken mugs and glasses, empty bottles of rum and bourbon, and sacks of flour, rice, and overripe red apples. A few piles of worn linens that were questionable in origin lay scattered on the shelves.

Stanley jumped out of his skin when a large yelp of glee echoed in the saloon. Jacob smothered a snort of laughter at his jittery nerves. Stanley had to take a deep breath. With any luck, Jacob had discovered where Charlotte and Bertha's captors had gone, and they'd catch them before they could do more harm to them or anyone else. He just couldn't figure out how they were connected to Marcus. According to Charlotte, Marcus had been determined to keep her safe and had warned her to stay away from Mr. Smith.

"What's going on?" Stanley whispered after

his heart stopped beating like it was going to burst from his chest.

"I caught up with one of 'em. The one who took your little lady."

"She's not—" He paused when he saw the smirk on Jacob's face. "How do you know it was the one who took Charlotte? She couldn't describe him."

"The man squealed like a pig in slop when I snatched him off his horse. Seems as though he wasn't as tough as he wanted to be after I got ahold of him. After a bit of persuading, he agreed to tell me where Marcus had gone."

Stanley shook his head. Jacob was a force to be reckoned with, and few men would take him on when it came right down to it. "What did you do with him?"

Jacob grinned. "Oh, he's trussed up like a turkey in the jailhouse, waiting for the sheriff to arrive. The deputy willingly took him off my hands after I told him how he took Charlotte and threatened to harm her."

"What about Smith?"

"I think he was the one on the horse that got away. I caught a glimpse of red hair, but I never saw his face. I can't be too sure, but it fits. Smith is likely behind all of this."

Stanley slammed his fist against the wall. "Dammit!"

"Hush, you've got to keep your voice low," Jacob hissed. "We don't know who might be out there, and last thing I want is to let them know we're onto them."

Stanley scowled. "Did you ask the man about Smith?"

"Yes. Fear like nothing I've ever seen crossed that man's face, but he did tell me that Smith was going back to the hotel to grab Charlotte and bring her back here."

Stanley grabbed Jacob's shoulder and stopped him. "Charlotte's safe in the hotel. We just left her and Bertha there not less than an hour ago."

"Is she?" Jacob said, gently removing Stanley's fingers. "I'm not too sure about that, not anymore. Your little lady needs our help, and us jawing back here isn't gonna help. They have every intention of selling her to a man who peddles women. I'm thinking you don't want that to happen. If we don't move quick, we'll likely lose catching the man and stopping him forever."

"Sell her?" Stanley was horrified. Jacob had to have misunderstood.

"You can't be that surprised. It's common enough practice, unfortunately."

"Until recently, I would've never thought this actually happened." The thought sickened him, although considering it was the trade his ex-wife had participated in, he shouldn't be too surprised. While Michael was in town, he had informed Stanley of all of her misdeeds. Stanley hadn't listened while he'd been in Helena last Christmas, but he'd finally sat down and heard everything Michael had to say about the woman who had upended their lives.

"Not all women inside whorehouse walls *want* to be there," Jacob said, his voice low and angry. "You can't imagine that any woman would welcome the idea of letting hundreds of men between her thighs, doing what they want, how they want, and when they want, giving women few choices in the matter."

Jacob's frank words were a reminder that sometimes Stanley lived with his head in the clouds. It was time to brush that away and be the man his pa had raised him to be.

"Let's go. We don't have much time." Jacob reached for his revolver, pulled back the hammer, and placed his ear against the door. He muttered under his breath and gestured for Stanley to follow his lead.

Cold sweat trickled down the back of Stanley's neck, but he was determined to end this. Charlotte meant the world to him, and he would do anything to keep her safe from harm.

Whatever was behind that door couldn't be good, but the two of them would face it together.

Chapter 25

May 19, 1901

Charlotte stood petrified next to the red-haired man. The scariest man she had ever seen in her life was mere feet in front of her. He was tall with wide shoulders. Red, jagged scars crisscrossed both cheeks. He had a thick neck that blended into his chest and a salacious look in his eyes. He opened his lips to reveal rotting teeth and flared his nose with ripe anticipation.

She shuddered in revulsion, and an evil grin lifted his ruddy cheeks when he saw her shiver. A sweat-stained shirt rested across his shoulders, and he yanked up loose trousers that had seen better days before crossing his arms in front of his chest.

"Smith, ya told me ya had two of 'em," the man said.

Her instincts were right. It was Mr. Smith. No wonder her father had warned her away, but it was too late.

He sneered. "Don't you worry, Zeke, I'll get you the other one. It'll just take me a few more days."

"I don't know," Zeke said, lumbering toward them.

Charlotte trembled when Zeke walked around them as though he were inspecting his new prize. Mr. Smith stood next to her, holding her tight. Bertha had warned her, and while Charlotte hadn't believed that she was lying to her, a part of her had hoped that Bertha had misunderstood. Charlotte had been a fool to believe that escaping from the old house would be the end of it.

"She's awfully scrawny," Zeke drawled. He

grabbed her chin and twisted it back and forth. "How are her teeth?"

Charlotte yanked her head away. "Don't touch me."

"Oh, she's feisty. I'm gonna enjoy breakin' this one."

"You can do whatever you want... *after* you pay," Mr. Smith said.

"Not sure she's worth the sum you're wantin'." Zeke scowled. "Especially since there was supposed to be two of 'em."

"I said she'll be here soon. Don't you worry none about that." Mr. Smith's voice had a decided edge to it. He scowled. "Now, are we going to get on with this or not?"

"Char... Charlotte? Where are you?" Aunt Martha's weak voice came from behind her.

Charlotte tried to turn around, but Mr. Smith clutched her arm, digging his fingers into her soft skin.

"I don't think so, young lady," he said. "You ain't going anywhere."

"But my aunt."

"She's fine," he muttered.

"No, she's not." Charlotte had to see how her aunt was doing. After Mr. Smith hit her aunt, a few drunken men had dragged her inside, not taking care to keep her from further harm. Charlotte was worried she wouldn't recover, although it was likely too late for both of them anyway.

Charlotte pulled hard, and he loosened his grip. He muttered obscenities but didn't stop her. She ran to her aunt and dropped to the ground. Martha lay curled on the floor against the wall. Catching Charlotte's eye, her aunt lifted onto one hand and managed to sit.

Charlotte pushed her aunt's hair away from her face. A massive purple bruise had bloomed on her cheek.

Charlotte raised her fingers to her lips. "I'm so sorry, Aunt Martha. If I had known—" She gasped when Zeke yanked her off the ground and away from her aunt. "Let me go!"

He ignored her screech and threw her onto a sofa on the other side of the room. "The first

thing you'll learn is that you'll do as you're told."
Zeke curled his lip at her look of outrage. "If you
don't listen, that bruise on your aunt's cheek will
be the first of *many*."

The door slammed open.

Charlotte burrowed farther into the sofa.
Before she could see who had burst inside, Mr.
Smith ran across the room. The fury that crossed
his face was far more dangerous than anything
Charlotte had ever seen before.

"I'll kill her," Mr. Smith roared.

Charlotte froze as he shoved the cold metal
gun against her skin. She had no doubt he would
pull the trigger if enraged any further, and he'd
have no guilt in doing it.

"I'll kill him"—her father pointed to Zeke—
"and shoot you next. Let her go!"

Charlotte gasped. She thought her father was
in cahoots with Mr. Smith. What was going on?
Her father held two revolvers, one in each hand,
and pointed them at Mr. Smith and Zeke.

"You crazy old fool," Zeke growled. "I don't
know who you are or what you want, but if you're

looking for a good ole time, just visit Ms. Noelle. She'll give you the girl without these theatrics."

Her father scowled, shuffling his feet. "I don't want a girl. I want her." He waved the gun at Charlotte. "Now release her."

Mr. Smith chuckled with revulsion. "You're too late, Marcus. You should've listened and done what you were told. Instead, you had to interfere, and now your precious girl will pay the price."

"I'll kill you," Marcus snapped, tensing his jaw, his hatred for Mr. Smith seeming to ooze from his pores. The fierce man standing in front of her was not the father she remembered. Too much had changed over the years.

Zeke's men started to move forward, but her father shouted. "Keep your men back. I ain't afraid to use these guns."

"No, you won't." Mr. Smith's hand was steady as a rock. He pushed the barrel farther into Charlotte's head. "You aren't getting her without giving me something. She's worth a lot. I wonder"—he paused dramatically—"how much she's *worth* to you?"

"More than money could ever buy," Marcus roared. "Let her go, or I'll pull the trigger and not regret killing you."

"You shoot me, and I'll shoot her." Mr. Smith's voice had grown flat, unemotional. He had nothing to lose.

If Charlotte's father shot his gun, there was no guarantee his aim would be true, while Mr. Smith could pull the trigger and not miss.

"Leave or I'll end her pathetic existence," Mr. Smith said, a low and forbidding tone to his voice.

Her father's hand shook as he gazed at Charlotte. His agony at the impossible situation caused her heart to break. While they might've had a tumultuous past, his desire to see her unharmed told her far more. He had come for her, but it was too late. Zeke and Mr. Smith had everything to gain and nothing to lose. If her father did as Mr. Smith demanded, he would die.

If he didn't, Charlotte would. Either way, someone was going to meet their maker tonight.

"I'll say this one... more... time." Mr. Smith pulled back the hammer, the snap loud in the quiet room. "Leave now or you'll have nothing left of her except a pile of blood and bones."

Her father's face fell, the horrible realization of the situation they found themselves in seeming to infiltrate his skin. He dropped his arms, and the revolvers hung limply by his side. He was defeated.

A wide, evil grin lifted Mr. Smith's lips. Pure, unadulterated pleasure poured from his eyes. "Hand those guns to Zeke's men. You can go on your way, and we can forget this ever happened."

Mr. Smith was lying. He wouldn't let her father go, not anymore. Her father had interfered, and once he was divested of his guns, he'd be killed. She couldn't let that happen. Her life was over either way, but she could try to save both him and her aunt.

Mr. Smith looked away, giving Charlotte the

chance to fight back. She grabbed the barrel of the gun and shoved it away from her face, yelling, "Don't give him your guns."

But it was too late.

Ripping the gun from Charlotte's fingers, Mr. Smith swung the barrel back and slammed it against her head. The force snapped her neck back. She moaned and collapsed against the back of the sofa as pain pierced her skull.

"Don't touch her," her father yelled, but Mr. Smith ignored his pleas and Zeke's men subdued him. Soon Zeke moved in and held him against the wall with a knife against his neck.

She had failed.

"I've had enough of you and your antics, Marcus." Spittle flew from Mr. Smith's lips. "You should've never double-crossed me."

Marcus glared at him. "You're crazier than I thought. I didn't double-cross you. There was no gold."

Mr. Smith's skin was flushed. "There is, and I know you've got it. If you want your daughter to live, I suggest you tell me where you hid it."

Marcus shook his head, his shoulders falling as Zeke pushed the knife deeper into her father's neck. A line of blood dribbled down his skin.

"Don't hurt him," Charlotte yelled.

Mr. Smith swiveled his head to look at her. His eyes were black and devoid of any emotion. "Oh, shut up, you sniveling brat. I'm gonna enjoy killing your father and your precious aunt. You'll watch as I drain every last drop of blood out of both of 'em. Then what happens to you will be far worse, and I'll enjoy watching you suffer. You *will* regret defying me."

Charlotte raised a hand to her cheek. "If you're going to kill me, then do it now and get it over with. I'd rather die at your hand than go with that… that man."

"Oh, you'll die all right… *after* Zeke and his men have their way with you."

Chapter 26

May 19, 1901

Charlotte watched in horror as Zeke and his men hung her father from the rafters. His alarming glee at what he had planned for her father was pure evil. As they tied Marcus's arms high above his head, Zeke described in great detail what he was going to do to her father. Zeke yanked on the rope and pulled his body up until he couldn't touch the floor, his arms straining from the weight of his own body. She could do nothing but watch as her dreams about the future were eviscerated.

Mr. Smith yanked her back to the sofa and shoved her onto it, the flat cushions doing nothing to soften her fall. "Watch, little girl. This is what happens when you interfere."

In the corner, her aunt struggled to stand but collapsed back onto the hard wooden floor.

"Please," Charlotte said. "Let me help my aunt. She's hurt and—"

Mr. Smith slapped her again, and her neck snapped from the force. He ignored her pleas, strode to the door, and spoke to someone harshly on the other side. A few seconds later, two rough-looking men came inside, grabbed her aunt by the arms, and dragged her out of the room.

Charlotte jumped up from the sofa to stop them, but Mr. Smith pushed her back. "Don't move or I'll have them kill your aunt."

She watched the men unceremoniously leave the room with her aunt and slam the door behind them. Her aunt's cries of agony echoed in Charlotte's ears. "Where are they taking her?"

"Enough with the questions," he snapped. "Zeke, get on with it."

Zeke's malicious smile was ominous. He sauntered to a wardrobe on the other side of the room and pulled it open to reveal numerous weapons: guns, sabers, swords, knives, and various other items that she couldn't identify but were all sharp and lethal.

He picked up a long knife, ran his thumb along the edge, and cackled with malice. "This is gonna be enjoyable."

Zeke sliced her father's shirt open and let it hang from his shoulders. He then ran the knife slowly along his chest, not yet piercing the skin. It was as though he was just getting started and was going to enjoy every last second.

"Please," she cried. "Don't do this."

Her father screamed as Zeke pressed the knife deep into his skin. His knife crisscrossed Marcus, going deep enough to draw blood. Her father's skin hung open like Zeke was filleting a fish. Zeke didn't stop as her father's screams continued to build into a crescendo of epic portions. Blood poured from her father's chest as he peeled him apart, inch by inch.

The squeals of pain grew louder and louder with each passing second. Zeke was doing enough damage to cause him to slowly bleed out but not enough for him to pass out. It was as though he had done it before and knew how far he could torture someone while at the same time keep them alive and coherent enough to feel every single slice.

Charlotte tried to go to him, but Mr. Smith held her back, satisfaction lining his face.

"Why are you doing this?" she cried.

Mr. Smith's red hair was slicked back, and his black suit contained not one wrinkle. He looked like the perfect gentleman except for the pure wickedness in his eyes. There was no doubt in her mind that Mr. Smith was enjoying the torture more than Zeke, and he wasn't even the one holding the knife. It was as though the torment her father experienced was exhilarating, mind-blowing, almost the best thing he could have ever witnessed.

Before Mr. Smith responded to her question, the door to the room burst open, and Stanley and Jacob came roaring inside. Jacob's arms were held wide, and a menacing glower twisted his face. Stanley ran toward her and Mr. Smith while Jacob rushed toward Zeke. With one broad stroke of his wide powerful hands, he snatched Zeke up by his neck and threw him against the far wall. The knife in Zeke's hand flew through the air, twirling and swirling as though a tornado had picked it up and was showing the world that it was the one controlling the situation and not the knife. Zeke's body collapsed hard against the ground before the knife did, the force of Jacob's blow immense and powerful.

Mr. Smith grabbed her by her hair and tried to drag her back, but she screeched with outrage. She was not letting him take her. Her father needed her. She twisted and pulled away as Stanley fought off the other men between her and Mr. Smith. Stanley's growl was fierce as he pummeled one man and then the next before he reached them.

Stanley pulled his fist back. "Let her go!"

Mr. Smith's eyes widened, the pupils expanding like fireworks in the sky, and he released his grip on her hair. She fell forward, but then scrambled to reach her father who hung limp and unmoving from the rafters.

"Father," she screamed.

Jacob ran to her side, his bulky body towering over her. She tried to hold up her father's body. Slick blood ran down him, coating her fingers and arms. She was more of a hinderance than a help, but she had to try. Jacob cut the ropes and gently lowered him into her arms.

Her father was paying the ultimate price for trying to save her. The wounds on his chest were too great, and she could see the life draining out of him. He lay limp in her arms, his eyes filled with acceptance to his ultimate fate. She was helpless and had to choke back her sobs.

He cupped her cheek and rubbed away her tears.

"I love you, Charlotte, my sweet baby girl. I'm

sorry it's come to this." His eyes closed briefly as he coughed, blood trickling from the corner of his mouth. She grabbed his shirt trying to stem the bleeding from his wounds, but there was nothing she could do.

"Father, don't leave me," she cried, knowing in her heart that it was too late.

He opened his eyes, his gaze weak but filled with affection. "I... I couldn't be prouder of you. I love you."

Her father's eyes slowly shut as the gurgling in his chest quieted, and he took his last breath. The only sound in her ears was the rapid beating of her heart. She had found and lost the man who had been such a presence in her young life. She had never expected it to end this way.

* * *

Stanley fought with Smith, trying to gain the upper hand. For a tall and lanky man, Smith was scrappy and put up a good fight, slipping from

Stanley's grasp and getting in a few good punches.

When Charlotte screamed for her father, Stanley took his eyes off Smith for just a split second. Smith took the opportunity and slipped out of the room. Stanley started to follow him but the pain in Charlotte's screams stopped him in his tracks. He could find Smith later. Charlotte needed him.

Jacob stood guarding her and her father as Stanley knelt at her side. He scanned the wounds on Marcus's body, but he had been cut too severely and had lost too much blood. Marcus wouldn't be long for this world.

When Marcus took his last breath, she raised tear-filled eyes to his. Stanley swallowed back the lump in his throat. She trembled and let him pull her into his embrace where she grasped the front of his shirt and sobbed. He murmured in her ear, holding her tight against him, and ran his fingers over her tangled curls, trying to soothe her pain the best way he could. Unfortunately, he couldn't offer anything more than his support.

"Why?" she cried. "He tried to save me. If I had done as Mr. Smith said and left town, then none of this would happen."

"You couldn't have stopped what happened," he murmured.

"I could have," she said, pounding her fists into his chest. "How do I go on without him?"

Stanley couldn't answer her question and nothing he could say would ease her pain. "Let's get you out of here." He didn't want her to see Marcus's ravaged body any more than she already had.

"No," she said, wiping away her tears. "I have to take care of him." She sniffled and sat back on her heels.

He was immediately bereft without her near him, but he would give her the space she needed. Stumbling to stand, she covered her mouth. "Oh, no." Her head swiveled sharply. "Where's Aunt Martha? They took her before you and Jacob..." She hiccupped, tears blooming once again.

Stanley took her hand. "She's all right. Jacob

and I found her before we came inside. She's resting comfortably in a room with one of the harlots."

"But how do you know they aren't working for that man?" She pointed to Zeke who sat cowering against the far wall. The other two men Stanley had fought sat next to him. Jacob hadn't taken his eyes off of them, his club held in his hands.

"Jacob knew the gal, and she promised to lock the door and keep her safe."

"But—"

He pushed a lock of her hair behind her ear, his thumb brushing against her wet cheek. "I promise. We wouldn't have put her in any more danger. I can take you to her if you'd like?"

"Yes, yes," she said, "but my father…"

"Jacob will take care of him, right, Jacob?" Stanley caught Jacob's gaze.

Jacob nodded, crossing his arms against his chest. "Yes. Little lady, don't you worry about a thing. I'll make sure your pa is taken care of. Why don't you go with Stanley and see to your aunt?"

She nodded, clearly conflicted but she let Stanley lead her away. As they stepped out of the room, she halted, her shoulders shaking in grief. "What am I going to do?"

Stanley stared at her for a long moment, not sure that anything he could say would ever make her feel better but he had to say something. "There aren't any magical words that'll make your heart heal any faster, but… but I want you to know that I'm here for you and that whatever you need, I'll do my best to give it to you."

She stared at him, tears streaming down her cheeks. Her agony over her pa's passing was a painful reminder of how he'd felt when he realized he was the one responsible for his pa's death. It wasn't the same as she couldn't have stopped what had happened to Marcus, but the pain was still real.

"I won't let you go through this alone, Charlotte." He tugged on her hand and pulled her close. This woman had somehow snuggled into his heart and he wasn't sure he ever wanted to let her go.

Chapter 27

May 21, 1901

Two days later, Stanley stood in the hallway outside Charlotte's hotel room and hesitated to knock. The past few days had been remarkably sad.

Watching the last moment Charlotte had shared with her father reminded Stanley that he'd not had the same luxury, although to call it a luxury was inaccurate at best. It was awful and unfair, and there was no way he could ease Marcus's painful passing. Only time would do that, though he had yet to find peace after his own pa's passing, and he couldn't tell Charlotte when it would happen for her.

The sheriff had arrived at the hotel yesterday morning to question both Charlotte and her aunt after he'd spoken with Bertha and her parents. The sheriff had told them the saloon owner was in jail, and he was sure the man would spend the rest of his life rotting in prison for murdering Charlotte's father. The sheriff seemed convinced they'd catch Smith soon enough. Stanley wasn't sold. Smith was slippery as an eel, and Stanley had an eerie feeling things weren't over just yet.

While he didn't want to leave Charlotte and Martha alone to deal with Marcus's passing he had been delayed for too long. He had an obligation to his family and had much to fix and plenty to make up for. He'd changed his train ticket to leave the next morning and it was only right to tell Charlotte that he was leaving. Martha had insisted that they would be fine when he had spoken to her the day before, but he was uneasy all the same.

Suddenly, the hotel door opened, and a high-pitched shriek emanated from Martha's lips.

"Oh my!" She waved a hand against her face. "I didn't expect anyone to be standing there." She patted his arm. "Mr. Seymour, it's so nice to see you. I was hoping we could say our goodbyes before you left. Please come inside. Charlotte will be pleased to see you."

Holding his hat in his hand, he twisted itat the brim. He shouldn't have come. It'd been a mistake, but it was too late to leave after Martha had found him standing like a bumbling fool in the hotel's hallway.

Charlotte was huddled on the sofa, a thick blue and white quilt around her shoulders, her back to him as she faced the fireplace. She appeared to be unaware he was near. Martha was wrong in thinking she'd be glad to see him. He was nothing more than a common acquaintance. There was nothing significant between them, and it'd serve him well to remember that.

"I'm sorry, Martha," he whispered. "I didn't mean to come by at a bad time. I just wanted to see how you were doing and express my condolences again for your loss."

She blinked and gingerly touched her cheek, the yellow and purple bruise a stark reminder of what she had narrowly escaped. "We're taking it one day at a time. You're kind to look in on us. I'm surprised you're still in Pocatello. Weren't you supposed to be on the train back to Helena?"

"I rescheduled and I'm..." He swallowed hard. "I'm leaving tomorrow. I just hate that I wasn't able to find Charlotte's father before..."

"No need to apologize, young man. My dear niece wouldn't have been able to say her goodbyes without your help."

Stanley continued to keep his voice low. "He tried to save her and died doing so."

"I'm well aware of what happened," Martha said, cocking her eyebrow in irritation.

He feared he had offended her.

"I'm angry that blasted Mr. Smith escaped."

She brushed away a stray hair from her cheek. "He intended to sell Charlotte to that saloon owner like she was a prize bull. If he'd carried through with his plans, he would've tried to grab young Bertha again and done the same to her."

He cringed at the implications. "It's a shame Smith got away, but he'll pay for his plans one way or another."

"How can you be sure about that?"

He cleared his throat. He didn't know if he had an answer for Martha, but he didn't want to look the fool. "When I talked with the sheriff, Bertha's pa had already visited, raised hell, and insisted the sheriff do something about it. The sheriff sent telegrams to all the nearest stops on the railroad. Someone'll see him. I have no doubt."

"I'm glad he did." Martha leaned heavily against her cane, but she swayed, the cane not doing a good enough job of holding her up.

Stanley caught her arm before she fell. He worried he'd overtaxed her. "Let's sit."

She nodded. Gently supporting her, he led

her to a chair on the opposite side of the room, away from Charlotte.

Once Martha was settled, he said, "I worry that Smith will come after her, Martha. If I hadn't been looking for Charlotte's father, none of this would've happened."

Martha placed her palm on Stanley's knee. "Nonsense. This wasn't your fault."

"Yes, it was."

She squeezed his hand. "And are you always able to control those around you who are trying to cause harm?"

"Well, no, but—"

"No buts, Mr. Seymour. You tried your best. She doesn't blame you for what happened, and neither do I. Without your help, we would've likely never found Marcus. While it ended badly, Charlotte was able to say her goodbyes."

He hung his head. While Martha had good intentions, it didn't absolve his guilt.

"Stanley, look at me."

He raised his head. She rarely said his first name, always being proper and polite by using his surname. Her gray hair was mussed, but a sincere smile lined her lips. She was likely concerned for his well-being when it should've been the other way around. He hadn't just lost a member of his family.

"That wasn't the first time Charlotte had spoken to her father. They'd spoken a few days ago. She kept it from me, as she was unsure what to do, and I'll venture to say she hadn't mentioned it to you either. I think she was trying to decide what to do." She raised a hand to her forehead. "While they didn't resolve the past between them, she was able to express her love to him."

"While I may not have found Marcus, my questions and pursuit of Marcus likely emboldened Smith to take Charlotte and Bertha. My poking and prodding almost sent them both into a life too horrible to contemplate." He pounded his fist into his palm.

"You can stop now." Martha gripped his fingers. "Being angry with yourself won't make Charlotte feel any better. In fact, I know she'll feel worse if you blame yourself." She let go and clasped her cane. "Now, why don't you go speak to Charlotte? I imagine you're eager to head home, and she'll want to speak with you before you do."

He wasn't sure about that, but he would appease the woman. It was the least he could do. "Thank you, Martha. It's been a pleasure getting to know you. I just wish I could stay longer to help you in any way you might need."

"You've helped us greatly. Now go talk with her. I'll wait here." She picked up a pot of tea and poured herself a cup.

He braced his hands on his knees to gather his courage. Charlotte still hadn't noticed he had arrived, or if she had, she didn't care that he was there. The loss of her father likely consumed her thoughts, and nothing he could do or say could take away that pain.

* * *

Stanley and Aunt Martha whispered behind her, but Charlotte ignored them. Instead, she stared at the fireplace, watching the red, yellow, and orange flames fighting each other to the top. It was quite warm wrapped in a thick quilt, but she didn't notice the heat. Tears slid unheeded down her cheeks, but she didn't bother to wipe them away.

When Stanley arrived, it would've been polite to turn and acknowledge his presence, but she lacked the energy to do so. She feared he blamed himself, but both he and Jacob had done all they could. First by trying to find her father and then by saving her from Mr. Smith and that horrible saloon owner, Zeke. Charlotte needed to thank him, but uttering the words required energy she no longer possessed.

She lost track of time, her focus on the flames while her mind clamored to make sense of everything. But nothing did. The pain of the past few days dulled her enthusiasm to see him. It was too late. The two of them were going their separate ways, and she'd never see Stanley again. She would return to St. Louis, and Stanley would return to Helena. If things had turned out differently, perhaps their last moments together would've been a precious memory to savor, but instead, they were tainted and ruined forever.

Stanley sat across from her, staring at her with sad eyes. He opened and closed his mouth a few times, as though trying to frame his words carefully for her sake. She hated that he felt uncomfortable in her presence, but there was no way to repair that. In the months they had known one another, there'd never been hesitation, but now there was. It was as though a large chasm had burst open like a mountain splitting from the top down, and no amount of dirt or rocks could repair the damage.

"How are you feeling?" he asked, the words stilted and awkward for them both.

She dropped her stocking-clad feet to the ground, slowly unfolding herself to face the man who meant the world to her. This was her last chance to tell him how she felt, but she didn't know if she was brave enough.

"I'm…" She reached for the tall glass of water on the table next to her and took a sip to wet her dry mouth. "I'm about as well as can be expected, I suppose."

He avoided her gaze, bouncing his knee before he cleared his throat. "I wanted to express my condolences. We haven't talked since… since the other day. I wanted to… Well, I mean… I'm leaving tomorrow. I didn't want to leave without saying goodbye."

"I'll be fine with time, I'm sure." She tried to smile but failed. It was hard to find joy in the depths of her suffering, although she was alive and shouldn't wallow in her misery. "Thank you for coming by. I hoped to see you, but I didn't want to presume."

He raised his hand as though he were going to touch her, but then he stopped and pulled it back. "I wish it was under better circumstances. Charlotte, I… I need to apologize—"

She held up her hand, her trembling fingers embarrassing, but she was determined to stop him. "Please don't."

"If you had never met me—"

"If I hadn't, then I likely wouldn't have been able to tell my father how I felt. For that, I will be forever grateful." She truly meant that, as hard as it was to accept she'd never see her father again.

"But because of me—"

"Because of Mr. Smith," she snapped, "my father is no longer with us."

Stanley winced.

She tried to soften her tone. "You tried your best to keep me from harm and could've been killed." She scooted to the edge of the sofa, the blanket falling forgotten to the ground. She reached for his hand and rubbed her thumbs against the rough skin of his palm, wishing things were different. "Stanley, I..." She bit her lower lip. It was too hard to say, but she had to find a way. "I appreciate everything you've done for me. My life has become richer, fuller after spending time with you. If things were different, I had hoped... Well, I had hoped more would develop between us."

The dark circles of his eyes widened until

they were almost black, eliminating the brown, but he stayed silent.

She had said too much, but it was too late to swallow the words. They were out there, and it was up to him to respond.

When he continued to look like a deer who'd been caught by a grizzly bear with nowhere to run, she filled the silence. "Thank you for saving me and doing your best to ensure my safety."

He finally opened his mouth to speak, but she shook her head to stop him.

"Please say nothing. You'll forget about me with time, but I wanted you to know that you'll forever hold a place in my heart." She paused for a long moment, resting her fingers against her lips before they dropped away. "I fell in love with you, Stanley Seymour. I don't expect you to return my feelings, but I couldn't let you leave without telling you."

As the words fell from her lips, she was surprised she had said them. His shuttered expression told her she likely should've said nothing, but the words were out there, and she couldn't take them back. If she were totally honest with herself, she wasn't sorry she had said them. If it was to be the last time she ever laid eyes on him, then it was better to be honest and not hold anything back. It wouldn't change anything, but at least she would have no regrets.

Chapter 28

May 22, 1901

Stanley dragged himself to the pitcher of water resting on the nearby vanity. His mocking reflection told him he'd made a huge mistake, one he'd never recover from. After pouring himself a glass of water, he downed the liquid before taking a solid breath. It helped his mouth and throat but did nothing to ease the throbbing behind his eyes or in his soul. He needed something stronger than water to curb that problem. Grabbing his pocket watch, he squinted at the time and groaned. It was a few minutes past seven, and he still needed to get a bite to eat for the long train ride home, although he wasn't sure he had the appetite to put anything in his belly.

Sickened with his appearance, he moved to stare out the window and squinted at the sun that had already started to rise from its slumber. The events of the night before still raced through his mind. After he left Charlotte and Martha, he had returned alone to his room. Conflicting emotions tore through his soul—emotions he wasn't prepared to face.

The night before he'd sat alone in the dark, watching the flickering lights from the saloons while the men inside played cards, laughed, and drank. Trying to analyze Charlotte's words, he couldn't come to terms with them. He could only surmise that she was distraught over her father's death and hadn't been thinking clearly.

His heart had about stopped with shock when she said she loved him. There was no way she could. It wasn't possible. His involvement in her life had caused her nothing but pain, and yet she held no animosity toward him. She had to be confusing gratitude with love.

After her words, he'd been embarrassed and unable to respond. Instead, he had mumbled something incoherent and escaped from their room faster than a hare being chased by a raccoon.

Pushing away from the window, he dropped heavily into a chair, rested his elbows on his knees, and hung his head. His heart and mind were torn in two different directions. He had been on a mission to find Connie for years, not allowing himself to feel or grieve his pa's passing. When he discovered Michael had killed Connie, he should have been relieved, but it had only compounded his guilt.

He had been running from his problems, staying far from his family for fear they blamed him for his pa's murder. When, in truth, they didn't. He just hadn't wanted to trust in their love. Instead, he'd chosen to believe that his family didn't want him. It was almost as though

Connie were still whispering in his ear that he didn't need them and that they didn't want him.

Yet he still felt anxious and unsettled. He stood and paced, sweat building under his arms and rolling down the middle of his back. Stanley didn't know what was wrong with him. He didn't have any injuries from the scuffles, so it wasn't physical. He wondered if it wasn't simple and had everything to do with Charlotte.

Are my feelings for her more than I want to admit?

She was beautiful, both inside and out. Her smile, her determination, her quick wit, and her ability to fight back all packaged together to make the perfect woman.

Why am I so afraid to explore what she clearly wants from me?

There was a soft knock on the door. There was no telling who could be behind it at that time of the morning. While he didn't think it was anything to be concerned about, he couldn't be too sure. He still didn't know where Smith had gone.

He grabbed his revolver and held it behind his back as he opened the door. It was Jacob. He relaxed and placed the gun back on the table.

"Jacob," he said. "It's right early. Is something amiss?"

Jacob pushed past him and stalked to the window. "So, you're leaving then?"

"Yes. You knew I was."

"I did." Jacob dropped the drapes and turned back to him. "But I didn't think you were stupid enough to do it without taking her with you." He plopped into a chair and slapped his hat onto the table.

"I don't know what you mean," Stanley said, although he *absolutely* knew what Jacob meant.

"Don't be obtuse. I've watched you with Charlotte. The two of you have something special, but you've let your obsession with Connie color everything in your life."

"I haven't—"

"Yes, you have." He tipped his head back and looked at the ceiling. "For almost eight years, you've been hunting without taking the time to mourn your pa's loss."

"That isn't—"

"Stop, Stanley!" Jacob's tone deepened.

Jacob never called him by his given name. He'd only heard that sound twice in the years he had known Jacob, and they were memories he'd like to forget.

The first time, he had been young and angry with his pa. He'd gone to Jacob, thinking he'd understand and be on his side. He'd underestimated Jacob's reaction and had been scared beyond measure when Jacob grabbed him by the scruff of his neck and dragged him back to Thundering Mountain Ranch to apologize to his pa. Stanley hadn't wanted to talk to his pa, hadn't wanted to do what Jacob demanded, but Jacob had insisted.

The look of relief on his pa's face when Jacob threw him into his study after two days of letting him worry would forever be imprinted in his brain. His pa had been angry and relieved, but Stanley had been obstinate and out of sorts, blaming both his pa and Jacob for making him do things he hadn't wanted to do.

The second time had been when Jacob had saved him from the group of outlaws who had robbed a bank, and just like the first time, the sound of Jacob's voice was soul-searing and not something he wanted to hear.

"You're acting like a fool, and I didn't think I'd have to knock you upside the head to get you to figure that out," Jacob said, reminding him once again that he was making another mistake.

"Charlotte's returning to St. Louis, and I have to get back to Helena. You know my family needs me."

"Your family wants you to quit wallowing and be happy." Jacob rested his hands on his knees.

Stanley bit the inside of his cheek. "You don't understand." He wanted to shout at someone, and Jacob was handy. "You haven't been to the ranch in over ten years, long before Pa died, so you have no right—"

"You know there were reasons for that." Jacob frowned, the lines deepening near his lips.

"Reasons you never told me when you disappeared."

Jacob pinched the area between his eyebrows. "Your pa and I had our differences, that's for sure, but he meant the world to me, just as you do."

"How do I know that's true?" Stanley rubbed his hand across the back of his neck. "You didn't even come to his funeral."

Jacob slammed his fist onto the table. "I didn't know he'd passed until months later. By that time, I wasn't welcome anywhere near the ranch. You treated me the same as your brothers when you made them leave."

A sour taste filled Stanley's mouth. "Don't remind me of how horrible I was. I'm perfectly aware I acted erratically in doing what Connie wanted. I regret that more than you'll know." Anguish tore at his soul for his stupid decisions.

"Then why are you still punishing yourself?" Jacob leaned forward and rested his elbows on his knees.

Stanley squeezed shut his eyelids. "I'm not."

"Are you sure about that? You helped Charlotte get what she needed, and yet you're still running away."

"I'm not running away, dammit! My family needs me."

"Anne's home safe. They don't need you to give up another important person in your life. You pushed away the love of your family and the comfort they offered, all to find the woman who pulled you away to begin with. You've let Connie control your actions for the last eight years. It's time to stop. Your family would understand if you were to stay another few days."

"Stay here to do what?" Stanley mumbled.

Jacob pushed from his chair and stalked toward Stanley, grabbing his forearms and holding him steady. "Don't pretend you don't know exactly what I'm referring to. Go to her. Tell her how you feel and make her your own."

Stanley shrugged out of his grasp. "What if she doesn't want that?" Although he was being ridiculous if what she said wasn't a sign that she wanted something more of him. She said she was in love with him for heaven's sake.

"And what if she does?"

Stanley dug his fingers into the back of a nearby chair. He didn't deserve whatever Charlotte might want to give him. He had given up the right to happiness the moment he caused his pa's death.

"Quit overthinking it." Jacob's voice grew soft, as though he realized he might've pushed Stanley too far. "Do the right thing." He paused and picked up his hat. "Give your brothers my regards. I'm leaving in the morning. Perhaps one day I'll visit the ranch. For now, I wish you all the best."

After Jacob left, Stanley washed, pulled on a clean set of clothes, and did a quick check of his belongings, making sure they were tucked into his carpetbag and that he'd left nothing behind. When he left his hotel room, the snap of the lock sent a finality through his spine.

After returning his key to the hotel clerk and having him hold his bag until he was ready to board the train, he turned and was shocked to see Charlotte running toward him, fear etched all over face.

"Is everything all right?" he asked, scrutinizing her.

"Thank heavens you're here. We need to call for the sheriff." She fiddled with the lace of her bodice.

"What? Why?" He raised a hand to her cheek and swept away a tendril of her hair.

"Mr. Smith was just here."

Stanley hadn't even seen the man. "Damnit! Stay here."

He ran out the front doors of the hotel, pushing his way through a crowd waiting for two trains to pass. He looked both ways and scanned the throngs of people but didn't see any man with red hair.

He slapped his hand on his hip. Smith had slipped away again. He's mistakenly assumed Smith had left Pocatello. They had all assumed that, and clearly they'd been wrong.

After continuing to look for a few minutes, he

found no sign of the man. Stanley had no idea where Smith had gone, but he couldn't leave Charlotte inside alone for much longer. He likely shouldn't have run out without making sure one of the hotel clerks was aware of the potential danger she might be in.

Back inside, he found her pacing in front of the dining room doors. "Charlotte," he called.

Her head whipped around, and she visibly sighed with relief. "He got away again, didn't he?" she asked as soon as he stepped near her side.

He nodded, his breathing hot and heavy after running through the thick crowds. "I don't know where he went. There was no sign of him."

Charlotte touched his arm. "It's my fault. I shouldn't have come down here when I got the note, but I thought—"

"What note?"

With shaking hands, she reached into the pocket of her skirt and pulled out a crumpled piece of paper. He took it from her and quickly scanned it, muttering under his breath. Smith had clearly written the note pretending to be Stanley. He had even signed it with a signature that looked remarkably like his. The man was becoming more and more brazen, not to mention extremely dangerous.

"What did he want?" he snapped, his voice curt and angry.

She startled at his tone but didn't let his outrage further ruffle her feathers. It seemed to embolden her, instead. "What do you think, Stanley?"

He gripped the front of his vest but slammed his mouth shut.

"He was demanding that I tell him where the blasted gold was."

"Smith isn't going to leave you alone until he finds that gold." Stanley was sick to think what Smith would do to her if he were to get his hands on her again.

"I don't know where it is. My father didn't tell me," she cried.

"I know."

"What if he... Oh! No!" She grabbed her

skirts and took off running toward the wide staircase.

"Hell!" It hit him like a ton of bricks.

Martha! Charlotte was worried about her aunt. He should've been as well. If Smith had gone upstairs to Martha instead of outside toward the trains like Stanley had assumed, they could be too late. It hadn't even crossed Stanley's mind that Smith would've gone after Martha, but he had tried it just days before and had almost succeeded in killing her. Would he try again?

Chapter 29

May 22, 1901

Charlotte and Stanley rushed up the stairs. She careened to a stop in front of her hotel room and fumbled for the key in her pocket, finally pulled it free, and then promptly dropped it. Her terror over her aunt's safety caused her to tremble like a scared little girl.

Stanley nudged her out of the way and unlocked the door. He rushed inside, a revolver in his hand. She hadn't even seen it. Her focus on getting to her aunt overrode anything else.

"Martha!" Stanley yelled.

"Whaaaattt?" Martha screeched. Her knitting flew from her hands like a rock from a slingshot, but instead of hitting an opponent, it hurtled back to the earth and hit Martha in the head before flopping to the ground. "Ouch!"

Charlotte slammed to a stop, straight into Stanley's strong back. His grunts echoed in her ears, but she stumbled around him and fell to the floor in front of her aunt. "Are you all right?"

Aunt Martha rubbed at a spot on her head and glared at Charlotte. "Of course, I'm all right. Or I was until you two came running in here like the devil himself was chasing after you." She frowned. "What in heaven's name is the cause of all this fuss?" She bent and picked up her knitting. "Look at what you made me do. How many stitches have I dropped? I'll have to start all over."

Charlotte started laughing hysterically. Her aunt was all right, but the look on her face had been too much. Giggles erupted out of her mouth like a volcano. All the worry and anxiety over what could've happened to her aunt made her lose her composure in a ridiculous fashion.

"I don't know what's so funny, young lady," Martha muttered. "Ruining my knitting is not something I appreciate."

"I'm so sorry, Aunty, but I thought…" Giggles erupted again. She was being uncommonly rude, but she'd rather be laughing. The alternative was too horrible to contemplate.

The hotel door slammed shut, and Stanley threw the lock.

"What is wrong with you two?" Martha asked.

Stanley didn't answer but strode to the window and pulled back the drapes, the revolver held near his ear, a stern expression on his face. He stared out the window for a long moment before he sighed and shoved the revolver into the back of his trousers. "I think we're safe. He doesn't appear to be anywhere near here."

Martha grabbed her cane and struggled to stand. "All right, you two, what is going on?"

"Aunty, please sit." Charlotte scrambled to

her feet and went to grab her aunt's elbow, but she waved her off.

"Do not patronize me, young lady. I've been through a nightmare this last week." Her sharp tone snapped into Charlotte, the rebuke clear.

Charlotte cringed and turned her gaze toward the dark bruises surrounding her aunt's eye and across her cheek. Her aunt had been through too much—all because of her and her quest to find her father. She should be more considerate.

"You're right." Charlotte took a deep breath, a thick lump in her throat. "You have, and I'm sorry if we scared you."

"You didn't scare me, but you did startle me and ruined my knitting. Now, I ask you again— what is going on?"

Stanley strode across the room and took her aunt's elbow. "Let's sit and I'll explain."

"No, I'll explain," Charlotte said, bristling at Stanley's authoritative tone.

He swung his thead toward her, but he didn't stop helping her aunt. Once her aunt was settled on the sofa, Charlotte picked up the ruined knitting and placed it on the table.

"Thank you, my dear." Her aunt patted Charlotte's hand.

Deciding her aunt would not appreciate her dancing around the issue, she said, "The note I received this morning, I thought it was from Stanley, but it wasn't."

"Who sent the note?"

Charlotte and Stanley shared a glance. He cocked an eyebrow as if saying, *you didn't want me to explain so go right ahead*. Irritation crawled through her when he smirked. He was giving her the floor, and yet she wasn't saying a word.

"Charlotte Ann McVicker, who sent that note?" Martha's voice sliced across the room like a scythe across ripe wheat.

She gulped. While telling her aunt what had happened would be the right thing to do, it didn't make it any easier. "It was Mr. Smith."

Aunt Martha's cheeks reddened, and she tightened her fists in her lap.

"Nothing happened, though," Charlotte said. "He tried to hold me against the wall but—"

"He was holding you against the wall and nothing happened?" Aunt Martha snapped.

"Aunty—"

"Don't you aunty me, young lady. This situation has grown even more precarious. I already had reservations about us heading back to St. Louis without any protection after everything that happened, and now this has just cemented my fears. Mr. Smith is determined to find that gold and believes you are the key to it."

"I'm not. I have no idea where that gold is, and even if I did, I certainly wouldn't tell him."

"We all know that, Charlotte," Stanley said. "But Smith believes you do, and until he finds that gold or you are out of his reach for good, you and your aunt are in serious danger."

Those ominous words hung over the room like a pall at a funeral—heavy, dark, and foreboding.

"I can't live my life being afraid of him," Charlotte said.

"No, you can't, but I can't protect you either," Aunt Martha said, her eyes downcast. The strength she had shown just moments before seemed to be sucked out of the room at an alarming rate. It was as though she realized she couldn't stop the train wreck that was occurring before her.

Stanley crossed his arms across his chest. "You and your aunt will come with me to Helena."

* * *

As soon as the words fell from his lips, Stanley knew he was right. It was the obvious choice and the safest route for Charlotte and her aunt until the authorities could arrest Smith.

"No, that is ridiculous," Charlotte said, jumping to her feet. "Going to Helena is *not* an option. I need to return home to St. Louis. I can't continue to put you in the middle of this mess. I've caused you enough trouble."

"If Smith hadn't lured you to the lobby this morning, I likely would've agreed with you."

Charlotte pursed her mouth into a thin line. It was as though he'd gut-punched her, but she quickly shuttered the pain, trying to hide her true feelings from him. He'd hurt her once again.

She had to realize that he wasn't good enough for her and never would be. He ran his hand through his hair. She was a temptation he didn't need but one he had nonetheless. "It isn't safe for you to travel alone, not anymore."

"I won't be traveling alone. I'll be with my aunt."

"You're being impertinent. Mr. Seymour is only trying to help." A gleam brightened Martha's eyes. She was no doubt thinking the turn of events would work in her favor. He wasn't immune to the fact that Martha wanted the two of them together, but Charlotte deserved someone much better than him, even if a part of him wanted to love her in return.

"No disrespect to your aunt, Charlotte, but she can't protect you from Smith."

"Humph," Martha muttered.

"If he wants to hurt me, he'll find a way," Charlotte snapped.

"Which is why you need to come with me."

"Helena is not on the way to St. Louis. It's south, not north."

Her stubbornness was going to be the death of him, but he couldn't in good conscience leave her and Martha to fend off the man. She was at Smith's mercy, and it was up to Stanley to keep her safe. It might also be the only way to save himself, to know there was good in him and that he was worthy of the love his family proclaimed to have for him.

He reached for Charlotte and gently placed his hands on her shoulders. She stared at him defiantly.

"I understand that, but it'll confuse Smith. He'll expect you to head to St. Louis on the southern route. If you come with me to Helena, we can lose him." She tried to twist away, but he held firm. "I know this isn't what you want and isn't ideal… But for the sake of your aunt, please do as I ask. You can stay at my family's ranch until we can be assured Smith is no longer a threat. At that point, I'll escort you to St. Louis and into your grandfather's hands."

Chapter 30

May 26, 1901

The wagon rumbled underneath the tall, wide pine arches of the sprawling Thundering Mountain Ranch. Charlotte couldn't believe how truly beautiful the place was. The trip to Helena had been long and almost surreal, but the open, green spaces had been certainly more magnificent than any place she had ever visited. She wasn't sure if it was because of the area itself or because of the man sitting beside her. Stanley oozed confidence as they inched closer and closer to his home. His strength, his determination, his pure masculinity made her salivate. If she wasn't careful, she'd jump into his arms at the first sign that he might be interested in her, and that would not do, not at all. She had already bared her soul and he hadn't returned her feelings.

As they came through the opening to the ranch, Charlotte asked Stanley if the sign above was the original one. He nodded and then had the ranch hand slow the wagon to a stop.

"It's weathered," Stanley said, "but still as strong as the day Ben and I helped Pa lift it into place."

A snow-peaked mountain range stood tall and magnificent in the distance, and pine trees lined the road, some looking like they had been there for years while others were freshly planted.

"Why is the ranch called Thundering Mountain?" Aunt Martha asked.

"Ma thought it was proper considering the mountains over yonder." He pointed to the mountain range Charlotte had just been admiring. "And because when we arrived, a huge thunderstorm was blowing through. Pa told us Ma saw the lightning flashes striking the mountain and decided it was a fittin' name. Ma's word was law, and Pa agreed when she said she wanted to call it Thundering Mountain." His sweet smile softened his face as he gazed up at the sign. "All of us decided years ago that we would name our own spreads in the same manner. Luke calls his place Thundering Ridge, and my brother-in-law calls his Thundering Meadows."

"What would you call your home?" Aunt Martha asked.

Stanley grinned. "I've always been partial to Thundering Snow myself."

"And why's that?" Aunt Martha said.

"I've always loved snow, and one of my favorite things to do—besides playing in it, mind you—was sitting on the front porch watching the snowflakes drop from the sky. I'd sit outside for hours. There'd be times when Ma would drag me inside, my hands and feet near frozen to death, but a big ole smile stuck on my face. It might've been frozen there, but I didn't care. I've always loved it." He rubbed at his scruffy chin. "No one else has claimed the name so when I finally settle on the piece of land Pa left for me, I think that'd be what I name it."

The memories of that day brightened Stanley's cheeks, and he relaxed his shoulders, the tension of the past seeming to ease out of him as he stared across the wide-open space.

Charlotte's ire with Stanley had slowly disappeared over the past few days of traveling, but she wasn't willing to tell him that he might've been right about her and her aunt traveling to Helena. She didn't want to admit that maybe, just maybe, Mr. Smith scared her far more than she had at first realized. Instead, she'd rather make Stanley stew a tad bit longer. His heavy-handedness in insisting she and her aunt follow him to Helena had irked her to no end. After he told her aunt she might be in danger, her aunt had agreed almost too quickly and had shuffled her out of that hotel room and onto the same train as Stanley before she had a chance to completely think it through.

Her aunt was no doubt still trying to throw the two of them together, but she kept those thoughts to herself. There was no hope for a future between them, no matter how much her aunt wished it were different.

As the wagon moved closer to the ranch house, Charlotte's nerves were strung thin. They were imposing on Stanley's family, regardless of what he said. He hadn't even had a chance to send a telegram informing his family they were coming. She was sure they'd be shocked and dismayed at the intrusion. Even the ranch hand had been surprised when he'd arrived, expecting to find just Stanley, but instead, he'd found two women and a stack of trunks along with them.

If it had been up to Charlotte, they would've stayed in Helena, but both Stanley and her aunt outvoted her. She'd quit protesting after her aunt silenced her with a vicious glare, but if there was any sign his family felt they were imposing, she'd insist they leave and head back to Helena. If needed, she would telegram her grandfather and ask that he send someone to guard them on their return to Helena.

Finally, the wagon pulled to a stop in front of a rambling three-story ranch house, the remnants of the fire that ravaged the home the year before still evident. Black scorch marks ran up the far side that had yet to be painted. The blackened wood was next to fresh cut planks. Some of the porch posts were new while others that were clearly weathered had survived the fire. A few men were putting in new windows and there were even men on the roof, hammering in shingles.

It appeared they'd made significant headway in fixing what had been destroyed. Stanley had told them to be prepared, but he looked shocked at the progress his family had made in repairing it. She couldn't imagine what it had looked like before, but if what she saw was any indication, it was a magnificent home that held a lot of love.

The sun was dropping behind the mountain range, streaks of red and orange illuminating the sky, but there was still enough light to see. The front door opened, and a stream of people emerged. Stanley jumped from the wagon and was engulfed in one man's arms before being passed into the arms of two other men—one of them being his younger brother Michael. The resemblance between the four men was uncanny. Stanley belonged to that family.

A few words were spoken between Stanley and the men before a woman with a thick brown braid draped across her shoulder joined them, a beaming smile on her lips as she pulled Stanley into her arms.

A pang of jealousy soared through Charlotte, but then the woman pulled away and moved near one of the other men. He put his arms around her waist, and Charlotte instantly felt better. She wasn't used to such feelings of jealousy for a man who sent tingles to her toes, a song to run through her heart, and a quiver of anticipation deep in her belly whenever he smiled at her.

Embarrassed they'd arrived without notice,

Charlotte wished she'd put her foot down and insisted they stay in Helena. But before she could say a word, the ranch hand helped her Aunt Martha down from the wagon. Her aunt's smile was a mile wide, her enthusiasm infectious. Her aunt would find nothing but joy in their latest adventure. Charlotte, on the other hand, was afraid her feelings would be evident for everyone to see, feelings that Stanley would never reciprocate.

* * *

As soon as Ben approached, Stanley pulled him to the side and explained why he'd arrived with the two women in tow. Being the host and protector he was, Ben was quick to agree. Elizabeth then enveloped him in a warm embrace. She had brought nothing but joy to his brother's life and made him smile.

Stanley had always wanted a wife like Elizabeth. She was pure, loving, and giving.

"It's so good to see you, Stanley," Elizabeth

said, releasing him from her arms. "I'm so glad you've come home."

"It's good to be home, Elizabeth." Looking at Ben, he asked, "Where's Anne?"

Ben's gaze was solemn, and he pulled Elizabeth to his side, wrapping his arm securely around her waist. "She and the children are inside. She's glad to be home but is still somewhat afraid to venture from there."

Stanley frowned. "Is she hurt?"

"No. At least not physically." Elizabeth squeezed his hand. "But we can discuss this later. Let's get you and your friends inside where it's warm. I'm sure you must be exhausted. Are you going to introduce us?"

Stanley had been remiss in not immediately doing so. "Let me help Charlotte from the wagon and then I'll introduce you."

Charlotte was trying to find the best way to climb out of the wagon and while he wouldn't mind having another glimpse of her legs, he didn't think she'd want to show them to his brothers.

She grasped the top of his shoulders and let him lift her out of the wagon. Her hair brushed against his nose, and a hint of fresh roses tickled his senses. He rested his hands on her tiny waist far longer than was proper, but he couldn't help himself. The longer he was around her, the more he craved her presence, but his family eyed them closely. It was best not to look like a lovesick fool, although he was afraid he'd already done that without intending to.

He was afraid he was making decisions based on her feelings toward him instead of the real threat. He had no doubt he needed to keep her safe, but was his insistence on bringing her to Thundering Mountain because he feared Smith would follow or because he couldn't bear to hurt her? But he feared he'd hurt her more if she thought there was even a modicum of a chance that he would make her his. There was no future for them and better for that to be clear.

His brothers Michael and Luke had welcomed Martha, and she was busy discovering Luke's secrets within moments of meeting him. Luke looked a bit stunned at the nonstop questions, but Michael just grinned and encouraged her questions, if only to drive Luke to distraction. Of course, Michael had already met Martha just weeks before and he'd already been pumped for information. Martha had set her sights on Luke and was determined to discover all he held dear.

Leading Charlotte to where Martha stood, Stanley said, "Martha, Charlotte, this here is my family." He pointed to each person and recited their names. It'd take time before the two of them got everyone straight, not to mention plenty were still missing. "Everyone, this is Charlotte McVicker and her aunt, Martha Evans. They'll be staying with us for a few weeks."

Elizabeth greeted them, a bright smile on her lips. "Welcome to our home. Please come inside. I'm sure you're hungry and would like to freshen up." She took each of their hands and squeezed affectionately. "I imagine the trip was long, and you could use the rest. We can get to know one another in the morning."

Both Charlotte and Martha followed Elizabeth, with Martha chattering ceaselessly in Elizabeth's ear.

Once they disappeared, Luke turned to Stanley, his face solemn. "We're sure glad to see you, Stanley."

He swallowed. Without the presence of the women, he could no longer hide behind the pain his distance had caused. "Let's go inside and I'll tell you what's been going on."

"It's about time you've come home. You've been gone long enough," Michael said. "Things have been right boring around here without your sappy face."

Michael laughed and slapped Stanley on the back of his shoulders, trying to soften his words, but Michael was right. The years since his pa's death had been difficult. It was time to end the hurt, step up to what he'd done, and ask for their forgiveness. Maybe then he could start to live his life again.

Chapter 31

May 26, 1901

Charlotte and her aunt were ushered inside and led to a large room at the back of the house. Elizabeth asked if they'd be all right while she prepared two guest rooms.

"Of course," Charlotte said. "We've imposed. Please don't go to any trouble on our account."

Elizabeth grabbed her hands and squeezed. "You're not. If Stanley brought you with him, then you're important. You're welcome to stay as long as you need."

"Thank you." Charlotte blinked to keep the

tears at bay. *Why am I suddenly teary-eyed?* "I'm sorry. It's been a long couple of days, and much has happened." She raised her hand to her mouth to cover a wide yawn. "I think it has finally caught up with me."

Elizabeth gestured toward a plush sofa, waiting for her and Martha to sit. "You've nothing to apologize for. I won't bombard you with questions, but I want you to know you'll be safe here."

Elizabeth's words were needed, more than she'd realized. Tears leaked from under Charlotte's eyelids. She bowed her head and tried to wipe them away, but she had no doubt that Elizabeth likely saw.

Instead of commenting on the tears, Elizabeth said, "Rest now. I'll add fresh linens to your rooms and get you something to eat. I'm sure you're quite hungry, as the railroad isn't known for its fine cuisine."

Charlotte chuckled. "That would be much appreciated, especially for my aunt."

"Tsk, tsk, young lady. I'm perfectly fine."

Martha removed her hat, placed it next to her, and undid the buttons of her coat. She leaned her head back against the wooden scrolls at the top edge of the sofa and, a moment later, was sound asleep.

Charlotte stood and followed Elizabeth to the hallway. "She's plumb tired and won't admit it, but the trip has been hard on her. My aunt's getting older, you see. She means the world to me, so I…"

Elizabeth took her hand. "Family is special. We need to keep those important to us close. I understand that more than you'll know." Letting go, she rested her hands on her hips. "Now, I'll get those rooms freshened up and have Sophia whip up something tasty for your aunt. Does she like anything in particular?"

"Please don't go to any trouble."

Her gaze kind, Elizabeth said, "It's no trouble at all."

"Then perhaps some hot coffee and a slice or two of warm bread. She prefers not to eat this late, but I worry she hasn't had enough to keep up her strength."

"That is easy enough."

"Thank you."

Elizabeth tilted her head to the side. "What about you?"

"Oh, I don't need much. That'll do." It was bad enough they'd arrived unannounced. She didn't want them to go to any trouble on her account.

"Maybe it will, but I'll ask Sophia to prepare cold meats and cheeses too. She might have something else stuffed in the pantry. She's always got something delicious packed away somewhere."

"It's late. I'm sure she'd rather be sleeping than preparing food for uninvited guests."

"Nonsense. If I know Sophia, she has done it without me even having to ask. In fact..." Elizabeth's eyebrows rose as she looked past Charlotte. "She's right behind you with a tray full of food. She's a magical mind reader."

Charlotte turned and smiled at a woman with

black, curly hair, bright blue eyes, and a wide smile.

"Miss Elizabeth, I hope you don't mind, but I thought your guests might be hungry. I prepared something for them to eat." She held up a tray and tilted her head.

"She is a wonder." Elizabeth followed Sophia back into the room where they had left her aunt. "Sophia single-handedly keeps this family from falling apart. Can I help?"

"No, no. Just tell me where to place this. I'll bring you hot coffee and tea in just a moment."

Elizabeth pointed to a table on the far side of the room. A few minutes later, Elizabeth and Sophia left to freshen a couple of guest rooms. Charlotte didn't want to wake her aunt, but she also didn't want her to go to bed hungry.

When Charlotte gently shook her on the shoulder, her aunt snorted and sat up, rubbing at her eyes. "Did I fall asleep?"

"Yes, Aunty, but it's all right. It has been a long couple of days. They've brought us some warm food." Charlotte pointed to where bowls and platters waited for them. Her belly rumbled.

Martha struggled to stand but managed it with help from Charlotte. She pulled off her coat and dropped it across the back of the sofa. "I'm sorry I fell asleep. That certainly wasn't my intention." Fatigue lined her aunt's cheeks, and she leaned on Charlotte's arm.

"I know. Why don't we get you something to eat?"

An hour later, after eating their fill and meeting more of Stanley's family, they were shown to their rooms. While it'd been a joy to meet them, Elizabeth had caught the yawns both she and her aunt were trying to hide and had wrapped the evening to a close.

While Charlotte had been tired earlier, a surge of restless energy poured through her veins. The house had quieted as the children were nestled into their beds, and the women had disappeared into their rooms. The men were still ensconced in Ben's study and would likely be there for some time. Charlotte was sure Stanley was sharing why he had arrived with two women, as well as the escapades they had gotten into while in Pocatello.

Unable to settle the thoughts racing through her head and deciding fresh air was needed, Charlotte grabbed a shawl and found a door that led outside to the wraparound porch. The sky was dark, but bright stars twinkled high above them. There was something compelling about the night sky in the wide-open spaces of the West. It was something to behold and made you realize how small you were.

She sat in a rocking chair at the end of the porch and pushed off with her stockinged feet. She had kicked off her shoes before leaving her room, and her toes appreciated the freedom. Her thoughts raced to the horrible way her father had died. She didn't want to become maudlin, but she'd had no time to mourn his death and hated that she hadn't been able to bury him properly.

The day before leaving Pocatello, Charlotte had made arrangements with the local mortician to have him buried there. Her grandfather wouldn't finance shipping her father's body to St. Louis, and it was easier to leave him there. While not ideal, the mortician had sworn he would care for her father and that he would receive a proper burial. She had to take comfort in that. She could visit his grave one day in the future. If not, then at least they had made their peace before he'd taken his last breath.

As she sat on the porch, the moon moved out from behind a dark cloud, and while not a full moon, it shined brightly. When she was young, long before her father had left her in her grandfather's hands, her father had taken her outside and had sat with her on their porch, pointing out the stars and talking about how bright the moon was. He had made her smile, especially being wrapped in his powerful arms. He had always smiled and laughed, never raising his voice to her, and always loving on both her and her mother. Why things had deteriorated was something she'd never understand, but she still had happy memories she could hold near her heart, and nothing could ever take that away.

The back door opened and closed. She didn't turn to see who it was, for she had no need. She recognized the sound of his footfalls and, when he stepped near, his scent. It was woodsy, smelling of fresh pines. Stanley said nothing for a long while, instead rocking in the chair next to hers, the squeaking of the rails against the wooden porch the only sounds in the quiet night.

His hand eventually touched hers, and she didn't know what to make of it. Not wanting to disturb the moment, she kept the questions that burned inside her soul to herself. She didn't pull away, but she wanted to rail at him, yell at him for turning down her obvious invitation for something more. He had dragged her to Montana, insisting it was for her safety, and yet she had to know if there was more to it than that, but she wouldn't ask.

A moment later, Stanley cleared his throat. "Is

there anything I can do? I know it's been a long couple of days between the travel and with… Well, with…" His chair creaked to a stop, and he turned to face her. "I fear it's been a tad overwhelming meeting my whole family tonight."

She squeezed his hand. "I'm fine. Your family has been a welcome distraction. They are a friendly bunch, but I'm not sure I'll remember all their names. There are more people than I expected."

He chuckled and turned his gaze away. "Yes, everyone's here. We're full to the brim." He dropped her hand and rested his on his knee.

Her gaze darted to his long, slender, strong fingers. Heat circled her belly. Her thoughts were inappropriate. She took a shallow breath and tried to focus on his words.

"With as many people here, it's a good thing Ben built a third story to the house after the fire last year. Otherwise, we wouldn't fit."

She stopped rocking and turned to face him. "Oh, no. We took two of the rooms. I knew we should've stayed in Helena. I shouldn't have listened to you and insisted."

He had a reassuring smile. "You aren't. There's no need to fret. There are plenty of bedrooms. Frankly, I was surprised by how much the place has changed, and I was here just over Christmas. Ben planned well, and there are a few empty rooms from my last count. If it'd been a problem, I would've stayed in the bunkhouse with the ranch hands. My brothers would've done the same."

She sighed, her breath steaming from the cooling air. "I just don't want us to be an imposition." She pulled the wool shawl tight across her shoulders. While she'd been blazing hot a moment before with her unsuspecting attraction, it had been replaced with chills from the cool air.

"You aren't. Trust me on that. You're welcome here. In fact, I'm glad you're here." His voice grew low and husky and awakened something deep within her. They'd had no time alone together while traveling to the ranch, and she didn't want to read anything into the moment, but a part of her couldn't help but do so. She searched his face for signs of what he meant, but under the porch awning, she wasn't able to see his features as well as she'd like.

"Your family's home is beautiful. Are you planning on staying here now that Connie is gone?"

He abruptly stopped his chair.

She had just ruined the moment. "I'm sorry. It's none of my business."

He stood and leaned over the porch railing, bracing his arms against the wood.

Why did I ask him that? Will I ever learn to be quiet?

"Thank you again for everything you have done for me and my aunt," she murmured.

He shook his head. "The genuine hero was your father. He died trying to help you. I should've done more and likely was the cause of his death by not getting to you sooner." He fisted his hand and slammed it against the wood.

She could hear the pain in his voice, and it

broke her heart. "No, Stanley." She walked to his side and placed a hand on the small of his back. When he didn't pull away, she left it there, trying to lend her support. "If you hadn't gotten involved in my life, as you say, I would've never found my father."

"But—"

"But nothing. My father died, yes, but not at your hands and not because of you. He died because of that evil man. Mr. Smith is the one who caused my pain. And while I hate to admit it after my stubbornness over the past few days, I'm even grateful you're trying to protect me from him. As you know I wasn't thrilled with your edict of my coming to Montana." She smiled, trying to ease the tension. "It seems I've caused *you* nothing but heartache."

"You don't understand. If I'd been able to find your father sooner, then none of this would have happened. It seems as though I'm always the messenger of pain!" He roared in the silent night, the sounds bouncing against the barn, causing even the horses inside to neigh with distress.

She shook her head. "I—"

He turned and grabbed her by the forearms, digging his fingers into her soft skin. She didn't pull away. He needed the comfort, and she could give it to him as distress poured from him like a waterfall after a harsh summer's rain.

Stanley shuddered and must've realized he'd been piercing her skin because he released her, brushing his fingers against the spots where he'd gripped her too tightly. Then he dropped his hands. He ran a shaking hand through his hair, a dull pain in his eyes she recognized all too well.

He brushed tendrils of her hair away. She should move away, not let him near, but she was frozen in place. He pushed them behind her ear, resting his palm on her cheek.

"You've caused me nothing but joy, Charlotte. I'm the one to blame for everything. I shouldn't be this close to you, but..." He dragged in a breath, held it for a long moment, then exhaled. He shook his head, his unkempt brown hair falling across his forehead. "I'm sorry, I shouldn't..."

Before she could take a breath, he pulled her into his arms and placed his lips against hers. The movement was swift, hard, and sinfully delicious. She shouldn't enjoy it and should resist, pull away, but swirling passion ran unchecked inside of her. She had wanted him to touch her again, and her wish had come true. She would enjoy every last second of it, no matter how long or short it lasted.

His lips molded against hers while he tightened his arms around her waist, pulling her against him. Goose pimples pierced her skin. She moaned and tugged at his collar, trying to pull him close, wanting to feel his skin against hers. He ran his hands across her back, one hand tangling into her hair, while the other skimmed along her side.

Then, without warning, he stopped and pulled away. Her chest rose and fell with unsuppressed desire. She wanted to pull him back, but common sense prevailed.

She stared at him for a long moment, hoping

he would say something, anything, to let her know how he truly felt.

He took a few steps back, widening the distance between them, both physically and emotionally. "I'm sorry. I... I overstepped. It's getting late. We should head to bed. We can talk more in the morning." The words rushed out of him quicker than a tornado dropping from the sky. He turned and left her standing alone on the porch, wondering what had just happened.

He kept running from her, and there was nothing she could do to stop him.

* * *

Stanley muttered obscenities under his breath as he stalked inside. He couldn't believe he had kissed her again. He had told himself he wouldn't touch her, no matter the circumstances, and once again, he couldn't seem to control his actions. While he thought he had brought her to Thundering Mountain to provide her a safe haven, he wondered if he had just dropped her into a viper's nest. One where he was the viper and she was the prey.

It had been a mistake to bring her there. He should put her on a train to St. Louis immediately. Ben would provide the men to ensure she and Martha were escorted safely into her grandfather's hands. Being around her was too much of a temptation. He wasn't sure he was the type of man she could rely on. He had to get out of her life before he hurt her further.

His anger at Connie had subsided slowly in the months since she'd been killed, but he still didn't trust himself or his actions. He had made several mistakes over the past few years and didn't know if he was making smart decisions when it came to Charlotte. His heart insisted she was perfect for him, but his head told him he was a fool to pursue a woman whose home was thousands of miles away. His home was here in Montana, and Charlotte could never be happy on a ranch. She was meant for high society with balls, operas, high teas, poetry readings, and any other number of events that took place in St. Louis. Helena would never compare.

For a moment eight years before, he'd thought he would enjoy being a cattle baron, owning the largest ranch in Montana, until he'd realized it was not his to begin with and never had been. He'd been jealous of Ben without realizing his pa's true will had left him a substantial piece of land just over the mountains. It was the perfect plot of land for him, as he could make it whatever he wanted. He could either build his own ranch or sell it and do something else entirely. His pa had known what he needed long before Stanley did.

He didn't need to complicate his life with a woman he couldn't even protect or offer a roof over her head. He had nothing to give her except perhaps his love, and he wasn't sure that was worth much. He couldn't be in love with her, especially since he didn't even know what that meant, not anymore.

Needing a drink, Stanley headed to Ben's study where he kept a cabinet of the finest liquors. Stanley shouldn't go in there without Ben's permission, especially considering all that had happened in 1893, but Ben would forgive him for the slight if he knew why he was looking for a drink.

Inside the study, he pulled on the cord for the gas lamp, stalked to the cabinet, pulled out a decanter, and poured himself a hefty drink. His movements were abrupt. The glass cracked against the decanter, the liquid sloshing over the sides and wetting his fingertips. He downed it in one gulp. The liquid burned his throat but warmed his insides at the same time.

"Going to get yourself drunk, I see."

Stanley spun around. Luke was sitting in an armchair in the corner, a glass of whiskey in his hands. He didn't appear to have drunk much of it, but Luke had never been a big drinker.

Grimacing, Stanley nodded. "I guess I'm joining you." He pointed to the glass in Luke's hand.

Luke took a sip. "Yes, it's a night for spirits."

"I didn't expect to find anyone in here. The light was off."

Luke shrugged. "It was still daylight when I sat down. I just hadn't moved to turn it on yet."

Stanley poured more into his glass before sitting in the leather chair across from Luke. "Can you believe it's finally over?"

Luke didn't ask what he meant. He didn't need to. "No, it doesn't seem real. Those months of chasing her were hard, but in the end, I found Louisa, and for that, I'll be eternally grateful. Some part of me is disappointed it was Michael who ended her, but if he hadn't, I'd likely be dead in the ground, so I really can't hold a grudge."

"I'm just as angry that it wasn't me who ended her. She hurt all of us."

"She sure did." Luke took another sip of his whiskey, a pensive smile on his lips. Luke's smile was one Stanley hadn't seen since before Connie came into their lives and upended everything. It was nice to see his brother happy again. They had his wife, Louisa, to thank for it. While Connie's death might've lifted the pressure on Luke, Stanley believed it was Louisa loving Luke that made the real difference. If only he had the same.

"She's gone, Stanley." Luke leaned forward, resting his elbows on his thighs, stroking his fingers along the edge of the thick beveled glass. "It's time to let it go. You've tortured yourself enough over the years. What will it take for you to forgive yourself?"

Stanley lifted the drink to his lips and took a long gulp. The whiskey burned his throat and gave him a moment to answer Luke's question.

"Drowning your sorrows won't solve it, either."

Stanley dropped the glass onto the table. Luke was right. He had eased up on the liquor over the past few weeks, but giving in and kissing Charlotte tonight had undone his tenuous control.

"Ben'll do anything to keep you from leaving. You know that, right?" Luke asked.

Stanley rubbed his forehead. "Ben does prefer to save us from ourselves, doesn't he?"

Luke peered at him. "I know things have been difficult between you two for years, but he doesn't hold a grudge. I'm not sure he ever did." The glass twirled between Luke's fingers. "Sure, he was plenty upset when he discovered what Connie did, but he doesn't blame you." He held up a hand to stop Stanley's protest. "He might've at first, but he was quick to get over it. It helped that Elizabeth stepped into his life and filled a hole he didn't know was missing. I was angry with you as well, but my anger was misplaced. I'm ashamed that I treated you so abominably."

Stanley listened carefully to Luke and wanted to believe that Ben didn't blame him. Sure, Ben had told him plenty of times over the years that he hadn't, but how could he not? "It was my fault."

"No, it was Connie's. She had a vendetta and was going to try to ruin our family, regardless. She latched on to you first. It could've been Ben if she could've found him before you. No offense, brother dear, but your brothers are a tad bit more handsome and, dare I say it, more charming than you."

Stanley laughed. "Kind of surprised you'd say that. I'd expect Michael to make a joke, not you."

Luke ran a hand through his hair and then leaned back in his chair, the glass resting on his knee. Amused eyes stared at him. "Guess the love of a good woman is changing me."

"Guess so." Stanley pushed to stand. "Need a refill?"

Luke shook his head.

"I should've seen what she was up to." He placed his empty glass next to the decanter. He really wanted another drink, but he'd abstain.

Luke waved his hand in the air, brushing away Stanley's words. "That's all in the past. As far as seeing her diabolical plans, I didn't see it either. Remember, I'm the distrusting one."

"Maybe, but I was married to her. I should've known her better than anyone else, and because I didn't see what she was up to, Pa's gone."

"You're right. He is. But we can't change it." Luke placed his glass on the table and crossed to the bookshelf, running his fingers across the book's spines. "Pa always loved to read. Both of them did. I wish I would've listened to him more and not fought him as much as I did, but he never held a grudge. He always forgave us, no matter the transgression." Luke pulled a book from the shelf. Placing a finger against the cover, he said, "I remember a time or two when you pushed him to his limits, and he always welcomed you home with open arms. You can continue to blame yourself and be miserable, or you can pull up your boots, clean yourself up, quit drinking, and cease your endless wallowing. Eight years of self-recrimination is long enough."

Stanley hung his head. "You've given me plenty to think about."

"Good. Now, tell me about this woman you brought home. She's a pretty little thing. Not as beautiful as my Louisa, but she suits ya."

"Oh, it's nothing like that between us." Heat climbed up his neck. *Why am I lying? She does suit me.*

Luke chuckled. "Who's lying to themselves

now? It took me months to realize what I could've lost in my haste to end Connie. Don't make the same mistakes I did."

He'd love to make Charlotte his, but it wasn't the right time. "Not sure I trust myself around women. I don't have an impressive record."

"You were young and stupid. Now you're..." Luke smiled wide. The gas lighting sent a glow across the room. "Well, now you're just old."

Chapter 32

June 1, 1901

Stanley pulled on the reins, rested his elbows on the pommel of his horse, and stared at the piece of property his pa had left him. He hadn't been there in years. There had been only one person he wanted to see the piece of land with, and she rested on the horse next to him. He didn't have to turn to see that Charlotte was likely beaming with joy. She'd been extremely excited when he agreed to take her for a ride that morning.

They'd been back at Thundering Mountain for almost a week. He had tried to convince

Charlotte and Martha to return home to St. Louis, but Martha refused, insisting she wasn't up for the trip after everything that had happened and needed the rest. Charlotte had studied him hard but hadn't said a word, waiting for him to explain why, in one moment, he wanted them to be there and, in the next, insisted they needed to leave. He hadn't fought Martha's wishes. He truly didn't want Charlotte to leave, but he didn't know how to tell her.

Charlotte's aunt then made herself right at home and demanded, with a charming smile and twinkling eyes, that the ranch hands show her every inch of the place, from the cattle that roamed in the far pastures, to the vegetable garden that Sophia and her husband maintained, to the horses in the barn. She'd even sweet-talked their foreman, Sam, into showing her the bunkhouse where the men slept. She was full of questions, and her inquisitive nature made the men smile and do her bidding with no question.

Of course, she also regaled them with stories of her youth and the escapades she had gotten into during the War Between the States. The ranch hands and Martha would sit in front of a firepit until the wee hours, laughing and having a good ole time. She could certainly hold her liquor and gave a few of them a run for their money.

Charlotte spent most of her time with his sisters and sister-in-law, but that morning, she'd found him working with the horses in the barn and asked if he would take her for a ride. He agreed, unable to deny her anything, and hours later, they ended up on what was his land. He hadn't meant to go there, but they had landed there, regardless.

After dismounting, he tied his horse to one of the many pine trees and then turned to help Charlotte, but she'd already slid off her horse, the reins held loosely in her hand. She wore a white cotton blouse with delicate lace around the neck and sleeves. Sturdy boots adorned her feet, and a brown sensible skirt was tucked around her waist.

Not giving him a second glance, she handed him the reins and walked forward into the meadow of wild yellow, orange, red, and blue flowers. It was a place unspoiled, fresh as the day it was created.

Gushing waterfalls fell from the peaks of the mountains behind them into a raging river that would keep his cattle well-watered and the lands moistened for any hay he'd need. It was the same mountain range that butted up against the edge of Thundering Mountain. His pa had planned well in ensuring each of his children had a decent-sized plot of land for when he passed. They'd be far enough apart but still close that they could see one another whenever they chose.

The property was more than he remembered. The dreams he used to have came to the forefront of his mind. This time with Charlotte in the picture. He'd likely already ruined any chance he had by running from her. She loved him, and he kept throwing that love back.

Gathering courage he wasn't sure he had for fear she'd hate it, he asked, "What do you think of the place?" He held his breath, waiting to hear what she thought.

She brushed her lips with her fingers before raising her gaze to his. "It's beautiful, Stanley. It's one of the prettiest places I've seen yet. Even prettier than your family's ranch." She placed her hand on his forearm. "But don't tell Ben that, all right? It might offend him." She giggled.

His breath swooshed out of him. "Ah, it might do him good to be knocked down a peg or two, especially if *you* were to tell him. If I said it, he'd tell me something was knocked loose between my ears."

She grinned but then walked away, her skirt blowing in the wind. A breeze had crossed over from the river, keeping them slightly cooler than normal, which only made the day more pleasant.

"What do you want to do with the land?" She faced away from him, resting her hands on her hips. Her long blonde hair streamed behind her in a mass of curls, and he itched to sink his hands into it. She had secured it with a yellow ribbon, but it had loosened during their ride.

"Not sure yet."

She pointed to a high clearing set back from the river. "You could build a nice house over there. You'd want it up on a slight ridge so if the snowmelt is high any year, the house won't be in any danger of flooding. Then you could put a barn over there." She walked in the opposite direction. "And you'd want a sturdy corral, an icehouse, and a decent bunkhouse for your ranch hands, as you'll need plenty of help to handle the thousands of cattle you'll want, I'm sure." Her enthusiasm was contagious as she continued around the meadow, pointing out different possibilities.

For someone who hadn't been raised on a ranch, she was remarkably knowledgeable about what he'd need to start a working ranch. She'd clearly been listening as her aunt interrogated Ben and the ranch hands, but he shouldn't be surprised. Charlotte and her aunt were tenacious and determined to learn as much as they could about the ranch operations for reasons he didn't quite understand.

"Can I ask you something?" Stanley came up alongside her.

Charlotte stood on the small hill where she thought the house should stand. Her gaze was open and guileless. "Of course."

"Why are you so interested in ranch life?"

She looked startled by the question.

He hurried to clarify. "I don't mean that in a bad way. It's just… Well, I didn't get the impression that you lived on a ranch in St. Louis, so I'm just curious as to your interest, that's all."

Charlotte turned in a circle before facing him. "Our enthusiasm and questions are overwhelming, aren't they?" She then walked toward something that caught her eye. "I was sheltered living in St. Louis. Mother and Father lived simply, and there wasn't enough money to do much of anything, but I was happy and loved." She paused for a moment as though reliving a happy memory. "Then, when I moved in with Grandfather, he was busy with his work. I didn't get to see much more than what I could find in books. Not that I'm complaining, mind you. I had everything most young girls could want." She extended her hands and brushed the top of the flowers and leaves, skimming them to get a feel but not endangering them. "I'd read as many books as I could, trying to see what the world was all about. When I was given the opportunity to travel with Aunt Martha, well, I just wanted to see if what I read lived up to my imagination."

"And did it?" he whispered.

"No."

He felt a tug of disappointment. A part of him had hoped that she'd love it there and never want to leave.

"What I've seen has been far grander and more majestic than what I read or could've ever imagined. So, to answer your question, I'm curious and want to know all about it. This may be my one and only opportunity to see something different. I want to soak it in and enjoy it before I have to return." Her voice had lost its luster and had grown hollow.

He wanted to share the world with her. "You

don't have to leave." The words slipped past his lips before he could stop them.

She halted and didn't turn for a long moment. When she did, rage burned from her eyes, and her lips were pursed. Her hands were curled into tight fists and were resting on her hips. If he were within swinging distance, she likely would've hit him square in the nose.

"We've been here for a week. You've avoided me, and now you're telling me I don't have to leave." She growled, her chest rising and falling from the depth of her displeasure. "Anytime I walk into a room, you find a reason to leave it."

"That's not true. I'm out here with you now," he said, knowing full well she was right.

"Don't even…" Her face was bright red. "You wouldn't have taken me here if I hadn't caught you in the barn. With nowhere to run or hide, you were forced to do as I asked. You didn't seek me out and offer to show me your land. In fact, I think you'd be happier if I'd disappear."

"I haven't been trying to hide—"

"You stubborn, obstinate, pain in my…" She

mumbled the rest of her sentence under her breath.

"I—"

"You dragged me to Helena because you were afraid that Mr. Smith would try to harm me. Then you tried to convince me to leave. Now you want me to stay?"

"I didn't mean to—"

She held up her hand. "Make up your mind, you—you..."

He had to suppress a chuckle at the look of pure consternation on her face but this wasn't funny, and he would do well to remember that. "I didn't mean to be confusing."

She groaned. "Why can't you just say what you want?"

He tugged at the collar of his shirt, his discomfort growing with each moment that passed. He couldn't avoid the conversation, not any longer, but he wasn't sure what to say or do. His feelings were all over the place, and he feared he was making another mistake.

Stamping her foot, she burst forward. Her

footsteps were sure and strong as she stalked toward him like a barn cat after a mouse. Her skirts flew through the rainbow of colors at her feet, scattering the flowers with the force. He took a step back, but she reached him before he could escape.

"I adore you, Stanley Seymour," she spat. She jammed her finger into his chest. "No, that's not it." She wrinkled her forehead, and pulled at her hair before she halted and released her grip. "No! I'm so in love with you, I can't think straight. I can't sleep. I can't go one moment in your family's home without wondering why you kissed me if you didn't have at least a modicum of desire for me."

Speechless, he stumbled back.

She spun around, hiding her face from him and tucking her hands into the sides of her skirt. "I shouldn't have fallen in love with you. I had no reason to do that. You've kept me at arm's length, treated me as a sister or"—she turned back, her flying hair a cascade of curls—"as a business arrangement." Sorrow filled her voice. "I made the mistake of thinking that perhaps you'd find a way to forgive yourself for what you believed was your part in what happened to your pa. I wanted to believe that after we found my father, you'd quit drinking, forgive yourself, and then open your heart to someone who stood right in front of you." Tears leaked down her cheeks, and she swiped at them with a quick thrust. "I need to leave here. I don't belong here. I never—"

A gun shot shattered the air. Stanley jerked, and a sharp, piercing pain split him in half. He looked down and then lifted a hand to his belly, touching a growing red spot on his side.

* * *

Charlotte screamed in horror when blood bloomed on Stanley's side.

"Get down!" Stanley ripped his revolver from his gun belt and ran toward her. Bullets flew through the air and hit the ground all around them. It was as though a hailstorm had just erupted.

She stood petrified. His words couldn't penetrate the fear circling her like a cyclone—fast, furious, and out of control.

Stanley slammed into her and lifted her off the ground. He ran like the pits of hell were licking at his feet and flew toward a thick grove of trees. She gripped his shoulders hard, and he grunted but didn't stop until they were somewhat protected by the wide tree trunks. They had been out in the open, exposed but within seconds, he'd moved them out of immediate danger.

Breathing heavily, he pushed her behind him. His body was taut with tension, and he seemed to be ignoring the blood dripping down his side.

"You've been shot," she cried.

"I'm fine," he said, peering around the tree trunks.

"You're not fine!"

Bark shattered and flew from the tree above their heads.

"Get down!" Stanley said.

She ignored him, lifted up her skirts, and grabbed at her petticoat, ripping off a long piece. She had nothing else to stop the bleeding, although he didn't seem to be too concerned with his injury. He was going to be the death of her, but he would not die while she stood next to him. Stanley meant too much to her, and while he'd never love her in return, that didn't mean she couldn't save him if she had the chance.

She inched closer to him. "Let me look at that wound."

"We don't have time for that." He didn't even look at her. Instead, he was focused on the bullets hitting the ground and trees around them. He scanned the area in front of them, and then a tight smile lifted his cheeks. "There you are."

He raised his gun and taking a strong stance, he pulled the trigger. The blast of the gun blowing right near her ear made her shriek, but he didn't even turn to look at her. His focus was solely on eliminating the threat.

Then silence reigned. There was no return of

gunfire. Had he ended their pursuer with one shot?

Taking advantage of the lack of flying bullets, she grabbed his shirt and lifted it before he even realized she'd touched him.

He glanced down at her and lifted an eyebrow. "Really, Charlotte? Right now?"

Another bullet slammed into the tree trunk above them, and he jumped a bit.

"Dammit!" He turned his gaze back to where the bullets were coming from. Stanley hadn't ended the threat. Whoever was shooting at them was not going to be easy to eliminate.

Ignoring him, she probed his wound. He sucked in a breath but didn't take his eyes off the meadow they had fled from.

Eyeing his side carefully, she said, "It looks like the bullet went straight through."

"I kind of figured," he muttered, wincing and pulling back slightly as she continued to examine it.

"Don't be a smart-aleck," she said.

He chuckled. "Smart-aleck, huh? Didn't think

I'd hear something like that come out of your beautiful mouth."

She stilled. *What did he mean by that?* She rested her fingers against his hot skin, the blood slowing but still needing to be staunched.

"Are you going to continue staring at my chest or do something about that blood?"

Muttering to herself, she shook herself out of her stupor and bunched the end of the long strip of cotton against his skin, pushing harder than she should have from the string of cuss words that flew from his mouth.

"Are you trying to kill me yourself?"

"Maybe I should, you stubborn blockhead." She quickly wrapped the cotton around his chest a few times before tying it into place. She took a step back and screeched when another bullet hit close above her head.

"Whoever is shooting at us has moved closer, I can feel it. We need to get out of here."

The horses had pulled from their ropes and had taken off. They had nowhere to go.

"Are you going to be all right?" she asked.

"I'll be fine. Thank you for binding my side." He looked down at her, his solemn eyes speaking volumes.

They were in a fine pickle. No horses, only the one revolver in his hands, and considering he hadn't shot but one tine, she'd venture to guess he had very few bullets in his pockets.

Not wanting to know the answer, she asked, "Are we in trouble?"

He sighed and brushed the back of his knuckles against her cheek. "Not if I can help it."

Charlotte took a few small breaths to try and calm her rapidly beating heart. She didn't know if it was because he had touched her or if it was because they were in danger of losing their lives, but she couldn't lose her composure. He didn't need to deal with a hysterical, crying woman on top of everything else.

"I'll get you out of here, Charlotte. I promise."

She nodded, clasping her hands to her chest. "What do you need me to do?"

Another bullet slammed into the tree near Stanley's chest, missing him by inches. Wood splintered from the tree. It wouldn't take long for their attacker to find his prey.

"Dammit!" he exclaimed. "We've got to leave now."

She didn't know where they were going, but she trusted Stanley with her whole life. He would keep her safe.

"Keep low and stay near me, all right?"

"All right." She gathered her skirts over her arm to free her legs and prevent herself from tripping.

He then took his free hand in hers. His warm palm was strong and steady.

A second later, they ran. Charlotte struggled to keep up with him, but Stanley didn't leave her behind. They weaved through the forest as bullets burst into the ground and tree trunks. The sound of someone stomping through dead leaves and brush could be heard from behind them.

Her burning lungs, aching legs, and stinging skin were worth the pain if they got out of it alive. Occasionally, he would push her behind him and try to take a shot, but he was methodical and only did it three times. His eyes were dark, and tension coiled from him like a poisonous snake ready to strike, but he seemed determined to get them out of there, although Charlotte wasn't too sure he could.

The sun moved behind the mountains. Shadows formed as a cold wind blew through the trees and bent the branches to the ground. Dry brush and leaves whipped up and blustered around them. The day had grown late, and a storm was brewing. Whoever was after them seemed to have an endless supply of bullets and hadn't given up.

Stanley stopped and pulled her against another tree, blocking her from the fierce wind and the man following them.

"What are we going to do?"

"Shh," he whispered. "I haven't heard anything in a few minutes."

"Do you think we lost them?" She spoke in a low voice, hoping it wouldn't carry in the wind.

"I don't know," he murmured. "I hope so, but I can't be certain."

"Where are we going?"

His gaze was sharp. He looked around them and pointed. "There's an old cabin, I think, just above that ridge."

She swallowed a groan. It was up a steep hill, and there wasn't anywhere to hide. No trees, no bushes, just an open expanse of rocks and dirt. "How are we going to get there? I don't think I can climb that hill."

He looked down at her, his expression softening. "It won't be easy, but we have to find shelter. I'm running out of bullets. If we don't get to someplace where I can barricade us in until my brothers find us, then…"

She shivered but immediately stilled as he pressed close. His breath was warm against her cool cheeks. The rough pad of his thumb lifted her chin, his movements slow. Now was not the right time, but it was also the exact right moment. He bent his head and brushed his lips against hers. The kiss so quick, so slight, she might not have realized it'd happened if it hadn't been for the crackle of chemistry that seemed to jump from his skin to hers.

"I'm so sorry, Charlotte," he whispered, dropping his forehead against hers. "I've put you in danger."

"No." She touched her fingers to his lips, effectively silencing him. "This isn't your fault, and I know you'll do everything to keep me safe."

He reached into his pocket and placed four bullets into the revolver's chamber. From his grim expression, she was afraid those were the last bullets he had, but she didn't want to ask. If she did, she might lose what remained of her self-control.

"Let's go," he said.

She took his hand and followed him blindly, placing all of her trust in the strong man who would do anything to protect her.

Chapter 33

June 1, 1901

The trust Charlotte placed on his shoulders was both exhilarating and frightening. Stanley had six bullets left, a crazed man following them who seemed to have an endless supply of ammunition, and only one chance to make it to the cabin where, with any luck, there would be a stockpile of weapons and bullets. The cabin he was aiming for was old and hadn't been inhabited in years. It was a hunting cabin that Jacob and his pa had used whenever they'd needed to get away. They'd always left a few things behind. He prayed it still had something left for them to find.

Stanley hadn't been completely truthful with Charlotte about how far it was. He had told her it was just over the ridge, and it was, but it was also at least two miles past the ridge. It could take them hours to get there, but it was the only solution. He couldn't leave her to go after whoever was shooting at them, and yet he couldn't push her any harder than he already had.

When he placed the last four bullets into his revolver, he had seen her look of terror. She knew exactly what they were dealing with but either didn't want to ask him how dire the situation was or had already figured it out.

His waning energy and his burning side concerned him, but he didn't want Charlotte to know that he was barely hanging on. They hadn't had any water or food in hours, and he wasn't sure how much longer he'd be able to stay on his feet. They needed a place to hole up until his brothers realized something was wrong.

When they didn't arrive at the ranch by nightfall, his brothers would come looking. He just prayed they wouldn't walk into an ambush. He didn't think there was more than one man following them, but he couldn't be too sure.

The bullets had come fast and strong for some time. Whoever was shooting at them was moving quickly or had an accomplice. Either way, they had to lose him or eventually their attacker would catch up with them and they would be outnumbered.

The sun had finally disappeared, and he had to rely on his memories of a place he hadn't been to in years. Stanley had to trust that he could find his way in the dark, as he couldn't light a match, for then they'd be an easy shot.

He looked over his shoulder and grimaced. Charlotte was struggling. Her skirts kept tangling in the thick brush and were keeping her from moving quickly. He pulled her behind a large outcropping of rocks and shoved his revolver into his gun belt.

"What are you doing?" She braced her hands

on her hips and took a big breath, sweat dripping down her cheeks.

"We've got to get those skirts off you." He reached toward her waist, but she pushed his hands away.

"No," she said.

"Charlotte," he said, sharpening his tone. "You keep tripping, and they're only slowing you down."

"I can't remove my skirt. What would people think?"

The notion was ridiculous. "There's no one out here to question whether or not it is appropriate, but we have to scramble up those rocks. Your skirts are only going to slow us down, not to mention make it extremely difficult for you to climb. I don't want you slipping and falling."

"But—"

"Do you want to die out here?" he snapped.

She swayed slightly from his harsh tone. "Of course not."

"Then remove your blasted skirts."

She glared at him but did as he bid. With trembling hands, she undid the buttons, shoved them down her hips, and stepped out of them, leaving her clad in her drawers, ripped cotton stockings, and sturdy boots. She grabbed her skirts and petticoats and held them in her arms. "I'm not leaving them."

He shook his head. "You won't be able to carry them as we scramble across those rocks. Just leave 'em here."

"No," she muttered. She wrapped them around her shoulders and tied them in a big knot across her chest.

"Heaven help me, woman." He reached to remove them, but she swatted at his hands.

"If they get in the way, then I'll lose them, but for now they're staying with me." She turned and stomped toward the rocks.

She was going to be the death of him, but he was impressed by her resilience. He'd leave it be, but the first moment they became a problem, he'd cut them from her chest himself. Following in her wake, he scrambled over the rocks and the makeshift trail that animals had foraged in the side of the mountain.

All was quiet around them. The only sounds were their harsh breathing and the occasional rocks tumbling down the steep incline whenever they dislodged them from the path. Whoever had been chasing them was either lying in wait somewhere or was waiting for a clean shot.

Hours later, they crested the ridge and continued in the general direction of the old cabin or what he hoped was the right way. The dark night sky and the overgrown forest made it difficult to know for sure.

Charlotte growled at him when he finally admitted that the cabin was farther than he'd led her to believe. She mumbled something incoherent but marched forward, her skirts still hanging from her shoulders like a thick cape. She grasped them tightly, not willing to give them up regardless of how much they weighed her down.

He trudged forward, his legs becoming heavier and heavier. His vision was starting to swim up and down like he was floating in a raging river. He paused a moment, taking a breath.

Charlotte stepped into his line of sight. "Are you all right?"

He blinked to try and clear his vision. "Yes, I'm fine." And then he promptly stumbled forward, straight into her arms. The only thing keeping him from falling was her slim form.

"Umph," she said, wrapping her arms around his waist.

He dropped his head onto her neck, resting for a moment before he took a deep breath and then pushed away. "Sorry," he mumbled, running a hand through his hair. "We really need to find that cabin."

"Yes," she said. "But let me check your side first."

"No. We don't have time. We have to keep moving."

She frowned. "But you're clearly not doing well."

She was right, he wasn't, but he had to stay

strong. "I'm all right, I just need to slow down a bit. The cabin has to be close."

"Are you even sure we're headed in the right direction?"

He hesitated. He didn't want to lie to her, but he didn't want to tell her he was afraid he had miscalculated and had gotten them lost. "It should be close. Let's keep going."

She grabbed his hand, offering her support. He marveled at her lack of complaint and pure determination. Charlotte was something to behold, and he'd be lucky to have her permanently by his side.

A few minutes later, he spied what looked like the old cabin, but he couldn't be too sure. It had gotten even darker the farther they ventured inside the forest. He hadn't heard their pursuer in some time, though, and Stanley hoped that meant that they'd lost the man, but he wouldn't feel comfortable until they were safely inside.

Pulling her forward, he pushed through the brush and sighed with relief when they stepped into the small clearing in front of the old cabin. It didn't look as derelict as he remembered and almost looked as though someone had been there recently.

Charlotte started to move toward it, but he held her back.

"Wait," he said.

"Why?" She scrunched her eyebrows.

"Let me make sure no one is waiting for us inside."

"You don't think…?"

He grimaced. "I don't know what to think. I still don't know who was shooting at us, and for all I know, they got in front of us and are waiting inside."

"That's ridiculous," she muttered but halted in place.

Reaching for his revolver, he wiped at the sweat on his forehead. He hadn't been sure how much longer he would've been able to go. Now he just had to have enough energy to clear the cabin and, if it was safe, get Charlotte inside. Then he could finally breathe easier and maybe find his strength after a bit of rest.

Reaching the cabin, he placed his ear against the door but didn't hear a sound. He slowly pushed open the door and found nothing but dust and dirt.

When he waved for Charlotte, she ran up to him and stepped inside the cabin alongside him and promptly sneezed, not once but three times in quick succession. She giggled, easing the tension that had been building for hours. Now that they were in relative safety, they both breathed easier.

He slammed the door shut and found a wooden door brace leaning against the wall as though it had been waiting for their arrival. After dropping it into place, he reached into his trouser pocket, pulled out a pack of matches, and lit one. Not much remained, but there was an old rope-strung bed in one corner, two wooden chairs that looked like they'd seen better days, and several shelves containing some metal plates, cups, and spoons and what looked like a couple of canned food items. He wasn't sure what they'd find, but it was more than he expected. If he remembered right, there should be a small spring behind the cabin to give them some water.

There should also be a lantern hanging on the wall. The match flickered as it burned the wood and then his finger. He flicked it, and the flame disappeared. Lighting another, he turned and sighed with relief. He grabbed the lantern and quickly lit the wick, turning the knob. The kerosene inside would keep them from living in darkness.

Hanging it back on the wall, he pointed toward the door on the back side of the room. "There should be a small spring outside that door. Let me go get us some water." He took a few steps but stumbled and fell to his knees. His fatigue and loss of blood had finally caught up with him.

"Stanley," Charlotte said, dropping to his side. "You're not going outside, not now. Let me help you to the bed. I'll go outside and get you some water."

"No." He shook his head. "It isn't safe."

She muttered something he couldn't hear as she wrapped her arms around his waist and helped him to stand. Leading him to the bed, she helped him sit and knelt at his feet. Raising his shirt, she cursed. "You're bleeding again. I need to get this cleaned and get a new bandage on it. You aren't going anywhere." She stood and pointed. "Lie back. I'll be right back."

Before he could stop her, she grabbed a pot off the shelf and went to the back door. After carefully opening it, she slipped outside. A moment later, she had returned, closing the door behind her and throwing the lock.

He watched her with fascination. She moved with single-minded determination. Her skirts, previously around her shoulders, were discarded. She pulled a small knife from her boot and tore another piece off her petticoat. At the rate they were going there wouldn't be much left of her petticoat if she had to keep replacing the bandage. He likely needed stitches, but they had nothing to do that with so they'd have to make do with the remains of her petticoat.

Nudging him back, since he had ignored her demands to lie down earlier, she unwrapped the bloody bandage and bit her bottom lip. She scrunched her forehead while she concentrated. After dipping a piece of cloth into the water, she carefully dabbed at the wound, cleaning it as best she could before wrapping a clean piece of her petticoat around him. "You've got to rest. You've lost too much blood."

He didn't argue with her because she was right. He wasn't feeling too good and was fighting to keep his eyes open. A moment later, cool water dripped across his lips. She lifted the back of his head and let him drink from a metal cup.

After he had his fill, he twisted away. "Thank you."

She nodded and helped his head to the soft pillow. Moments later, fatigue took over, and the last thing he remembered was her concern as she hovered over him like an angel. A beautiful, caring angel he couldn't seem to let go.

* * *

Charlotte watched Stanley fight to stay awake, but his swollen, purple eyelids were determined to shut. Moments later, he was out cold. Grabbing an old woolen blanket sitting on a shelf, she shook it out, coughing from the dirt and dust, but happy she had something to cover him. He had lost too much blood, and if they weren't careful, he could catch a chill. The fact that he'd stayed on his feet for as long as he had was a miracle.

With the glow from the lantern, she was able to take a good look around the cabin. She'd keep the lantern lit long enough to see if there was any food, weapons, or bullets. While looking for items to help them, she discovered a second wooden bar for the back door, but before she blocked them in, she grabbed two more pots and quickly went outside to get them more water. It would be better to be prepared if they ended up having to stay locked inside for days. With any luck, Stanley's brothers would've already started looking for them, and they wouldn't need it.

Once she had the water inside, she locked the latch and then dropped the bar into place. That was when she noticed the windows had interior shutters with holes made for rifle muzzles to squeeze through in case of an attack. Snapping them shut made her feel more secure, but it also eliminated the glow from the moon. All she had left was the lantern and what little kerosene rested inside. Whoever built the cabin had done it with care in mind. It was a nice stronghold that could keep them relatively safe for some time if the walls were strong enough to withstand a prolonged attack, but she wouldn't despair until she had to.

She picked up the different cans of food. Peaches, beans, chicken. Even a small bag of salt. It wouldn't be the most delicious bit of food she'd ever eaten, but it was something, and they wouldn't starve.

Stanley moaned as he shifted uncomfortably in his sleep. She watched him for a long moment to make sure he stayed asleep. Sweat beaded across his brow. She placed the back of her hand against his forehead and grimaced. He was growing warm. Grabbing a rag, she dipped it into the cold water and wiped his face, hoping to cool it. She then folded it and rested it against his forehead.

He opened his eyes and twisted his head around. His eyes were unfocused and a moment later they dropped close. He had shifted out from underneath the blanket. As she pulled it back over him, incoherent words came from his lips, but he didn't fully wake. After a moment, he quieted and dropped into a deep sleep. Sleep he would need if they were attacked.

Plopping into a chair, she took a deep breath for the first time in hours. Wind whistled through the cracks of the cabin, and tree branches brushed against the roof. She shook from both fear and nervousness. The temperature was dropping, and while it was the beginning of June, as high as they were, it was bound to get cold overnight. Realizing she was still wearing just her drawers, she glanced around and found her skirt and what remained of her petticoats on the floor. Grunting, she stood, her legs protesting the movement. She would surely be sore in the morning from all the unplanned hiking they'd done that day, but it would be worth it if they survived the night.

Picking them up, she slipped the remains of her petticoat on. While it was in tatters, it would help, and considering the wind was seeping through the cracks in the walls and under the doors, she would need all the clothing she could muster. At least her skirt was in decent shape. A bit dirty but better than nothing.

Her growling belly reminded her that she hadn't had a thing to eat since early that morning. She cracked open a can of chicken and beans. She'd love to start a fire to warm it, but the smoke would likely let their pursuer know where they were. Better to eat the food cold than give the man a clue as to where they were hiding.

Sitting on one of the rickety old chairs, she

slowly ate the cold chicken and beans and ran through the events of the day. She hadn't given herself a chance to consider who might have been shooting at them, but she wondered if it was Mr. Smith. Although they had been careful, he had likely followed them to Helena. It wouldn't have taken much after that to discover where the Seymour ranch was located. The family was well known, and anyone could have given him directions. He could have observed them for days and, when she and Stanley left, followed them until he found the right opportunity to take a shot.

She didn't know for sure it was Mr. Smith, but it couldn't have been anyone else. She was the one with an enemy, not Stanley. His family had eliminated the woman who had caused havoc, so it had to be Mr. Smith who'd shot Stanley.

Rubbing at her neck, she dropped the can of beans onto one of the shelves. She crossed her arms around her twaist and yawned. While her belly was full, the trauma of the day had finally caught up with her.

The lantern flickered, the kerosene likely growing low. She grabbed the remaining blanket from the shelf behind her and dropped it around her shoulders. Deciding she needed to preserve what remained of the kerosene, she twisted the knob, and the light disappeared. She tried to get comfortable on the chair, but there was no comfort to be found. The hard wooden spokes dug into her shoulders, and the rough seat had numerous slivers poking her backside.

Her eyes adjusted to the darkness. She briefly considered climbing in next to Stanley in the bed but shrugged off the thought. It wouldn't be appropriate. He wouldn't welcome her next to him even if he wasn't fatigued from the blood loss and potential fever. It was best to make herself as comfortable as she could on the chairs.

She scooted the other chair in front of her, raised her feet to rest on the seat, and tightened the blanket around her, but it was useless. There would be no sleep tonight. She could lie on the floor, but she wasn't too sure she wanted to curl up with spiders, mice, and who knew what else.

"Are you going to keep making all that noise or are you going to climb into bed with me?" Stanley's voice was low and hoarse.

She stilled in shock. It was a good thing it was dark, and he couldn't see her. She didn't know what to say.

"Well," he muttered, "neither of us is gonna get a good night's sleep if you continue to wrestle like an alligator over there."

"I'm not—"

"Charlotte, I'm in no condition to take advantage of you. We both had a hard day. Just climb in the bed. Nothing'll happen, and we can both get some sleep. We're going to need it."

She hesitated, but her scratchy eyelids and tired bones overrode any rational thought that might have won if she had been in a better frame of mind. She carefully moved to the edge of the bed, unsure if she should climb over him or encourage him to move against the wall.

"You're going to have to climb over me and

sleep against the wall. That way, I can get to the door first if someone tries to break in."

"That doesn't make any sense, Stanley. You're hurt and won't be able to stop anyone."

"Just do as I say," he muttered.

"No, scoot over, and I'll lie on the edge."

"Charlotte," he snapped. "I'm not going to argue with you. You're not going to be closest to the door. I won't allow it."

"You won't allow it," she snapped right back. "You don't get to tell me what to do."

He sighed, muttering something under his breath, but shifted to sit. He rested his hand against his wound. "Please," he implored. "Don't fight me on this." He held out his hand.

She didn't want to give in, but she also didn't want him wasting any energy fighting her. "Oh, all right, but I'm doing it against my better wishes." She lifted her skirts to climb in but then stopped. "Wait, are you hungry or thirsty? There are some cans of—"

"No food, but some water would be most welcome."

She nodded but he likely couldn't see her doing that in the dark. "Stay right there, I'll get you some."

"Thank you."

A moment later, she handed him a metal cup with some water. He took it and emptied it within seconds.

"Would you like more?" She wanted to touch his forehead to see if he was still warm but didn't think it'd be wise.

"No, that was enough for now."

Her fingers brushed against his as she took the cup back, and fire leaped up her fingers and straight to her belly from the innocent touch. She dropped the cup on a shelf and then climbed onto the bed, her face on fire. Stanley eased back against the bed and moaned. He shivered, patting the bed, likely looking for his blanket. She picked it up from near his feet and placed it across his long body. She rested her hand on his shoulder when he reached up and covered hers with his.

"Thank you, sweetheart."

His endearment sent a rush of love through Charlotte's heart. She didn't think he realized what he had said, but it calmed her nerves. Lying on her side, she pulled her knees up so her skirts covered her feet and pulled her blanket on top of her. She closed her eyes, and moments later, she too was asleep.

Chapter 34

June 2, 1901

Stanley woke with a start. He shifted his legs, and without thinking, he stretched his side, sending a sharp pain along his ribs, but he tuned his ears to the sounds around him. Charlotte lay warm against his back, her breathing deep and steady. Whatever he'd heard hadn't woken her but had definitely stirred him from sleep. Being careful not to shake the bed, he climbed out when the sound came again.

Whatever was outside was either an animal or the man after them. Neither was welcome, but one could cause more damage than the other. His hand reached for his revolver, and he cursed under his breath. At some point, Charlotte must've removed it and put it somewhere, but he didn't know where. It was too dark in the cabin to see but a few inches in front of his face. He'd adjust to the dark but not soon enough to find it without making noise and alerting the man outside that he was awake.

A loud crash sounded on the other side of the cabin walls, and the choice was taken out of his hands. He had to find his gun.

"Charlotte," he whispered, shaking her shoulder.

"Hmm," she murmured. She opened her eyes and gazed at him.

If he didn't know better, he'd think she was dreaming about him, but he wouldn't let that thought take hold. He had to eliminate the threat before he could fix what had gone wrong between them. "Where's my gun?"

"What? Why?" She sat, rubbing at her eyes.

She hadn't gotten enough sleep. Neither of them had.

He didn't want to frighten her, but she deserved to know what they were up against. "Someone's outside."

She covered her mouth with her hand but then scrambled off the bed. She tripped and crashed to the ground.

"Charlotte," he said, kneeling next to her. "Are you hurt?"

The two of them were a mess, but they had to address the threat outside the four walls. Neither one of them could afford to be hurt any more than they already were.

"No, no," she said. "I'm fine. Embarrassed but fine."

She looked at him, her love for him in her eyes, and his heart burst wide-open. That woman had done everything in her power to keep him safe after he'd been shot. Thinking only of him, putting herself in greater danger, and doing everything he'd asked without complaint. She was a remarkable woman—smart, strong, stubborn, resilient. And he'd been stupid to think he could actually let her go. What a fool he'd been. He had to fix the mess he'd made and convince her to stay. He couldn't imagine his life without her.

She was everything he could have ever wanted and more. Her beauty was more than just on the surface. Her kindness toward others made her even more beautiful. She had healed a broken part of his heart without him even realizing it.

Before he could consider that it was not the most appropriate time, he pulled her to her feet, wrapped his arms around her waist, and pulled her close.

"What are you doing, Stanley?" she said, pushing at his chest. "Someone's out there."

"I know," he murmured, "but I have to do this first."

"Do what—"

He dropped his head and kissed her silent. Her soft lips were pliant under his. She tasted better than he remembered.

A moment later, he pulled away, heavily breathing, and spoke the words he'd been holding inside of him for far too long. "I love you, Charlotte."

She gasped. "What? You don't mean that."

"Shh," he said, placing a finger against her plump lips. "I do, and I'm so sorry it took me this long to realize it."

She shook her head. "You're delirious. The loss of blood has addled your brain."

He chuckled. "I'm not, I promise."

It was going to take some time to convince her he truly did mean what he said. In that instance before the bullet hit his side, he had known he loved this woman with everything in him, but he hadn't examined it until just then. Seeing her standing on his property, talking about all the things he should build and where to put the barn and the house, made him realize it wouldn't be home without her by his side.

"Don't laugh at me." She tried to pull away from him, but he didn't let go.

He had to make her understand, even it

wasn't the safest time to do so. "I'm not laughing at you. You mean the world to me. I have every intention of convincing you, but now isn't the time. We *will* talk everything through." He kissed her forehead softly, and she shivered. "But can you tell me where you put my gun?"

"Your what?"

Running his fingers along her chin, he said, "My gun."

"Oh, yes, yes, your gun." She turned and raised her hand to her forehead. "I put it on one of the shelves under the cans of food. I'll get it for you."

"No." He gripped her elbow. "I'll get it."

"Don't be stubborn. You're still hurt, and I know where I put it." She scurried to the other side of the room. A few seconds later, she'd struck a match and lit the lantern. Luckily the light was dim. She handed him his gun, touching his hand for a moment before she pulled away.

"Did you happen to notice any other weapons or bullets?" he asked as he flipped open the chamber to check how many bullets he actually had, as though the number would have grown in the hours since they'd arrived at the cabin.

"I started to look when we first got here, but then I got distracted with getting water and food and… I'm sorry. I should've looked and been prepared. I wasn't thinking, and now we're going to be killed." Her voice had climbed in pitch.

Placing a hand on her shoulder, he squeezed. "It's all right, my love. We'll be fine. I won't let whoever is out there get to you."

"I'm not worried about me," she mumbled, shrugging out from under his grasp. "And don't call me your love. You have a bullet wound in your side, have lost a lot of blood, and are likely running a fever. Not to mention the fact that you haven't eaten, and I'm not too sure you can stand for very long."

"Shh, Charlotte. I'm fine, I promise."

"But—"

"But nothing. I need you to listen to me." He gazed at her, trying to convey how dangerous their situation was. He didn't want to scare her, but things could go wrong fast if they weren't careful. "Whoever or whatever is out there is likely trying to find a way in here. I need you to do what I say without question. Can you do that?"

"I don't…" She looked carefully at him and then slowly nodded. "Fine, but when we get out of here, I have a few things to say to you."

Stanley smirked. He was looking forward to whatever she had to say because he had plenty to say and do to her. It would be an enjoyable discussion that would ultimately give them what they both wanted, a future with one another.

* * *

Charlotte watched as Stanley strode to one of the windows she had latched shut and looked over his shoulder.

"Yes, I closed them and locked them." Her tone was curt.

He grinned, and she bristled with irritation. She shouldn't be annoyed with him, but she couldn't seem to help herself. He said he loved her, but she wasn't sure she believed him. She wanted to, but after everything that had happened, it was too hard to understand. Losing all of that blood had to have addled his brain. It was the only thing that made sense.

"I wasn't going to say anything other than thank you for looking out for both of us."

Startled, she took a step back and wrapped her arms around her waist. She was being unreasonable, but her emotions were tumbling down a dangerous path. What he said was such a turnaround from everything he had done in the past few weeks that she didn't know from one second to the next if what he was saying was how he truly felt or if it was just a fever raging inside him making him say things he didn't mean.

The door rattled, and someone tried to push it open. She stumbled back with fear and crashed into the rope bed, falling backward and hitting her head against the post. Stars exploded, and pain radiated across the back of her head.

"Charlotte," Stanley said.

The door rattled again.

"Dammit!" he said, looking behind his shoulder and then back toward her.

"Go," she said, pointing to the door. "I'll be fine."

Although the ringing in her ears and the pain shooting down the back of her neck made her think it might take a few minutes before she would be fine, the pain paled in comparison to whoever might be behind that door.

He bent and brushed his lips across the top of her forehead before moving back to the window and trying to peer out the small rifle hole in the shutter.

She touched her forehead where his lips had just rested. The thought of his kiss taking away all her pain rang through her mind. She prayed that they'd get out of there alive. Then she could really and truly know if he meant what he said and maybe get her happily ever after, after all.

Chapter 35

June 2, 1901

Stanley pulled back the hammer of his revolver, flicked open the lock on the window, and carefully pulled it open. It was still dark, and he couldn't see much of anything except the thick forest and a dark blue sky.

A gunshot blasted through the night and exploded into the wall near his head. He slammed the shutters shut and threw the latch as a barrage of bullets hit the outside of the cabin.

Charlotte shrieked with fear and scrambled to the far corner of the room.

He turned to look at her. "It's all right. They can't get inside."

But he was afraid he was just giving her false hope. The cabin was old and wouldn't hold up against an onslaught with no end. He had no idea how the man had found them, but he had.

Charlotte was crouched in the corner, covering her ears with her hands. She had been so strong, but that might have been the last straw that had finally pushed her over the edge. While he longed to pull her into his arms and tell her that they would survive the night, he couldn't, at least not yet. Whoever was coming after them wasn't going to let them go without a fight. He just wasn't sure if it was Mr. Smith or someone from his past, but whoever it was wouldn't stop until they got what they wanted or Stanley stopped them.

"Charlotte," he said.

She didn't reply, just sat rocking back and forth, mumbling something under her breath.

"Charlotte," he said with more force.

She suddenly stopped, looked up and then down, and then stumbled to stand. "I'm so sorry," she muttered. "I don't know what came over me. That isn't like me. I just..." She swallowed hard and then ran her hands down the front of her skirt. "You don't need a hysterical woman on your hands. You need help, and I... I can help. I'll look for more bullets while you see to the varmint outside."

She rushed to the shelves and started digging through the items stacked in haphazard piles. Hiding his grin and being extremely proud of her, he stalked to the other window, and being a bit quieter, he opened it to peek outside. All had grown quiet, and that was more unnerving than the man shooting at the cabin. Where was he?

"Stanley, I think I've found something."

He latched the window closed. She had found a small metal trunk under the rope bed. It had a latch but opened easily. He crouched next to her and lifted the lid. He breathed a sigh of relief. It contained two six-shooters and boxes of bullets. The guns were old but looked well cared for. They likely hadn't been used in some time, but the bullets were still in good shape. They had a fighting chance. Jacob or his pa must've left the trunk the last time they'd visited the cabin.

Charlotte clapped her hands and then threw her arms around his neck. He fell back on his haunches as she crushed her body against his. He grunted but wrapped his arms around her waist and held her tight. It was worth it to feel her against him, even if his side screamed in agony. He buried his face in her neck and pressed his lips behind her ear. She shivered but surprised him when she kissed the hollow of his neck.

"I love you, Charlotte McVicker."

She smiled into his skin, and while he couldn't see it, he could certainly feel it. Perhaps it wouldn't take long for him to convince her that he meant every word he'd said.

Charlotte kissed him again, resting her lips against his neck for a long moment, sending zaps of awareness through every inch of his skin.

Then she slowly pulled away, running her hands along the back of his hair and then to his cheeks. She gazed at him for a long moment.

"And I love you, Stanley Seymour." She then blushed, her cheeks becoming bright pink. Scrambling out of his lap, she bumped against the bed and then stumbled to her feet.

The roar of gunfire erupted again outside. Wood splintered outside, and a few stray bullets managed to work their way inside the cabin, hitting the ground next to them.

He jumped up, ignoring his wound. Blood once again trickled down his side, but fixing that would have to wait. Snatching up a box of bullets, he strode to the window. Enough was enough. Whoever was out there wanted a fight, so he was gonna give 'em one.

* * *

Hours later, the sun had finally crested over the mountains, but the thick forest cast shadows in every direction. The man after them was slippery and had been near impossible to find. Every time Stanley thought he saw the flash of a muzzle, he'd shoot in that direction, and then a moment later more bullets would fly in from a different direction. Stanley was relatively positive there was only one man outside, but he had no way to determine for sure.

Charlotte stood against the other window, a gun held in her hand. She had shot her fair share of bullets out her window as well, but her lack of sleep and worry were evident. She was barely standing. He didn't know how much longer she'd be able to sustain the onslaught they were being subjected to.

Their attacker wasn't giving up, but neither was Stanley.

"Charlotte," he said. "This has gone on long enough. I have to go outside and track him down."

"No," she said. "You can't. He'll kill you."

He shoved his revolver into his gun belt and strode to her. Taking her hands in his, he squeezed gently and pulled her close until she grabbed his shirt front, nestling into him. He held her close for a long moment, her warmth seeping into his skin. That woman meant everything to him, and he was angry at himself for taking as long as he had to realize how much.

"We can't sit here any longer," he said, rubbing circles on her lower back. "I have to go outside and see if I can't catch him unaware."

"No, he'll kill you," she said, pulling back. "I can't lose you, not like this."

"You won't lose me. I promise." He took her hand and kissed her knuckles, trying to comfort her as best he could.

She looked him in the eye. "You can't promise me that."

"I can and I will. Now that I've finally come to my senses, I have too much to live for. If I stay here, he'll eventually find a way to take us down, and I won't let that happen. Not if I want to live a long and happy life with you."

She blinked back tears, a trembling smile on her lips, but she slowly nodded. "All right, but you'll need me to cause a diversion, am I right?"

He shook his head at her pure stubbornness. "I don't want to put you in any danger."

"I won't be. You promised."

He chuckled. "I guess you're right. I'm not sure I'd be able to stop you if I tried."

"You couldn't." She moved a lock of hair from his forehead, her soothing touch a boon to his battered soul. "Please be careful. I can't lose you."

"You won't." He dropped his head and gave her a sweet kiss, one filled with promises and hope.

He pulled her to the bed, where they sat and quickly talked through several scenarios before deciding on their best chance at getting out of there alive. If he did things right, this would end soon, and they could make their way back to his family's ranch.

If things went wrong, she was to stay inside the cabin until nightfall and then try and make her way back to Thundering Mountain. He gave her directions and made her memorize particular landmarks. He had her repeat the directions numerous times until he was sure she could make it there if need be. He didn't want to leave her, but they had no choice. He just prayed he had made the right one.

* * *

Charlotte tried to hide her shaking hands when Stanley slipped out the back door of the cabin. He had given her one last glance before blowing her a kiss. It was such a tender moment, she almost burst into tears. It could be the last time she ever saw him. She was so afraid their plan would backfire. If he were killed, she would be next. There was no way she could fight off the man hunting them, regardless of Stanley's insistence that she could make it back to the ranch alive.

While she was scared, her heart was also bursting with joy in knowing Stanley loved her. His innocent touches, his sweet kisses, and the way he looked at her all but convinced her he was telling her the truth of his feelings. She still felt they needed to discuss plenty, but they would have time to do that if they could manage to get out of this mess alive.

Following his instructions, she carefully put the wooden bar into place once he had gone outside. He had told her to give him five minutes before she started to shoot out the window. It was the longest five minutes of her life. She paced back and forth, muttering to herself, but she was determined to give him the diversion he needed. Their plan had to work.

When the five minutes were up, she took a deep breath, peeled back the shutters on the window, and started shooting in every direction, hoping their attacker would return fire. He did, and Charlotte hoped it gave Stanley a chance to pinpoint where the bullets were coming from. She continued to shoot in various directions, hoping she wouldn't inadvertently shoot Stanley.

After shooting for a few minutes Charlotte dropped to the ground and quit firing. Stanley had told her to only shoot for about five minutes.

He thought that would give him enough time to find the man. She prayed he was right.

Everything was silent, and as the minutes passed, unease crept up her spine. She wanted to look outside, but Stanley had made her promise that she wouldn't. No matter what, she was to stay out of sight, regardless of what she heard. If he didn't come back by the time night fell, she was to leave. He had even packed a bag for her to take, filled with a few cans of food and hopefully enough bullets to keep their attacker at bay.

"Charlotte," a male voice sang. "How about you come out now? Your hero ain't gonna be able to save you."

She raised a fist to her mouth. It sounded like Mr. Smith, but she didn't move. There was no way Stanley would've been caught by him. Stanley was too smart, too strong, too determined to let something like that happen. He was just trying to confuse her, to get her to reveal herself. He must've figured out or seen Stanley and was just trying to lure her away from where she was safest.

"If'n you don't come out soon, you're gonna regret it. I aim to cut your man apart piece by piece unless you show yourself and step outside."

"Never," she yelled, praying he didn't hear the fear.

"Not very smart, girl. He's already bleeding from the bullet wound I gave him yesterday, and the cuts on his arms and head are bleeding quite deliciously from him being stupid enough to think he could sneak up on me. I'm too smart for that, and now he's gonna pay the price."

Her heart stopped. Did Mr. Smith have Stanley? Was she putting his life in danger because she sat inside the cabin all snug as a raccoon who'd found the perfect hidey-hole?

"How do I know you really have him?" she yelled.

Mr. Smith's laugh cackled with evil, the sound seeming to grow closer with every passing second. "Why don't you pop your head up to that open window and see for yourself?"

"How do I know this isn't a trick and you're standing right there with a gun to blow off my head?" She wasn't completely naïve. If she looked out the window, he could take her out with one pull of the trigger.

"I guess that's a chance you'll have to take, but if you don't do it soon, I might lose my patience and end your lover boy's existence."

Charlotte didn't know what to do. There was no way Stanley would want her to do anything that could harm herself, but she couldn't in good conscience let Mr. Smith hurt him if she had a way to stop it. She started to stand, then stopped. Mr. Smith was expecting her to peer out the window above her head, but she could go to the other and look through the rifle hole instead. It was daylight, and if he was standing in view of the open window, then she should be able to see him.

Being careful not to make a sound, she crept to the other side of the cabin and inched up the wall until she was almost eye level with the hole. Taking a deep breath to calm her nerves, she looked outside and had to contain her gasp.

Her worst nightmare *was* playing out in front of her.

Stanley was on his knees in front of Mr. Smith. His hands were bound behind his back, and a rag had been stuffed into his mouth. Blood ran down his forehead, and numerous cuts and bruises marred his face, chest, and arms. In trying to catch Mr. Smith, Stanley had been caught instead. His injuries must've taken more out of him than they'd realized because Stanley would have been capable of taking care of Mr. Smith if he had been healthy.

Stanley's head hung, but he slowly raised it. He examined the outside of the cabin, and then he looked straight at her. His eyes seemed to communicate with her through time and space. A slight shake of the head was likely his way of telling her not to come outside. He was still trying to keep her safe at a cost to himself.

She sank onto her haunches, her mind trying

to come up with different possibilities. If she went outside, she had no doubt Mr. Smith would kill her or perhaps something worse. Stanley couldn't help her. He was tied up, and his injuries had been made worse. If she tried to fire the gun, Mr. Smith would likely kill Stanley before she got off the first shot. Yet she couldn't stay inside the cabin. If she did, he'd for sure kill Stanley. She couldn't let that happen. She loved Stanley far too much to let him die because of her.

Perhaps she could convince Mr. Smith to let Stanley go if she told him she would show him where the gold was. Leading him on a merry goose chase would give Stanley time to get away, find his brothers, and come after her. That might be the only way to keep Mr. Smith from killing them both.

Resolved to do what she must, she eyed a knife sitting on the shelf. Mr. Smith would likely demand she drop the gun, but he'd be less likely to check her boot or her corset for any hidden knives. She quickly grabbed a knife and stuck it in the boning of her corset. She still had a small knife tucked inside her boot. It wasn't much, but it would be enough if he tried to harm her before Stanley found her. Picking up the gun to distract Mr. Smith, she took a deep breath and walked to the door.

"Charlotte," Mr. Smith yelled. "I'm tired of waitin'. You have ten seconds to show yourself or I'm gonna start cutting him until he's dead at my feet."

Holding the gun at her side, she removed the wooden brace from the door. "I'm coming out. Don't shoot."

Praying the man was crazy enough to keep her alive to find that elusive gold, she slowly opened the door and stepped outside.

Chapter 36

June 2, 1901

Stanley pulled at the ropes holding his arms tight behind his back. He thought he had seen Charlotte peering out the rifle hole of one of the windows. He'd shaken his head, hoping she would understand that she wasn't to come outside no matter what, but the stubborn woman had ignored everything he had told her and had instead walked outside. Her need to protect him overrode her good sense.

She walked outside, holding the gun in front

of her as though that was going to stop Smith from taking everything they both held dear.

Smith cackled with glee. "Drop that gun, missy." He pressed the muzzle of his revolver into the side of Stanley's head. "I ain't afraid to kill him."

Charlotte slowly bent and placed the revolver near her feet. "Let him go."

"You ain't the one holding the gun. You'll do as I say." Smith was growing more agitated by the minute. It wouldn't take much to send him off the edge.

"What do you want?" she asked.

"What do I want?" he screamed. "What I've wanted for months. I want that gold. You took it from me, and I want it now."

"I don't have it with me," she said.

Stanley glanced at Smith. His face was bright red, and sweat rings had formed under his arms and down the middle of his back. The man was nervous and skittish as a baby deer who'd lost sight of his mother. It likely wouldn't take much for Smith to kill Charlotte or Stanley if he felt any threat come his way.

"But," she said, "I can take you to it."

Smith's grin was pure evil. "Oh, you're gonna take me to it all right or I'm gonna kill him. I may kill him just for fun so you'll know I ain't playing."

"No, please. If you kill him, I'll never tell you. I'll do what you want, just leave him. We can go now."

Stanley's heart near stopped. What was she doing? It was already bad enough that she'd come outside. Now she was telling Smith she knew where the gold was. There was no way she could fool Smith for long. She didn't have a devious bone in her body, and Smith wasn't stupid. He'd been smart enough to track them down. There was no telling what he would do if he even had a hint that she was lying about the gold.

Stanley pulled at the ropes once again, but Smith grabbed him by the back of his neck, and squeezed. "I suggest you stop trying to get away or I'll kill her slowly, peel her skin away inch by inch, and make you watch. Then I'll do the same to you until your blood drains out of your body."

Stanley stopped fighting at the wickedness emanating from the man's eyes. Smith was dangerous, unholy, and he would carry through with his threat.

"Let him go!" Charlotte barreled toward them without care for her own safety.

Smith lifted his gun, and before Stanley could react, the butt struck the back of his head.

* * *

A blast of gunfire burst through the air. Bullets struck the dirt and trees around Mr. Smith. With a scream, Charlotte dropped to the ground and covered her head. What was going on?

When Mr. Smith hit Stanley with his gun, horror filled her, and it was all she could do not to choke. She had thought she had been doing a good thing coming outside to appease Mr. Smith, but clearly, it hadn't been enough. He was angry, deranged, and determined to find the gold. When he discovered she was lying, he was going to kill her.

Charlotte started to run toward them when gunfire halted her in her tracks. Mr. Smith yelled, spun around, and shot wildly in that direction. Charlotte scrambled to her feet, searching the forest in front of her. She didn't know who was shooting at them, but she had to get Stanley out of there. He was in danger.

She picked up her skirts and ran toward him, falling to the ground near his head and throwing herself over him as the gunfire continued to explode all around them. Mr. Smith ran wildly toward the forest as bullets slammed into his frame, but he was crazed enough that his momentum carried him forward until one last bullet pierced his skull. He fell forward and crashed to the ground. Then everything went blessedly quiet.

Whoever had been shooting at Mr. Smith stopped. Charlotte looked down at Stanley and touched his head. A thick lump was on the back of his head, but he stared straight at her. She ripped the rag out of his mouth so he could breathe.

"Stanley," she whispered. "Are you all right?"

He moaned and pulled at the ropes still binding him. She ripped out the knife she had stuffed into her boot, the metal gleaming in the light, when a man stepped out of the forest and pointed the gun straight at her.

"Don't move, Charlotte." It was Ben.

She gasped. "I'm not going to hurt him." Her voice shook. "I was only going to cut the ropes around his wrists."

"I don't know what's going on, but you need to get away from my brother right now." His face was boiling red, his mouth was in a thin line, and his voice was low, piercing, and downright ominous.

She was ashamed. Ben thought she would hurt his brother. She carefully placed the knife on the ground and slowly scooted away from Stanley. It was the last thing she wanted to do, but considering the questions Ben likely had, she'd best do as he asked. It had been a rough night and an even rougher morning. She didn't want to make things worse.

Michael and Luke stepped out of the forest, following Ben. Their eyes were solemn, and they held their weapons ready. They all believed she had caused this, and in some ways, she had but not the way they likely believed.

Ben strode to Stanley and picked up the knife. With one eye on her, he carefully cut the ropes around Stanley's wrists. Stanley groaned, his hand going to his neck and to the back of his head, likely to rub at the pain emanating from the many wounds Mr. Smith had inflicted on him.

Stanley muttered something to Ben that she couldn't hear. Ben's lips moved in response, and Stanley's eyes narrowed. Stanley waved his brother away and pushed to stand.

"Charlotte," Stanley said. "Please come here."

Ben said something, and Stanley pushed him back. Ben slapped his hat against his leg and stalked toward his younger brothers.

Crying with relief, she ran to Stanley's side.

He pulled her into his arms and hugged her tightly.

"You're hurt." Pulling slightly away from him, she ran her hands across his chest and down his side. She carefully touched the area around the bullet wound. It was bleeding again. As she bent to grab her petticoat, Stanley stopped her and grabbed her hands.

"I'm fine, Charlotte. A few bruises, but I'll live now that I know you weren't harmed." He bent and kissed her softly across the lips. A moment later, he pulled away and glared at her. "What were you thinking coming outside? I told you to stay inside no matter what you heard."

She wasn't about to listen to him yell at her. "What did you expect me to do?" she hissed. "I wasn't about to let him kill you."

"And what if he had killed you?" he said, his tone harsh.

"It was my fault he shot you to begin with."

"It wasn't your fault. I brought you to the ranch to keep you safe from him. I should've known he would find us." He grimaced and brought his hand to his wounded side.

"You can't keep me safe from a madman," she muttered.

"Dammit, Charlotte," he roared. "I love you and didn't want to see you hurt."

"I didn't get hurt," she snapped. "You're the one full of bullet holes, scrapes, bruises, and a big ole cut on the back of your head. I'm just—"

"All right, you two," Ben said, interrupting her tirade. "I think we can continue this conversation back at the ranch. Stanley's about ready to fall over and needs to see a doc. We can discuss what has been going on when we get back to the ranch."

"Not now, Ben," Stanley said, completely focused on her. She couldn't read his expression but feared he was furious with her.

"Don't argue with your brother, Stanley," she said, although she wasn't too certain she wanted to have that conversation with Ben. Something had changed his opinion of her, and she wasn't sure she was going to like it. "Let's get you home."

"I need to talk with you." Stanley took a step forward and started to sway. "I can't let you think…"

His eyes rolled into the back of his head, and he promptly fell forward straight into her arms. She grunted from the weight, but she wouldn't let him go. While he might be angry with her, she was furious with him. He wasn't supposed to have gotten hurt again, but he had. Now, he could still die, and it would be her fault.

Chapter 37

June 6, 1901

Charlotte paced back and forth. Dirt clumps flew around her like a dust cloud from the force of her kicks. She was anxious, afraid, angry, and frustrated that Stanley would not wake. She had been nothing but a noose around his neck, and because of her, he could die. He had finally told her how much he loved her, and she'd likely never hear those words again.

Louisa, Luke's wife, had insisted he would make a full recovery once she'd had a chance to tend to his wounds after the frenzy they caused when they returned to the ranch. Louisa's father had been a doctor and had trained her well. She was even attending medical school in the fall and would become a fine doctor.

Louisa had tended to Stanley's wounds with diligence and proficiency, or at least that was what Elizabeth had told her. Charlotte hadn't been allowed in his bedroom until Louisa had done all she could for him. Even then, Ben had glared at her and argued with Elizabeth when she insisted Charlotte could go inside.

Ben had stood at the door with his arms crossed, watching every move she made. His disgust was unnerving, but she had stayed until Elizabeth pried her away from his sickbed and encouraged her to take a bath and to get something to eat.

After she washed, Stanley's brothers had insisted she meet with them in Ben's study. They'd been cordial, but they'd had a lot of questions. She'd tried to answer the best way she knew how, but it hadn't ended well. That had been four days ago, and Stanley still wasn't awake.

Twisting her hands in front of her, she continued pacing next to the barn, out of view of the house. With any luck, no one would discover her. She hadn't wanted to see the continued censure in Ben's gaze, for she had caused the latest turmoil in their family. It seemed she was a beacon for tragedy. Michael and Luke had seemed to accept what she had told them that night, but Ben had been wary and said he wanted to talk to Stanley first.

The barn doors creaked open, and she flattened herself against the wall. With any luck, whoever was there wouldn't see her, and she could resume walking in peace. It was likely a ranch hand, but if it was one of Stanley's brothers or sisters, she'd rather stay hidden from their view. They blamed her as much as she blamed herself.

"Charlotte?"

"Stanley!" She ran around the corner and straight into his arms.

"Humph." He fell back against the wall, but his strong arms were sure as they grasped her around the waist. "I didn't expect that kind of reaction," he murmured, tightening his arms and holding her close. He kissed the top of her head.

"You shouldn't be out of bed." She'd flattened her ear against his chest. She could feel and hear his heartbeat. It was rapid but seemed to slow the longer they stood holding one another.

"Maybe not," he said a moment later. "But no one could find you. Although I'm not sure Ben was too keen on finding you."

"He's angry with me," she said, tears filling her eyes. She hadn't wanted to disappoint his brothers, but they didn't trust her, especially Ben.

"He didn't understand what happened. I explained everything, and he wants to apologize."

"He does?" She pulled away.

He gazed at her with solemn eyes. "Yes, he does. With all that's happened over the past few years, he gets a little protective." He tenderly brushed away something from her cheek. "Turns out, a lot happened the morning we left for our ride, and Ben wasn't sure what to believe. He blames himself for not trusting his instincts, but when he found me hurt, his good sense was overridden by concern."

"I'm so sorry."

"You have nothing to apologize for." He swayed and leaned back against the barn wall.

"You need to sit." She took his hand and led him to a wooden bench.

He moved slowly but seemed determined to stay on his feet. Once they sat, he placed his arm around her shoulders and pulled her close. She melted into his embrace.

"Ben said you received a telegram from your grandfather this morning. He wants you to return immediately."

"I did," she said, tracing the seam of his shirt pocket. "He's concerned and says I need to come home."

"Did you send a response?"

"Not yet," she murmured. "I didn't know what

was going to happen with you and… and I know we said a lot of things, but I wasn't sure…" She was bumbling badly. She hadn't been afraid to tell him how she felt before, but things were different. Too much had occurred, and she didn't want to assume that he still felt the way he had claimed.

"Charlotte," he said.

She kept her gaze on his chest and touched the smooth edge of the pearl buttons running along the seam of his faded blue chambray shirt.

"Look at me, please."

She shook her head. She was afraid if she did, she'd be disappointed and hurt.

"Please."

She shuddered and then slowly raised her head.

His brown eyes were full of concern. He swallowed a few times before any words slipped past his lips. "My feelings haven't changed."

Her heart stopped. *Does this mean what I think it means?*

"I love you so much, Charlotte. I want to

spend the rest of my life with you." He reached into his pocket and pulled out a small black velvet box.

Her breath hitched, and she rested her hand against her throat. He fumbled to open it but finally did. He shifted until he was facing her and started to drop to the ground, but she stopped him. Shaking her head, she said, "No, you don't need to do this."

He smiled tenderly at her. "Yes, I do." He then got down on one knee, grabbed her hand, and held the ring out in front of him. "I love you so much, Charlotte. Meeting you was the best thing that could have ever happened to me, but I didn't see it. I didn't think I deserved someone as special as you."

"Stanley—"

"Please let me finish. I was stubborn and foolish. Seeing you standing on the land my pa always intended for me to have hit me hard. You belong there. I'll never be happy living there without you by my side. I'll never be the man my pa wanted me to be if you aren't with me. I want to be the man you deserve."

She quirked an eyebrow. "And who says I need a man? I've been perfectly fine without one until now." She was giving him a hard time, but she had to be sure. He had rejected her love twice already.

"You're right. Maybe you don't need a man, but…" His forehead wrinkled. "Perhaps you could still let me love you the way you deserve."

She curved her lips into a smile. "I don't know. What's in it for me?"

Still holding her hand, he stood and pulled her up. Slowly, he placed his hand at her waist and rested his forehead against hers. "Not much except the chance to build a ranch with me on a lovely piece of property. You did say it would be a nice place to raise a family."

"Did I say that?" she asked, inching her hands up his chest and around his neck. She loved this man so much, but she wasn't going to make it easy on him. "I don't remember saying those exact words."

His impish grin made her heart sing with joy. "Maybe not those exact words, but there was something about a house on the hill, an icehouse, and even a large barn in that meadow," he murmured, sliding his finger up and down her arm.

"Hmm, that sounds slightly familiar. What were you thinking of calling the place?" She was being mischievous, but she couldn't seem to help herself.

He tilted his head as if considering it very carefully. "I was considering Thundering Snow if…"

"If what?" she said, smiling with mirth.

"If that's agreeable with you, of course."

Their breaths mingled. He cupped her cheek, moving a strand of hair behind her ear before he brushed his thumb against her lips. He then bent and placed his lips against hers. Heat rushed through her, tingles zipping to her toes, lights exploding in her brain. He was tender, loving, and everything she had always wanted and more. The kiss was sweeter and more poignant than any other, for it was the first time they both knew that they shared the same love for one another.

A few moments later, he lifted away and ran brief, light kisses along her cheek until he reached the soft lobe of her ear and whispered, "Does this mean what I think it means?"

She giggled. "I don't know. Have you asked me anything yet?"

"I've been remiss," he said, kneeling before her.

She gasped. "I didn't mean to suggest—"

"Shhh," he said. "I'm not doing anything I don't want to do. Charlotte McVicker…" Sweat gathered across his brow. His gaze begged for the answer she was sure she would give him. "Will you do me the honor of becoming my wife?"

She stared at him for a long moment. "On one condition."

"I'll give you anything you want."

Possibilities of the future filled her mind. He

had finally forgiven himself and opened his soul to her.

She grinned and touched his chin. "That you'll let me help you build that ranch you've always wanted for us and our children."

A bright smile lined his lips. "That can most definitely be arranged."

"Then yes," she murmured, "I'll most certainly marry you."

The answer would've always been yes, but she needed him to realize how much he loved her and was glad he had discovered it on his own. She dropped to her knees, placed her hands against his cheeks, and that time, she kissed him. A searing kiss that sent lightning strikes from her lips to his.

Epilogue

September 30, 1901

Stanley lifted the ax and slammed it through the log, splitting the wood in half. The sun was high in the sky, but a cool breeze blew through the pine trees and across the river. The temperature was starting to drop, but with any luck, he'd have finished the house before the first snow fell. It wasn't large like the main house on Thundering Mountain Ranch, but it would serve him and Charlotte well, especially once they started having children.

They were getting married next month, and

he'd been working around the clock trying to get it done before they said their vows. Charlotte had insisted that he complete the barn and corrals first. Her selflessness was something he hadn't been prepared for but was extremely grateful for. Once the outbuildings were completed, he'd started on the house. They'd sat at the kitchen table with Ben and Elizabeth sketching out all the things they wanted, laughing, smiling, and imagining their future.

Charlotte and Elizabeth were coming out to the ranch that morning. Charlotte would be surprised to see how much he'd accomplished. The pleasure on her face was worth the long days he'd been working since she'd accepted his hand in marriage.

A wagon rumbled down the dirt road, the four horses straining under the load they were pulling. He dropped the ax into the hard stump, pulled out a handkerchief from his back pocket, and wiped the moisture from his brow. It wasn't hot outside, but he had worked up quite a sweat. It wasn't Charlotte and Elizabeth, as there was only one person who sat on the seat of the wagon. He wasn't expecting anyone else, and from the glare of the sun, he couldn't tell who was driving until the wagon pulled to a stop next to him.

It was Michael.

Stanley grinned. "Whatcha doin' out here, little brother?"

Michael set the brake, wrapped the reins around the handle, and jumped down. "I have something for you."

Stanley shoved the handkerchief into his pocket and followed Michael to the rear of the wagon. Michael lifted the canvas from the bottom of the bed, and Stanley stared in shock at what was lying inside.

"Did you do this?" Stanley asked.

Michael's thumbs rested in the belt loop of his trousers, and he rocked back and forth, a smirk on his face. "Yes. I thought it was only fitting. You've done all this work to have the house and barn ready for Charlotte, I figured you hadn't considered making one. Pa would've wanted you to have something like this."

"It hadn't even crossed my mind." A thick lump grew in his throat. "I don't know what to say."

"You don't need to say a word. It's the least that I could do," Michael said. "Of course, if you don't like it, I can—"

Stanley shook his head. "I love it. Charlotte's going to be thrilled."

"Well, help me pull it out of the wagon. It's gonna take the two of us. It's mighty heavy."

A few minutes later, after a bunch of curses, groans, an almost broken toe, a couple of bruised shins, and muscles that'd likely hurt like the devil in the morning, the two of them managed to pull the large, intricately carved, wooden and metal sign out of the back of the wagon. They leaned it up against the fence.

"This reminds me of when Ben and I were with Pa the day he put up the sign to mark the name Ma had picked for the ranch," Stanley said.

Michael grinned. "Pa loved to tell that story, didn't he?"

"Yes, he did." Stanley's heart didn't hurt like it had just months before when he remembered his pa. Having Charlotte in his life had changed his perspective and made him remember his pa with fondness instead of pain. The memories were something to treasure, and he did. He had finally forgiven himself for his part in bringing Connie into their lives. While he'd made mistakes, he had more than paid for them, and it was time to let it go.

"He'd be proud of you, Stanley," Michael said, nudging him in the side.

Stanley blinked and swallowed hard. "He'd be proud of all of us, wouldn't he?"

"Yes, he would," Michael said, grinning. "Although I'm sure he'd be the proudest of me since I was his favorite." He puffed out his chest like a proud peacock.

Stanley playfully shoved Michael on the shoulder. "I don't know about that. I'm sure I was his favorite."

"Oh, I don't think so," Michael said. "If I wasn't his favorite, then it had to be Katie."

Stanley laughed. "Yeah, you're probably right about that. He surely loved her something fierce."

"But I definitely came next, big brother."

Before Stanley could set his brother straight, he saw another wagon in the distance, dust and dirt flying around it as it came down the long drive.

"Who do you suppose that is?" Michael asked, holding his hand above his eyes to protect them from the bright sunlight.

"It's probably Charlotte. She and Elizabeth were going to come by this afternoon to measure the windows for new curtains and take measurements for some furniture. Elizabeth is letting her have some of Ma and Pa's old things that were stored in the attic."

"I thought everything burned in the fire," Michael said.

"No. Ben said the fire didn't reach that part of the attic. They were able to salvage a few pieces."

"I'm glad to hear the fire didn't ruin more than

it did. Ma and Pa would've liked you to have some of their things."

"I hope you're right."

"Of course, I'm right. I always am." His amused grin was a reminder that they could still have fun in their lives despite all the tragedy.

Stanley shook his head.

Michael pointed to the sign. "Do you want me to cover it so you can surprise her with it later?"

Stanley looked at the sign for a long moment. "No. She'll want to see it and thank you properly, I'm sure."

Elizabeth pulled their wagon next to Michael's and set the brake quite efficiently. Elizabeth was wearing her favorite trousers and had even convinced Charlotte to don a pair. Stanley shouldn't be surprised. Elizabeth had a mind of her own and would wear trousers whenever she worked on the ranch. Years ago, Ben had a mighty hard time with seeing his wife in men's trousers but, over the years, had grown used to it and would have a bemused smile on his face whenever she put them on.

"Michael, what a surprise," Elizabeth said, using the large wide wheel to climb down. "I didn't expect to see you out here today."

"I wanted to surprise Stanley," Michael said, giving her a quick hug.

Elizabeth patted his cheek and then looked around the meadow in front of the house. "My, oh my, Stanley. You sure have made a lot of progress." She rested a hand on her hip while the other waved to the area in front of them. "Ben and I didn't think you'd get the house done in time, but you're sure proving us wrong."

Stanley chuckled and gave her a quick hug as well. Her sisterly embrace was something he treasured. Having Elizabeth in their lives had been a blessing in so many ways. She had stepped into Ben's life just when he needed it the most. They'd had a few ups and downs, but Ben was lucky to have her.

Stanley reached for Charlotte's hand and gave her a quick kiss on the cheek. His eyes roamed across her slim frame, and he couldn't help but admire her backside in the trousers she was wearing. He didn't mind one bit seeing his soon-to-be wife in them. They definitely accentuated her long legs and... He shook himself from his thoughts. There would be time enough for that later. He only had one more month until they were married, and he could officially make her his.

She grinned at him and glanced down at her legs, giving him a knowing smile. She likely knew exactly where his mind had gone. They had already had a few moments where they had pushed the bounds of propriety, and they were both anxiously awaiting their wedding night. They had both agreed, however, that they were saving themselves for that night and would patiently wait—or not so patiently in his case.

Her smile was generous, and her plump lips beckoned his touch. He'd have preferred to take her into his arms and kiss her silly, but with his brother and sister-in-law watching them like hawks, he held off. There'd be time enough for that later. He'd catch her after dinner and give her a kiss they'd both remember. Grabbing her hand, he tugged her forward. She stumbled but kept up with his long steps as he took her to where he and Michael had put the sign just a few minutes before.

"Stanley," she said, laughter in her voice. "What are you doing?"

"I've got something to show you." Stopping in front of where the sign rested along the fenceposts, he pointed. "What do you think?"

She let go of him and covered her mouth with her hands. Her eyes had filled with tears. "It's beautiful, Stanley. When did you do this?"

"I didn't," he said.

She raised her eyes to his and tilted her head. "You didn't?"

"No." He paused. "Michael did."

She turned and found Michael standing behind them, his hands behind his back, rocking on his heels. "Michael, it's beautiful."

She threw her arms around Michael's neck, giving him a quick squeeze before turning back to the sign and running her fingers along the carved metal and burned wood.

It was an elaborately carved sign that said *Thundering Snow Ranch.* Michael had somehow managed to convey snow-covered mountains in the backdrop with lightning strikes made of metal. It was beautiful and would mark their new home in just the same fashion as the Thundering Mountain Ranch sign had for years.

Stanley placed his arm around her waist and pulled her close. Her soft curves nestled against his. She rested her hand against his chest, leaning into him.

"It's something, isn't it?" he said.

"It is. Your brother is purely talented."

"Darn right I am." Michael walked up alongside them.

They all laughed, their chuckles ringing through the quiet air. Stanley, Charlotte, Michael, and Elizabeth stood quietly looking at the sign for a long moment before their soft murmurs of what needed to be done next on the ranch soon took their attention.

Days later, Stanley, Ben, Michael, and Luke would hang the sign in memory of their parents.

It would stand for years to come and continue the tradition of naming their spreads in the same manner their ma had when she and their pa found Thundering Mountain all those years ago.

* * *

My Dear Reader,

I hope you enjoyed Stanley and Charlotte's happily ever after. If you'd like to learn more about me and my novels, sign up for my newsletter at www.nicoleneiswanger. substack.com.

All my love, Nicole